THE
FOURTH
HOUSE

THE
FOURTH
HOUSE

KERRY ZUKUS

MADISON
PARK
PRESS™
NEW YORK

Published by Madison Park Press, 15 East 26th Street, New York, NY 10010. Madison Park
Press is a trademark of Bookspan.

Book design by Christos Peterson

ISBN: 978-1-58288-248-2

Printed in the United States of America

With love, to my mother

PREFACE

OUSE IS A term used by astrologers to define a set of twelve sectors of the sky that are similar to the zodiac's twelve signs but may differ in size and location as to where the sector begins and ends. In the heavens, the sun, the moon, and the planets are each traveling through a sign and a house at any given time.

The *fourth house* represents the childhood home and all that it implies. It is the place of our deepest personal roots and what we feel sentimental about; our subconscious memories, habits, and fears learned in childhood.

The fourth house also represents the most private area of our psyche, the opposite of our public image. It is concerned with all the things brought from our past, our roots and family history. It symbolizes ancestry and blood relations, particularly parents, and where we come from. It signifies the foundation of our security, the derivation of our identity, and our sense of where we belong. The ancients also considered this place to be a contributing factor in one's ability to have children. In addition, the fourth house shows one's relationship with the parent of lesser influence, usually the father.

Neptune in the fourth house governs orphans and orphanages, as does Saturn, if one is afflicted or debilitated. While it may not mean that the native is adopted, he or she may *feel* that way. The father may have been a nebulous and confused person who seemed to disappear when needed, or perhaps became completely estranged from the family. Thus the native is often left without a sense of belonging, being ignorant of his or her lineage.

If Mars is the lord of the fourth, the native may be a miner of raw minerals. Because this place is hidden beneath the surface, the native may be adept at covering tracks or at uncovering secrets.

THE
FOURTH
HOUSE

ONE

Two teenage boys stood atop a black mountain and looked down upon the glimmering lights of their kingdom. Each with a bottle of beer in hand, they toasted themselves and the good fortune of being alive on such a night. Far enough from the small town below, the stars twinkled unimpeded by streetlight. It was summer, and the night air was cool, but not too much so. Since they took the advice of an older guy (which every young teen needs if he wants to get booze), they had bought Kaiers instead of the more expensive Yuengling, and so they had more than enough to get one hell of a buzz on. Life was good.

Indeed, the town below was their kingdom, as each successive class of teens had that one year during which they seemed to command all that they surveyed. And within each class were always the chosen few who ruled over all others via divine providence. The two boys on the black mountain were among those blessed. They were handsome, athletic, witty, funny, and danced better than any other boys they knew. Girls dug them and they knew it. They were cool cats.

As the night wore on, they retreated back to their sleeping bags, drank some more beer, and discussed the deepest concerns of the day.

"This Kaiers ain't bad."

"I think it's because we brought it up early and put it in the stream. Even the worst beer in the world tastes better when it's freezing cold. When it's cold, it just flows; you know what I mean? It just flows." He kept saying the word "flows" as if it was a magical, almost religious thing. So awe-inspiring was this word as it described the perfect beer that it began to sound like he was pronouncing it wrong, contorting his mouth and adding syllables that did not belong.

The shorter of the two boys made himself more comfortable. "When I sleep out, I like to get naked. It feels great."

"Do you sleep that way all the time?"

"Naw, I share a room with my brother. He'd tell on me."

"Your brother's a prick sometimes."

"Yeah, I know. He's always getting me in trouble." Unabashed and unrestrained, the shorter boy stripped to total nudity in the moonlight, not even exhibiting the modesty to do so within his sleeping bag.

"What are you doing?"

"I told you. I'm sleeping naked."

"Yeah, but prancing around like that, someone could see you."

"Man, we're outside of town, up on a mountain in the woods. There's nobody around to see us. You think people are in their houses with binoculars looking to see if there're guys dancing around naked up here?" To make his point, the boy did, indeed, begin dancing around, his genitalia flopping about in a way that looked almost painful.

"Stop that. You're gross."

"Hey, I feel free. I'm gonna go to one of those nudist camps."

"What?"

"They have these camps where people dance around naked all day. They're called nudist camps."

"No they don't."

"Sure they do. I've seen pictures."

"I've seen pictures of naked people, too, but I didn't know they had a camp for them."

"Yeah. And it's not just pretty girls either, like in Playboy. It's, like, everyday people, just sitting around, reading the paper, mowing the lawn . . ."

"Bullshit. You can't mow the lawn naked. You'd hurt yourself."

"I don't know. So maybe I'm making up the lawn-mowing part. But they really do have these nudist camps."

"Man, I'd love to sneak up to one and watch."

"Yeah, I hear there's one up near Erie."

"Erie. That's pretty far away."

"Yeah, but if we knew there was a nudist camp there, we could borrow a car sometime and drive up and see if we could see somethin'."

"Yeah, that would be neat."

There were neither three houses nor four. Rather, there was simply block after block of row houses built in pairs going on for about half a mile, each almost humanlike with identically matching arms and legs. But no brain.

The name "Good Street" was a joke if ever there was one. Not even "Good" spelled "Goode," or even some ethnic variation such as "Gud," but just good old "Good," as in "What's so good about it?"

The little bungalows raised an immediate issue, which could only emanate from someone on the outside looking in, regarding their architectural reason for existence. With so much unused land spreading out in every direction, here were these teeny little half-homes squashed up against one another, with yards the size of postage stamps in front and an envelope in the rear.

Historically, most black silt hamlets like Mountain City, Pennsylvania, had been mining towns; communities formed only because of the existence of anthracite coal beneath them. The mining company owned the land upon which stood the assorted shanties built for the poor immigrant workers they employed. As many of these clusters were named after the company or some mining term, they became known as Shaft, Cork, Tunnelville, Rocktown, or anything one could think of involving a black hole in the dark ground. This was the world into which Jordan Matino was born.

Despite the somewhat condescending prose with which Jordan or those who escaped the locale referred to the place, it was still home. In most cases, the remaining inhabitants actually encouraged that escape. "Escaping the mines" originated as a phrase when mining was one of the few occupations one could pursue. Mining was also a fifty-fifty proposition for death; sometimes quick, sometimes slow. Once the mining industry left town and double-digit unemployment took its place, the flight was simply to bigger and better things.

Jordan's parents' generation had taken enormous pride merely in graduating from high school. A few even managed to attend college—"attend" being the key word, as completion of college was a much rarer accomplishment. The local shopping mall was staffed almost entirely by those who had known the honor of "attending" Penn State, Bloomsburg, or Kutztown, if only briefly during their college-age years.

College completion became more frequent with the generation of Jordan Matino, Mountain City Regional High School class of 1986. Prior to that, one of those rarest-of-the-rare from the previous generation who had managed to complete a college education was Rick George. And Rick George hated Jordan Matino. This last statement could never quite be confirmed, is most likely overstated, and could have existed only in the mind of Jordan Matino.

Rick George was Jordan's next-door neighbor as well as his godfather. Mountain City is a place where being chosen as a godparent is still taken quite seriously. This, along with the neighborly proximity, closeness of family intertwinements, and the fact that Jordan grew up without a father, is what drove Jordan Matino to expect so much from a man who gave him so little.

As time went by, Jordan tried to put a finger on exactly what it was that made this man, this larger-than-life personality, give so much to the rest of the world and so little to him. Rick George possessed exceptional amounts of gregarity and charm. That and his well-groomed style made him seem as out of place in Mountain City as a brand-new, hand-polished Jaguar in a demolition derby.

Every day of his adult life, Rick walked ten blocks to work, as if for the need to strut. His clothes, like everyone else's in Mountain City, were obviously purchased off the rack, yet on him they looked custom made. The walking was exercise, which kept him in great physical shape for his age, but it also conveyed an attitude. Rick George gave a big "Hi-hello" to every man, woman, and child in Mountain City. One might have thought he was campaigning for something.

Rick was a pharmacist but one who usually only poured pills from one big bottle into a smaller bottle and handed them, smilingly, to some little old lady in a babushka. That was Rick George's job and life in Mountain City, population 4,000 and shrinking.

Rick had attempted but failed to become a doctor and did not even own the little drugstore. Southern's Pharmacy was still owned by Cal Southern, who was well into his eighties and hardly worked anymore. Most of the town had to wonder why Cal hadn't retired completely and sold the business to Rick, who had been with him since the day Rick got out of pharmacy school. Some thought that cocky, flirty Rick simply had a personality that rubbed Cal the wrong way, being as how it ran so contrary to his own boring, pedestrian ways. Some had even told tales of the old man bossing Rick around right in front of customers, just to show whoever might be wondering exactly who was the top dog in that gone-to-the-dogs little mom-and-pop drugstore. That had to make someone with an ego as big as Rick's a little sore. But why did he only seem to take it out on his godson?

When pressed, Jordan admitted to his mother, the only person with whom he ever discussed it, that he might just be overly sensitive about the whole thing. Hate usually invokes some act of gross severity, like a punch to the jaw or a kick to the groin. Or in a more civilized setting, perhaps an anonymous call to the IRS or the local police over some petty nothing. No, this hate was more ambivalent, more a name hung upon a gut feeling that someone unquestionably disliked you. Frankly, even the thought of Rick George becoming a surrogate father to him in his real father's absence made Jordan chuckle derisively.

His father had not died but had disappeared shortly after Jordan's birth. Perhaps he *was* dead by now, as information was quite limited. No one had spoken of seeing him in decades.

The story Jordan had been handed was that his father had gotten into some financial quandaries, compounded by your basic run-of-the-mill marital troubles. His solution, rather than to stay and persevere, was to disappear. He was eventually found and the fiscal matters somehow negotiated. But his lack of desire to remain as a husband and father had been blatantly exposed. He then vanished for good, not under a cloak of darkness or through some obfuscation, but by simply packing up his things and walking out the front door in broad daylight.

Jordan often wondered how that scene had played out. Did his father kiss him good-bye? Were there tears? He'd been far too young to remember. He had also forgotten to ask.

Nonetheless, out the door he went, and that was the last anyone saw or spoke of him. Opal Matino bragged of her insistence that she and her baby receive no child support or alimony from the man. In later years, Jordan came to look at this source of Dutch pride as being, in practical terms, financial foolishness. How much better they could have lived. How much easier things could have been.

Instead, Opal Matino worked job after job, usually a few of them at a time, in order to keep food on the table and a roof over their heads. Jordan's maternal grandparents, who lived a few blocks away before they both died last year, helped with Jordan's care. So did the Steins next door and, to a lesser degree, his godmother, Eleanor George. For those were the three adjacent houses of Jordan's youth: his house being in between his godparents'—the Georges—on one side; and Jack and Mildred Stein's on the other.

In Jordan's opinion, the Steins were more suited to being his godparents than the Georges. Not that he had any trouble with his godmother, Eleanor. She was, in fact, an early source of his adolescent sexual fantasies. Of course, this may have been a rather Freudian impediment to his ever accepting her as a mother and parent. But Eleanor George was a rather perfect fit to swaggering Rick. Jordan could easily picture them as the homecoming king and queen of some long-ago year. Eleanor did not grand-stand like Rick, but looking as good as she did, it wasn't neces-sary. Doing so would have also prompted far too much gossip in a town as small as theirs. Eleanor had wavy, wild, just-had-sex blond hair topping sleepy cat eyes, a flawless nose and chin, and a model's high cheekbones. And those weren't even her best as-sets. Eleanor George, looking into the face of sixty, could still weaken the knees of a man half her age.

It was the recent deaths of his maternal grandparents that made today, Thanksgiving, feel strange and awkward for both Jor-dan and his mother. There is an old sight gag, used in far too many films dealing with the über-wealthy, where two people sit at a mile-long dining table looking and feeling absurd at the osten-tatiousness of it all. The Matinos' kitchen table was modest and fit only four comfortably, six if you put in the optional leaf. But for a holiday meal that had always featured four, it felt just as in-hospitable as if it were made for forty.

This was Jordan and Opal's first Thanksgiving alone, and while they had visited each other since the funerals, today felt wanting and empty. Their conversation was somewhat strained, as if this was another black crepe day.

Thanksgiving was not just any meal but one of those circle-the-date feasts that brought Jordan back from Philadelphia, where he was now living. Philadelphia was just far enough away for bachelor Jordan to feel like an independent adult, yet close enough that he could be helpful to his still-single mother.

Opal Matino made every attempt to have this dinner be a replica of all the Thanksgiving meals her mother had made be-fore. There was the requisite turkey; beyond that, though, things took on a more local flavor. The gravy had giblets, as did the stuff-ing. Mincemeat pie drenched in whiskey joined the traditional yet commonplace pumpkin pie. And where else but in "the region," as expats affectionately referred to it, could one find kielbasi served as a complementary second meat to the turkey?

Jordan had always felt it was the rampant alcoholism of the area that set it apart from more refined society. Yet discussions with people from the full gamut of the socioeconomic and geographic expanses of the world made him realize it was, in fact, the kielbasi. It was served endlessly.

Jordan broached the obvious. "Strange this year, isn't it?"

"Yes," his mother replied wistfully, "just you and me."

Each smiled sadly. They were close, and both had been equally close to Jordan's late grandparents. Because of their daily routines, with Opal working all the time and relinquishing many of her parental duties to her mother, she and Jordan were sometimes as much like sister and brother as mother and son. This was further enhanced by there being just the two of them, both of them only children.

Opal Zimmerman Matino had never seen her parents share a bed. Not once. From the time she was born, she could only recall her father working third shift—nights—and her mother keeping normal daytime hours. Their bedroom had two small single beds. Once Opal married, her mother moved out of that room and into Opal's old room. She said it was to escape her husband's snoring. That certainly raised questions in Opal's mind, since their schedules were so different. When exactly would they find themselves in that room together in order for his snoring to bother her?

The night-shift situation, the twin beds, the flight from their shared room, and her father's gentlemanly yet strict prudishness in all matters involving sexuality often led Opal to wonder how on earth she had been conceived by these two. Nevertheless, here she was, alive and certainly not adopted unless the entire world had been searched for the ideal baby to grow into the particular nuances of both her parents' physical and temperamental features.

Opal's situation was easier to explain. No man; no more babies. Opal dated off and on while Jordan was growing up, which was a lot stranger back then in Mountain City than it probably is today. No other kid's mother was going out on dates at the time, at least any that he knew.

Jordan was never too wild about the men his mother brought home. Once he became older, he tried to analyze his behavior toward them in an attempt to judge whether or not he had a complex about the whole thing. Was he predisposed toward disliking these suitors? Jordan took pride in being very self-aware, and his analysis provided him with this conclusion: No, he was not subconsciously sabotaging his mother's relationships. She *was* dating bozos, or at least borderline bozos.

Thankfully, there were no full-fledged melodramatic scenes in these dalliances. No drunks or batterers, which, given the male talent pool in the vicinity, was quite impressive. It was more like a short parade of double-knit, leisure-suited, white-shoed dorks without the slightest idea of how to have an intelligent conversation with an erudite person of any age. Some were good for a bag of candy or a game of catch, but little more. Each lasted awhile and then disappeared.

On the nights when she was to break up with one, Opal would confide in Jordan her plans and then later ask, "Did he mind?" Mind? Christ, he couldn't care less.

The thing Jordan never really thought about, basic as it was, was whether she might ever marry one of these paramours. It could happen; it could *have* happened. Yet these boyfriends of hers were nothing more than background scenery. They were simply her hobby, no different than stamp collecting or antiquing. No bozo, background scenery, or hobby was on the scene today, nor had there been in a year or two.

Jordan thought his mother might be getting a bit weepy-eyed, so he gave her a sincere, loving smile. Big hugs and long dissertations weren't necessary. Germans or Dutch or whatever the hell they were did not put on big, showy displays of affection. Volcanic anger on occasion, yes, but they weren't overly demonstrative with other emotions.

German or Dutch? For an area with major distinctions made between various Slavic countries of origin—Polish or Russian, Lithuanian or Czech—those of Germanic descent referred to themselves as Dutch one day, German the next. Most of them had no idea, since tracing one's roots was a hobby just starting to catch on around there. The confusion most likely stemmed from their phonetic-only translation of the native word, *Deutsche*. Thereby, "Pennsylvania Dutch" in most cases really meant "Pennsylvania German."

St. John's Church, attended regularly by the denizens of all three houses, might now be referred to as a sanctuary of the United Church of Christ, but prior to that it was affiliated with the Dutch Reformed Church. Opal Zimmerman became, at age thirteen, the church's organist and at age eighteen, choir director, positions she continued to hold throughout her entire life. Jordan sang in the choir, as did Rick George and his only daughter, Heather. The Steins were stalwart parishioners as well, though neither they nor their three sons were musically inclined.

For Jordan, singing in his mother's choir was an experience marred only by his godfather, Rick. Each Sunday and at each rehearsal, Jordan knew that he would have to see him and sit by him. There's good-natured joking and then there are cutting remarks that are thoughtless and meant to cause hurt, and Rick always seemed good for the latter.

Rick George was considered the best singer at St. John's, although Jordan could never understand why. Yes, unlike most people in small-town choirs, he could carry a tune. But he had this manner of singing, completely germane to his personality, that sounded as if he were channeling Dean Martin. While others sang, Rick George crooned. As Dean Martin, at least to Jordan's knowledge, never released an album of gospel music, Rick's artistic approach was quite incongruous with the material being served. Jordan approached choral music in the more traditional fashion and, thanks to Opal's genes, was quite good at it. Perhaps therein lay the rub. Jealousy—that had to be it. Rick once aspired to be a doctor, but for whatever reason, had settled for becoming a pharmacist. Jordan *had* become a doctor. And if Rick was the aging Clark Gable of little Mountain City, Jordan was a young, handsome, single physician in Philadelphia with no trouble attracting the ladies.

The jealousy theory seemed applicable for about 98 percent of all conflicts Jordan had with his godfather, and that might be about as good as theories get. The 2-percent margin of error was based upon the fact that Jordan could never remember a time when Rick George was not a son of a bitch, bully prick to him. Jordan had not joined the adult choir until his voice changed after puberty. He was still young enough to recall events long before that and could never remember a time when Rick George acted any nicer toward him.

All this talk of Rick George might lead one to believe that he was a major focus in Jordan Matino's life, but truly he was not. Especially now, when life was medicine and Philadelphia, cash in pocket and lovely young ladies. Today, Rick was more of an irritant associated with a place, the place Jordan was in right now: his hometown. It was more akin to an oft-frequented gas station manned by a friendly halfwit who always told the same lame joke. Yes, just an irritant.

Like most in the region, the Matinos served Thanksgiving dinner as a noontime meal. Upon finishing dessert, Jordan cleared and Opal set about packaging leftovers. The house was small, and the smell of cooking could literally become nauseating, especially once one was stuffed full, as Jordan was every year. When he told his mother he was going for a walk, she replied, "Good!" in the enthusiastic way one would respond to a loved one announcing they were quitting smoking or going on a much-needed diet. While Opal Matino was a single working woman who dated and had only one now-grown child, she still had a lot of classic "Mom" in her. She was downright hokey at times.

Bouncing down the wooden front steps of his childhood home on this brisk yet pleasant fall afternoon, Jordan was only slightly surprised not to find more activity outside. Neither Eleanor George nor Mildred Stein were sitting out on their front porches, as they often did. But this was Thanksgiving, and great activity was going on inside each of the Good Street homes.

The town park was only a block away and seemed a fitting destination. As a young child, Jordan found it a place of frolic on the slides and teeter-totters. When he was older, it was a place to flirt with girls and make out behind trees after baseball games played on the diamond just above it. As he approached now, the park was mostly empty, no games being played, no young children either.

A young woman with her back toward him swung slowly, alone on one of the old swings. The closer he got, the more familiar she looked. Funny, when Jordan was younger he could actually recognize another local kid simply by his or her coat, as they were all rather poor in Mountain City and usually owned only one or two pieces of outerwear each.

It was Heather George, his "cousin." That was another inside joke in the region. His godparents had always been referred to as "Uncle Rick" and "Aunt Eleanor," although they were not blood relations. Odder still, the Steins, not even his godparents, were known as "Uncle Jack" and "Aunt Mil." Initially Jordan thought it was an oddity of his family alone. But other kids his age were all doing the same thing, until it became difficult to know who really was related to whom in this quirky little town.

His gait altered to a discreet slither as he sneaked up behind the cousin-who-was-not-his-cousin.

"Horny Heather."

"Jordy Jerk-off."

He had first laid the nickname on her when he was about eleven and she was ten. The alliteration just sort of popped out one day. It was ironic because he, as well as she, barely understood the meaning of the word "horny" at the time. Yet he knew from that very moment that it upset and embarrassed her, so he incessantly kept it up. To that very day, no one else had ever called her that. So too, his being called "Jordy Jerk-off."

Like he and his mother, Heather was an only child, rather strange in Mountain City, where birth control seemed as foreign as time travel. Families of all faiths regularly had broods of at least three or four, usually more.

Despite how he felt about his Uncle Rick, Jordan loved Heather as a brother loves a sister. They teased, they fought, they defended each other, and they hurt each other's feelings and spent days not talking. In short, they were like every brother and sister they had ever known.

Once they were old enough to know the meanings of words like "horny" and "jerk-off," Jordan was not blind to the fact that Heather was growing into a beauty. But those thoughts were, within him, regarded as verboten. For what sort of person lusted after their sister/cousin/god-something-or-other? Only a creep.

As a child, Heather had the face of a porcelain doll topped with Shirley Temple curls, an advertiser's dream of a beautiful baby girl. Many wondered if growing up would do her looks more harm than good. But no, she developed well and was quite popular with the boys. Some even tried approaching her through Jordan, as one would a sister through a brother. He treated it like a brother would, giving a steely glare to anyone who sounded disrespectful of her virtue. So too, although they were each other's best friend of the opposite sex, he did not care to discuss sexual matters with her, nor she with him, "Horny Heather" and "Jordy Jerk-off" aside.

He asked, "Did you scare the other little kids off the swings?"

"Yeah, that's why I'm here all alone."

Glad as they were to see each other, there was no hugging or kissing, for that would have been much too weird. That air-kissing bit was big in Philly, but here in Mountain City the only times Heather and Jordan had embraced were at his grandparents' funerals.

"Seen anyone?" he asked.

"Naw. How's Philly?"

"Sweet."

Standing alongside her, he began to do something odd. As she faced him, he started moving around behind her.

"What are you doing?"

"Seeing if you can still hear me if you can't see me."

"Asshole."

Heather was a teacher of the deaf and therefore an excellent lip reader. Jordan knew one of them would be the first to start the inevitable teasing, as he was a urologist. Only proctologists and gynecologists got more abuse in the medical world.

It was her turn. "Grabbed any big ones lately?"

"They all look small to me."

Joking and cutting up was safe ground between them.

Once, *once* they were at a basement rec-room New Year's Eve party, years before, while home from college. Jordan was stag, and Heather was with some guy who had no personality whatsoever, an outsider she had brought home to Mountain City. Jordan had no idea what the deal was with them, serious or not, the sleeping arrangement, whatever. But shortly after midnight Heather was much the worse for wear, and Jordan was worried.

"Who's driving?" he asked.

"Who said I was going anywhere?"

She was totaled. Jordan looked around for her date. He saw him off in the crowd, still wandering about with not much to say and no one to say it to. He felt a bit sorry for the guy, as most everyone there had known each other since diapers. But unlike most shy guys in this situation, he wasn't hanging all over his date for social support. Jordan couldn't figure out the dude.

"What's-his-name looks better than you do. Make sure he drives."

"You think he looks better than me? What are you, gay?" She laughed drunkenly at her own joke. Then she leaned in to him as close as two people can get. "I want *you* to take me home."

This was not phrased as some random drunk would say it to a random designated driver. There was sexual subtext here.

"Take me home, Jordy. I wanna be with you."

Her lips were a millimeter from his, and the extreme proximity caused her face to become indistinct to him—close enough to reveal every pore, yet too near for the individuality of perspective. For the first time that he could remember noticing, her eyes had that sexy, sleepy, sultry look of her mother's. The moment seemed to last forever, until he realized he was about to kiss his best female friend in the world, which made him pull back in horror. Luckily, no one noticed the discomfort he felt. Not even the unkissed Heather. He jerked his head back slightly and gave a discreet chuckle so as not to make the young lady feel embarrassed at her forwardness. But he knew. He knew. She wanted him. If only for that one moment on that one night, *she* had wanted *him*.

He managed to grab hold of her errant escort and instructed him to drive her home carefully. The entire time, Heather kept gazing at Jordan and not at her boyfriend with that same lustful, come-hither smile. She wanted him, not as a friend, a big brother, or a cousin that night, but as a lover. God, for whatever reason, that moment had become etched in his mind as brilliantly as any real sexual conquest of his life.

He never mentioned it. Never. Not the next day, although he did come over to see that she was all right. Not ever. But that was ten or twelve years ago, at least, and what did it matter today? Especially since Jordan had no handle on what exactly it had meant to him.

"How long you in for?" she asked.

"The weekend. Unless I get off early for good behavior."

They had always had a good rhythm together. How many awful, awful dates had he been on with women who had no sense of humor whatsoever?

"What about you? Spending the weekend?"

"Yep. No school tomorrow. Maybe I'll hit the mall."

"Not the one up here, I hope. I hear they closed K-Mart because the clothes were too haute couture," he joked.

Heather lived and worked in Reading, which was about forty minutes away, and where there were certainly much better places to shop. Her closer proximity to Mountain City also allowed her to visit home more often than Jordan.

"What are you going to do for four days? Any of your crew still around?"

"Probably. Maybe if I'm lucky they won't find me." By this time Jordan had slid onto the swing next to her.

"So Jordy, making the big bucks now?"

"Yeah, finally. Unfortunately, the student loans will be paid off around retirement time." He paused for no other reason than to think of what to say next so that he would not say what he *wanted* to say next. And then it came out anyway. "So, do you want to go out and do something some night?"

There it was. Now, *he* knew he didn't mean it the way it came out, but would she? All these years as friends, they had done millions of things together, but it had always sounded like, "There's a party at Danny's Friday night. Me, Kev, and Bear are going. We heard you and Cheryl and some of your friends were going, too. Are ya?" It never quite sounded like he had just put it. He had accidentally made it sound like a date.

"Sure."

Oh geez, he thought. She was smiling. They were both single. Now he didn't know what to think. Heather was a pal to him, nothing more. On the other hand, she had many of the attributes that could make for a tolerable evening back home. She had a brain, she wasn't an alcoholic (though after that New Year's Eve episode, he'd have to recheck his intel on that), and she was fun and funny. Could be a good time, if there were no expectations of it being something more. There was so damn little to do back home. The mall cinema had only three screens, and he wasn't really in the mood for a movie anyway. Going out to dinner was a date thing. Besides, it was Thanksgiving and there would be leftover turkey and kielbasi in both their homes for days. That left bars, nightclubs. On Thanksgiving. "Any clubs open tonight?" he accidentally asked out loud.

"I don't know. I hardly go out around here anymore."

"Doing something some night" had suddenly become "tonight," for whatever reason. If it was to be barhopping, it occurred to him that if they stayed in the park catching up for too long, they'd have little to talk about later.

"Pick you up around eight?"

"Can you find the place?"

"Fuck you." Damn, he thought, suddenly even the ol' smilin' "F.U." made an uncomfortable tickle in his throat. Jordan still cursed far too much. He'd been working on curbing it since med school. Heather was neither a slatternly trashmouth nor some born-again priss. Just perfectly in the middle for a woman, profanity-wise, as far as he was concerned.

"See you later," she said, as Jordan turned to leave.

He'd only been out of his house perhaps fifteen minutes, and here he was heading back down the hill toward home. He figured that if he went in any other direction Heather would have wondered why he was leaving at all. But he understood his own reasoning.

So where were they going to go? What would he wear? What was *she* going to wear? Ooo, that was a good one. That would certainly tell him what she was thinking. On a first date, Jordan could often tell if he was getting lucky just by what the lady was wearing. Any overt slut-wear and he knew that he was golden from the word "Hello." But geez, this wasn't a damn date. This was Heather. This was home. This was an alternative to staying in with his mom watching sitcoms or calling up guys he'd gone to high school with, hoping they were still single or between bad marriages.

Calling the guys was becoming a game of diminishing returns. Marriage was banishing most of them to the proverbial bench. Yes, he could still go over and hang with the J.C. Penney's photo families they had become. But the differences between them and him were getting too stark, too fast. There was an entire menu of annoyances to choose from. The sermons on the joys of matrimony. The guy pulling him aside, telling him what hell it really was. The wife pulling him aside and saying the same thing, but with a leer in her eye that meant she was "open for business" if a better offer came along, hint, hint. The fix-up offers. The "why aren't you married yet?" bullshit. On and on.

At thirty-two, Jordan's life was sometimes odd. He had really just reached the point of simply *being* a doctor, whereas most of his contemporaries were already well defined by their occupations. Jordan had just completed almost a decade and a half of college and residency and thus still possessed somewhat of a college student's social mentality. Most other doctors his age were also single. Most other *people* were not. Often, the world seemed jealous of his title, even in Philly, even though he had just begun earning some of the good green.

As he rounded the corner to the most infamous row of houses in his personal history, there he was: Uncle Rick. Oy. His best friend in Philly, Paul Zeiss, would be pleased: Jordan was even *thinking* in Yiddish now, as Paul's influence invaded Jordan's being.

"Well, the prodigal returns."

"Yup."

Jordan was glad Heather had not returned with him. It would have been uncomfortable. Now that he was an adult, Jordan had less compunction to take what Rick might dish out. Over the last few years, he had no problem returning Rick's sarcasm and was prepared to really tell the sonofabitch off if he crossed the line.

"C'mere a second."

More posturing in the war of the minds. Jordan had to come sit on Rick's porch, Rick's home turf, albeit ten feet away from Jordan's. They sat on the old glider, a strange piece of patio furniture that was part porch swing, part outdoor sofa, and part rocking chair. Vinyl covered, it held about three people and glided back and forth on a metal runner. The Georges, the Matinos, and the Steins all had one.

Rick leaned in conspiratorially. "Viagra's selling very well."

"Pfizer thanks you." Aha! Aha! He got one in first. Damn, times had changed. Rick was unfazed.

"I hear they're working on some newer things. Patches and stuff. What do you know about that?"

Rick George was not a studious pharmacist engaging in scholarly shoptalk with a doctor. Rick George simply insinuated sex into every conversation. This was another thing that always made Jordan uncomfortable. For years he had heard Rick brag about "wild nights" with his gorgeous Eleanor. His talk always seemed to drift toward accoutrements such as vibrators, lubricants, Frederick's of Hollywood, and all sorts of things that Mountain City gentlemen did not discuss in public. Rick seemed to want the world to know how virile he was, as if he was the only man in the world having regular sex with his own wife. It would be boorish in any context, but particularly so if you lived next door to him and were his godchild.

"Yeah, our practice participates in studies from time to time. There's a lot going on in that area right now."

"Yeah, yeah, I've heard that." Rick sounded like he was getting insider stock tips. "Things have come a long way since pumps and Papaverine, haven't they? You ever try that Papaverine?"

"No, Uncle Rick. I primarily work with prostate cancer patients, although I get some sexual dysfunction work on occasion."

"Well, if you ever get some samples of any new stuff . . ." Rick's leer said the rest.

"You having some problems in that area, Uncle Rick?" Damn! He was killing him today, absolutely murdering him. A lifetime of losing these verbal battles and now he was standing tall and strong.

"No, no, not me. You should come up to the bedroom. I just bought one of those chair things. You know those chairs?"

"What kind of chair do you mean?"

"You know, those swinging chairs with the holes in the bottom. You hang it on a chain, you know?"

Suddenly the picture was clear in Jordan's mind, from some long-ago porn flick or soft-core cable thing. Rick was back on top because yes, this was not a visual Jordan wanted to deal with. Aunt Eleanor, nude in some swinging wicker chair, hovering above a prone, naked Uncle Rick with his erection perpendicular to his body; pushing up through the bottom of the chair while she . . . spun around on him? Oh geez . . .

"That's okay."

"You haven't seen our new bedroom, have you? I redid it in these wild, jungle prints. Now we walk around like Adam and Eve. With Heather out of the house, no need to be discreet. Know what I mean?"

The guy was a total, smirking, arrogant perv. This was not some drunk at a bar bragging about unknown, faceless women. This was the man who was supposed to become his father if his own father had failed to live up to his duties, which is exactly what had happened. And he was talking about Jordan's own godmother, no less! Why did he do this? Jordan had heard similar garbage from Rick's mouth over the years, not just directed at him but at anyone else who would listen. To Stein. Everyone, including his own wife, Mildred, referred to Uncle Jack Stein simply as "Stein." Poor neighbor Stein had to have heard this trash for ages and couldn't have liked it any more than had Jordan. Stein would never talk about sex or his wife to anyone in public the way Rick George did. Stein may have been the one with dirt under his fingernails, but in some ways he had more class than white-collar Rick by a mile.

As Jordan retreated into the safe haven of his house, the one to the right of the Georges', he wondered how Uncle Rick would feel about him going on a date with his precious daughter that very night. Damn! There it was again. He was not going out with Heather. She was just a pal he'd known his entire life. Two people in this burg who could spend a platonic evening together and conceivably have a very good time.

Jordan's mother looked up from her cleaning. "You're back soon. See anyone you know?"

Funny question. There was no one in Mountain City whom he did not know. But it was Thanksgiving, and there was food on the table and football on the tube. The streets and sidewalks were so vacant that birds could be heard cawing hundreds of yards away. A ghost town on a chilly day.

"I ran into Heather."

"Oh, that's nice."

His mother would have said "Oh, that's nice" if he had told her he'd discovered a dead body under the leaves by the park swings. No, in all fairness she would have instead replied, "Ohhhh . . . that's not good," and continued to carve up turkey into neat little foil-wrapped packages.

"We're going out tonight; see what's happening."

"Oh, that's a good idea. That's great."

She had to have assumed it was not a date. Had to. Her entire tone had an "I'm so glad you're playing with Johnny-the-hemophiliac," sound to it.

She was so damn proud that her son was the first in her family to complete college that Jordan pretty much got to skate on everything else. She never asked "When are you going to get married and give me grandchildren?" Most of his other high school classmates were already onto their second or third child, or even their second or third marriage by now, but that was okay by her.

Funny how Heather hadn't gotten married yet, either. What was her excuse? She was attractive, bright, had a decent job, and this was about the tenth time Jordan had mentally listed her attributes since he saw her.

Strangely enough, their little tête-à-tête in the park was one of the longest conversations they'd had in years. They went to different colleges and settled in different cities but kept similar "coming home holidays." Yet mostly they were like planets passing in separate orbits. He might see her on Thanksgiving; he might not. Ditto Christmas or any random day he chose to drop in. If they did see each other, it frequently involved nothing more than a "hi/bye" as one or the other departed for places unknown. This did not indicate a frost in their relationship. They were simply into their own new lives and, perhaps, took their lifelong friendship somewhat for granted.

Jordan thought that if it weren't for the sexual overtones, this could be a very good evening ahead. She was bright, she was fun, and here he was listing her attributes again. Damn!

Barhopping was something Jordan did semi-frequently. He went to bars for the same reason most single people do—sex. Despite all the negatives postulated about singles bars, Jordan rather enjoyed them. To him it was an advanced study in American urban sociology. Like some perverse sportscaster, he got gassed watching the mating rituals and narrating them to himself or his compatriots of the evening.

"She's beautiful and she knows it. Dressed to kill. She makes eye contact with no one, except to order a drink. In a room full of people, how can she still manage to find a place to look where there are no other eyes? It's like a magic trick or something. Occasionally, she looks toward the door and then quickly back to staring at the posts holding up the ceiling. It gives the impression that she's waiting for someone, someone better than anyone who's here, but that person never comes."

"So she's available?"

"Go up to her and find out."

"And get shot down? No way."

"Why?"

"Because she's waiting for someone."

"No she's not. She just wants you to *think* she's waiting for someone. If she was really waiting for someone, she'd look longer at the door."

"How do you know these things?"

"I'm a urologist. We study this in school."

Granted, Jordan had other ways of meeting eligible women, but most of them he abhorred. Dinner parties thrown by couples with him and only one single woman invited. He hated that. Socially acceptable voyeurism with him as the show. At singles bars there was still the feel of stalking prey, of unlimited choices and possibilities. Despite the naysayers, Jordan had actually met and dated—sometimes for quite a substantial amount of time—a number of women he'd met in bars and clubs. There is a certain conundrum in the rantings of anti-bar believers. In order to conclusively postulate that relationships could not be found in these places, they had to have tried it themselves. Thus, they essentially were living proof that all types of people looking for all sorts of things could be found on a given night in a given bar. This was Jordan's Singles Bar Theory of Random Possibility.

There was also *the issue.* The single doctor issue. He and Zeiss joked about their prestigious memberships in the DDL—Doctors, Dentists, and Lawyers. Even rude, ugly doctors were in demand. It was like being a movie producer.

In Philly, he was always meeting women who had turned marriage into some sort of goal, something one would put at the top of a "to do" list. Especially getting married to a doctor. But what Jordan particularly loathed, the thing that made him leave skid marks on a moment's notice, was when a woman he had just met told him, "I'm really looking for a committed relationship." If he were feeling spry enough, he would debate them on the notion.

"With just anyone?"

"No, not with just anyone."

"So how would you know?"

"I don't understand what you're asking."

"You said you're looking for a committed relationship. That means you want exclusivity and yet you don't even know this person yet."

"No, but if they're the right person, I'd want a commitment."

"But how do you get to know if they're the right person?"

"We'd go out."

"And if he wasn't the right person?"

"We'd stop seeing each other."

"Sounds just like 'dating around' to me."

"No, it's different. It's dating a person who's ready to make a commitment."

"But to who? Maybe to you; maybe not to you. You'd have to go out awhile in order to find out, right?"

"Right."

"Would you sleep together?"

"I don't sleep around. I told you, I'm looking for a committed relationship."

"But what if you were sexually incompatible? What if he was into S&M or something?"

"I wouldn't stand for that."

"But you'd never know that until you got naked together, would you?"

He could drag this on for hours. Not that he enjoyed arguing, but he'd been through this cliché so many times it stuck in his craw.

And so, Jordan Matino trolled singles bars for sex and absence of commitment. He trusted no woman, a casualty in the battle of the sexes and utterly sick of the game. Entering the DDL, he swore off love as a nun swears off marriage. Another time, perhaps.

TWO

———— ✺ ————

There's a point when flirting reaches a crest of do or die. Stop and be thought a tease, continue and be thought a fool, or forge ahead and do something wonderful or terribly wrong. Tonight is that point of no return.

I'm attractive. I know I am. I'm young, I'm pretty, I'm full of life. And that life is dying on the vine.

I can't take the fighting anymore. I'm tiptoeing around and nothing I say or do is ever right. I fight back and feel horrible and insensitive afterward. I apologize and it almost seems to make matters worse. I try to understand, but I can't and there's no one around I can talk to about it. Some things you just have to keep to yourself. You do it for him. You do it for your marriage.

And then I flirt. It brings back my ego. It reminds me that I can. It reminds me that I'm still who I was before I became this unhappy person.

I don't do it around every man. That would be wrong. I've never been that sort of girl, even when it would have been all right. I was *never raised to be that forward and brash. Besides, the boys came around anyway. They liked me. Lots of them liked me. I had my choice. It's just that now I have to flirt in order to remember.*

I like him. I've liked him for a while. I chose him for that reason. I also chose him because he seemed like the most unlikely person to let it go too far. The fact that it's gone this far amazes me. Maybe a lot of it's in my mind. But no, I'm not that naïve. He's playing with me and I'm playing with him. We're both playing with fire.

He's not stupid. And he's a good man, too. He must be doing it for much the same reason I am. We both dance around it, like we dance around each other. Either of us making some big, dramatic confession about how miserable we are would be out of character. Movie stuff.

But we keep dancing. Flirting. Smiling. Being suggestive. Finding excuses to be in groups together. Finding excuses to be like we are right now—alone together. Pushing the limits.

Isn't this enough? He's obviously attracted to me. Case proven. I can stop now, right? But the other one claims he's attracted to me, too; at least that's what he says. But he never shows it. At least not how I want him to show it. But this one does, I bet. This man won't stop at simply saying it. I can feel it.

I stand so close to him as we talk. I lean back into him as I point something out. That's the flashpoint. That's the moment when I feel what it would be like to be his lover. I'm that close. My breath is trembling. I'm trembling. He's trembling. I'm not a tease. He doesn't think I'm a fool. Something terrible or wonderful is going to happen right now.

At eight o'clock, Jordan walked out onto his front porch and, for the first time in his life, hesitated before approaching the house next door. As a kid, he sometimes hopped over one porch banister and onto the Georges', a distance of a few feet. The Matinos

and Steins shared one double block, the local term for the paired
row houses; the Georges and a succession of various families over
the years shared the other. Jordan wasn't climbing banisters or
jumping anywhere tonight, but was he supposed to walk up their
porch steps and ring the doorbell like a common suitor? A date?

As if on cue, Heather came out onto her porch as well. She
looked good. No slut-wear, just fitted black slacks and a bulky
blue turtleneck under a nice black-leather jacket. Jesus! He was
wearing a blue shirt, black chinos, and a black-leather jacket.
They looked like twins.

"Nice outfit," she said. "Did you watch me getting dressed
through the window or something?"

"If I tell you what color underwear you're wearing, do I get a
prize?"

"You'll get a slap."

"Want to take two cars or one?"

She looked at him with a scrunched-up face that was meant
to convey, "What kind of stupid question is that?"

He knew what he meant, even if she didn't, or if she was just
playing dumb. It was a common ploy he and his pals used. Take
more than one car. That way if someone got lucky, they could
split up and not have to worry about leaving someone stranded.
Jordan was still straddling the differing mind-sets of this being a
date or just a night out with the guys, even though this guy had
breasts. As Jordan looked at grown-up Heather George, he realized he might have a hard time finding a better-looking woman in
Lantenengo County on this or any other night. This was true internal conflict.

Heather didn't seem to be buying the two-car thing. "That's
your Lexus, isn't it?"

"Yeah." Upon getting a position at one of the best private

urology practices in Philly, he had done his first yuppie thing by
buying himself a luxury car.

"It could be worse. If you'd bought a 'Vette, I'd know you
were a total eunuch."

Heather's father, Rick, had often talked about buying just that
kind of vehicle, a perfect complement to his suggestive macho
pretense. It probably would have been bright yellow.

"We could take your car. What do teachers drive these days?
Skateboards?"

"I like a Lexus. I don't usually get to ride in cars this nice."

This seemed more like a date every second. All they needed
now was for their parents to be watching from their front doors,
waving like they were going to a damn prom together.

Settling into the car truly sent it over the edge. She smelled
good. Too good. *Date* good. Makeup, too. Her face looked beautiful, absolutely stunning. This was not the way a woman dressed,
perfumed, or made herself up for a night at a bowling alley with
the girls. This was date dress, date smell, date makeup. He was in-
toxicated.

"Where do you want to go?"

"You're the guy. Where do *you* want to go?"

"*I'm the guy?* What's that supposed to mean?"

Suddenly, her look changed. It was nothing gigantic, but her
face showed a broken mood and a tipped hand. According to her,
he was "the guy" and she was "the girl." Those were dating roles.

As gently and affectionately as possible, he countered with a
smile. "I haven't been out around here in awhile and I thought
you might know what's hip and happening among the coal
banks." He leaned toward her, not close enough for a kiss, but
close enough to demonstrate attraction as well as empathy. "Is the
Alley still open?"

"No."

"The 'Fink?"

"Closed years ago."

"So you can understand my problem."

Why didn't he take that awkward moment to be direct and simply ask, "Are we on a date? Are you attracted to me in that way?" Yet he did not, because he was a coward and a lecher, and he was intrigued enough to let it play out in real time.

He felt in equal parts wholesome and perverse. There was absolutely nothing wrong with them dating. It was not a sin for him to feel tantalized by her. Tantalized by her mother, that was probably a sin in most cultures. But by Heather, no.

"There's a place called Club 21 in Gibbsville. Ever been to it?" Heather seemed to be getting over being hurt or offended or whatever.

"No. Where is it?"

"Twenty-first Street."

"Original name. Is it a dance club?"

"No idea. I just heard it's a hangout."

"Is it nice?"

"Afraid of getting mugged?"

"No. I'm with a tough chick in a leather jacket. I'll be all right. She probably has tattoos, too."

There are two types of bars in the United States: singles bars and "guy" bars. Gay bars are also singles bars, as people obviously go there in search of luvin'. Even sports bars are becoming more singles-oriented. Guy bars tend to open at daybreak, entertain no more than a half dozen denizens at any one time, and have the same absence of spirit as a chemotherapy ward.

Lantenego County, here in the coal region, had more guy bars than singles bars by a hefty margin, one on almost every corner.

That fact alone might paint the best and simplest picture of the place. Bleak. Something from which to escape.

Club 21 will never be confused with the famous "21" in New York. The building was falling down, almost leaning to one side. White paint was peeling. It did not stand alone but was in a commercial-residential mixture of connected row buildings. Not double blocks; just a long string of shack after shack. One match and the whole damn thing would go up like dried leaves. There was one very tall, large, and crooked step a person had to negotiate in order to get to the front door. Jordan imagined the scores of drunks who had tripped on that very step over the years. If he was a personal injury lawyer he could plant himself there day and night in order to pick up clients as they crashed to the pavement.

"This is the place?"

"So it says," replied Heather, with a hint of embarrassment.

"Who told you this was a good place?"

"I forget. A lot of people."

"Did they have teeth?"

The best was certainly yet to come, as Jordan had ambient dread whenever he entered a region bar. He tended to stand out, for he had bathed and shaved, and his clothes were clean. This was not necessarily a rich-versus-poor thing. Some of these guys had decent-paying jobs. Hell, coal mining, what was left of it, paid damn well. It would have to for people to do it today. No, this was some other sort of cultural glitch, some odd macho thing that Jordan never understood or felt a part of.

"You want to go in?" he asked.

"The only other places I know of are up toward Hazelton and Wilkes-Barre. Ski lodges and stuff."

"Okay, here goes nothing."

They climbed Mount Front Step and opened the windowless

door. Everyone in the room it seemed, turned to face them, two strangers allowing street light into a darkened opium den. If there had been live music, it would have ground to a halt. This was *High Noon* and Jordan was Gary Cooper, with none of the townsfolk watching his back.

It was almost triple the size of a typical region guy bar. There was a jukebox playing and a TV showing sports, so it lacked that total feeling of hopelessness and despair. The male-to-female ratio was about ten men to every woman. There were "hosey women," the kind who belonged to volunteer fire company ladies' auxiliaries. There were also bowling league ladies and softball wives. The differences were subtle, but Jordan's eyes were trained and keen. None of them appeared to be single. The place had a British pub ambiance, with wives accompanying their husbands for a pint as their only means of seeing them at a decent hour.

As for the men, he had not seen so many covered heads since he went with Paul Zeiss to a Jewish wedding. Jordan hated wearing a hat and had always felt that outside of the Orthodox, those who chose to wear them indoors were covering up either bald spots or lobotomy scars. When he had last entered a place like this, most of the indoor hats were emblazoned with the logos of sports teams, beer brands, or machinery companies. Tonight, they were almost all featuring automotive companies and racecar drivers. Oh, no. Lantenengo County had become part of the NASCAR nation. It only made sense.

He listened to the music on the juke. Country. *Country!?* Only yesterday, everything here was either polkas or heavy metal. An entire generation of coal region baby boys had been proudly named Lemmy, Angus, or Axl. Country?! They were well above the Mason-Dixon Line. Jordan had never heard country music around here.

As nondescript twanging filled the room, he even spied a few cowboy hats among the NASCAR apparel. *Cowboy hats!?* There were no cows, horses, or rodeos in Northeastern Pennsylvania. Never was. What the hell was going on?

"Want to stay?" Heather asked, pensive as he.

"Yeah, I'll try to behave."

All eyes watched as the out-of-towners found an empty table. Bars around here had no cocktail waitresses, not even when they had discos, which was ten years after everyone else in the world had grown tired of doing the Hustle.

"Think they'll have white wine?" she asked without a hint of irony as Jordan pulled out her chair. Obviously she was telling the truth when she said she hadn't been barhopping around Gibbsville in awhile.

"No."

"Think they'll have red wine?"

"No."

"Hmmm . . . what are you having?"

"Something other than beer, which could be a challenge."

"I'm easy. Get two of whatever you're having."

He strode up to the bar a few feet away. Jordan smiled and nodded at those still staring. Just like dealing with a strange dog, he thought. Show no fear; make no quick movements.

He looked behind the bartender, to where most bars display bottles. Funny how that's taken for granted everywhere else in the world. But here, the bartender stood in front of one half-empty shelf—a wooden plank sitting on cinder blocks about two feet off the rancid floor.

In the dim light, Jordan leaned over, trying to figure out what was in those dusty old flasks. He thought he knew most liquor from the bottle shapes alone. But here, he could hardly even decipher the colors of the vessels. One of them looked clear. That meant either vodka, gin, or empty.

"Tanquer . . ." Tanqueray was his gin of choice, but that bottle of clear stuff or no stuff was not in a green Tanqueray bottle, so he caught himself just in time. He'd learned years ago that in a region bar what you saw was what you got. There would be no Tanqueray gin hiding in some special safe place waiting for him.

"Got gin?"

The bartender looked at Jordan as if he had asked him for money. Slowly, he turned to the nondescript ancient bottles. Just as slowly, he turned back.

"Yeah."

"I'll have two gin and tonics."

Now he got an even worse look, like he was foreclosing on the guy's house. Even more slowly, the man turned and walked away. Simply walked away. It was surreal. Jordan wondered if this meant he was not going to be served at all.

The slow-moving old bartender returned with what appeared to be his boss. Geez, was this going to be trouble? Over gin and tonic?

"What can I get you?" The boss seemed a bit more of this world. By now Jordan was downright skittish about what and how to place a drink order in this joint.

"You got gin?"

The boss turned to look. "Yeah."

"You got tonic?"

That seemed to throw him. "You mean soda?"

"No, tonic. Quinine." Unfortunately, "quinine" must have sounded like an illegal narcotic or something.

"No, nothing like that."

Jordan knew he was outnumbered, but he also had his pride

and did not want to be thought a fool. "It's a popular combination. I really can't think of much else to mix with gin, can you?"

The boss and his near-mute bartender-assistant looked at each other for an answer that would never come.

"Tell you what. You got bourbon down there?" Jordan had a med school pal from New Orleans who drank nothing but bourbon and Coke. The darker stuff in one of the bottles had to be some kind of whiskey, and he *knew* they had heard of Coke.

"Got whiskey." He picked the bottle up. "Blended whiskey."

"It'll do. I'll have two of those with Coke."

The boss placed two glasses of whiskey and Coke in front of him. Without ice. Jordan knew not to expect a slice of lime or a swizzle stick. But ice was pretty basic. He contemplated starting in on this new issue but thought better of it. Whiskey and Coke, neat. It would have to do.

Jordan felt every set of eyes at the bar boring through the back of his skull as he returned to Heather.

"Hope you like warm cocktails."

"Is the glass clean?"

"I wouldn't bet on it."

Luckily, Heather felt much the same as he did about the region. Some of his ex-cohorts hated it, absolutely loathed the place, and vowed never to return. Jordan may have escaped and embraced the city, but he always had to have this place within his life. It reminded him of where he'd come from and how far he had gone. Some who, like him, had left and became—in a sense of the word—*successful* returned to gloat. But Jordan was almost shy about the M.D. after his name. Back here, he never referred to himself as Dr. Matino. It was just plain Jordan. Jordan from Mountain City.

Eventually, Heather gave up the goodies about her personal life. She'd been in love a few times. Once, she lived with a guy for over a year, but she had never been engaged or married. She loved her job and had lots of friends. For his part, Jordan did not go into his relationship philosophy-of-the-moment.

This was a date. He was having a good time and so was she. They'd had a few drinks by now, and their bodies spoke the language of flirtation. Jordan no longer felt strange, and Heather apparently never had in the first place.

For no logical reason, Jordan wanted to reach across the table and hold her hand. He had no idea why. It had been years since he touched a woman for touching's sake. Handholding with the right person used to make his insides warm. Such a simple gesture, yet for him it was true affection. But he held his impulses in check, feeling that if he made such a romantic movement Heather would laugh in his face and say, "Jerk-off, it's me! Get your freakin' hands off me."

"Music. I must hear different music or my head will explode." Jordan got up and went to the jukebox. Scanning about, his eyes finally lit up. Amidst the country and polkas he found a treasure, one glorious musical gem.

Returning with a pickpocket's smile, he commanded, "Let's dance."

There was indeed a modest-sized dance floor. Perhaps on a night other than Thanksgiving some couples used it.

"No one else is dancing."

Jordan offered his hand, though, and she took it. This was so unlike him, unafraid to be the first on a dance floor. But this was a rare moment of impetuous inspiration.

"Who cares? We *must* dance to this."

She had no idea what was coming. With his offbeat sense of

humor, she knew he could have just put on something by Weird Al Yankovic.

Instead, it was a slow, old, country ballad with which she was not immediately familiar. The vocal began and it was not some drawling, southern-sounding wannabe but a soulful black man. Jordan guided her into his arms.

"Brother Ray," he whispered reverently into her ear.

> *You give your hand to me,*
> *And then you say, "Hello,"*
> *And I can hardly speak,*
> *My heart is beating so.*
> *And anyone can tell,*
> *You think you know me well,*
> *But You Don't Know Me.*

They danced the first verse politely and tentatively. She looked into his eyes and smiled with all of her face and he with all of his, unable to repress reciprocation. By the second verse they were embracing like lovers.

> *No, you don't know the one,*
> *Who dreams of you at night,*
> *And longs to kiss your lips,*
> *And longs to hold you tight.*
> *To you I'm just a friend,*
> *That's all I've ever been.*
> *'Cause You Don't Know Me.*

Jordan did not see her expression when he turned to kiss her. He did not need to, nor did he need any other permission to do so than the way their bodies were moving together. It was, quite simply, the only thing to do.

> *For I never knew the art of making love,*
> *Though my heart ached with love for you.*
> *Afraid and shy, I let my chance go by,*
> *The chance you might have loved me, too.*

If not for the need of breath, they might have held that kiss forever. Squaring with her face, that beautiful face he had known eternally, Jordan was truly gazing at a completely new person, a person who felt so right, so damn right in every way. Hard as it was to look anywhere else but into her eyes, he glanced past her for only a split second. Just long enough to see every hosey woman, bowling lady, and softball wife in the place staring at the two of them as if they were watching a classic romantic film. He returned to her kiss.

> *You give your hand to me,*
> *And then you say, "Goodbye."*
> *I watch you walk away,*
> *Beside the lucky guy.*
> *To never, ever know,*
> *The one who loves you so.*
> *No, You Don't Know Me.*

The music may have ended; he couldn't really tell. Corny as it sounds, there was a smattering of applause from the ladies' auxiliary. Jordan gave an impish grin and nodded his head in modest acknowledgement as Heather held both his hands and giggled ever so slightly. He finally broke the silence. "I think we should go."

"Yeah?"

"A good performer knows to leave his audience wanting more."

She kept grinning as they returned to the table for their coats. They were now handholding, and socially acceptable touching was occurring, and he actually liked it.

Carefully descending Mount Front Step, they came to Jordan's car, parked directly in front of the bar. She leaned back against it as he engulfed her with another deep, passionate kiss.

Once inside the car, they immediately attacked each other with athletic lust. This wasn't a naughty little peck of a kiss and a promise for later. This was "I've just spent ten years in prison and must crush myself against you in every way possible until I can't think straight anymore."

Cooler heads prevailed just long enough to realize that they could not consummate these feelings right there, under a street-light directly in front of Club 21 at ten o'clock at night. Jordan reached for his keys and silently started the car, not breaking the mood for the obligatory, "Where can we go?" They knew they had nowhere to go. Neither lived nearby, and they were staying under their parents' tiny roofs. A motel seemed crass.

Driving up the street a bit, Heather did not question anything he did or what he was thinking. The only sound was of their heavy breathing.

Not totally sure of where he was going, he remembered all those "parking" places he had gone to as a teenager. Old abandoned coal strippings and pole lines—high-tension electrical towers planted across mountains on the outskirts of town with dirt roads running underneath them. Jordan ventured that he had yet to have sex in a bed as often as he had in a car. Such were the passions of youth.

They made it all of three blocks. The street was residential and dark. Lust would not allow Jordan to drive farther. Something in the sound of Heather's breathing said she felt much the same.

Swerving quickly into a parking space, he shut off the engine. God, he was completely out of his mind. Nothing made sense, nothing mattered, and he couldn't care less if the Gibbsville police found them buck-naked in flagrante.

There were still no words outside of the occasional, *Oh God* and *Oh God, yes!* For God must certainly have felt loved and appreciated on this night. This was . . . Jordan didn't know what to call it. It was lust *and* love, wholly uninvited, exploding together and refusing to separate within his mind.

They literally tore off each other's clothes. The rib-shattering center console provided the only moment of clarity. The front seat would not do. Pulling each other, they fell together, still wordlessly, into the back.

Every part of him was touching a part of her. This was loving sex. Full-body, contact-high sex. The car was chilly inside, and he warmed every part of her with a part of him. Despite the cold, they were drenched in sweat as they groaned together in climax.

Like earthquake survivors, they both experienced aftershocks. Neither could bring themselves to speak coherently. Along with the *Oh God!*s and the moans, there were no *Fuck me!*s or *Come! Come with me now!*s. This was a different kind of passion. Jordan wanted to break the silence in only one way, and that was by saying, "I love you." But while it was something he felt, it was too bizarre, too outside of what was on his mind as recently as that very afternoon. Love was a complication, a conundrum of wanting to feel and express feelings that, for him, had become a sticky morass of agendas and timelines.

With great profundity, he finally uttered, "I don't know what to say."

"Then don't," Heather glowed, still in his naked embrace.

"How did that happen?"

"*I* know."

"Share."

"I know how it happened, I know why it happened, and if you care, I don't want you to say anything."

"Okay."

"It happened because *I love you*," she whispered. Her voice shivered and cracked, making it barely audible. "Don't say a word. I don't want you to say anything because you think it's what I want to hear."

Now he knew he was in some parallel universe, some fifth dimension. They kissed and cuddled, then began to dress. Jordan's mind was reeling with questions and the desire to make proclamations of his own, his self-protective defenses obliterated by this person he had trusted since memory began. Yet he respected her ground rules.

"How long?" he asked.

"Forever." She paused just long enough to reiterate, "Don't say a word."

Had he been so dense all these years? Jordan couldn't even remember them teasing each other about such a thing. It simply seemed outside the realm of possibility.

"When was I going to find out?" By now they were more or less fully clothed, and he started the car again.

"I always thought the day would come. There was no grand plan. Just a feeling. Fate."

"Don't tell me that's why you're still not married."

"Not really. If something outside my control had happened,

so be it. Same thing if you'd gotten married. I'd have always had
these feelings. I just would have had to deal with it."

Jordan drove a bit more until he found himself heading
toward the sexual playgrounds of his youth. As he veered off-
road, she said, "Hey!" as in, "Hey, what the hell do you think
you're doing?"

"If I can't say certain things, I've got to occupy myself somehow."

"You can talk. You just aren't allowed to say three little
words."

Oh God, she was cute. Cute, bright, sexy, beautiful . . . he was
making lists of her attributes again, and they were naked once
more in a matter of moments. This time was slower. Throughout,
he wanted to say, "I love you," but bit his tongue or simply thrust
it into her warm, luscious mouth in order to restrain himself.
This was a problem he'd never had before.

"It's not fair." Silence seemed to make him more uncomfortable than her.

"What?"

"That I'm not allowed to talk."

"I keep telling you, you can talk. Within certain limits."

"Cruel, harsh mistress."

She laughed. "Do you want to see me again?"

"Are you coming home for Christmas?" She gave him a com-
ical, wide-eyed, "Oh, you bastard!" look and he rejoined, "Just
kidding. Yes, I want to see you again. That's if tonight ever ends."

"I think it'll have to, eventually. They'd be too weirded out."

"Are you going to tell them?"

"What do you think?" she said unsarcastically. On this subject she did not appear to have a secret master plan.

"I don't know. Maybe we should play it cool."

He regretted putting it that way as soon as it left his lips, for it could have been interpreted as being as cautious and conservative as he honestly felt. Jordan knew if they were to parade this new relationship in its entire splendor in front of their parents, how horrible it would be if something went wrong, if it did not work out.

If it did not work out. Was this really love? He'd said those words in eight previous relationships and had meant them in about three. In each, he had an inkling from the first moment. Yes, he did believe in love at first sight. He just made sure not to say it out loud. But this was by no means first sight. He looked at her, *really* looked at her, still naked in his arms. Isn't your wife supposed to also be your best friend? *Wife?* This was the best and worst feeling in the world.

If he couldn't tell her how he felt, he could still compliment her. He'd never done it before, so there were quite a lot of accolades stored up, especially after tonight. She blushed, "aw-shucks"-ed him, and reiterated that he was crossing the line she had drawn about saying things only to be reciprocal. He kept one single declarative statement out of his monologue, maintaining his end of the bargain. But she would not end this evening without knowing she was every incredibly great thing he thought she was.

Heather started to cry. She buried her head in his shoulder and he felt wet tears on his naked chest.

"What? What?"

Since he was getting no answers, he had to content himself by holding her lovingly until the moment passed. Once she had composed herself, he slipped into the front seat and started the car.

"I'm not dressed."

"Neither am I." The car began to move.

"We can't drive around naked!"

"Trust me." He was taking a calculated risk since he still had no idea what her crying was all about.

Still off-road, Jordan appeared as knowledgeable as someone driving a familiar highway. Through the laughter of hitting rocks and potholes while driving starkers, he slowed to a halt alongside a golf course. A golf course!? Lantenengo County was not known for its golfers or golf courses.

"What's this?" Obviously Heather was not as familiar as he with Mountain City's more interesting lovers' lanes.

"Stan Burke's. Didn't you know he had his own golf course here? One hole."

Stan Burke was Stanislaw Burstokowicz. In every town, no matter how small and impoverished, there's still one rich guy. In Mountain City, it was Stan Burke. He changed his name soon after learning English and starting his own textile business. Eventually, he became a very wealthy man. He was a benevolent king who gave a lot to charity and was known as a friendly, down-to-earth sort. He also had this one-hole golf course out in the middle of nowhere, way in back of his huge estate. Jordan knew his way around it quite well and not as a duffer, either. Doctor or no doctor, Jordan had still never had a golf club in his hands. But he certainly had spent some time on Stan Burke's putting green late at night, working on his short game.

Naked as the day he was born, Jordan turned the car off and got out. Heather was laughing hysterically, still in the backseat. He opened her door. "If it were warmer and I had a blanket, I'd invite you out here."

"What are you doing?" she asked in fine-spirited incredulousness.

"Just lay back."

She did, as he stood naked on the well-manicured grass. Kneeling before her, he found yet another way of not saying, "I love you." Verbally, anyway. Eventually, they made love for the third time in barely as many hours. This was not the sort of Olympic performance he put on much anymore. She simply inspired him and it was out of his hands. They made love in the chilly moonlight, and it was erotic and beautiful. *She* was erotic and *she* was beautiful and this would not end tonight or any night soon. This was the best.

When they finally fixed themselves up for reentry into the real world, they were parked and fully clothed in front of their side-by-side homes. "*Now* I'm shy."

She knew what he meant. They could have been seen by any number of people that evening, including various members of the law enforcement community. But making out where they played hopscotch together as toddlers made them both uncomfortable.

She leaned in and gave him one more deep, passionate kiss. "That's it"—Heather's declaration that "last call" had been announced on sexual activities for the evening.

"You mean we can't do it again right here?"

"No!" she laughed.

"I want to see you again tomorrow."

"Me, too."

"Know any other great places like Club 21?"

"No, but then I also don't know where to make love in the great outdoors like you do."

"Tomorrow I want to take you out on a real date."

"Oh, tonight was just a fuck?" she snickered.

Suddenly, he loved how the word "fuck" sounded when she

said it, especially after they had, finally . . . In fact, he thought he felt something move again. It was probably just his member begging for some sort of balm to nurse it back to health.

"Tonight will never be forgotten as long as I live. Can I drop by in the afternoon? We'll make plans."

"Yes." She got out of the car, leaned back in, took his face in her hands, and whispered, "I love you," followed by, "Don't say anything," sternly wagging a finger.

He smiled as he watched her walk ahead of him and up the steps of her porch.

THREE

"*SHUT THE FUCK UP!*" *Each word was punctuated by a thrash of an arm upon whoever was within reach. Being as how Jack Stein was almost too drunk to stand, this took far more time than one might imagine.*

"*Dad, stop!*" *Jerry Stein, almost fifteen, attempted to be heroic, but he was too physically immature to take on his father. This did not stop him from trying. He moved into the slow-motion buzzsaw that was his father's arms and fists. "Stop!"*

Mildred Stein was crying. Her eyeglasses had been ripped from her head with one glancing blow, and they cut her as they fell down her face. Despite the sight of blood, Jack Stein continued his perpetual motion, his lyrics now a symphony of incoherent rage and vulgarity. "Shut the fuck up! Cunt bitch, tell me what to do! Fuck bitch, oughta smash yer face in . . ."

Jack "Buddy" Jr., all of twelve, raced up the stairs, following his older brother's lead. Futile, obviously, but necessary as his hulking father continued this tirade against his mother with no end in sight. It was not the first time in his short life Buddy had seen his father this way, but each episode seemed more menacing and dangerous than the last.

Among the three of them, they tried less to fight him than to simply restore some semblance of peace. Each battle began with little in the way of provocation except for the massive amount of drink inside the man. When they were extremely lucky, he would simply fall dead asleep somewhere, anywhere. Today was not a lucky day.

Sean Stein was unlike the young child who hides in his safe room until the boogeyman is gone. Ever curious, ever competitive with his older brothers, the seven-year-old tentatively, yet steadily, moved closer and closer to the horrid action.

Stein was swinging wilder and wilder now. His family's attempts to wrap him up and calm him down were only making him angrier. Sean got too close. Another flail of Stein's fists caught the little boy flush on the forehead, sending him reeling backward down the stairs.

"Aaaaaaah!" Mildred's shriek could pierce pottery. Her baby, her youngest, lay crumpled in a heap at the bottom of the stairway. Everyone was making too much noise and movement for her to know whether he was breathing, moving, or crying. But the picture was the most horrific a mother could stand.

Opal Matino hardly knew the couple next door. She had heard the fights ever since she moved in but never paid much attention. This was a working-class town with a bar on every corner. Drunken fights between men, as well as men and their women, were as commonplace as flies. She'd been blocking it out of her perception her entire life. But this was bad, very bad. This Jack Stein character was a mean drunk, meaner than her father had ever been. Daddy could knock back enough to be an embarrassment now and then. But there were never any sounds like the ones she heard from these neighbors.

The last scream sent Opal over the edge. She was a petite woman, *barely five feet tall, and svelte. She had no idea what she could do, but she knew she had to do something. Calling the cops would have been a joke. They'd probably show up an hour later, half tanked themselves. They also tended to side with the men; at least that's how it always seemed to her. Charlie was at work, Daddy was sleeping, and Reverend Paulson was the only other man she could count on. But she didn't want to be a bother. No, she had to do something on her own.*

It occurred to her once she was halfway out the door that she'd just found out she was pregnant. Oh my God, pregnant women are supposed to be careful, she thought. Suppose this Jack Stein punched her in the belly? She was almost ready to go back when she saw the little boy lying on the floor inside. He was a rambunctious little kid, Huckleberry Finn incarnate. Now he was in a tangled clump that did not look anatomically right.

Her maternal instinct took over. The door was wide open, explaining some—but not all—of the elevated noise level. Opal tried to announce her presence, but nothing came out of her throat except a whisper. Terror and emotion had shut down her vocal chords. The screaming and pounding continued from the second floor, heard but not yet seen. When she got to the boy, she took a quick glance up the stairs. There in the afternoon shadows she saw figures that were difficult to distinguish and differentiate. One of them had to be that drunken bastard Stein.

There was an odd silence. She'd been noticed. The biggest figure started coming toward her, shouting expletives as he clomped down the steps like an inebriated Frankenstein. Fight or flight? Fight or flight? Neither. Protection. She gently laid herself on the hurt little boy. It came without forethought, like a war hero throwing himself on a grenade. Sense would have told her to protect her own unborn child. But it was too late now. She wrapped up the little boy and used her back as a shield against whatever was to happen next.

Eleanor George lived two houses down from the Steins, but she had never heard such a calamity before in her life. It was summer, and everyone had their doors and windows open. Kids, cars, and birds made noise interminably, but these sounds of screams and fighting cut through everything. She thought she heard her friend Opal wandering outside. Curiosity made her do the same thing, as she stepped out onto her porch. Opal wasn't there, which seemed strange. Eleanor had no inclination to get directly involved but thought to run down her steps and up Opal's to see if she knew anything more about this than she did. Running on tiptoe, Eleanor peered through the front door but saw no Opal. She didn't want to call out for fear those hell-raising neighbors would catch her snooping.

The sounds quieted, then grew louder again at the Steins'. "Don't you touch her! Don't you touch her!" It wasn't one of the boys shouting that; it was a woman, probably that redhead who took such a beating all the time from the louse she was married to. Eleanor had to look. Standing on Opal's porch, she had no trouble leaning sideways and looking in. There she saw a man, two young boys dangling off of him, making his way down the stairs toward . . . something. It looked like a person all curled up. It looked like . . . Opal! She recognized her friend's summer blouse. Without a thought, she ran in. Opal was her husband's best friend's wife, and the four of them found these houses together on Good Street, the first homes of their newlywed lives. Everything was good, except for these noisy, low-class neighbors. She'd hoped Rick, her husband, would have set them up in a better neighborhood than this.

Rick George walked slowly from his job at Southern's Pharmacy. Damn old asshole, he thought. Goddamn jerk. Rick thought he'd come back to his hometown like some conquering hero after pharmacy school. Start up his own business and run Southern out of town. But there was no money for that right now, not with all the college bills and the new wife who wanted to set up housekeeping. Should have done what Charlie did—enlisting and then going to college on the G.I. Bill. Not that that's how Charlie played it. Charlie had no plans for college. He just figured he'd get drafted anyway, so he took his typing skills and hoped he'd avoid the worst of things. He was right. Charlie was the fastest typist Mountain City High ever saw. Strange for a man. But that's what attracted Rick to Charlie. The guy was a walking party. A contradiction of everything that made sense. Crazy cat.

About a block from home, he heard what sounded like a slaughterhouse in full operation. Men screaming, boys screaming, women screaming. Cursing, pounding, crashing. Wow, this had to be something. Rick quickened his pace until he found himself running. The closer he got, the less exciting and more dreadful it seemed. It was right by his house. Where was his wife? There were too many women's voices. Not good.

Rick ran past his house and up the steps to the Steins'. What he saw was Jack Stein—his two oldest boys hanging onto him, his wife throwing things at him from above on the stairs, his own wife, Eleanor, slapping at him from in front—and what looked like Opal Matino curled up in a fetal position about to be crushed by his steel-tipped boots. Rick blew through the screen door and ran straight at Jack Stein. He smacked him good, real good. Harder than he'd ever hit a man before. He clubbed that bastard two or three times until he fell backward upon the steps leading to the second floor. Good solid shots to the jaw that Stein was unable to block for the mess of people pinning his arms. Enraged at the sight of his wife having to physically defend herself, Rick wanted to keep ramming and hammering away on this drunken fuck, but once he was down, he seemed down for good. No need to kill the man. Let the cops straighten it out.

The only one still making a sound was Mildred Stein, wailing *something or other. Rick turned around to see Charlie's wife, Opal, lying crumpled on the floor. She began to rise, revealing the half-unconscious little boy beneath her. Jesus Christ, he thought. Jesus fucking Christ.*

Jordan awoke awash in guilt. Had last night really happened? Did he have sex with Heather George? Did she tell him she loved him? Did he feel the same way? Did she think he loved her?

Everything had changed. Thanksgiving morning, he had simply looked forward to a pedestrian day of Mom, turkey, and boredom. Today, he wondered if he wanted to marry the girl next door. What a difference a day makes, indeed.

The breakfast inquisition was no more intrusive than any other, thank God.

"Did you have a good time last night?"

"Yup." He'd had the best sex of his life, but he doubted his mother wanted to hear that.

"Did you run into anyone you know?"

"No." Well, he didn't *run* into anyone, but he was certainly *into* someone—body, soul, and mind.

"How's Heather?"

Sore, bowlegged, and probably as confused as he.

"Fine. She likes her job. Teaches deaf kids." His mother already knew all of this, but he was being sociable. By doing so, he hoped he wasn't letting on that he was hiding anything.

Opal had the day off, so they ran around together doing this and that. Domesticity and the loyal son. He could hardly wait to go over to Heather's and make plans for the evening.

Years ago, Jordan wouldn't have thought to use the doorbell. But as he wasn't as frequent a visitor these days he didn't want to startle the Georges. Eleanor answered. He immediately wondered what and how much she knew. From her look, it appeared she was as much in the dark as Opal. Although they hadn't seen each other since his grandfather's funeral four months ago, he was greeted with a pleasant yet blasé "Hello."

Invited in, Eleanor began the perfunctory, "How are you? How's work? Are you a full-fledged doctor by now, or are you still interning or going for more training or what?" The usual "blah" questions. Eleanor would have known most of the answers from firsthand experience had she and Rick been better godparents. They did not attend his high school or college graduations, let alone his graduation from medical school. There was always some convenient excuse, and for this he never forgave them. The Steins, ironically, managed to attend all his special days. Of course, he put most of the blame on Rick, for Eleanor seemed to have no issues with him, now or ever.

Heather was home, and she joined him on the sofa. Was the electricity between them evident? His anxiety was palpable. Did it show? If she sat on his lap, giving him a "hello" peck on the cheek, he'd know that last night was not a dream. But Heather sat no closer to him than did her mother, who eventually got up and went back to whatever she had been doing.

Jordan whispered, "Did you tell her anything?"

"No. What about you?"

"No, my mom doesn't seem to suspect a thing."

Heather smiled mischievously. "This is wild."

Phew! Good thing she felt this way, Jordan thought. The mystery was *why* she felt that way.

Unfortunately, this house was Rick George's house, the sofa he was sitting on, Rick's as well. It reminded Jordan that he had always felt more at ease with Heather when they were anywhere but here.

When Jordan was a kid, Rick would summon him in church and say, "Here, let me fix your collar." Then he'd take Jordan's perfect collar and flip it up in the back so that he looked like an idiot. Or else he'd say, "Here, you have your tie tied all wrong. Let me fix it," and completely ruin the thing on purpose. As it was, Jordan had to teach himself to tie a tie. He learned it from a book, as he had no father and because neither Stein nor his late grandfather ever wore one. His mother was also tie-challenged. He'd sooner wear a clip-on than ask Uncle Rick for help, as he preyed upon Jordan's lack of confidence like a schoolyard bully.

Opal would console him and tell him that this was Rick's way; he was just being funny. But this kind of funny was hurtful to an insecure, awkward kid, and Jordan hated Rick for it. Although Jordan could not recall witnessing it, Opal apparently went to Rick occasionally and chastised him for these cruelties. His insincere, sarcastic apologies, though, were often worse than the transgressions themselves. Jordan welled up with tears sometimes when he talked to his mother about it. But he never cried. Never. The first day of kindergarten, he was the only kid in the entire class who did not bawl for his mommy. No idea why. Pragmatism, he supposed.

Once. Check that, but yes, there was one time he recalled crying. The Little League Baseball Father and Son Game. All the kids were informed that after the July Fourth triple-header there would be a father and son game and to remember to bring along their fathers to play. He was not singled out in any way, nor did the coach say anything about not being able to play if one didn't have a father. But Jordan looked around and realized that he *was* the only fatherless boy. He walked home that night feeling more sorrow and paranoia with each step. It was completely illogical, and some part of him had to have known that. But on this night, this one night of his youth, it all came crashing down on him that he *was* different. More different than he had wanted to be.

By the time he approached his block, he was inexplicably running and wailing hysterically out of control. His mother was away at choir practice, but he was loud enough to cause Mildred Stein to come out onto the porch. She immediately embraced him until his shaking and crying stopped. Through stammering tears, he was eventually able to say what had upset him so. Mildred hugged him again. Hugs *did* exist in Mountain City. They were simply held in reserve for when they were truly needed.

"So, you promised me a real date tonight," Heather said to him.

"Absolutely. Let's go out to dinner and a movie like good little kids are supposed to. Give me a chance to show you my suave."

"I think I saw a lot of suave last night," she purred.

"You have to allow me to pull out all my magic tricks before you toss me out with the trash." He sounded confident and full of wit, instead of confused and full of shit.

"What makes you think I'm planning on tossing you out any-time soon?" After a quick head turn to make sure her mother wasn't watching, she scooted over and kissed him quickly, then remained in her new and friendlier seat next to him, their thighs touching. "What time?" she asked.

"Let's try around six. That'll give us time to catch a movie."

"You really want to go see a movie?"

"Yes. It's a nice, wholesome 'date' thing. I'm a traditionalist." She looked at him strangely, but he knew that negotiation would indicate he was unsure of himself. And he had never been more unsure of himself than today.

"Mom, Jordan's taking me out to dinner tonight, okay?"

The "okay?" part was a considerate child letting her mother

know not to set another place for supper, rather than a request for permission. But Jordan knew this was also the first salvo lobbed over the horizon onto an unsuspecting Eleanor George. Which in turn meant that it had been thrust upon the denizens of all three houses. Eleanor responded by coming to a complete halt of whatever she was doing and returned to the living room for a face-to-face confirmation.

"Dinner?"

"Uh huh," Heather replied.

"Tonight? Who's all going?"

"Just the two of us."

Jordan was staying out of this conversation.

"Oh. Okay." As Eleanor turned again to leave the room, her last look at them was quizzical—a person slowly digesting an absurdity.

Well, that was that. They were outed.

Later, as Heather and Jordan were en route to dinner, the Three convened on the Matinos' glider as if some previously scheduled meeting was now in session. *Macbeth* began with three witches mixing a brew. Opal Matino, Eleanor George, and Mildred Stein were not witches, but they stirred the same cauldron anyway.

Heather's mother began. "It's a date."

To which Jordan's mother replied, "Really?"

"I'm sure of it. They're on a date."

Mildred chimed in, "When you stop to think about it, it's kind of amazing they never did it before." The other two stared at her, prompting her to continue. "Seriously. They're about the same age and they've always hung around together. I was always expecting to find them smooching behind a tree somewhere. Weren't you?" she asked of whomever was willing to answer.

Opal bit. "I never thought it was that sort of thing between them. Heather was like one of the boys. That's how my Jordan always treated her."

"Well, she's a damn beautiful girl. Did you think he was blind?"

"Thank you, Mildred," answered Eleanor proudly.

They digested their thoughts for a moment as the glider squeaked slightly with every rhythmic movement they made. It was a cool late-fall evening, but they wore only light jackets and sweaters. These were hearty mountain girls who didn't much mind the cold.

"I don't think it's a *real* date," said Opal finally.

Eleanor added, "You mean kissing . . . ?"

". . . Sex?" said Mildred, finishing the thought. As her two friends glared at her, she brought up the other thing that was on all their minds. Facing Eleanor, she asked, "Have you told her yet?"

Eleanor's mouth could not be made to open any wider had she been sitting naked on a block of ice. "NO!"

Well, that certainly was emphatic. Mildred gave Opal the same question. "Did you ever tell Jordan?"

"I don't think so."

"YOU DON'T THINK SO?!" Eleanor was getting hyperploxic. "You can't remember for sure if you told him or not?! Are you getting senile?"

"I try to tell Jordan everything."

"But we promised not to tell anyone about this. We promised," said Eleanor in a distressful tone.

"Probably not. Not the stuff about Heather anyway. But I do try to always be open and honest with him. If I did tell him about Heather, I doubt he would date her. I mean *really* date her. But that doesn't mean I'd ever lie to him."

"So, let's just say that Jordan doesn't know, because I know Heather doesn't know. What if they really *are* dating?" asked Eleanor.

"Want my recommendation?" asked Mildred, who intended to give it anyway. "I say let it run its course. You obviously don't want to tell Heather. But if you get in the middle of this, you'll have to. I say shut up and sit back. What are the chances it'll amount to anything?"

"But what if it does?" asked Eleanor.

"Cross that bridge when you get to it."

Jordan had indeed found a nice restaurant. He and Heather sat across from each other and held hands by candlelight. If the picture was cliché, so was the food. Jordan, who had done internships and residencies in Philadelphia, Boston, and New York, was of the theory that cities were great for expensive as well as inexpensive dining experiences, while places like Lantenengo County were most unique for their greasy spoons. Yes, some of them might do nothing more than spread disease and dysentery, but others featured some fabulous spins on genuine home cooking. As for "fancy" restaurants, they were fine but pretty forgettable out in fly-over country. But this was a *date* date, and chili dogs and pierogis wouldn't cut it.

Conversation with Heather still flowed effortlessly, much to Jordan's relief. He had a lingering fear that tonight would be one of those uncomfortable "about last night" nights, where one of them would feel strange that they had let sex ruin a good friendship.

Dragging her to the cinema at the mall, they selected a film that would perhaps be mildly entertaining. Looking around the lobby at the other couples, Jordan recalled past trips he'd made back to the region since his escape. One time he had brought some college friends home with him. They visited one of the only touristy spots in the area, a coal mine that was open to the public. Once deep down inside, his pals began asking intelligent and serious questions that those who had not been raised around the mining industry might wonder about. Nothing sarcastic; they were quite on their best behavior that day. The first response from the grizzled old miner giving the tour was "Is youse from the city?" Jordan cracked up laughing. As if the rest of the planet was indeed "the city" and that the city was a strange and foreign place, as were its inhabitants.

Yet in retrospect, there was poignancy to the moment. The coal miner's hands reminded Jordan of his grandfather's. Callused, but most particularly, black. Hands black as soot, blacker than an African's. The coal dust refused to come off when day was done and those hands were washed with as strong a soap as could be produced. Technically, the hands were clean, but they never, ever looked it.

Jordan loved his grandfather but hated his hands. His entire life had been spent vowing to never have those hands. That day, standing inside a vein of coal, his hands were not the hands of a miner. Neither were the hands of his cohorts. All were white and soft. Staring at his friends, he noted their dress. Clean, new, blue jeans, but more specifically, jeans that had been ironed and creased. What a laugh the old miner must have had at that, in his blackened, wrinkled coveralls. Jordan's jeans were unironed—casual out of the dryer. There remained differences. But his was now the life of a man straddling two places and cultures. He was able to travel within both but was not fully accepted in either.

In the sparsely attended theater, Heather and Jordan sat safely tucked away without anyone too nearby. In darkness and lacking the thrall a better film might have provided, Jordan was sixteen again. They held hands; he put his arm around her. They made out for a while. Being with this woman cut his age in half.

When the lights came back on and it was only ten o'clock, she asked him the inevitable. "What do you want to do now?"

"Do you trust me?"

"No."

"Good answer."

Hand in hand, they went to his car and kissed until their lips chapped. There was that feeling again, that nostalgia for a more hormonal time, yet without the pressure to go further, to conquer.

Minutes later they were lying between the two old handmade comforters he had stolen out of his mother's attic and surreptitiously placed in his car trunk. They stared up into the full moon sky on Stan Burke's putting green. Jordan promised Heather he would make no jokes about holes-in-one, putters, or handicaps. While not a bed, this was a move up from the backseat of a car and still much more all-American and romantic than a motel. The night canopy was beautiful, and so was she. Jordan thanked God for the absence of rain. It was all so right that he wondered what could go wrong. Life always has that yin and yang to it.

Returning home that night, they *did* make out on Heather's front porch. All three homes were dark. Jordan's mother had gone to sleep early. Unless they were doing their Adam and Eve bit in the dark, Heather's parents must have been sleeping as well. So, too, were the Steins. A part of Jordan expected one or more of them to be awake in order to get a late-breaking news report, being as how he and Heather were probably the only local item of note.

The next morning, the inquiry finally began.

"So, you're seeing Heather a lot since you've been home."

"Yup."

It was inevitable. While Opal rarely pried into Jordan's Philadelphia social life, he knew only a gag and muzzle could prevent her from asking about his recent evenings with the girl next door. This is what mothers live for—a ringside seat to their children's love life, a vicarious reliving of their own.

"Are you two dating?"

Which did not mean that Jordan felt any more comfortable discussing it with her.

He gave a high-pitched, noncommittal, "Hmmmm," followed by a strategically placed, "What have you heard?" playing it as close to the chest as possible.

"Well, it *looks* like you two are dating."

"Depends on your definition of dating, I guess. Did she say something?"

"She hasn't said anything about it to me, but I was just wondering."

"What did she say to Aunt Eleanor?"

"Nothing that I've heard. Why are you being so coy?"

"I just don't like to discuss my social life when it's still somewhat undefined. If I ever have a major announcement to make, I promise to let you know. Does Aunt Eleanor think we're dating?"

Opal had to answer that one. "I think she thinks you're dating."

"She have a problem with that?"

"No, no. No."

A double "no," followed by a pause and then a third "no." That had to, of course, mean, "yes" on some significant level.

Jordan had no clue as to why, and strangely enough, he didn't much care. He was far more afraid of finding *Macbeth's* three witches together on a glider looking over wedding stationery.

Opal continued, "So you *are* dating."

"Yeah, I guess you'd say that. Just the last two nights. Going out again tonight. Don't want to jump to any conclusions. Look, the only reason I'm being coy is that I know it must be kinda weird for everyone and I don't want it to be a big deal. Just want to take it a day at a time, like the alcoholics say. So, if you don't mind, I'd prefer not to talk too much about it, okay?"

"I never butt into your personal affairs."

"No, you're right. You don't. But this is different. It could build up expectations."

Opal replied with nothing more than a slight, tentative smile. It revealed little, no different than if it had been caused by indigestion. Jordan was simply relieved that the topic, for the moment, was closed.

As Saturday night's date gave way to a sunny Sunday morning, Jordan dutifully dragged himself out of bed early enough to get to church. So, too, did Heather, albeit from separate beds in separate houses. For as they were visiting the homes and beds of their youth, they were treated as the children they once were. Both families, and the Steins as well, walked down their front steps in their Sunday best, or what passed for that. Eleanor and Rick looked good enough to be from "the city." Mildred and Opal dressed handsomely. Jack Stein, as always, was somewhat disheveled and tie-less. He walked with a bit of a limp from some long-ago work-related injury. Stein installed siding, roofing, and rain gutters. He owned his own company, which did not make him wealthy by any means but placed him on a level of particular esteem in this poor community, much as Rick George's professional title did for him. The limp did not impede Stein's activities. He continued to work every day, retirement be damned.

The Steins were about ten years older than the Georges and Matinos. Their three grown boys had long ago moved away. Unlike Jordan and Heather, they were rarely seen back in Mountain City, even for Christmas.

Heather looked stunning to Jordan. Had she always? Or was it that she looked stunning before, just not to him? Or was she not really stunning but just seemed that way because he was falling in love with her?

This descending of the steps in unison was a weekly Sunday ritual. But today it was, of course, far different. Jordan and Heather were gazing at each other as never before. Eleanor looked definitely uncomfortable. Rick appeared to be sneering. He sported a mustache, which made many of his glances look like sneers or smirks. Or perhaps he really did sneer and smirk a lot in Jordan's general direction. Who knew? Mildred Stein seemed natural and normal, yet Jordan knew that if his mother thought to ask about him and Heather, all three of the Good Street ladies shared the same curiosity as well as information. Stein was simply Stein. He most likely knew nothing.

Stein had one foundation upon which his life was built, and that was work. Employment. Stein often said, "Don't ever criticize a working man." This was fine and good, as it put a heavy stress upon the Christian work ethic. But in Stein's book, it also meant that the world was divided into two camps: workers and non-workers. Workers could and should be forgiven a multitude of evils because, at the very least, they were not a drain upon society.

Stein was thus out of the loop on a lot of things, as his wife and her two best friends could and did gossip about everything and everyone, albeit discreetly. He was also not the best of friends with Rick George, perhaps because they had little in common. Stein had his hunting and fishing buddies who came by to hang out in his basement wood shop from time to time. That and work pretty much defined Jack Stein. Rick, ironically, had far more in common with Jordan. He enjoyed music, theater, and movies. Despite that, they actively shared none of those interests *together*, except for Rick's trying to one-up him on knowledge of entertainment trivia or something similarly irritating.

Jordan loathed hunting and felt only slightly less offended by fishing. A hammer felt foreign in his hand, and he feared that a lathe or a bandsaw could end his career as a surgeon. Despite this, Stein was patient and did not insult Jordan for his disinterest in these manly pursuits that Stein obviously loved. Perhaps it was because Jordan had a job. Even when Jordan was a young boy, though, Stein had always found time for him. He was mellow with him, which was a nice contrast to a lot of the adult men Jordan knew. Stein was introverted and quiet, and so, too, was Jordan when they were alone together. The conversation never ran too deep or profound; it was just peaceful and workmanlike. Jack Stein was the guy Jordan turned to when he needed tips on camping, lessons in using a nail set, or help making his Pinewood Derby car.

In a perfect world, he would have gathered this knowledge from his own father, but that was never to be. In an accommodating world with a backup plan, he should have had this relationship with his godfather, who lived right next door. But Rick George couldn't be bothered. So in a world of make-the-best-of-it, Stein became his male mentor. They respected each other's differences. And in complete contrast to his relationship with Uncle Rick, Jordan had always felt that Stein was quite proud of him.

The trip down the steps to the three respective family cars went along amicably, although some appeared to be eyeing others a little suspiciously. None of the Good Street homes had garages or driveways, so everyone parked on the street. Arriving at St. John's, about six blocks away, all three parked again and proceeded inside. Rick George would usually never drive this short a distance, but Eleanor and Heather rarely chose to walk that far in heels.

Once inside, Opal and Rick rushed into the rear dressing rooms to change into their choir gowns. Jordan and Heather had always joined this group, but now, as visitors, they preferred to sit in the peanut gallery with everyone else. For a few years, Opal had bugged Jordan to throw on his old gown and join the choir up front when he came home for a visit, despite his not having practiced with them. But as he no longer had much confidence in his sight-reading ability, he always begged off with dignity. Besides, he'd have to sit and stand next to Uncle Rick, who was sure to mock him every time he hit a wrong note or botched a word of some song he'd never sung before.

This was Jordan's first trip to the church of his youth since he had helped bury his beloved grandfather a few months before. Since moving away, he had always sat with his maternal grandparents on the center aisle, right side, third row from the rear. Today was a first, one that he had not counted on. For the first time ever, he would be neither in the choir loft nor with his grandparents. Jordan Matino had nowhere to sit.

He knew what the natural answer was. Heather and her mother sat midway down the right-hand side, also on the aisle. He was dating Heather. Eleanor was his godmother. He should sit there.

Jordan took notice of the whereabouts of the Steins. They always sat on the left side, third row from the rear, and on the far aisle rather than the center. He had never sat with them, or with the female Georges for that matter. But today was a new beginning.

Jordan followed Eleanor and Heather to their seats. Heather always had the aisle, her mother the inside. Heather turned to see Jordan behind her and gave him a big, fabulous morning smile. Eleanor on the other hand, either through habit, bewilderment, or something else, plopped down in the same second seat she had warmed for all her years. Thus, Jordan was given the choice of either sitting on top of Heather or moving to another row. Dumbfounded, Eleanor looked up upon realizing she had to shift over in order to allow Jordan in. Jordan never knew Eleanor George to be a big emoter or face-maker. She was the cool, unflappable type. The look she gave him now, coupled with the one she had given him as they descended to their cars earlier, was very strange indeed. What was she thinking? What was he doing wrong? These were not glowingly happy future-mother-in-law looks. Quite the opposite, if anything.

The look on Heather's face was as beatific as that of a bride strolling down the aisle. Jordan—guilt, confusion and discomfort dissipating with every moment—grinned as smugly as his godfather, Rick.

As services ended, the other parishioners greeted Heather and Jordan as if they were returning heroes, for this is true church hospitality, far different than coming home and going to a bar or a mall. This pilgrimage meant that those returning still had a sense of religious and community roots. It felt nice, and Heather glowed.

The first words Jordan and Heather actually spoke to each other came as they made their way out of the chapel. He asked, "When are you leaving?"

"No big rush. What about you?"

"I was going to hit the road soon after dinner." Coal-region Sunday dinner was at noontime rather than evening time, just like Thanksgiving dinner. "Come over once you're done eating. I want to talk." He made sure to say it nicely enough so that it did not convey ominousness, "I want to talk" being one of the world's most nerve-wracking phrases.

"Great. See you then."

While enjoying leftover turkey, Jordan's mother broached the subject he knew he'd be discussing in only a few minutes with Heather. "So, now that you're going back, what about you and Heather? Or was this just a weekend thing?"

"Weekend thing?" he chuckled. "That wouldn't be nice at all."

He meant that sincerely. If you're going to have a fling, you don't do it with the girl next door whom you've known your entire life. You especially don't do it once she's professed her love for you.

"No, I suppose it wouldn't. So what are you going to do?"

"Well, Reading isn't that far from Philly. I'm going to be talking to her shortly and I plan to suggest getting together once we're back."

"Okay."

That "okay" was tentative as hell. Eleanor's looks earlier in the day and Opal's voice now added up to reactions he would not have expected. Jordan had to ask, "What's the matter?"

"What?"

"What's going on? I know it's weird that Heather and I are dating after all these years, but you guys are really acting strange."

Opal searched for an answer. The pregnant pause only made Jordan more paranoid.

"Mom, what's the matter? Did I do something wrong?"

"No, no, you're fine. I just don't want to see either of you get hurt, that's all. This isn't like you just dating some girl. This is fam . . . this is different. We're all neighbors here and if something doesn't go right, it would feel uncomfortable for everyone, and I don't want that."

"You're right. It would be. That's been on my mind a lot, too. All I can say is, I'm being very careful to prevent anything bad from happening."

"But Jordy, you can't control the world like that. People have their own feelings. Just because you think you're letting someone down easy doesn't mean they're going to take it that way."

This was the deepest discussion of relationships he'd ever had with his mother. It was strange yet poignant.

"I agree. I'll be careful. Besides, who said anything about breaking up? Maybe we won't."

"You think this relationship is serious?"

She was certainly serious right now. Deathly serious. "I think it's a little premature to call it serious or to call it anything. That's my opinion." He lied.

"What's her opinion?"

"I think she's looking at it kinda that way, too. Maybe a bit more serious. I don't know. I'm going to talk to her after dinner."

"Honey, just be careful, okay? That's all I ask."

"You sound like you wished we'd never gone out."

"Maybe that would have been better."

Thud.

"Mom, I can't believe you're saying that! We're both single, we come from nice families, we've known each other forever, we've always gotten along. Hell, we even go to the same church, and her parents are my godparents. What more could you ask for?"

"I've said all I'm going to say. I think you heard me. You two do whatever you're going to do. I won't stand in your way."

"*What the hell is going on*?! You sound like you're warning me that if I date Heather, I'll be left out of the will or something. I'm not doing anything bad. We like each other. We're free to do this," he said angrily. He almost wanted to throw down his utensils and bolt from the dinner table in order to make a point. But this was near the beginning of the meal, and a Zimmerman-Matino did not walk away from a table full of good food. They chewed silently throughout the rest of dinner, occasionally exchanging the bare minimum of courtesies in order to pass food or condiments. Jordan stewed.

The knock on the front door could not have come sooner. Jordan sprang up to answer. It was Heather. Instead of asking her in, he said, "Let's take a walk. Wait here while I get a coat." This may have been mildly rude, but he didn't want Heather to pick up on his mother's bad vibes.

Hand in hand, they strolled down Good Street. "I like walking. You?"

"Sure," she said.

It was a slate gray, cloudy afternoon. The town was beginning to look wintry. Jordan was not making idle conversation when he said he was a walker. Rick George may have enjoyed strutting the same daily path from Good Street to Southern's Pharmacy on Nahas Avenue. But during his youth, Jordan had walked every square inch of Mountain City.

Being an only child, Jordan had not had that built-in best friend in the form of a brother or sister. He had friends growing up. Lots of them. But there were days when no one was home or someone was sick or whatever. And on those days, Jordan walked. He walked and he daydreamed. He covered every street and every alley in town. Every single nuance of every house and every yard, he noticed. He could name which street signs were missing and which were rusted to a point of being unreadable. From those walks, Mountain City belonged to him. That is why he would always keep it in his heart, if not his permanent mailing address.

"Have your parents been acting weird since we've been seeing each other?" he asked.

"Yeah. I can't really put my finger on it, though. It's like I can tell they're not happy about it, but I can't figure out why. They won't commit to anything. They asked what we plan to do after we go back . . ." She stopped there; realizing she and Jordan had not actually broached the subject themselves. That was far more important than what their parents thought.

Jordan gladly took the bait. "I was going to talk to you about that, too. I know you were only hoping for a Thanksgiving hookup, but I'd love to see you some more. What do you think?"

"Jerk-off, I'd love to see more of you. I thought you knew that."

"I was hoping you did."

They walked a few more silent paces, each with a shit-eating grin that nothing could possibly remove. Jordan switched from handholding to putting his arm around her. The warmth of their bodies on this nippy cold day felt good. More than that, it again felt perfect. Perfect in which body was next to which body, of all the bodies and of all of the people in the world.

Jordan slowed their already leisurely gait to a complete halt. Turning to face Heather, he took her face in his hands, looked her in the eye, and finally said, "I love you."

She returned the remark wordlessly with a deep, expressive

kiss. The word *finally* was in his thought. "Finally" in this case meant all of four days. It only felt like "finally" because he had felt it like a thunderclap on Thursday evening. In a way, this was all very fast and much too soon. By his late teens Jordan had already learned the "strategies" of dating, the "strategies" of relationships. This declaration of love, three days after the first rendezvous was unheard of.

"You didn't tell me I couldn't say it today," he whispered, ending the kiss.

"No, it's all right now. You didn't say it right after I said it and you didn't say it right after sex."

"I mean it."

"I know you do."

And finally his mind was firmly wrapped around it. Without reservation, Jordan Matino was in love with Heather George. He'd never been so happy in his life. All the details would work themselves out.

They walked some more, talked some more, kissed some more. When they finally returned to Good Street, they boldly kissed and embraced on the same sidewalk where they'd scraped knees together as far back as either could recall.

"I'm going in to pack. I'll call you tonight from Philly. We'll make plans."

"Can't wait," she said, smiling.

Jordan quickly slapped together his things and began loading his car. When he came into the kitchen to say good-bye to his mother, she handed him a care package of turkey, kielbasi, and various holiday leftovers. He made a conscious decision not to engage in further argument or discussion about Heather. He did not want to leave on a sour note. His mother may have doused his spirits, but she didn't deserve lingering anger. Maybe it was just the "weirdness" factor. Perhaps she simply had to live with the idea for a while until she could warm to it, as had he.

Thanking his mother warmly for the leftovers, he hugged and kissed her goodbye.

"I love you, honey."

"I love you, too, Mom."

Opal waved to him as he drove away. The smile she gave him was not as big and warm as usual, but it was a smile nonetheless. It was melancholy, if one needed a word to describe it, identical to the last two smiles she had given as he drove away after the funerals of his grandparents. Perhaps that was it. Maybe she was still feeling out of sorts, not fully adjusted to being without them. He would let it go and focus on Heather and where that all would lead. All things considered, the ride home to Philly was a bit better than usual.

FOUR

In most every life there is a Golden Age. A specific period of time with a definite beginning and end, uncommonly good and poignantly memorable. The next month became the Golden Age of all Golden Ages for Jordan Matino.

That very night, he called Heather from his co-op in Philadelphia, and they talked for over an hour. Jordan hated long phone conversations, so doing this and actually liking it was uncanny. As he was not on call that Tuesday night and was off on Wednesday, he arranged to visit her in Reading. Although he'd hoped that their first out-of-coal-region experience would be on his turf, he took the soonest opportunity he could get.

Heather greeted him at her door with an amorous, deep kiss he was pleased to return with ardor. Their lips still locked, she backed up until she fell backward onto a couch. Finally, she pulled her head away long enough to blurt out, "Wait." Slipping out from underneath him, she took him by the hand and led him down the hall.

"We are going use a bed like adults, for once," she panted.

They pulled and tugged at each other's clothing carefully, yet directly and emphatically. No one was being coy. Neither cared to be casual. Naked together at last, they reveled in each other and in being, finally, in a nice, large, cozy bed.

They needed no instructions about each other. A simple shift of movement, a moan here or there, and the other followed. Together, they were magical. Tonight's lovemaking was more primal, more vocal, more raw in its sexuality. It was bliss.

By the time they were done, both were drenched in sweat and looking for traces of blood and bruises, much like their first time in the backseat of his car.

"I won't have to hit the gym for a week," she finally gasped. Snuggling next to him, she pulled up a sheet over them as they came back down to earth.

"God, that was good. That was the best."

"The best? I'm the best?" she gleefully asked.

"Yeah."

"You really mean that? Or is that part of your shtick?"

"No. I mean it. Really. The best. World Champion."

She laughed out loud and hugged him even harder, pleased as someone who'd just won a million dollars. "It's usually not that good right away with two people."

"You mean it's better with three or four?"

She giggled in exhausted pain. "No, you know what I mean. Most people, it's okay the first time, but that's just lust. Even if everything isn't perfect, the lust carries you through enough to make it all right. Then the next few times, you notice the faults and try to teach each other your likes and dislikes. You get into a rhythm together. Then, if you're still attracted to each other and try hard enough to listen and please each other, it can be good. Better. Know what I mean?"

"I have no idea what you're talking about. I was a virgin until Thanksgiving," he said, dryly as a funeral director.

Jordan knew fake laughs, but Heather's were sincere. "You are way too good to be a virgin," she said.

"How would you know?"

"I've been around. Not a lot, but enough."

"What's 'enough'?"

Heather curled more and more into his body, a child returning to the comfort of the womb. "What are you doing? Making me sound like a ho?"

"I'm teasing you. I've always teased you. Why should I stop now? Unless you've always secretly hated it."

"I always secretly loved it. It meant you were paying attention to me, which you rarely did."

"I always paid attention to you."

"Bullshit. Attention like a kid sister. I didn't want to be your kid sister. I wanted to be like this." She rubbed against him for emphasis.

"Horny Heather."

"That's right. But just for you, baby. Just for you."

Baby? Such a clichéd pet name, but the girl next door had never called him "baby" before. And now it came from the throat of an incredibly sexy blonde who made love like a fantasy.

Heather returned from a visit to the powder room. Jordan asked her to stop just before crawling back into bed.

"What?"

"You're naked. I just want to look at you."

"You've seen me naked before."

"Not like this. Not head to toe, all at once. Just let me look at you."

She chuckled uncomfortably, "You're making me nervous."

"Turn around." She obeyed. "You're beautiful. Absolutely perfect."

She climbed back into bed and onto him. "Oh God, I love you, Jordy. I love you so much."

It mattered not what "perfect" meant, nor how subjective the word was. In Jordan's mind, she was perfect and beautiful. He usually went for shorter girls, but Heather was about five-seven and well built. Not too skinny, but without an ounce of fat on her. Her breasts were full, firm and . . . *perfectly* shaped. Her ass was round and porcelain white, as well as porcelain hard. She was fair with a childlike cuteness about her still, a smiling, laughing, sexy cheerleader.

He spent the night. They talked little about their parents and their peculiar ways. The hours spent together were so exhilarating that Jordan had trouble sleeping for fear he'd miss something.

She had school the next day, while he was off. He didn't know whether to go back to Philly or stick around. She told him she could make a point of coming home quickly after school, around three-ish, so he decided to stay. It was an odd day for him indeed, as he tended to work, work, work. But by checking and answering his e-mails, he felt less guilty and more productive.

He knew he couldn't stay another night, as he had appointments early the next morning. They made the most of their late afternoon and evening together before he left, around 11:00 p.m. It was splendid, every single moment.

From then on, every second they were able, they were together. Heather drove into Philly as soon as school let out on Fridays and finally got to live in Jordan's world. She loved it. She glowed in every activity and in every moment. When he had rounds or was covering for another doctor, they worked around it and she had the run of his place. She went shopping; she bought him little gifts. This was, indeed, the Golden Age.

On her second visit to Philly, Jordan arranged for dinner and drinks with Zeiss, which was akin to meeting the parents, had their particular parents not been who and what they were to each other. Zeiss quickly took to Heather. Because he was Jordan's best friend, this was important. Jordan and Zeiss's friendship was such that they were brutally honest when it came to assessing the other's romantic interests. This is never easy for friends to do, but they felt they owed it to each other. When lusty fog envelops a friend's mind, it often disallows rational thinking.

Zeiss admitted some initial skepticism prior to meeting her. "Why are you doing this?"

"What?"

"You move out of Hooterville, go to medical school, live in the city, and have hot young ladies throwing themselves at you left and right."

"My life is a dream. I know."

"I never picked you for one of those class reunion types, Matino."

"I'm not following you, Zeiss."

"The class reunion type. The person who spends every five-year period between class reunions planning and preparing for the next one. They have to reach certain career goals. They need the right car. Then about a year before, they hit the gym and the tanning spa so they can walk in looking like a million bucks. And you know who they do that for?"

"I imagine you're going to tell me."

"The girl next door, that's who. Or the head cheerleader.

Whoever they couldn't get in high school and still want to impress."

"Paul, I haven't thought about her since . . . I haven't thought about her, period. It was all a surprise."

"Didn't you say you always wanted to bang her mother?"

Truth was, Jordan had indeed rolled that one around in his dirty little mind. No, whatever adolescent fantasies he had about Eleanor never entered into how he felt about Heather today. "Let's not go there. She's not a junior version of her mother."

"Uh huh. I think I hit a nerve, perv." Zeiss was never gratuitously mean-spirited. But he was funny and direct, and he never feared the ramifications of his honesty.

Much as they ranked and rode each other, Jordan latently wished he *were* Paul Zeiss. Zeiss of the beautiful suburbs, the topshelf private school education, and the wealthy, well-connected family. These were the attributes someone like Jordan could loathe and envy as easily as aspire to. But Zeiss, a doctor like Jordan, had it together. He was not a jerk. Jordan truly liked him. Sometimes he imagined himself today as being Zeiss, only one generation behind. His children would grow up to be the Paul Zeisses of tomorrow. Perhaps they would be as class-blind as Paul and someday befriend a coal cracker or a similar culturally deprived sort such as he. That would be good.

Days stretched into weeks, and Jordan Matino was madly, passionately in love, as was Heather George. For each of them every single moment brought an obsession of thoughts about the other until the next time they were together. They went out to shows, dinner, and dancing, but most of all, they stayed home, talking and making love. Jordan had experienced other Golden Ages amid the throes of eros. If there was a distinct difference from the outset, it was that he and Heather knew each other's complete personal history. Neither worried that the other was a seething bowl of rage, a substance abuser, or a compulsive liar. Any flaws either had were pretty much known to the other. The only mystery was the lovemaking, and neither had ever had better. Which left . . . nothing.

Shortly before Christmas, they discussed holiday plans. Jordan had some time off, as the partners in his urology practice were split almost fifty-fifty, Jew to gentile. The Jews worked Christmas and Easter; the gentiles took Yom Kippur, Rosh Hashanah, and Passover. It was a good system. If your urinary system was in poor working order Thanksgiving or New Year's, you were in trouble. Heather, of course, had Christmas break.

What Heather did not know was that Jordan was considering the most drastic decision of his life. They'd been dating for less than a month and Christmas was still about ten days away.

Jordan wanted to ask her to marry him.

It hit him the morning after the first night Heather had stayed with him in Philly. Funny how inspiration arises at the oddest times over the strangest of things. She walked into his kitchen, opened the refrigerator door, and let out a scream. This is not unusual when a woman surveys a man's apartment. Jordan never claimed to be a neatnik. As for refrigerators, women are frequently taken aback by a bachelor's choice of provisions.

"What?" he asked, wondering what had so offended her sensibilities.

"Is Smuckers the only jam you have?"

That's a question he'd never gotten before, prefaced by a scream. "Whatever's there. Why?"

"Willard Scott."

"Willard Scott?" he asked. "What about Willard Scott?"

"*The Today Show*. I watch it every morning. Willard Scott shows these pictures of hundred-year-old people and they're mounted on a Smucker's label. Every time I see Smucker's jam, all I think about are thousand-year-old fossilized prune people with no teeth and Willard Scott saying 'Isn't she adorable? She's 107 today and she doesn't look a day over 93.' It grosses me out."

Jordan cracked up. "Hey, some day if we're lucky, we'll be that old."

"Yeah, but I don't want my gross pictures on *The Today Show*, superimposed on a Smucker's label."

"You don't want to see me when I'm a hundred?" he asked.

"I'd *love* to see you when you're a hundred."

"I'll be a gross old prune person."

"But so will I. Plus, I've seen your baby pictures. They say when people get really old they look like their baby pictures. You were a cute baby."

Jordan tended to think fairly fast on his feet. "Any pictures you've seen of me were taken after you were born. That meant I was at least a year or two old. That's not really a baby."

"No," she responded, "I've seen pictures of you from before I was born. You were cute."

"How?"

"My parents are your godparents, remember? I've got pictures from your christening."

In all his years, he had never directly broached the subject of Rick George with Heather. And now they were lovers. What better time than the present?

"Why does your father hate me?"

"He doesn't hate you." The response came back autonomically, as he sort of expected it to. She continued, "What makes you think he hates you?"

"I don't know. Lots of things. Let's forget 'hate.' Let's just debate as to whether or not he likes me. He doesn't like me. Rebuttal?"

"I've never heard anything negative about you in my house, ever."

"Ah, c'mon, Heather. He mocks me. He's hurtful, sarcastic. What's up with that?"

"Overprotective father?"

"Naw, not just now; now that we're dating. I mean forever. For as long as I can remember." Jordan got more agitated as he spoke.

Heather appeared taken aback. "I think you're blowing it out of proportion. You two never struck me as the best of buddies, but I'd never say he hated you."

"You never saw it? The digs? The attitude? The hurtful practical jokes?"

"Give me an example."

"If my mother ever gave me a solo in church, he'd be like, 'Nepotism.' Or once he said, 'Matino's got a solo. Save a few pews on Sunday for all the dagos.' "

"Ethnic humor was part of their generation. Give him some slack. We've said ourselves that teasing was a way we showed we liked each other."

"Maybe it's just me, then. I guess I just expected more from him because I didn't have a father and he was my godfather."

"My turn to ask you a question. Speaking of your father, why don't you ever speak of your father?"

He had to admire the wordplay. "Why bother? There's nothing to say."

"But you're here complaining that *my* father was a poor father to you. I would think you'd be ranting more about the guy whose job it really was."

Aw, thought Jordan, she didn't understand. She loved her father and she wasn't going to stand around listening to him getting dissed.

"I don't want to say this, Jordy, but it sounds like you've been taking out a lot of your feelings toward your father on *my* father. I love you and because I love you I have to tell you that. It doesn't make you a bad person. I just think you've got some issues and you have a right to them. But my father never ran away . . ."

"Hey!"

Heather wasn't backing down. Jordan couldn't intimidate her even if he tried. "So you're defending your father?"

"No," said Jordan irritably.

"Either you are or you're not. I'm not saying this to hurt you. I told you that. Work it out. I'll help you. But if you're sticking all your feelings of abandonment on my dad, I think you're hitting the wrong target." Heather came to him and placed her arms around his hips. Touch tranquilizes. "I get the impression this has been on your mind for a long time."

"Yeah. Years."

She pulled him closer. "I'm sorry. My dad has a way, you know? He jokes around a lot. You do, too."

He returned her embrace. Jordan had rarely experienced a girlfriend consoling him. "So you say he doesn't hate me?"

"It would be news to me and I think a secret like that would be pretty hard to keep in our little house. I'm sorry you feel he let you down as a godfather. You came out okay, though."

"All right. I'll try to deal better."

"I love you, Jordy."

"I love you, too."

Simple conversation, short period of time. But they were talking about seeing each other at one hundred, and he was discussing deep, personal issues he housed inside of him like a malignancy. Consequently, he found himself thinking about his far distant future and Heather being a part of it.

It may have been less than a month on paper, but this was a lifelong friendship. Jordan kept telling himself it was not as bizarre as it appeared. He had drunk from the cup of life, chug-a-lugged from it on quite a few occasions, in fact. He no longer had any financial reasons to avoid marriage. He could provide as well as almost any man his age. Having children of his own and being a good father was an aspiration that lingered prominently in the back of his mind. Time was creeping up on him. Slowly, but creeping nonetheless.

It had already crossed his mind a few times to go out and purchase a nice ring, get down on one knee, and do the whole classic proposal thing. He was convinced she would say yes. If he had any worries at all, it was about their parents. And not just Rick.

During this Golden Age, he and Heather stayed rather blithe and vague with their parents concerning their continuing relationship. They seemed to be handling it similarly. Neither would bring it up unless asked or unless they absolutely had to. They were neither keeping secrets nor lying. Both admitted to still getting fuzzy feelings of oblique negativity. Since things were going so well, though, they agreed to not allow parental oddities to bring them down.

Jordan made a mental promise to confront Opal, Rick, and Eleanor in person at Christmastime. Get things out in the open. Until that happened, he would postpone talk of marriage. At least that was today's plan.

On a flowered sofa somewhere in a room with stenciled wallpaper—which it did not quite match—in a home on top of a mountain full of coal about one hundred miles northwest of Philadelphia, sat a blonde, a brunette, and a redhead, all of matronly age. No men were in sight.

"They're still dating," said Opal Matino.

"I know. I think it's more serious than just dating, too," said Eleanor George.

"What are you going to do about it?" asked Mildred Stein.

"You're the one who said to let it run its course," replied Eleanor.

"I guess I didn't see it coming," Mildred said. "I thought maybe they were spending time together over the holiday 'cause they were each other's only port in a storm. I never thought it would go much beyond that."

"I always lived in dread. Always. Doesn't matter what you do or how you do it. Nobody really gets away with anything. It's all just a matter of time." Eleanor had rarely sounded so hopeless.

Opal reached out a hand and placed it upon Eleanor's knee. "We'll work it out. It'll be fine." Opal was being thoughtful and motherly, but in truth, she had no idea, nor did any of them, exactly how they would work it out or how they would make it okay.

"Have you reconsidered telling Heather? I think she could handle it. She's older now and she's got a good head on her shoulders," Mildred suggested to Eleanor.

"No, no. That was Rick's condition. As long as he lived, she was never to know."

"Then talk to Rick. That's what he said years ago. It's water under the bridge now. All this worrying is his fault," said Mildred, trying to make headway.

"His fault? God, Mildred, you have a short memory," Eleanor

shot back in disbelief. After a mournful pause, she turned to Opal. "Anything you can do from your end?"

Opal did not have an answer. "Like what?"

"I don't know. I was hoping you'd a-thought of something by now."

Mildred rejoined the fray. "Well, what you're both worried about is that they'll fall in love, get married, and have kids. You really think that could happen? I think you're both getting ahead of yourselves."

"I think it could happen. Girls talk more about their feelings. I think Heather loves him. She hasn't come out and said it, but I can tell. I can tell," said Eleanor.

Opal finally had something. "If marriage is the worst that could happen, they wouldn't do it if we didn't give our blessing."

Mildred had trouble containing her incredulity. "Your blessing? This isn't the old country, Opal. Kids do whatever they damn well please today. Jesus!"

"Not an only child. Not my Jordan and not Heather. If we said no, they wouldn't go through with it. It's different with an only child," repeated Opal.

"Maybe. Heather always wanted to get married in our church and march down the aisle with her father. With Rick," said Eleanor mournfully.

"So when you withhold your blessings and they ask why, what the hell are you going to tell them, if you refuse to tell them the truth?" asked Mildred.

"I have no idea," responded Eleanor, in as deep a funk as she could possibly be. "I have no idea."

FIVE

The smaller boy finally finished his moonlight dance to the gods of nudism and got back inside his sleeping bag. "Hey man, did you ever jerk off?"

"What?"

"Jerk off. Did you ever jerk off?"

The tall boy hemmed and hawed and made all sorts of noises that did not mimic human words, as he attempted to avoid answering the question. Finally, he realized that the best defense was a good offense. "Did you?"

"Yeah." It came out hesitantly, as the boy who started the discussion wanted to buffer himself against possible moral outrage.

"When?"

"What do you mean, 'when'? Like, when do I do it, or when did I do it?"

"I don't know. I guess I meant, when did you start doing it?"

"A while ago."

"A long time ago?"

"Not too long."

"How did you learn how to do it?" It was an odd question, not one the smaller boy expected.

"Chicky showed me how," he said hesitantly.

"Chicky?"

"Yeah, Chicky. Chicky showed me when we were at scout camp." The veracity of his answer, just like his tale about the nudist camp, was questionable.

"Chicky showed you how to do it at scout camp? Weren't you afraid of getting caught?"

"It was dark and it was late at night. Everyone else was asleep. We were real quiet."

"Man, I'd be afraid of Mr. Kerlavage catching us and telling my parents." The boys were best friends, but one was Catholic and the other Protestant. As the town had two scout troops, one for each of their religions, they did not go to camp together.

"It feels really good. You should try it some time." The tall boy silently considered this advice, when he looked over and noticed his friend's sleeping bag bouncing up and down in the middle.

"What are you doing?"

"I'm jerking off. I told you."

"You didn't tell me you were going to do it right now!"

"Yeah, it's perfect. We're up here all alone and we can do whatever we want."

The taller boy continued to lie on his back, staring up at the sky, frequently glancing over at the inexplicably enticing sight of his best friend beating the inside of his sleeping bag with great intensity.

"You should try this. It feels great." The smaller boy never missed a beat as he spoke, his voice vibrating from the rapid activity of his right hand.

"I don't know. I never did it before."

"Oh. You want me to show you?"

"I don't know. I feel funny about it."

The smaller boy kept selling the idea. *"It's really great. Here, watch me,"* and he threw back his sleeping bag to show himself in full tumescence. The boy's small stature was consistent in his other body parts, but he was almost inhumanly erect. Now the taller boy understood where the word "boner" came from. Show-and-tell continued, and the taller boy found it hard to look away. *"Now you do it."*

"I don't know."

"Know what? Anyone can do it. Ever go to the Philadelphia Zoo?"

"Yeah."

"The gorillas do it all the time and they don't care who watches. Ever watch them do it?"

"Not that I remember."

"Well, if even a gorilla can do it, I'm sure you can."

Gingerly, the taller boy unzipped his sleeping bag as well as his pants. The other boy began moving his own sleeping bag closer to him. The tall boy's member was larger than the shorter boy's, but it had nothing on the other boy's insofar as stiffness. *"Mine doesn't get big like yours does."*

"It will. Think of something."

"Like what?"

"Sophia Loren."

"Sophia Loren?"

"Yeah, or anybody. Anybody that makes you horny. Don't you ever get horny?"

"Sure."

"Then think of what does it for you and watch how hard you get." The tall boy tried, jostling himself at the same time, yet nothing much happened. *"Want some help?"*

The offer took the tall boy aback. "What?"

"I said do you want some help?"

"No!"

"Just asking. That's how Chicky taught me."

"What?"

"Chicky showed me. I told you that. He's older. He knew more than I did. He helped me."

"How?"

"He got me started a little. Watch, it feels real good," and the smaller boy boldly yet tentatively reached over and touched the tall boy's penis. "See, I'm not gonna hurt ya. It feels good, doesn't it?" The tall boy seemed too frightened to answer. "Really, I swear, I'm not gonna punch ya in the balls or anything. This is really great." And the tall boy relaxed the tiniest bit and allowed his friend greater access. "See, you're getting harder now."

"I tried that by myself a few times, but it never seemed to work very well."

"Yeah, well when someone else does it, it's just like if you were with a girl. That's what makes it better. If you don't have anyone else around, you can use your left hand instead of your right. It's almost as good."

Jordan doubted that he, let alone any other kid, went through grade school saying, "When I grow up, I want to be a urologist." He had never even heard the word until he was in college. And even then, despite being in a pre-med program, he never imagined it was the specialty he would be in today. Specialties were like a list of fun extracurricular activities or the choices on a diner menu with six or eight pages. Jordan loved choices. He reveled in researching the pros and cons of each one, eventually wanting to choose them all, if it were somehow possible.

As his medical training progressed, some ideas passed by the wayside, while others sprung up. When he began to explore urology, it was prostate cancer that first grabbed his interest. Oncology itself was a consideration. Yet it was in urology that he found a special feeling and humanity. A humanity that was particularly his own.

Being raised without a father, he felt very comfortable in the company of women. Only women had ever seen his childhood vulnerabilities. So too, he had rarely seen the vulnerabilities of other men or boys. He was heterosexual beyond a doubt, for whatever part that played in all of this. He never worried for a second about his sexual identity, although his mother had confessed to him that it had plagued her. On one of her parental-reading kicks, she had come across some now-lampooned theory that boys who are only children raised in a fatherless environment were more likely to "become" homosexuals. God, how that made him laugh today. But for a short time, Opal kept dragging him into a chair to discuss his "feelings" about girls and boys, and ugh! The whole thing made him wince as he recalled it. The only good upshot was that she never gave him any grief about playing sports, as if somehow playing sports made you like girls instead of boys. So he participated in good heterosexual activities like wrestling and football. One, where you simulated rough sex with another boy, the other, where you and other boys took turns jumping on top of each other.

Exploring oncology, he met both male and female patients who were suffering from cancers. They were upset, afraid, and vulnerable, as one might expect. But in urology with mostly male patients, the prostate and testicular cancers he primarily saw also had frequent sexual side effects. Between those, as well as male infertility and other sexual problems, he saw men at their most vulnerable, their vulnerabilities in most men's minds akin only to the issues of actual life and death. Jordan felt strange at first. Strange, yet incredibly empathetic. These were men without their drinking buddies; men not talking about hunting or fishing or cars or basketball. Scared, frightened men. Men he wanted to put his arm around. Men who needed someone who was not going to play drill instructor or football coach, telling them, "Buck up. Be a man. Be a good soldier." Men who needed someone to say, "Hey, I know. It sucks. Let's see what we can do together to make your life all right again." That was what had made Jordan become a urologist. That and Jeff Stroncavage.

Stroncavage was a few years ahead of Jordan in high school. Football hero. Star halfback. Hard to imagine it when first meeting him, as "Strong" was only about 5'6" and built like a bowling ball. With that and his red hair, he did not match anyone's typical image of Mister Touchdown. But Strong had all the intangibles. He was a leader on and off the field. A man who, as they said about Gary Cooper, old folks wanted as a son, men wanted as a pal, and women wanted as a lover.

One lasting visual in Jordan's mind was when he was a lowly sophomore on the football team and Strong was the senior star. As Jordan stood on the sideline during a particularly hard-fought game, Strong came barreling down that same sideline with the ball. Jordan was close enough to see that Strong's mouth was as red as his hair. Redder, as his mouth was obviously gushing blood. Once he was finally brought down right by Jordan's feet, he bounced up quickly as he always did, grabbed the two nearest offensive teammates he could find and screamed, "Blocking! We need some fucking blocking!" His blood splashed into their faces, humiliating them into giving greater effort on the next play. That was Strong.

But on this day years later, Jordan's being handed a patient chart with the name Jeff Stroncavage on it meant nothing at first blush. Then a young man with red hair, a bit of a paunch, and a slightly receding hairline came into his examining room.

"Strong?"

" 'Tino?"

Jordan was surprised that Stroncavage, the older football icon, would have known his name at all, because at the time their paths last crossed, they were like royalty and peasant. Yet that, too, was Strong. He was the type to remember the little people.

Today, their roles were reversed. 'Tino was now the doctor and Strong was a young man with testicular cancer. Jordan wished he had more time for reminiscing, but he knew his job and tried to do it to the best of his abilities, neophyte physician that he was. He ran through his routine, taking the hand-off, as it was, from the previous doctors who had examined Strong and run some tests. It was now up to Jordan to give his prognosis and options. Had Stroncavage been wealthier or had better insurance, he would not have been having this talk with a doctor as inexperienced as Jordan was that day. Yet for this patient, Jordan was determined to do his job as well as any doctor twice his age. He was going to give Strong some fucking blocking.

As their session stretched on, Jordan knew he was going beyond the amount of time he was supposed to spend with one patient. But for the first time in his young medical career, he didn't care. Jordan wasted no time talking about long-ago touchdowns or ample-breasted cheerleaders. He gave Stroncavage incredibly well-thought-out, clearly communicated options and recommendations. He gave him his home phone and beeper numbers. He made him copies of some new journal articles he had recently read. Strong's case was not an easy one. There were complications. Cancer was spreading, and things such as the ability to have more children or even normal sexual relations with his wife were now in danger.

Stroncavage must have known he was getting care above and beyond the call of Jordan's duty. Despite their shared personal history, Jordan was not making light of any of it. Nor did he pump him up with false hope. It was the best and worst consultation of his young medical career. When Stroncavage got up to leave, they shook hands. Then Strong did something that Jordan never saw coming. He pulled him closer and bear-hugged him soulfully and sincerely. "You're a great fucking doctor, Jordan."

That was the first time Jeff Stroncavage had called him by his first name. It was one of the first times any guy he had grown up with had used it. None of the guys back home ever used first names. It was a defining moment for Jordan as a doctor. For in that one session, he discovered what kind of doctor he wanted to be and how he wanted his patients to feel and be treated. He would be a doctor to men: straight men, gay men, black, white, young, and old men. He was as confused and befuddled by women as any male. But somehow he felt that underneath every man, every kind of man, there was a common denominator that he understood and could somehow connect with. A common denominator that often only presents itself at the worst possible times. To these men, these patients, he could be brother, son, father, friend, as well as physician.

Maybe Christmas, thought Jordan. Maybe. After he had all but dismissed it, he realized that with work and all the time they were spending together, he'd not yet purchased a Christmas gift for Heather. There'd been simply no time. She had probably gotten him something fabulous and thoughtful by now.

It was only a few days before Christmas Eve. They were planning on driving up to Mountain City together on the twenty-fourth. He was off until the twenty-sixth. Her holiday was longer, but she decided she'd rather spend it at his place than back home, even if he were working much of the time.

They were into semi-cohabitation by now. Jordan loved watching her tromp around in an old football jersey and sweat pants as much as seeing her in an evening dress. He saw her with no makeup; she watched him scratching himself. True love. He even bought a different brand of jam.

Christmas gift, he thought. Yes, many couples get engaged around Christmas. Jordan already knew that he wanted to marry Heather George. Everything else was just protocol.

As soon as he left work, he headed downtown to Bailey Banks & Biddle, the most prestigious jeweler in Philadelphia. He wondered whether it was better to propose first and then have her pick out her own ring. But he loved the image of her opening that special box to see a diamond inside, gleaming like heaven. If he blew it with his choice of stone or setting, he could always exchange it. He was sure that happened all the time.

It was a snowy early evening that looked much later for the shortness of December days. The streets pulsed with holiday shoppers. Jordan had not done his homework. This sort of Christmas shopping was typical for him, this last-minute stuff. But for the kind of purchase as important and expensive as an engagement ring, he was usually an inveterate planner. Working within his normal system, he would have first bought a few books on the art of diamond purchasing, asked a few knowledgeable friends, and gone online for recent articles. Instead, here he was—completely unprepared and about to plop down an extraordinary amount of money on the most important purchase of his young life.

How much do they say an engagement ring should cost? Two and a half months salary? Or is it three? If he asked the salesman on commission, he'd be bound to get a high figure. Not a wise choice. Jordan was making decent money at this point, but he hadn't set any aside for this. He guessed most guys did, once they'd been dating a girl for, oh, three years or so. But three weeks?

Just recently, he'd put together the down payment on his co-op. Zeiss and he had been roommates, doing the young bachelor thing together for a few years. When they both hit thirty, they suddenly felt they were getting so old that their continuing to co-habitate would make young ladies wonder about their sexual proclivities. Zeiss's father, who was rich and well connected, found them a co-op building with two single units available. A pulled string here, a pulled string there, and the two young doctors were suddenly no longer within the world of renters. Did Zeiss's father know any jewelers that did creative financing? He probably did, but Jordan was already standing in front of Bailey Banks & Biddle, credit card at the ready. He knew that presenting a ring to Heather in a BBB box would cause her to melt into a puddle of sweet goo. Boxes are of incredible importance when it comes to jewelry. This box would contain his heart.

At about this same time, a handsome, mustachioed man approaching sixty years of age was fiddling with tools and a home-improvement project in a small master bedroom with jungle-print wallpaper. His wife entered, to find him nearing the end of construction, putting the finishing touches on the thing that occupied his attention.

"You finally got that thing out of the box that's been sitting in the corner for six months?"

"Yeah. It's almost set."

The attractive blonde got into the wicker-basketlike chair and began swinging. "Weee!"

"Don't do that. I don't know how much it can hold."

She was laughing and giggly. "Then how the hell are we supposed to use it if it can't support me? How's it going to support you?"

"It's not supposed to support *me*. I'm not sitting in it! How the hell would that work? Stop swinging it a minute. I have to measure."

"Measure what?"

"Clearance."

"I don't get it."

"It has to be set at just the right height so we can use it."

Eleanor George sat in the now-motionless hanging chair and waved her hand underneath it. "You mean clearance here?"

"Yeah."

She kept waving her hand underneath the chair. She was still giggly. "What's going on under here? Hey, there must be two or three feet between this and the bed. What the hell are you putting under here that's going to reach up and poke through the holes in the bottom of this thing? I never saw anything long enough to reach *that* far." She was hysterical, yet Rick was dead serious.

"*I* go under there. Not just my thing. *Me*. Here . . ." He lay on the bed underneath the chair. "See, I take up room, too. Now check the clearance."

Eleanor started to swing again. "*Would you like to swing on a star? Carry moonbeams home* . . . She sang, off-key and giddy.

Suddenly, she crashed to the bed. "Aaaaah!" Had Rick been directly underneath her point of landing she might have broken his pelvis. Luckily, Eleanor dropped just aside of him. He did an "Ompf!" as the wicker-basket chair landed only partially upon him.

Plaster was falling from the ceiling, and Eleanor was laughing so hard she feared she would wet her pants. Rick remained unamused. "Look what you did! Look what you did! You could have killed me and you nearly brought down the whole ceiling!"

Eleanor tried through her laughter to put up an argument. "But think about it. If that's all it took to make it fall down, aren't you glad it happened now and not when we were doing it, naked?" Just imagining it caused her to roll into a ball on the bed, continuing her convulsions of laughter.

Rick was still far from jovial. Collecting herself finally, Eleanor rolled over by her husband and took his face in her hands. "Richard, I love you. We don't need chairs hanging from the ceiling or crazy stuff like that. It's okay. Everything's great."

Rick George gazed past her, depressed.

She asked, "What?" He gave no response. "Is this about Heather and Jordan? Hmmm?"

"I don't want to talk about it."

"Richard George, you're the guy that I love. Thirty-six years together. Still together. I'm the luckiest girl in the world. Stop worrying about everything." She kissed him, but her kiss was not returned.

"I haven't been myself since they started seeing each other. I don't want to go back there again. Things have been good for too long."

"They'll still be good. Don't worry about it," Eleanor lovingly reassured him.

"I worry."

Exiting another house two doors away, a man of about seventy walked his two hunting dogs while sneaking a smoke. In the dark, with only his lit cigarette for illumination, he did not carry or use the now-requisite plastic bag for picking up dog crap. Clandestine smoking; clandestine dog walking. The actions of the oppressed yet defiant. Jack Stein enjoyed the night air but wished that so many of his activities did not have to be done surreptitiously. He frequently altered his route so that the dog droppings were equally spread among his neighbors' lawns and sidewalks. Some might not notice the piles at all. Others were less prone to investigate if only a stray piece was found here or there. Even the most banal forms of lawbreaking still had to be properly planned.

When he returned the dogs to their small kennel in the backyard, for his dogs were not allowed indoors on orders from Mildred, he went inside the house to get their food and water.

"Did you wipe your feet?"

"Yes," he replied.

Mildred came out to the kitchen, which was just off the back porch from where Stein had entered. "Look, you're dragging in mud again. You didn't wipe them good enough. You never do."

"Sorry," he answered contritely.

He went back to his ministrations, taking care of his beloved dogs. When he returned to the house, he made a more concerted effort to clean the bottoms of his shoes. In fact, he took them off, but only for a moment. "I wanna go back to the shop. I gotta fix some scaffolding."

"Now?"

"Yeah, now," he answered. "Don't know when else I'll get a chance."

"Go, go. Just don't stay out too late or wake me up when you get in. You never want to spend an evening at home. You're sixty-nine years old and you just want to work all the time."

Without replying to her criticisms, he carried his shoes to the front door and silently put them back on. Shutting the door behind him, Stein went out to his pickup truck parked half a block away. The family car was parked right in front of his house, but he did not dare take that for fear of dirtying the seats. He also did not dare park his truck in front of the house, as there was only enough space for each family to park one car on the street directly in front of their door. That meant it was the spot for her car, not his truck. Stein limped in the silence and darkness.

He gunned the truck in the direction of his shop, about six blocks away. Parking and unlocking the shop door, he went in. He turned on the lights and made sure the answering machine was set to pick up on one ring. He grabbed a beer from the 'fridge and slugged down a few mouthfuls before heading back outside and into his truck. Then he drove off.

SIX

THE SUN WAS setting as Jordan approached Reading. Each mile closer to his destination made him more agitated. Turning now from highways to streets, he thought he would have to pull over from a bout of nerves.

Mind over matter, he finally reached Heather's door. He was determined to make his every move, his every word and inflection, something to be remembered forever. A movie that needed no second takes.

She greeted him already bundled up, her overnight bag packed and ready to go. He was immediately thrown off his rhythm.

"Um, can I come in for a bit?"

"Gotta pee?"

"No. Well, yes, actually I do."

"Give me your keys. I'll put the suitcase in your trunk and wait for you in the car. Use your key to lock up."

"No . . . stay here."

"Why?"

Ugh! Why was she making this so hard? "Just sit down. Please. I'll only be a second. I want to talk to you."

"Can't we talk in the car?"

Never in all the time he had known her did Heather frustrate him so. Yet she did it so innocently that he could not show anger, not at a time like this. "Humor me. Have a seat. I'm a bit tired from driving and I'd love to sit and hang a bit before jumping back in the car again. Okay?"

"Okay," she said as she pulled her suitcase back into the apartment.

Pretty good thinking on his feet, that last one. The problem and beauty of life is the lack of control over its intangibles.

He came out of the bathroom. There sat Heather on the sofa. Was this where he wanted her? It seemed natural, a piece of comfortable furniture where they could sit together. But then he would have to turn to talk to her. Somehow he had envisioned facing her, not turning toward her. Was he becoming some sort of obsessive-compulsive? If he sat in a chair opposite her, she might think that this was bad news. That's the way you fire someone or break up—seated far enough away so you can escape flying fists.

He joined Heather on the sofa and kissed her hello. "If we're staying awhile, why don't you take off your coat?" She smiled, as he noticed she had done likewise.

His coat remained on because its large pockets could hold the ring box comfortably without it cutting into his body or protruding strangely. He knew that taking off the coat, then reaching back toward it and digging into it for the box would be clumsy and awkward. God, this was like trying to negotiate a straight line after consuming a fifth of gin! He couldn't make a single move without planning it first, for fear he would fall flat on his face.

The coat stayed on. Open, but still on. "I know Christmas isn't 'til tomorrow, but I wanted to give you your present privately because once we're back in Mountain City, nothing we do will be very private."

She smiled nervously and silently allowed him to continue. "I just wanted to tell you that I love you and that these past few weeks have been incredible. I don't want them to end. I really want us to be together all the time."

Suddenly, and without any pre-planning, Jordan slipped to one knee in the same motion with which he stuck his hand into the coat pocket that contained the ring box. Is this why guys got on one knee? He was doing it because it allowed him to face her more squarely while sitting next to her on the low couch. Was this the secret behind that maneuver? He had always thought the one-knee thing was some symbolic gesture of gallantry as opposed to physical logistics.

As he looked up into Heather's face, he couldn't help but notice that her feet were no longer on the floor. For she was now crouching upon the sofa and edging backwards like a person escaping gradually rising floodwaters. Was this a good thing? At first blush it would not appear so, but she did not look angry or disappointed. Pensive, though. Pensive and nervous.

He pulled the box out of his coat pocket, and her eyes widened. Jordan could think of little additional purple prose befitting the moment. The box was doing all the talking for him. He offered it up to her and she tentatively took it and started to open it. Like a coffeemaker, she began to percolate. He watched silently as she opened the box, carefully yet quickly and purposefully, exactly as they had first removed each other's clothes in this very same apartment a few short weeks ago.

Finally, the lid opened and she looked inside at what she

could not have been expecting. Or was she expecting it? It could have just been a nice pair of earrings, right? That would have been a great, *very* great Christmas gift from a guy she had only been dating for a few weeks.

Now her mouth was open as wide as her eyes, and Jordan felt he had to make some sort of statement. He opened his mouth to speak, but there was a catch as he struggled to talk through welling emotion. "Heather, will you marry me?"

"Oh my God! Oh my God! Oh my God! Oh my God! Oh my God! Oh my God!" He rose up toward her, and she hugged him. She was crying; his neck became moist with her tears. He lost count of the, "Oh my Gods," but they were the only thing she seemed capable of uttering. Suddenly, it was perfect, and it would be remembered forever and ever as being the most perfect of perfect moments.

Realizing that "Oh my God!" did not legally indicate an answer of "yes," Jordan pulled slightly away to say, "If you need time, or if you're unsure, you can still keep the ring. I want you to have it. I bought it for you because I love you."

She was quick on the uptake. "Yes! Yes, I want to marry you! Yes, my answer is yes! Yes! Yes! Yes! Yes!" And now "Yes!" had replaced "Oh my God!" and he again lost count. They again embraced, and the rest of the world ceased to exist.

Jordan's heavy coat was making him sweat even more than the life-altering moment he had just experienced. He broke the clinch just long enough to remove it and get comfortable. They kissed, they smiled, they laughed at themselves. Finally, they were ready to make the trek from Reading to Mountain City in time for St. John's Christmas Eve service.

The ride up Route 61 to Mountain City was unlike any other. Heather held her left hand aloft staring at her ring perpetually, long enough for Jordan to wonder how she could keep it up without losing all circulation. "Does it fit okay?"

"Yes. It fits fine. How did you know my size?"

"I didn't. I figured a little bit larger than my pinky should do it. They said they could size it better if you liked."

"It's fine. It fits great."

"Do you like it?"

"Like it? I love it! It's perfect."

"No, I mean not just the thought and what it represents. I mean, as a ring, a piece of jewelry. Do you like it?" Jordan was sounding like he needed stroking, but he didn't care. He wasn't asking for compliments on his sexual performance or his choice of cologne. He had spent thousands on that damn thing and if it didn't get some "ooos" and "aahs" he'd be quite disappointed.

"Yes. It's the greatest. I love this ring and I'll never take it off. Never ever," she laughed.

"What's so funny?"

"I'm so happy. I'm engaged. I'm getting married to Jordan Matino. I've dreamed of this day my entire life."

"Getting engaged?"

"Getting engaged to you."

"What?"

"I've loved you ever since I could remember and now I'm marrying you. Whenever I dreamed of my wedding day, I dreamed I would be marrying you. Ever since I was a little girl. And now it's happening and I've never been so happy in my life," Heather laughed from the bottom of her soul. Joyous laughter you couldn't help but get caught up in.

"Well, you kept a great secret."

"Yup."

"You don't think this is too soon, do you?"

"If I did, I wouldn't have said yes."

"You're sure? I mean, you wouldn't have maybe said yes because you didn't want to hurt my feelings when what you really wanted to say was, 'Yes, but not right now. Maybe sometime later?'"

"Is that what you think?"

"Which part? The part where I think that you think it's too soon, or the part where maybe I think it's too soon?"

"You're confusing me. You ruminate more than a Woody Allen film. Do *you* think it's too soon?"

"If I did, your Christmas present would have been a gift certificate to the Gap."

"I *like* the Gap."

"Want me to take the ring back and get that instead?"

"NO!" she paused. "Could I get a Gap gift certificate, too?"

As Route 61 turned into Nahas Avenue in Mountain City, he asked, "When do you want to tell our parents?"

"I say, let's get it out of the way as soon as we get in. I'm not taking off this ring. Never."

As they parked on Good Street, he recalled old pictures of himself. He was just learning to walk and was holding onto the edge of a bassinet and looking at Heather as a newborn baby for perhaps the first time. Imagine telling that little one-year-old boy, "This is Heather. You're going to marry her some day." He probably would have wet himself, but with *feeling*.

Heather was giddy, temporarily forgetting the strangely negative attitude their parents had been giving them since Thanksgiving. Jordan, on the other hand, felt he was walking up the steps to the gallows. Maybe Heather had it right and he had it all wrong. He *was* thin-skinned and oversensitive. Perhaps that's why he thought Rick George hated him all these years.

Heather turned to him, "It looks like your mom is home. Grab her and bring her over to our place. I'll put my gloves on. Hurry."

Jordan tapped on his front door before entering. It was open, as it always was when his mother was expecting him and even when she wasn't. Crime was a rarity in Mountain City. The rumor was that the borough police had only one bullet, Barney Fife-like.

"Mom, I'm home."

Opal came out from the kitchen. "Hungry? I have a platter set up for you. Kielbasi and bleenies." He should have known.

"Come out here a second."

"What?"

"Just come out here."

"Do I need a coat?"

"No, we're just going next door a minute."

"Why?"

"Just come on."

Dutifully, she came out and saw Heather standing on her front porch steps.

"Hello, Heather." It was pleasant enough, but not with the special warmth Jordan thought appropriate.

"Hi, Aunt Opal." With that, Heather stepped forward and kissed her on the cheek. This, of course, is completely proper behavior between a son's fiancée and her future mother-in-law. But Heather had never greeted Opal this way before. Slightly taken aback, she tried to recover quickly enough so as not to draw attention to the matter.

Together, the three of them knocked once on the Georges' front door and then walked right in. Jordan looked at his mother and could see she was finding this entire adventure perplexing.

Rick George was sitting in his leather recliner. "Hi, Daddy,"

Heather said as she moved quickly over to him and gave him a big, happy hug.

"Hi, sweets," he responded. Glancing up at Jordan and Opal, he looked quizzical rather than out-and-out surprised. "C'mon in," he motioned to them.

Eleanor came down the stairs and got the same big hug thing from Heather, who was downright flighty enough to make everyone suspicious that something of special importance was afoot.

"Sit down, everybody," Heather said to her mother and Opal. It is universally known that "Sit down, everybody"—or a variation thereof—is an introduction to a cataclysmic event, pleasant or otherwise. Jordan noted that Rick had not gotten up to shake his hand nor did Eleanor acknowledge his presence, not that Heather had given either of them much of an opportunity.

Once all were eyeing one another nervously, Heather dropped the bomb: "Mom, Dad, Aunt Opal . . . Jordan has something to tell you."

Gulp. *He* was going to announce this? Crimes of passion toward his new fiancée filled Jordan's mind.

Given the stage, he reluctantly stepped up to give a completely unprepared oration. "As you know, Heather and I started seeing each other last Thanksgiving . . ."

"*This* Thanksgiving," his mother interrupted.

"That's what I meant. *This* Thanksgiving. Thank you. Anyway, I'm sure you heard we've continued to see each other since then. While I know this has been a very short time, we've known each other since birth. Not just casually, but as friends—close friends."

Jordan looked into the faces of his audience. No smiles, but perhaps that was only indicative of their apprehension. "So while we've only been dating a short time, we've been talking about making some major decisions about our future together and . . ."

The "and" seemed to hang in the air for a lifetime.

"Get to the point," growled Rick George. Jordan knew he was being somewhat obtuse, but he didn't need hecklers.

"Heather and I are getting married."

If silence is golden, he had just become King Midas. As if on cue, Heather dramatically pulled off her left glove, holding out her hand with the big, beautiful engagement ring upon it for all to admire. Yet not an eye gazed in its direction.

Rick got up from his recliner, peeking painfully through squinted eyes and a surly, wordless grimace, and exited the room. Both mothers were soundless and in shock. Heather finally acknowledged the mood and cried out "Daddy!" before chasing after her father.

Jordan looked at the open-mouthed expressions of Opal and Eleanor, their eyes reflecting the look of crisis. Angrily pointing in the direction of the departed Rick he said, "I guess that was all in my head, too."

Heather caught up with her father in the kitchen at the rear of the house. He stood with his back to her, looking out the window of the back door, staring at dark nothingness. He seemed to be trying to decide whether to dramatically blow out the door or stay inside his own home. Most certainly, he'd made it abundantly clear he did not want to be in the same room as the others.

"Daddy, what's a' matter? Why did you do that?" Rick wasn't talking, nor was he even turning around to face his only child. "Is it Jordan?"

After a long pause, he finally answered, "Yeah," still not looking in her direction until another moment passed and he reluctantly turned toward her. "Yeah, I don't like him."

He delivered the line while gazing at the floor in her general vicinity. For that reason, he did not immediately see that Jordan had followed her into the kitchen.

Rick's point of focus must have finally reached a different pair of shoes as he looked up to see Jordan standing there. He raised his eyes to stare directly into the face of his godson, the boy next door whom he had held during his Christian naming thirty-two years ago. Rick George's expression was perplexing. It displayed neither anger nor disdain as much as it seemed bereft of anything—a blank look from the dead eyes of a shark.

He did not seem inclined to expand upon his statement nor did he move to retract it. Jordan returned the stare, though his was more of a glower, the type a prizefighter gives his opponent as the referee gives them final instructions. He had never wronged this man. "Yeah, I don't like him." Even minor acquaintances avoid saying something so simple, hurtful, and blunt. Rick's words would ring in Jordan's ears forever.

Heather turned and looked at Jordan, then back at her father. Jordan knew of nothing he could say, only things he might later regret. Selfish as it was, he had to get out of there. He needed clarity of thought. He turned and walked out of the Georges' kitchen, straight on through the living room. Striding past his mother and Eleanor, he never stopped to look at their faces. He was completely inside his own head, oblivious to anything or anyone else around him.

Hitting the cold night air, he bounded down the steps at the same pace he had flown down them as a child. The night was frigid, colder than he'd expected. Not a night for long walks unless one was bundled up for arctic trekking. Jordan was not. He walked around the block, going behind the Good Street homes. Then he decided to detour into the backyard of the Steins. In the three families, coming in through the back door was as common as entering through the front. Despite walking only a short bit, Jordan was freezing. No amount of anger or hurt was going to change the weather.

He banged on the back door and was greeted by Jack Stein, who was hanging around in his kitchen, doodling with a project of some sort. Small tools were strewn about the table. Stein gave him as big a smile as he could, for while he was the stone-faced type, he seemed sincerely happy to see Jordan.

"Can I come in?" asked Jordan.

"Sure. Sit down."

It would have been out of character for Stein to ask too many questions. He figured if you had something on your mind or a favor to ask, you'd get around to it eventually. Jordan plopped down and watched him fiddle with his tools for a while, not paying enough attention to know what he was working on and too self-absorbed to care.

"How was the ride up?" Stein broke the silence, figuring he had to be the one to prime the pump of conversation for once.

"All right, I guess."

"Been here long?"

"Just got in."

The old man looked up at Jordan, his poker face not betraying his thoughts. Jordan figured the guy had to be wondering why he was sitting there in his kitchen instead of in his own. "Uncle Jack, is there something about me that's unlikable?"

Stein stopped what he was doing and gave Jordan the strangest, quizzical look. "Who doesn't like you?"

"My godfather."

"Rick? What makes you say that?"

"He just did. He just said it. Not sorta said it; he just said it. Out loud. With me right there."

"How'd it come up?"

"Heather and I came up together for Christmas. We've been going out. We're engaged."

Stein wiped his mouth thoughtfully, pondering his next move. "You know how fathers can be with their daughters."

"Maybe. But this was way out of line. When your boys came home to tell you they were engaged, did you give them grief about it and make their girlfriends upset?"

"That's different. They're boys. They weren't coming to me for nothing." Neither man spent much time musing on the fact that Stein's boys never *did* come back to him for anything. Ever.

By this time, Mildred had heard voices in the kitchen and stopped in to investigate. "Look who's here! Merry Christmas!"

Jordan got up to hug her, and she picked up right away that this was a "hold me, I'm upset" embrace.

"What's a' matter?"

"I'm engaged."

"To who, Heather?"

"Uh huh."

Suddenly her face drooped, too.

"What's going on? I come home, I announce I'm engaged, and everybody acts like I've got lice. What's the problem?"

"Maybe they just think it's too soon. Ever think about that?"

"Yeah, okay, maybe. But we've known each other forever. It's different."

"Jordy, nobody knows everything about each other. Not after only dating a few weeks. At your age, you don't even know yourself yet."

"I know myself! People come to me with their problems every day. I save lives. I'm old enough to get married."

"Well, maybe. I don't know. I'm not unhappy with you. You

have my blessing." With that, her husband shot her a look. As Jordan had turned somewhat away from Stein, it was an expression that he could not fully discern.

"Rick's reaction was to tell me he didn't like me."

Both the Steins jointly yet silently decided this was a perfect time to inspect the tops of their shoes. After a yearlong moment, Mildred finally said, "I don't know if he really meant that. Maybe he was just upset and taken off guard. You two aren't the best of friends, but I don't think he disapproves of you or dislikes you. You're just different."

"I'm different? Different from what?"

"Different from him. That's what I meant. Some people just don't mix well. Maybe that's just it. It doesn't mean you have to be enemies. You and your Uncle Jack don't have a lot in common, but you get along fine."

"Right, we do. That's the point. I have a lot less in common with Uncle Jack and he's always been great to me."

With that, Jack Stein gazed over at Jordan and smiled what Zeiss would call a *haimishe* smile, filled with *nakis*. Warmth and familial pride. Stein seemed to mellow more each time he saw him. God, he wished Stein was his godfather. Perhaps, though, that wouldn't have worked out much better. Maybe it was the title. Without it, Jordan expected nothing from Jack Stein, and Stein seemed to feel he owed Jordan nothing as well. Free of those expectations, they formed a bond of their own choosing.

Rick George had just ruined his engagement. How predictable, thought Jordan.

SEVEN

— ꝏ —

BACK AT THE Georges', Heather had isolated herself in her bedroom with her door closed to anyone who might upset her more. Jordan should have been there with her, she thought. But he'd run out. Run out just like his own father did when the pressure and pain became too much for him. Granted, Jordan had been gone only a few minutes, not a lifetime. And sure, Jordan hurt too, probably more than she did. She was not the one insulted so directly. But God, this hurt. This hurt so damn bad.

Downstairs, Rick George's anger was mixed with melancholy. "Is this how you're taking care of things?"

"How did we know, Rick? It's been a couple of weeks. Nobody does anything that fast these days. It isn't like he just got drafted or something," replied Eleanor.

"Rick, I didn't appreciate what you said to Jordan. That was out of line. It was uncalled for," enjoined Opal.

"Yeah, now I get to be the bad guy. The girl's upstairs crying and everyone can hate me. Like any of this is my fault," Rick said, defending himself.

"Well, it's not Jordan's fault. And it's not Heather's either. It's been over thirty years, Rick. Let it go. Tell her the truth and let the chips fall. She still loves you. She'll be more upset if you leave things as they are, telling her this is all because you don't like Jordan," Opal angrily replied.

"If I ever wanted Heather to know," he lowered his voice to a whisper, "it was not going to be this way. Not over this. Maybe someday if she was married to some other guy and we were all sitting around and everything was relaxed and I just wanted to come clean after all these years. But not like this."

"You could still do it, Rick. She'll hurt for a while, but she'll come around. I know she will," said Opal.

"No. *You* take care of it," Rick said as he sat back down in his recliner, making the point that he was done arguing.

"Take care of it how? You want *me* to tell Heather?" asked Opal.

"No! No one tells Heather. Anyone does that, I'm outta here." Rick was on his high horse. Whatever regret he had over upsetting his daughter had now passed. He was entrenched.

"You want me to tell Jordan?" Opal was looking for direction.

"I don't care what you do. Just don't tell Heather. And don't tell anyone who'll *tell* Heather either. It gets back to me that she knows, I'm gone."

During this entire exchange, Eleanor George kept quiet. Like a child within a group being reprimanded she seemed relieved to not be singled out for a personal verbal thrashing. Opal, though, was reclaiming her spunk.

"You know, Rick, I can understand how you feel. But you just hurt my son and I don't like it."

"Oh, get over yourself, Opal. Don't be raising a pansy. I didn't shoot him or anything."

Opal's disgusted grimace made no impression on Rick as she got up to leave. A sheepish Eleanor looked at Opal like a whipped puppy. "What are you going to do?"

"Try to fix things. Just like I always do. Try to fix things and make everything whole again." With that she turned and left. Onto Opal's shoulders, shoulders much stronger than one might imagine her to have, fell another burden. God only gives you as much as you can handle, indeed.

Inside her own house and its warmth, Jordan was waiting for her. So much for having enough time to formulate a plan.

"How long have you been here?" she asked.

"A few minutes. I was next door." By next door, he obviously meant the Steins'. That suddenly gave her an idea.

"Wait here a minute," she said as she slipped back out and knocked on the Steins' door. When Mildred answered, Opal signaled her out onto the front porch. "Come over. I need you."

"For what?"

"Jordy."

"He was just here. He's very upset."

"I know. I need you. For moral support."

"What are you going to do, Opal?"

"Tell him. Tell him what he needs to hear. I just can't do it alone. If you're there, he'll know I'm not making it all up."

"Is this what you really want to do?"

"It's the only way this whole thing is going to get sorted out. Once he knows, he'll understand what he has to do."

Slowly and filled with angst, the two friends walked the few short steps back into the Matinos' living room, where Jordan waited. He was subdued and more disgusted than livid by now.

Rick may have spoiled their announcement, but at least he hadn't forbade Heather from marrying him or anything outrageous like that.

Opal and Mildred had the same look on their faces that Jordan put on his when giving fatal news to a patient. The two slipped into a seating arrangement around him, landing so gently that they appeared like hens afraid of cracking eggs beneath them.

Opal took the floor. Mildred was present, indeed, for the simple, stalwart role of bolstering Opal's resolve. "Jordy, it'd be really easy to make you think that scene over at the Georges' was just about your Uncle Rick not liking you. But that would be dishonest. I know you have questions and I know you're hurt, but there's a lot more going on than you think.

"It goes back a long ways, back to when you were just born. We all lived here—us, Mildred and Jack, and Rick and Eleanor. Just like we still do today. But there was a fourth house . . ."

"What do you mean, 'a fourth house'?"

"A fourth house, on the other side of the Georges'. Your aunt and uncle lived there."

"Which aunt and uncle?"

"You don't know them. They're on your father's side. It was his brother Nick and Nick's wife Marianne." On the word, "Marianne," the most disdainful look crossed Opal's face, as if the word tasted like a bitter elixir on her tongue.

"Anyway, we all became friends. Except for Marianne, who we never really liked.

"Your father and I were buddies with Rick and Eleanor, and we double-dated a lot, went out to movies and dances and things together. Rick and your dad had been pals since grade school. Mildred here and Jack were a little older and we didn't know them until we'd been living here awhile." Opal glanced at Mildred, who returned a look of tentative approval.

"Your Uncle Nick and Aunt Marianne came along sometimes, too. Since none of us liked Marianne, when it came time to pick out godparents for you, your father and I argued long and hard about it, but I insisted on the Georges.

"Well, Rick and Eleanor began having some problems. Then Eleanor had an affair with your Uncle Nick."

Jordan's face shouted, "What?" but his tongue stayed quiet, for he could not interrupt this amazing story in which he had no idea what twist or turn might come next.

"Anyway, your Uncle Nick had an accident at work and damn near lost his arm. Put him in the hospital for a while.

"One day, Marianne was visiting Nick. They had taken him out of the room for physical therapy or something. The nurse came by delivering mail. Marianne took a look and saw there was a letter, not a card, but a letter from Eleanor George. She'd been suspecting something for a while, so she opened it. It was this long, tear-stained letter where Eleanor told Nick she was pregnant and that he was the father."

Opal stopped for effect. It had its desired result. Jordan's face betrayed the fact that he was already a step ahead of the story. Yet he still refused to verbally acknowledge it, for fear that if he did, it would all be true. Opal also knew the question that would come next if she waited long enough.

"*Was* he the father?"

"Yes."

"How did she know for sure?"

Finally Mildred chimed in. "Rick was impotent."

"You mean sterile?" asked Jordan.

"That, too," answered Mildred.

"He was impotent *and* sterile?"

"Yes," said Opal, continuing the story. "He had a lot of prob-lems down there."

This was too rich, thought Jordan. Strutting Rick the Prick had a defective dick? Couldn't be. "But what about all the sex talk? All the bragging he's always doing?" asked Jordan, growing more and more agitated and showing disbelief for the first time.

"This all happened a long time ago. They didn't have the medicines and stuff back then that you have today."

"He was impotent? He couldn't even get it up?" Jordan kept asking.

"Why are you focusing on that? So you can throw it up at him? You of all people should be more sensitive. Yes, it really was Nick Matino's child, and Eleanor didn't want to give it up because Rick *was* sterile. She was young and confused, and she felt unat-tractive and unloved because Rick was having his problems. That's why she took up with your uncle in the first place. But she never really wanted to leave her husband, and she certainly wasn't trying to get pregnant by another man. She made a mistake.

"All hell broke loose. The nurses had to restrain Marianne be-cause when Nick came back she tried to break his other arm. She was hysterical. Everyone's life was in a shambles.

"Eleanor was a wreck. She begged Rick to take her back. Good Christian man that he was, he agreed, and he raised Heather like his own. Nick and Marianne figured the only thing for them to do was move, because certainly neither of them could stay living next door to the Georges after all this. And your father was gone by then, so they didn't have that reason to stay either. That left me and you, Rick, Eleanor, and Heather . . . and Jack and Mildred of course. So, that's the story."

Opal let the news hang in the air for Jordan to put together.

It didn't take long. He did not wish to speak but wanted it to all magically go away. Finally, Opal could not allow her son's silence to negate the major point to be made. "Heather is your first cousin. You can't marry her."

Jordan was still too deep in thought to respond.

"Jordan, *say something!*"

Again, a silence of undetermined length. "Does Heather know?"

"No. If she did, would she have gone out with you? Gotten engaged to you? No, she doesn't know. I'd-a thought maybe she might've been told by now, but Rick won't allow it. He told Eleanor there were two conditions to his taking her back. One, that she never again be unfaithful to him. And two, that he'd raise Heather as his own so long as she never knew he was not her father and that no one else knew. All these years, the only people who knew are the people in these three houses."

"And the fourth house," added Jordan.

"Yes, of course, they know. They moved away, as I said. Marianne apparently gave Nick another chance, too, but I haven't heard from them in years. Not that I'd ever expect to. I know they're not around these parts at all. I don't know where they are exactly. And your father knows about it, I think . . . I guess. We never discussed it. I saw him once, maybe twice after that, when we finalized the divorce—your father, that is. The only person *I* ever told was Mildred, because she was my rock when your father left."

"I told Jack, that's it," said Mildred. "And Jack wouldn't say anything, even if he had a load on."

"And now there's you," Opal Matino said as she looked deeply into her son's eyes, feeling his pain, understanding his despair, and knowing that he was now faced with a world of trouble he had taken no part in creating.

Jordan's mind spun. He alternated between deep concentration and total confusion. Suddenly, he lasered in on one of the characters in this debacle who deserved to be blamed for at least part of it. "Rick George. Rick George. You know, any trepidation I had about getting together with Heather was all about him. How was he going to mess it up? How was he going to ruin it? Well, it was creative, that's for damn sure, but he did it. Son of a bitch . . ."

"Jordy, would you have done what he did? Would you have raised a child, loved a child who your wife carried but wasn't yours? And he loves Heather, he loves her with all his heart. You know how close they are."

"Is this why he hates me? And yes, I'm going to use the word 'hate,' because the cards are all on the table now."

Opal gave a deep sigh. "Put yourself in the man's shoes, Jordan. You're chasing after him, nagging him to be your father . . ."

"What? When the hell did I ever do that?"

"You did. More when you were a little guy, but you did, I saw it. You probably don't remember, you were so young, but you used to say, 'I wanna be like Uncle Rick.' You said things like that all the time. And even when you got older, even when you were telling me he did this bad thing to you and that bad thing to you, you still watched the way he dressed, the way he acted. You decided to be a doctor . . ."

"I didn't do that for him!"

"Yeah, but it made you feel good to come back here knowing you did what he set out to do and failed."

"Why are you doing this to me? You're trying to tell me this is all *my* fault?"

"Down, boy," said Mildred, butting in for her friend's sake.

"That's crazy, Jordan. That's not what I'm saying at all," said

Opal, getting defensive and agitated. "I'm saying that you wanted more from the man than he could give you. Can you buy that? Every time he looks at you, he sees your father and your uncle. You're a Matino, a Matino *man*. Every time he sees you, it reminds him. You'll never get him to admit it, but I feel in my heart that it's true. I'm sorry. It's not right, but he's never tried to be deliberately cruel to you. Maybe you disagree with that, but it's true. It just always kept him from being close to you, I think. I'm sorry. You didn't deserve that, but he was named your godfather before all this happened."

"But what about Heather? Why doesn't he hate her? She's a Matino, too. Huh?" He couldn't believe he just said that. Heather was a Matino, too? Only a few hours ago he got down on one knee and asked her to become Heather Matino. Little did he know she already was.

"Because he loves her. He sees her and doesn't envision her as being anything but his. He saw her come out of his wife's belly and he held her and fell in love with her. It's always been that way. He *is* sterile. He couldn't have his own child, so she's special to him. I know it's confusing to you, but I think a lot of it is because you're a boy and she's a girl. If Eleanor had a son, it might have been different. What do I know? I'm no psychologist."

"But how do they know for sure that she's not his? Did they get blood tests? Is he still impotent?"

"No, after all this happened, Rick started getting every kind of help there was for the sex thing. He and Eleanor worked very hard on that part of their relationship. He saw all kinds of doctors and therapists, urologists like you, and other things. They're happy now. But no, they tried to conceive a child of their own and they never could. He's still sterile. And at the time Heather was conceived, he was also impotent. So they hadn't done it around

the time she got pregnant with Heather. Eleanor figured it had to
be Nick's child."

"But what about DNA?"

"Honey, this is the coal region and it was a long, long time
ago. They didn't have that sort of thing. And Jordan, before you
keep going off on your Uncle Rick, remember that the people
who screwed up here were Aunt Eleanor and Nick Matino, not
him. And Eleanor is suffering greatly right now. Her heart is
breaking."

"*Her* heart? *Her* heart? What about Heather's and mine? We
want to get married. Screw her heart! She fucked up. We didn't."
Jordan had never used the word "fuck" in front of his mother before, but he was in prime form now and couldn't restrain himself.
His entire future was crumbling in front of him.

His mother allowed the profanity without comment. "I know
how you feel, Jordy," she responded firmly yet calmly. "But this is
what's what. You can't marry Heather. She's your first cousin."

That was the second time Opal said it. Jordan knew it was the
major point she was trying to ram home. His world was being
driven off a cliff, but he was still hanging onto the wheel, trying
to steer his way out.

Opal Matino loved her son far beyond words. She reached
across, putting her hand on his knee. Her son had just announced
his engagement, and she had told him he had to call it off. It simply wasn't fair.

Finally Jordan spoke. "What am I supposed to do now?"

"I don't exactly know. If you tell Heather, Rick will walk out.
He said so just a few minutes ago. Jordy, you can't do that to that
family," she said, getting more upset and emotional for people
other than herself again. "I know how you feel about him, and I
know you'll never look at Eleanor the same way again. But that

family has been through a lot and they're still together. It would be a sin for you to ruin that.

"Look, I know how you must feel about Heather, and I know this will sound cruel and unfeeling, but you've got everything going for you. You're young, you're handsome, you're a doctor, you live in the city. Someday you'll find someone else who'll mean just as much to you. And she won't be your first cousin."

Jordan thought that her last declaration deserved an accompanying laugh track. Real life did not feature such lines. Real life is mundane. People don't sit down to seriously debate wheather marrying one's first cousin is a good thing, a bad thing, or a thing at all. Average people simply didn't put themselves in a position of *having* to decide the legal, moral, or biological issues of such a matter.

After a moment, feeling he wanted to rebut his mother's comments about meeting someone else, Jordan instead said, "But you still haven't told me what I'm supposed to do. If you don't want me to tell her the truth, what am I supposed to say to her?"

"I wish I had the words for you, Jordy. I wish I could do this for you. It shouldn't have to be you. Think about it. You're smart, you'll come up with something. Just don't hurt her. Heather's a sweet girl. Try to do what you have to do so nobody has to feel any more pain."

This was real-life melodrama. It differed from someone finding out they were going to die. Sooner or later everyone is going to die. Jordan wanted to run, run as far as his legs could carry him or his car could drive. He needed time for bereavement. Yet how and where could he get that? He was back on Good Street, back in Mountain City, and it was Christmas. He had a responsibility to be with his mother. He had a responsibility to be back at work seeing patients in a few days. Mourning had no place in his schedule.

"I have to get ready for church. I'm going in early to rehearse the soloist. I'll see you there later," said Opal, collecting herself and moving on. This was the mother he knew best, the one who understood moving on and carrying forth like a good soldier.

"I don't feel like going."

"Now listen. You're a big boy. I know this is hard, but you always go to church on Christmas Eve. You're here. You have no excuses, not even this."

Jordan didn't put up much of an argument. He was drained of fight. But he did not want to go to church that night, and he sure as hell didn't want to talk to anyone—especially Eleanor and even Heather. For one thing, where the hell would he sit?

Next door, Eleanor knocked and then entered Heather's room without waiting for an invitation. Her daughter's back was toward her, but she was relieved to see that her shoulders were no longer heaving from heavy crying.

"Are you okay?"

"You can't be serious," Heather replied. Turning toward her mother, she sat up and thrust out her left hand. "Look at this. Look at this ring." Her eyes were defiant yet hurt.

"It's beautiful," was all her mother could quietly say.

"This had been a perfect day. A storybook day in every way. Every day of this past month has been perfect—like a dream. And this ring topped it off. Now look." Heather did not need to explain further.

"I'm sorry, honey. Please don't hate your father or me."

Heather looked at her oddly. "Why would I hate you? What did you do wrong?"

That one put Eleanor on her heels, but she tried to forge ahead into uncharted territory. "I don't know. I feel responsible."

"Why? That's stupid. It's all *his* fault. I thought Jordan was too thin-skinned. Now I see he knew all along. He's perceptive that way. He's sensitive and wonderful and I love him. He wants to marry me. I wanted you to hug me and love me and be happy for me. We'd get married in our little church in Mountain City. Daddy would walk me down the aisle and it would be perfect. Now it's ruined."

Midway through, Heather began to cry so much that her words were difficult to understand. Eleanor pulled her daughter close to her chest and tried to hug her tearful tremors. "Shhh, shhh . . ." was all she could come up with until the crying began to subside. She would have to think of something of greater substance to say. Something . . .

"I'm still getting married to Jordan. I don't care what Daddy says."

"He didn't say you couldn't get married. He just has some issues with Jordan."

"Like what? What is there not to like about Jordan?"

"Well." The "well" hung in the air for a long time as Eleanor tried to defend her husband. It would not be an easy task. "Did I ever tell you about Jordan's father?"

"Yes. That he had money problems and walked out on Jordan and Aunt Opal."

"Well, there's more to the story than that. Yes, he did have money problems. But he had a *lot* of problems. He had money problems because he didn't like to work much. That's one thing. The other thing is . . ."

"What?"

"He was a troubled person. He had psychiatric problems. Lots of them. He spent time in mental hospitals."

"Does Jordan know?"

"I don't think so. Maybe. I don't know if I'd come right out and ask him. Jordy never really knew him. But I think your father sees a lot of Jordan's father in him. Jordy seems to have turned out all right, I'll grant you that. But there's still a lot of Matino in him."

"What do you mean?"

Eleanor sighed. "The Matino boys were charmers. They were Italian. There weren't that many Italian boys around here and they were very . . . sexy. They were all great dancers. Charlie Matino looked like James Dean. He was smaller than Jordan, but much better looking. Gorgeous. And he had two brothers, Nick and Vincent. Vince was older. He passed away at a very young age, mid-thirties I think. Heart disease. See, that's another thing . . ."

"This is so ludicrous, Mother!"

"Mentally unbalanced, heart disease, dishonest, lazy. There's a lot of bad in those genes."

"Get out of here! You're ridiculous! Get out of here!" Heather started to literally push her mother out of the room.

Eleanor tried her best to not lose her own temper. "Honey, Charlie Matino had everything going for him. Everybody loved him. The money stuff . . . honey, not only did he not like to work, he stole. Embezzled. Opal was humiliated. If it weren't for your father and the Steins, she never would have shoveled her way out of it. Reverend Paulson at the church got her a raise. Everyone pitched in to help her. She's wonderful. It's just that damn Charlie. When he ran off, he had a nervous breakdown. Claimed he had amnesia. *Amnesia!* No one gets amnesia except on television. He made it all up trying to lie his way out of stuff.

"Opal went to see him in the hospital. She came in; she even brought little Jordan. He looked at them both and claimed he didn't know them."

Heather felt one hell of a heart tug. "And now you want to punish Jordan some more?"

"Honey . . ."

"Mother, Jordan is his own man. He's nothing like you've described. And I'm not getting into any 'nature versus nurture' arguments with you at a time like this. Is his father still in some mental hospital?"

"I don't know. In the end, the doctors thought they had him figured out. Told him he no longer had a son or a wife. That he was free to do whatever he wanted; go wherever he wanted. No bills, no responsibilities. Suddenly, like some miracle, he gets his 'memory' back. But he's never been the same. That's why he never visited Jordan or sent Opal child support. He can't even support himself."

"Mother, this is all very enlightening and very upsetting. But that still doesn't give Daddy the right to look Jordan in the eye and tell him he doesn't like him. Jordan never did a thing to Daddy to deserve that. Or to me. I love him, Mom. I want to marry him."

"Heather, all I can say is don't blame your father. He means well. He loves you. The sun rises and sets on you. Always has. Charlie Matino was a very screwed-up man and his brother Nick wasn't much better. Jordan's got those genes in him. And if he starts acting strange, don't be surprised. Charlie started off looking like a real catch, then he turned. I think that's what your father is afraid of for you. Just keep an eye out for anything odd. Like if he starts getting cold feet or lies to you or something. It's just a warning. And . . . and Vince had a bad heart. How would you like to be a widow after only a few years of marriage?"

Hurt and anger filled Heather, but all she could say was, "See my ring?" Suddenly, she was a little girl again. A little girl in her little girl's room with the flowered wallpaper and the color pink in abundance. A little girl who had painted a pretty picture and wanted her mother's approval.

"It's a beautiful ring, dear. Beautiful." Eleanor hugged Heather while squeezing her eyes tightly, trying to push away the pain and guilt she felt. No one gets away with anything, she thought. No one really gets away with anything.

EIGHT

"MY FATHER SAID he won't pay for the wedding and he won't attend."

"Sorry to hear that." Jordan adopted a stance of nonengagement as he drove back to Philly, his favorite music on the car stereo.

"They kept bringing up your father."

"What does my father have to do with anything?"

"They said bad things about him. They said they thought you would turn out just like him." Heather stopped short of saying they told her Jordan's father was a criminal and crazy.

Jordan silently counted to ten. Of course the Georges would have to give some excuse to Heather. So they picked invisible Charlie Matino. It was kind of creative, really. Damn the father-less boy for having an asshole for a sperm donor. Nice.

The rest of their trip was rather quiet, with little more of consequence discussed. Since the Christmas Eve Massacre, Jordan had taken on the countenance of a zombie. His mother and Mildred Stein had poked and prodded him to "do something" to end this relationship and thereby allow everyone to move on to the next chapter in their lives. But Jordan could not. Instead, he retreated into his turtle shell, procrastinating, stewing, ruminating, plotting, and doing what people do best when faced with catastrophe: nothing. He spent time with Heather but she, too, was off her game. She was still wearing his ring and even announced her engagement to her best friends—with a muted, doleful tone she hoped they could not read anything into.

He glanced over at her from time to time with a mixture of emotions. God, what she didn't know! But was it true? She was such a wonderful friend. And as his friend, this was exactly the sort of thing he'd have loved to talk out with her. But not this. Not now. In fact, probably not ever.

Jordan made mental to-do lists. By the time they'd reached his place, he wished he were alone so he could throw down his bags and go right to his computer to begin research. He could not completely alter his destiny on hearsay alone. He had to know everything. People lie. But aside from that were other major issues. If it was true, if Heather and he were cousins, could he thumb his nose at everyone and marry her anyway? Or would he have to break it off because it was illegal for cousins to marry because they'd have retarded kids? Was that part a fact or a rumor? Everyone seemed to know it, accept it as gospel, like it was something you learned in school. But he couldn't for the life of him remember it, even from medical school. Was it an urban legend? Who the hell has this data at their fingertips?

Heather was staying with him in Philadelphia through New Year's, almost an entire week. He had to work, but he would come home to her every night. Good as that had once sounded, it now carried an ominous dread, tinged with discomforting annoyance.

Heather commandeered some closet space and boldly moved some of his things around in order to clear a dresser drawer. It was, according to general relationship wisdom, a ballsy move, but she had the ring now. What might have been cute and endearing before was now irritating and nervy to him.

There was also Zeiss—his right hand, his guru, his best friend. How could he excuse himself and say, "Heather, I'm going upstairs to see Zeiss for a few hours. Alone. And I may reek of scotch when I return"? He had to consult with Zeiss. Zeiss was discreet, wise, and honest. He would also probably hang him out the seventh-floor window by his feet for getting engaged to someone after only a monthlong courtship.

The evening dragged on, and Jordan displayed all the social stimulation of a dead otter. It suddenly occurred to him that they would soon be disrobing for bed, ostensibly for sex. Having had sex—great sex—every night they'd spent together, she would certainly be expecting some on their first night alone as an engaged couple. During the entire Christmas visit to Mountain City, they had refrained from relations. Now he was supposed to have relations with his relation! Again! He began to feel ill. How could he participate in something so wrong? Wrong? Wrong. Wrong? And how many times had he already done so? Ugh, he needed Zeiss! He needed a shower. He needed a joint. He needed to go bungee jumping with too long a cord. He needed anything but to be expected to perform sexually.

Heather showered and slipped into a racy little Victoria's Secret number. Omagod, he thought. She smelled so good and looked so good; he was mesmerized. So of course he said, "I think I know where your mind's at. But I'm really beat from the drive and I have to go into the office extra early tomorrow. I'd like to just get to sleep early, okay?"

It was the first time Jordan had ever turned down sex with her, and Heather was stunned enough not to protest. Rolling onto his side, he pulled the covers over his head like a kid hiding from the dragon in the closet. Heather crawled in beside him, stroking his back and shoulders in a spoon position. That was okay, Jordan thought. You can't be sent to hell for letting your cousin massage your back.

He wasn't really tired. Truth was, his mind raced. He could not, though, show alertness or he'd be expected to perform. So there he lay, frozen as a corpse, staring straight ahead and away from her.

Jordan never had a female first cousin before, biblically or otherwise. Hell of an irony. Perhaps he had some on his father's side, but those people were strangers to him. He had no prior reference as to how he should or should not feel about having sex with a cousin. Theoretically, he knew he was supposed to be repulsed by the thought. Certain revulsions are printed upon one's genetic makeup from birth, like bestiality and necrophilia. Few people ever need to be pulled aside and taught that those things are bad. This, though, was different. He may have already *accidentally* had sex with his cousin.

At some point Jordan must have fallen asleep for real, for he awoke moderately refreshed and ready to face the world. By jumping quickly into the shower, he demonstrated he was in a hurry. Lord knows he did not want to have to fight off morning sex as well.

Given the time it takes for genetic testing and results, he knew it would be some time until he was clinically certain whether or not Heather *was* his cousin. That was priority number one. You're a scientist, he told himself. Think like a scientist. Believe nothing until it is scientifically proven. That was the noblest reason he had for not breaking off the engagement back in Mountain City. Less noble was that he loved her and didn't want to give her up. Unfortunately, he was clueless as to how he was going to get through the next week without making love to her.

Outside his building, the air Jordan pulled into his lungs felt like freedom, even if it smelled like wino urine. If he allowed himself to get deep inside his work, he could almost dream he hadn't a care in the world.

Most people start their day with a bran muffin and a morning paper. Jordan Matino started his with a vasectomy, the first surgery he'd be performing this particular morning. The vasectomy was followed by a testiclectomy, which led to a partial prostate removal, followed by a reverse vasectomy. Dr. Matino's day had come full circle. Being back on the job made him feel alive again. Gone was most of the self-pity he was beaten down by in Mountain City. Why did he have to go home to Heather and *the situation?* If he stayed at the hospital and slept on a gurney, he could be ready for action first thing the next morning.

He called Heather and explained that on his first workday after the holiday, he was backed up with reports and might be too late for dinner together. It was a lie. Somehow, he felt that having his fiancée standing behind him as he cruised the Internet for data on whether marriage between cousins was illegal did not paint a pretty picture.

Nick Matino. *Was* there a Nick Matino? Ah, now Jordan was really getting paranoid. The DNA results would take at least two to three weeks, and by then he'd be certifiable. He had to do something to fill the time. Maybe he'd also try to find this Uncle Nick character. What the hell?

Jordan paged Zeiss during a break in his day, and they hooked up for a brief between-patients consult. "Dr. Zeiss, I'm back. We need to talk."

"So talk, Dr. Matino."

"It'll take too long. Come by my office tonight after work."

Paul Zeiss was the same age as Jordan. He was a Franklin and Marshall undergrad, a native Main Line Philadelphian. A bit taller and thinner than Jordan, he had curly hair to Jordan's straight. They had nothing and everything in common. Zeiss was a non-practicing Jew, Jordan a skeptical Protestant. More potentially polarizing was Jordan's being raised dirt-poor, while Zeiss's family was rather wealthy. Jordan had no father or siblings. Zeiss had two parents who were still very much together, as well as two sisters and a brother.

Their similarities were far more important to them. Both were fun and funny and had a basic loyalty, goodness, and humanity that drew them to each other. Jordan knew he could call Zeiss in the middle of the night and say, "There's no time for questions. I'm in Vegas. I'm in jail. I need $10,000 cash and my passport. Immediately." Zeiss would be there within hours with everything he needed, as well as a change of underwear.

There was a chapel in the hospital. It hardly qualified to be called that, as it strove for the political correctness of not being associated with any particular faith—or with religious faith at all. Jordan had never entered it before. He had always been afraid that patients or visitors might see him there in his scrubs and think, "Oh boy, hope that's not *our* doctor, because he must have *really* messed up!"

Jordan needed a place to be, though. Since Christmas Eve, he felt he had not yet been alone, truly alone. Even lying in bed in his mother's house, he had tossed and turned with this absurd burden, unable to focus. He could not find his center, nor could he read into his feelings beyond dreaming up crazy strategies and hypotheses. This, then, was the perfect moment for a long sit on a park bench, but it was twenty degrees out, and the damp, wooden planks would chill the seat of his pants in seconds.

The chapel was empty, as it usually was as he passed it on his rounds. Stained-glass windows depicting no biblical scenes, just color, prismed in light from one side, while burgundy glass fixtures over incandescent bulbs gave the room a dim yet warm meditative ambiance.

Jordan sat. The pews were uncomfortable, and he was soon up and pacing. He kept looking toward the door, hoping no one else would come in. How did he *feel*? For some reason he wanted to make himself cry, but he couldn't, and the fact that he was trying and thinking about it took him back to his grandparents' funerals. He couldn't cry there either, although he had felt a rush of memories and wistful thoughts. Maybe he was incapable. He hoped this was not the case, for now he felt the need to purge his soul.

He kept pacing. Even without the religious accoutrements, he was reminded of the New Testament phrase, "Let this cup pass from me." This whole thing was too much. He couldn't deal with it. He shouldn't *have* to deal with it. *Somebody make it go away!*

He was startled from thought by a Sikh in a turban entering the chapel. Without thinking, Jordan said "Sorry," as if he was taking too long in the only bathroom stall.

"It is all right, doctor. I do not require privacy. You are welcome to stay."

Jordan's face must have betrayed befuddlement as he mumbled more variations on "Sorry" and "Excuse me" while making his way out of the small room.

"I hope nothing is troubling you, doctor."

Just as Jordan had feared, this was going to start a bad rumor about him. "Not what you think. Nothing medical."

The Sikh's face seemed incredibly placid and welcoming, unlike the faces of everyone else Jordan was used to seeing in the hospital. Not grief-stricken or anxious, nor lost in busy thought and in a hurry. "You help people all day long, doctor. May you let me return the favor and perhaps help you?"

"That would be nice." Before Jordan could thoughtfully weigh this offer, he impulsively blurted out, "I was wondering: If someone told you a terrible secret and it turned your world upside down, how should you feel?"

"This secret is about you?"

Jordan paused, looking skyward, "Mmm, yes."

"How did this person feel when they told you this secret?"

Jordan thought about this puzzling question. "Bad. I think they felt very bad. Why?"

The Sikh no longer smiled but looked at Jordan seriously, yet calmly. "Then this is a good thing. This person unburdened themself. You should make them feel good about that and show them forgiveness."

Forgiveness was a word that had not entered Jordan's mind since Christmas Eve. "But what if I know another person who is affected by this bad secret? Should I tell them?"

The Sikh shook his head slightly. "No, this is not your secret to reveal. You must encourage the keeper of the secret to unburden themself again. And then you must encourage this other person to also forgive."

Jordan felt like he was talking to some mystic or Buddha. The man even looked like a guru. "You've been very kind. I'm sorry to have taken up so much of your time."

His guru chuckled. "Please, I know how doctors feel about being asked for free medical advice. You look like the kind of nice young man who has given out his share of that."

"One last thing: What if I have doubts that this bad secret is true?"

The man in the turban took longer to consider this question than he had the others. "Truth. We are all on a journey for truth. But we also need forgiveness. These things are never bad. Find out your truth and be prepared to forgive."

"I'm listening," said Zeiss as he sat in Jordan's private office later that evening. Listening was one of Zeiss's best skills and a trait Jordan admired. Their profession had more than its share of windbags who loved to pontificate. Rarely did Zeiss blather or bore. Questions and challenges, yes. But at least that demonstrated interest in someone other than himself.

"Good news, bad news. Good news: Heather and I are engaged."

"That's not good news, you schmuck! What are you, crazy? I yelled at you enough when you started *dating* the hometown honey. Now you get *engaged* to her after what, a month? What the hell could be worse?"

"We're related."

Zeiss's eyes narrowed where words were not needed. He allowed Jordan to continue, figuring what was to follow would likely be one helluva tale.

"We might be first cousins."

Zeiss still wouldn't bite, the sign of a truly good listener. Any dummy knows that silence will bring out the rest—and best part—of a story. But this story so far had to be making Zeiss's cerebral cortex do the Macarena.

Jordan switched to ramming speed and delivered the entire sordid tale in the span of maybe a minute, not stopping for a breath. He'd been practicing this in his head all day long.

"Is that all?" Zeiss knew how to deliver the ideal line to make Jordan crack up at a perfectly inappropriate moment.

"What the hell am I supposed to do?"

"First off, you're going to have to put everything you just said into a print-out so I can follow it better. A syllabus perhaps?

"I don't want to belabor the point, but why did you rush into all this in the first place? I know you used to live next door to her, but we all grow up and change. She seems like a nice girl and she's bangin' as hell. But man, you're at your peak, dude. This must be God's way of kicking your ass."

"Is that the sum total of your professional opinion, doctor?"

"Jordan, buddy, you're supposed to break up with her but not tell her the truth? That might fly if she was some hotty you met in South Philly a month ago. But this one knows where you live, knows where your mother lives. Damn, she lives right next door to you on holidays. And you got *engaged* to her? Man, tell me you didn't buy a ring."

Zeiss wasn't the only one who could say a paragraph with nothing more than a look. "Ah, shit! You're nuts. You're absolutely nuts!"

"Paul, in a million years, how the hell could I have guessed she was my blood relative? Do you go up to every girl you meet and ask them for a blood sample?"

Zeiss was communicating with only his eyes again.

"You probably do, you paranoid germ freak."

Paul Zeiss, infectious disease specialist, chuckled at that one. In the ten years they'd known each other, a bitter word had never come between them, but if written transcripts were ever made available of most of their conversations, one would be led to believe they were mortal enemies. Blunt, brutal, profane, hilariously disrespectful honesty was what had brought them and held them together.

"J, let's talk about the breaking-it-off issue. I don't know how you're going to tell her a great lie and get away with it without mondo hard feelings. Women get crazy mad when guys break off engagements unless it's mutual. She'll pull a Glenn Close on you and boil your rabbit.

"I think you've only got a few viable options here. You could turn into a complete jerk in hopes that *she* breaks up with *you*. For you, that shouldn't be too hard. You could also be a jerk and create some sort of conflict where you have a big fight over something and *you* break up with *her* . . ."

"You seem to have an endless supply of scenarios where I'm a big jerk."

"I know what I'm working with. Continuing . . . you could just act really, really strange. The closer she gets to you, let her find out the more socially unacceptable quirks you have that normal people—like she and I—could never live with. Hey, have her see how crooked you cut your toenails and let them go flying all over the bathroom. That drove *me* out of your life."

"I take it you have very little of substance to offer me."

"Jordy, I still have trouble fathoming this. It sounds like science fiction. You can't expect me to provide truly helpful answers on the fly. Why couldn't you just get hoof-and-mouth disease? That I could help you with. There's no handbook on what to do when something this messed up happens."

"Paul, it goes without saying, this is a secret above all secrets. Me and you, period."

"I know. Oh, big question. I never heard you say you were definitely breaking it off with her."

Jordan didn't reply.

"It's illegal."

"You know that for a fact, Paul?"

"No."

"Neither does anyone else. Everyone just assumes it. I can't go by that."

"You sound like someone who has his mind made up about marrying his first cousin. Explain."

"First off, I'm not positive she's my cousin. Secondly, my mind isn't made up yet about anything. Let me ask you a question. If I did decide to marry Heather, would you give me your unconditional support?"

After his own thoughtful pause, Zeiss replied, "No. No, J, I wouldn't. I don't believe that's the role of good friends. I realize that flies in the face of many other people's philosophies, but that's how I define friendship. Being the person who's willing to tell you what you don't want to hear and sticking by it as long as possible. I'll still be your friend no matter what you decide, but I won't support and accept a decision that isn't upheld by good logic."

"I can live with that."

Jordan wanted to get right on to the DNA test, but for that he needed Heather, and she was still back at his place. Also, he had not yet figured out how to gain her participation. So once Zeiss left, Jordan instead decided to commune with his PC. For days, all he could think about was parking in front of this high-speed hookup and getting into as many libraries as possible. Medical school had taught him how to step back emotionally and sort through fragments of information in order to come up with a cohesive diagnosis. Now, he tried to research the legal issues but came up snake eyes, with no immediate hope for a definitive answer concerning state law. Pennsylvania had recently ceased to require blood tests for marriage licenses in response to fears that an applicant's HIV status might leak out. Those tests were done only to screen for disease anyway, not to investigate possible incestuous marriages. For the moment, that was good.

It also came as no surprise that few doctors were writing dissertations on the marriage of cousins. The only remotely relevant papers recently published appeared to be concerned with medical problems found in primitive and semi-primitive foreign cultures where intermarriage was only one of a number of factors, competing with lack of access to first-class medical care, nutrition, and exposure to numerous unchecked diseases. Jordan skimmed and found them fairly useless.

He then found reference to the anecdotal tales of American hillbillies. But they were more of the Ripley's *Believe It or Not* variety with, again, very little direct connection to the type of hard data he was looking for. The mere mention of the word "hillbilly" and things loosely referred to as "intermarriage" and "incestuous relations" caused Jordan to shudder. Coal crackers. Hillbillies. He'd spent his entire adult life trying to gain a modicum of respect in the world outside Mountain City. Now here he was, investigating this malady of the heart from which he suffered, linked most frequently to white trash who went barefoot and played the banjo.

With no great luck in either the legal or medical portion of his quest, Jordan felt it might be appropriate to begin another phase in his mission. It was time to find Nick Matino.

He thought about staying on the Internet, but there was an easier and more efficient method: Dominic Grasso. Dominic was a year older than Jordan and had attended Immaculate Heart

Academy, the Catholic companion to Mountain City Regional. Dominic was a badass. Being a badass has a very specific connotation in the region. Despite the athleticism required to beat up people all the time, badasses are rarely star jocks. They are, quite simply, the toughest, meanest S.O.B.'s in any given town.

Dominic had been Immaculate Heart's resident badass. Despite beating up on nearly every guy Jordan knew at school, Dominic had never laid a hand or even sneered a threat in his general direction. The two became friendly acquaintances, as friendly as a badass gets with a normal, straight-edge kind of guy like Jordan. On at least two occasions, Dominic beat the daylights out of people who meant Jordan harm for one reason or another. Jordan could lay no finger upon any good deed he had done this local thug to deserve such treatment.

One time, there was a Sunday afternoon pickup football game that Dominic was supposed to participate in, with Jordan and a slew of others. Despite his largess toward him, Dominic had never invited Jordan into his home. On that day, for one reason or another, Jordan rapped upon his door.

The biggest badass Jordan ever knew answered the door as sheepishly as a novitiate nun. "C'mon in. I'll only be a minute." Led into his living room, there were older people seated all over, a holidaylike visit of some sort on a random fall afternoon. "This is Jordan."

That was it. "This is Jordan." No last name, or anything else. Yet the older folks nudged each other and nodded hello. It was weird. Dominic the badass continued his incongruous imitation of a frightened English butler. As they exited, Jordan got up the nerve to ask, "What the hell was that all about?" Dominic finally spilled the beans: He and Jordan were cousins. Coal region cousins, anyway. It seemed that Jordan's father's mother's sister's son's sister-in-law was Dominic's mother. Even though that made them third, fourth, or fifth-time removed someone or another, they *were* related. Dominic had known this all along, while Jordan had not. That was the reason for his protection by the town bully.

Up until then, Jordan never knew any relatives on his father's side. Apparently, Dominic's living room had been full of them that day, which explained why he needed no last-name introduction.

"One question. Were any of them my father?"

"No."

"Okay."

That ended most of Jordan's curiosity. He tweaked his mother a bit for not telling him that Dominic was a relative. But frankly, his mother did not know that Dominic and he were acquainted. It's rarely considered a good move to inform your mother that the local badass is a pal.

Uncle Nick Matino was probably in the room that day, but Jordan couldn't have picked any of them out of a police lineup from that brief encounter. But now he needed him.

Dominic still lived in Mountain City. Most badasses remain in the town in which they reign unless they've been horribly beaten to incapacity or incarcerated.

"Dom?"

"Yeah?"

" 'Tino."

"Hey, what's up?"

"Need a favor."

"Anything."

"I need to know how to find Nick Matino, my father's brother. Can you help?"

"Yeah, probably. It'll take a few calls, but I'm sure I can pull it off. Easy. What's the problem?"

"No problem, really. Just need to get in touch for something. Looking primarily for an address, if it's not too much trouble." Jordan wasn't in the mood to make up some elaborate or even simplistic lie. He just wanted information and to hang up. Nothing personal against Dominic, but outside of asking who he'd beaten up lately, Jordan didn't feel they had much to chat about.

"Your name came up awhile ago, you know. Your grandmother died."

"Yeah. My grandfather too."

"No, I mean the other one. Our side of the family."

Jordan knew that his father's mother, his other grandmother, lived on the outskirts of Mountain City. His other grandfather had died when Jordan was quite young. Jordan was never encouraged to seek out the woman, just as he'd never been encouraged to look for his father. Nonetheless, he often wondered why his grandmother had never tried to create a relationship with him. Even as he got older, Jordan held steadfastly to a belief that it was her responsibility, not his. He was the child, even when he grew up. The onus was on the Matinos. The onus went unanswered.

"Yeah, I heard that, too." Jordan offered no elaboration. He felt nothing for this person.

"Your dad was there."

More silence on Jordan's end. As far as Jordan was concerned, Charlie Matino was another apparition who existed only in the same realm as Peter Rabbit or Spiderman.

Dominic continued, "I know things were messed up with your father, but a few people thought once you got older you would reach out, ya know? To him, your grandmother, somebody."

"Dom, I don't want to have an argument. Obviously there're two sides to every story. It's in the past."

"I got you. Hey, it's not my issue, you know? I'll make a few calls. Gimme your number."

"And Dom, do me a solid. Try not to tell the world I'm asking about him, okay? Trust me, I mean him no harm. You have my word on that. It's just a thing."

"Okay, dude. Stop by for a beer next time you're in town."

Jordan and Heather exchanged a few phone calls throughout the evening. Jordan's trick was to stay out so late that she would be asleep when he returned. It was night number two out of the eight they were supposed to spend together during her Christmas break. The way he figured it, unless she was a total doormat— which she wasn't—by about night number four she'd be throwing large objects at his head. With this in mind, why did he continue to court pain and suffering? A lack of better options. And hope springs eternal. Men are crazy like that. Every Halloween it was Linus, the cartoon omega male, who futilely sat out all night in the cold and dark awaiting the Great Pumpkin.

By the time Jordan turned the key in the door to his co-op, Heather was indeed sound asleep. Their phone conversations throughout the evening sounded sad and yearning. Hearing her voice, yet knowing this sword of Damocles dangled over the bed they shared, was painful. There she was, urging him to come home and be with her. There he was, dreaming this voice belonged to the same girl he knew a few days ago and not to someone who could perhaps cost him his medical license were he to marry her.

Looking at her slumbering, just as he'd hoped she would be, Jordan slipped under the covers and again played dead. Again, he wished he were.

NINE

❧

IT WAS RARELY a surprise when Opal Matino stopped over to
pay Eleanor George a visit, but since the engagement debacle
every encounter between them was like a Middle East summit. "I
just wanted you to know, I told Jordan the truth over Christmas."

"The truth?"

"Yes, the real truth."

"Which real truth?"

"Eleanor, the *real* real truth. About you and Nick."

"Oh my God! You didn't!"

"What else was I supposed to do? Tell Jordan I didn't like
Heather?"

"You're just saying that to get back at me. Is that why you told
him about Nick? Thanks. Thanks a lot."

"No, that's not why I told him. I told him because the truth
was the only thing he was going to believe. He's not stupid, you
know."

"Oh, and did you tell him other things, too? Did you tell him

about you and Charlie and the other stuff? Did you tell him
that?" Eleanor was nearly hyperventilating.

"Eleanor, I don't have to put up with this from you. I put up
with enough thirty years ago. This is baloney. My Jordan is heart-
broken."

"So's my Heather. What are we supposed to do about it?"

"I did my part. What more do you want from me?"

"Has Jordan told Heather?"

"I think we would have heard about it by now if he did, El. I
told him not to."

"Can he keep a secret?"

"I think he can keep a secret as well as anyone. That's not the
point. The point is why the hell should he? I wouldn't blame him
if he told Heather just to get back at Rick."

"He wouldn't!"

"What reason does he have to be loyal to him?"

"I thought we were friends."

Opal pursed her lips and shook her head. "*We* are. But that's
not the point, is it?" Despite being inside her toasty little home,
Eleanor wrapped her arms around herself, looking silently off
into the distance for something to save the situation. "What's
Heather going to do, Eleanor? Go live with Nick and Marianne?
Come on."

Eleanor had no answers, just needs. "I agreed with Rick to let
it be his way. It's been a good life, him and me. Maybe someday
he'll want to tell her. That's up to him. That's what I agreed to.
We're not going to live forever. Any one of us could die tomorrow.
Maybe then . . ."

"Maybe then what? We have to wait for Rick to die to let
Heather know who her father is? Rick's *been* a father to her—
that's all that counts. She can take it. She's a good girl."

"Yes, but Rick . . ."

"Honey, do you honestly think that Rick is going to walk out on you after all this time? Twenty-five, thirty years ago, maybe. Most men probably would have. But now? Where's he going to go?"

"I don't know. He's stubborn. He's got a lot of pride. He'd do it just to make a point. He won't go for it. He just won't."

"Well, I told Jordan not to tell Heather. But if he does, I don't know what I can do to stop him. He's an adult. He makes his own decisions now. I'm sorry. I'm really sorry. I could just see no other way."

As Opal got up to leave, Eleanor George remained glued to her sofa. Feeling more and more like a nudist in the midst of the fully clothed, she knew she was losing the battle as yet another remnant of her pride slipped away.

By the next morning, the seams were starting to fray on Heather's mood. Ever the moving target, Jordan insisted on breakfast out. What might have appeared romantic was, of course, just another way of avoiding sex.

Whatever calm familiarity Jordan had felt on his first day back at work was gone by now. All he thought about as he performed his professional duties was finishing up and getting back to his computer. He picked up a DNA kit. It would be dicey submitting the results to a lab using John and Jane Doe names, but he hoped that his track record up until then allowed him a little leeway when he did something a wee bit out of the norm.

Hitting the digital airwaves, it took him a few hours and then, boom! The Internet is like that. One minute a person is trying to research John Wilkes Booth and all they're finding are sites on toilets, former Lakers players, and places to make phone calls. A minute later, they find the John Wilkes Booth Fan Club, complete with T-shirts, refrigerator magnets, chat rooms, and essays on how Booth was set up as a dupe by the CIA.

Jordan's Valhalla was a site called cousinsinlove.com. He couldn't decide whether to laugh or cry. He was actually considering serious research at a site for guys who just love, love, *loooove* the girls they meet at family picnics.

The site was good though, really good. Well put together, easy to use, and chock-full of information, it contained most everything Jordan was searching for. It had a definite bias in favor of cousins marrying cousins, so he would have to cross-reference the medical data. But it seemed reliable and credible enough to be his initial base of exploration.

He never would have guessed that this cousins thing could be an entire underground movement. It brought with it a feeling of queasiness at involuntarily belonging to something that had a distinctly outlaw connotation. Sort of like waking up from a drunken stupor and finding yourself tattooed, an official member of the Hell's Angels, and surrounded by guys in leather calling you Spike.

Twenty-four states completely prohibit marriage between cousins. Pennsylvania was one of them.

Thud.

Nineteen states allow cousin marriage free of any conditions. Some of them weren't bad states either. Hawaii. He could dig practicing in Hawaii. But where do cousin-married Hawaiians go for vacation? North Dakota?

New York. Ah, good old New York. You can make it there with your cousin, but you can't make it everywhere. Although you *can* make it in Tennessee. Some things are just cliché.

Despite the legal setback, Jordan trudged on to the medical

data on cousins procreating. More of that good ol' male insanity. The primary argument the cousinsinlove advocates hung their hats upon was that birth defects are more prevalent in pregnant cigarette smokers, cocaine users, alcoholics, teens, and women over thirty-five than in first cousins. They made additional cases by mixing cigarette smoking with cocaine use and being a drunken, pregnant teenager. Jordan was familiar with the practice of expanding one's report to try to impress people with volume versus new and better substance.

All this looked rather convincingly in favor of marrying one's cousin. The Web site admitted that children conceived of first cousins have a slightly greater preponderance of recessive gene disorders, dominant gene disorders, X-linked disorders, and chromosomal defects than the baseline, meaning normal people, if there truly are such things.

This was all moot, though, if none of it applied. The tale was still a tall one. An uncle he never knew about and an incredibly long and well-kept secret. That was why the DNA test was imperative.

A breakthrough like this was cause for some personal decompression, though. Jordan inexplicably felt better than he had a right to, being that he would not be able to legally marry Heather in Pennsylvania if she were, in fact, his cousin. There is still a certain sense of relief when a problem gets sized down into a neater package. The negative variables were getting more specific and their numbers more finite. For the moment, that would do.

His private office line rang. Dominic came through with an address and phone number for Nick Matino. Once a badass befriends you, you've got a pal for life.

New Jersey. Thank God it wasn't far. Jordan's first thought was to just pop in on the guy. Then he remembered what Dominic had said about his father's side of the family wishing Jordan would make contact with them. Why not follow traditional protocol by phoning first? Either way, his Uncle Nick wouldn't know what was about to hit him.

"Nick Matino?"

"Yes."

"This is Jordan Matino. I think I'm your nephew."

"Oh my God! I don't believe it! What are you doing calling me?"

"Well, it's a long story, but I got your number from Dominic Grasso."

"We see Dominic from time to time. He and you were buddies, weren't you?"

That works, I guess, thought Jordan. "Yeah. Anyway, I know a lot of water has gone under the bridge, but I'm older now and I thought it might be about time to get to know more about the other half of my family. Dominic speaks well of you and I thought maybe I could come by sometime and have a cup of coffee. Nothing fancy."

"Sure. Anytime. I just retired and have a lot more time on my hands. We're in New Jersey, not too far from you."

"Yeah, Dominic gave me the address. I know this is short notice, but are you free tomorrow? I have rounds in the morning, but I'm free after lunch. I'm a doctor."

"Yes, we know. Tomorrow's good. We'd love to see you. Thanks for the call."

Jordan leaned back in his chair. Just the sound of "Uncle Nick's" voice made this nightmare even more real. His mother once said she knew that his father's family managed to find out just about everything about Jordan over the years. That always irked him. "We're in New Jersey, not too far from you." How the hell did they know where he was? The doctor thing as well. And why had Dominic known all along that the two of them were distantly related, while Jordan had been kept in the dark? If Heather *was* Nick's child, was this why his mother had never encouraged any relationship between Jordan and his father's family? For fear that someone would slip and he'd find out that the Heather of next door was, in fact, Heather, his first cousin? Perhaps Mountain City wasn't as boring as he'd thought. Jordan was glad he'd made his date with Nick for the very next day. Depending upon how fast the gossip express was running, Jordan worried that if Nick didn't know about him and Heather by now, he might find out if he waited too long.

Again, Jordan hoped he was returning home late enough to find Heather safely asleep. This time she was awake but groggy as a sedated surgical patient two seconds from total unconsciousness. He kissed her hello, and for the first time, she tried to express that she was angry with him, although she was barely audible because of her sleepy haze. Damn, this is where it begins, Jordan thought. Perhaps after ruminating on the cousinsinlove stuff he'd at least consider some slap and tickle with her. Maybe.

As she drifted back to sleep, Jordan left the bedroom and reached into his briefcase for the DNA kit. How the hell was he supposed to swab the inside of her cheek?

He had an idea. He forced himself to stay awake by watching television in the living room with the volume turned down to a whisper. After forty-five minutes, he approached the bedroom. Heather's breathing was rhythmic and steady. Jordan slipped his clothes off as quietly as possible and climbed under the covers, with Q-tip and sterile vessel in hand. If she awoke, he'd have one hell of a time explaining *these* bed toys.

She stirred the tiniest bit while he lay in the frozen state at which he was becoming quite adept. Another fifteen minutes passed until Jordan finally felt it was worth a go. Eyes adjusted to the dark, he turned toward her, again monitoring her breathing. Holding the Q-tip in his right hand, he placed the vessel on the bed stand. Just as he had hoped, she was lying on her back. Her mouth was slightly open. He would have preferred it expansive in full, bellowing snore, but that would have been undainty for such an attractive woman. With a surgeon's hands, he aimed his Q-tip as he would a probe or scalpel into a benumbed patient. Her mouth was open not much wider than the head of the cotton swab. His colleagues would certainly applaud his success if he could do this, considering the degree of difficulty with the darkness, a nonsedated victim, and his lack of sophisticated equipment.

The closer he got, the more he ceased to breathe for fear of waking her. Closer . . . closer. The cotton tip was almost past the gate of teeth now. A maneuver off to the side in order to catch cheek would prove to be more complicated than at first imagined.

Argh! Gag reflex. Heather started to spit out the foreign probe while still asleep. Jordan quickly retreated and shoved the Q-tip under the covers while desperately hoping he might get another try. Dream on. Even if he avoided the gag reflex, what about the inside-of-the-cheek tickle?

"Jordy?"

"What?"

"You awake?"

"Now I am. What's a'matter?"

Her eyes opened. "Were you sticking something in my mouth?"

He almost did a Ralph Kramden "homina-homina." "No, why?"

Now she was sitting up and ready for a lively conversation. "I felt something going into my mouth. Something long and hard. Were you . . . ?"

"What?"

"You weren't . . . ?"

"No!"

"Well, it's been a long time. I was starting to think you were getting kinky on me."

"No, I would never do something like that. No. Absolutely not. You must have been dreaming."

"This wasn't a dream. I can almost taste it."

"What does it taste like?"

"Hard to tell."

"Well, I did not stick my thing in your mouth while you were sleeping, if that's what you're thinking." What he didn't say was how insulted he felt that his penis was now being mistaken for a Q-tip.

"Jordy, why don't you make love to me anymore?"

"Heather, it's late. When I take a few days off, I get punished for it when I get back. I told you that before."

"If that were true, how come we did it constantly after Thanksgiving? Every day, every night, every minute you could squeeze away from your practice, we were making love. You'd drive to Reading and we'd be doing it the second you walked in the door. You never said anything then about being tired after long drives or long hours. You just wanted me."

"I'm still upset about your father."

"My father isn't in bed with us. Get over it."

He knew he deserved what she was dishing out and was silent, even though any idiot would have known that strategy was doomed to fail.

For her part, the now wide-awake Heather mounted him without warning, pulled off her nightgown, and rubbed her warm breasts all over his naked chest and face. She was arousing him and he had no more control over it than when he rode a subway car that bounced and rocked just right.

She aggressively seduced him. He was as participatory as a cadaver. When she finally slipped him inside of her, he even thought he heard himself whimper. After a while, he tried to be a good sport about it and grabbed her hips and thrust into her with enough authority to mimic passion. Shortly thereafter, she slid off of him.

After a few moments she said, "That fairly sucked."

He was at a loss. Yes, he really did suck that time and not in a good way. A mental tape loop had chanted "Sinner! Sinner!" throughout. "I'm sorry. I told you, I'm really tired. I'll make up for it," he said. Jordan rolled over, and eventually so did Heather. He was in big trouble now, no doubt about it. Damn it to hell.

Come daybreak, morning sex was no longer something Jordan needed to avoid. Women tend not to desire it from lousy lovers they're angry with. He tried to put on a civil face, for he was not at all cross with her, no matter what she'd said the night before. Any bile she doled out that morning he knew he had earned. His immediate mission was to keep her placid enough so he could use plan number two for the DNA test.

"Heather, there's a study I'm participating in at work. I need at least one more volunteer. Care to help me?"

"What do I have to do?"

"I need you to swab the inside of your cheek, that's all."

Someone with his intelligence should have known better than to try this tactic the very morning after she accused him of sticking something in her mouth while sleeping. Nonetheless, impatience caused him to throw caution to the wind in order to get the information he wanted as soon as possible.

"Sure."

It was going too well. He went to his briefcase to get another swab. "Just stick this in your mouth, swish it around the inside of your cheek, then give it to me and I'll seal it in this container."

Grabbing it, she said, "Did you stick this in my mouth last night?"

"No! Why are you still on that?"

"Jordan, it felt like a Q-tip. I couldn't put my finger on it until now. It was a Q-tip. You stuck a Q-tip in my mouth while I was sleeping."

"Heather, why would I do that? Why?" Put the onus of explaining the ludicrous onto the other person. That's the ticket.

"I don't know. You're acting so strange lately I'd believe anything."

"That offends me. I'm working. I'm dealing with stuff. Now you insult me. What the hell do I need with that?"

"We all have problems, Jordy. This self-pity crap is getting tired, you know? Last time I looked, we were both getting married, we were both going through hell with my parents, and we both had jobs. And don't compare our careers and tell me how you think yours is harder or more important because I'll walk right out. I don't need that."

Whew. If he could keep this up and get her to storm out, perhaps she'd call it off. His mission would be accomplished. But that wasn't *his* mission. That was *their* mission: the Good Street Puppeteers. No, *his* mission right now was the Q-tip. Damn it, he'd wrestle her to the floor and shove it in her mouth if he had to. The truth would set them free. Or not.

"I'm not going to play, Heather. I have to get to work. I'll try to get home early. We'll spend some time together, I promise."

"Thank God you didn't say 'quality time' or I'd punch you out, I swear."

"No, just time. The quality is up to you. Now I have to get going. I'm doing this, too. Watch, I'll show you." He proceeded to swab his mouth with a different Q-tip. Another bad move.

"Are you testing us? Is this a lie, this study thing? Are you conning me into doing some AIDS test or something? I don't like lies, Jordy. If that's what it is, you could've just told me. We're getting married. I wouldn't object to you doing things like that but don't lie to me."

He lied. He thought he had to. People getting married sometimes *did* get tested. Ugh! How could he have screwed this one so badly?

"I swear it's a study. I need a larger control group."

"But aren't control groups kept in the dark so they don't know they're *in* a control group?"

"Yeah, but that's so much bullshit. Do you really think if a group of people is given sugar pills and another is given the real drug that the sugar pill people could have unique drug reactions because they're so clay-brained that they can psychosomatically will them?" God, he was so desperate he was questioning the validity of the scientific method. What next, try to debunk gravity?

"Fine." She swabbed her mouth, less out of being convinced of Jordan's sincerity than of no longer giving a good goddamn.

Eureka! He had his two samples. However, the wait for the lab results meant a critical piece of the mystery would not be solved during this little vacation she was spending with him.

Male optimism allowed Jordan to imagine what it would be like to find out that the whole thing was facetious and they were not related. Sex? Yeah, they'd have some sex. Until then, he had to try to keep her from breaking up with him. That was getting more challenging by the minute. Tonight he'd get home earlier. After morning rounds, he'd blast out to Jersey and meet Nick. If he was efficient, he could be home in time for a late-ish dinner. Yeah, dinner . . . dinner out. Dinner and a movie. He'd never schemed so hard before to avoid nooky.

Jordan could have eaten lunch on the fly, but he hoped to run into Zeiss in the hospital cafeteria. The cafeteria setup was odd. Doctors and staff as well as the general public all used it. The doctors were cordoned off by a lowbrow version of the velvet ropes they use to keep riffraff out of the city's hottest nightclubs. Staff sat with the great unwashed, staring at the arrogant doctors in their VIP section. Everyone remained clearly in sight of one another, making it incredibly uncomfortable for the class-conscious Jordan. Guys from the region weren't used to getting beyond the velvet ropes anywhere.

Camaraderie and socializing were nothing like in a high school cafeteria, where everyone had a uniform lunch period. Doctors came and went pell-mell, beepers went off constantly, and ears were attuned to pages and codes over the loudspeaker. It was a lucky day when Jordan could get into a halfway decent conversation with a colleague lasting more than one or two minutes.

Cafeterias and restaurants are similar to singles bars when it comes to observing the wild Homo sapiens in their natural habitat. An impoverished-looking family sat close enough to the vaunted doctor's kingdom for Jordan to check them out. Fat, very fat, all of them. Jordan wasn't skinny, but like most yuppie doctors he had a prestigious gym membership he used as often as possible. He needed it to compensate for his coal cracker appetite: meat, cheese, fried foods, processed flour and sugar, and lots of it. But these people were huge, almost freakishly obese.

Beyond their appearance, only a few overheard words were needed to tell their story. They were a man and woman in their fifties and a younger woman about mid-twenties. They looked alike—obviously mom, dad, and daughter. With them were two little kids: a girl around two and a baby about six months old in one of those portable car seat thingamajiggies.

The kids were of mixed race. The adults were white. As they ambled toward their seats, the young woman hissed loudly enough for Jordan to hear, "I am *not* sitting near *her*!" pointing a stubby, crack-nailed finger in the direction of the woman who appeared to be her mother. The older woman looked down and away as if to pretend she'd not heard the slur. Barely squeezing into their chairs at the round dining table, the daughter did indeed arrange the seating so she did not sit next to her mother, nor did her small children. Throughout the meal, the daughter aggressively shot dirty looks toward the older woman, while the father acted blissfully ignorant and played with the kiddies. The mother pretended she was somewhere else.

The older woman was a racist. Had to be. Her daughter had married a black man and had children with him. The mother never approved. The daughter never gave an inch, firing away at her harshly, waiting until the older woman voiced some sort of sincere apology. It obviously had yet to happen.

The parallels to this imagined story sent chills down Jordan's spine. Narrowing his eyes tightly enough to make things a bit out of focus, he saw Heather at lunch with Rick, Eleanor, and the two children he and Heather would someday have together. Heather pointed her long, well-manicured finger at Rick, who did not acknowledge it so as not to give her anger the satisfaction. With limited enthusiasm, Eleanor played with her grandchildren, happy to be out of the line of fire. Jordan was busy bussing tables, having lost his medical license for knowingly breaking state laws concerning consanguinity.

Oh yes, Jordan had found out it had a name. "Consanguinity," the type of word one usually hears at the National Spelling Bee. The word sounded lazy and refreshing, like "sangria" or "sanguine." Consanguinity. The spell-check in his computer even had it in its memory. Fancy that. Must be there were many others who did it, others who found it titillating, or still others who dedicated their lives to tracking down and bringing to justice those who partook in it. Consanguinity. A word he had never before heard now haunted every moment of his existence.

Meanwhile, Heather was bored out of her skull. Making love, what the hell happened to that? What was this utter baloney about working late and still being upset about her father? They both were upset about that. They were both probably upset about the national deficit and nuclear threats from North Korea, too. That wasn't stopping other people from getting busy. It was also far too convenient that her mother said, "Watch out. He may get weird on you," right before Jordan did, in fact, start acting peculiar. What was up with that? Her mother had never demonstrated clairvoyance before.

And Jordan's MIA father? Why was that the only clue her mother gave for everyone's behavior? Since when were her parents so hung up on genetics? She was a woman, not a thoroughbred being prepared for the Kentucky Derby. And why would Jordan be so cool toward her if he, too, had just found out his fa-

ther was a crazy, lazy guy? Something was missing. There had to
be more. As she knew damn well that Jordan didn't have any
skeletons in his personal closet, then most likely it was something from the past. The far, far past.

Idle hands are the devil's playthings. Heather frequently used
Jordan's computer to check her e-mail and cruise the 'net when
TV got too boring. If Charlie Matino were the problem, she'd
track him down. She'd find out if he really was the loon her
mother had said. It couldn't be too hard. In the cyber world, no
one is anonymous.

Charles Matino was a common enough name to have a few
hits but not an unwieldy number. The problem was finding the
right Charlie Matino. Plus, not all of them had listed phone numbers. Jordan didn't even list *his* home number, but there were
multitudes of other ways to track a person down. Unless someone is truly trying to hide and not be found, they leave bread-
crumbs all over the place.

Checking out name after name, she managed to ascertain
ages by getting birth dates or graduation dates for each one. That
eliminated all but two names. Two names had complete addresses
and telephone numbers: One was in Arizona, the other in New
York.

New York. It had to be New York. From everything she'd
heard about Charlie Matino, he didn't strike Heather as the kind
of guy who'd travel extraordinarily far from where he was born.
Few coal crackers ever did, especially those from her parents'
generation. Her mom and dad always bragged about their high
school class reunions drawing such a high percentage of atten-
dees compared to the national average. The fact that most of them
never settled more than an hour away certainly didn't hurt.

Heather had two other compulsions she decided to stifle for

the time being. Her mother had mentioned that Charlie had one living brother named Nick. Maybe he would know Charlie's whereabouts. She nixed that idea, figuring it might cause too much suspicion. When a guy runs away from his wife and child and never looks back, it's most likely because he doesn't want to be found. The other idea was to let her fingers do the walking and call this particular Charlie Matino. Again, the same concern applied. She could scare off her prey.

It was road-trip time. Unlike a lot of her friends, Heather didn't mind driving alone on long excursions. When would she go? Whether he knew it or not, that would be up to Jordan. She had no intention of asking him to come along. She was the one on vacation, not him. Furthermore, she wasn't going to allow an argument with him to take up precious time she could be spending getting to the bottom of things. No, if Jordan came home late again tonight or continued his campaign of emotional solitude and sexual standoffishness, she was hitting the open road like Thelma without Louise. Not out of anger but to make a point that he had to turn this thing around. In her dreamworld, this week was to have been heaven. Although it wasn't quite hell, it certainly was purgatory. She was getting tired of spending days and nights waiting and waiting for nothing of consequence.

TEN

❧

THERE'S NEW JERSEY and then there's New Jersey. Nick Matino's town was neither of them. Of all the things that people dislike about New Jersey and all the things they love, none could be found where Nick lived. It was a place devoid of oil refineries, polluted swamps, horrible traffic, beaches, boardwalks, good Italian restaurants, skeeball, or Bruce Springsteen. It was distinctive by nothing whatsoever except for a series of very large, very tall roller coasters close enough to be seen from Nick's front step. It was winter, but in the summer the noise of people riding those things day and night had to be maddening.

Despite the circumstances, Jordan was not angry with Nick Matino, and he was too driven and focused to be scared of him. Harsh as it might be, Jordan viewed meeting Nick as nothing more than a means to an end. Jordan had had thirty-some years to flush himself of any feeling for the Matino clan.

He rang the doorbell, and a large man answered. Jordan's first impression was that he looked quite Italian. Raised by Zimmermans, Jordan, despite his lineage, never felt very Italian, so he searched further for any familial resemblance.

"Well, there's a lot more to you than Charlie."

With that, Jordan was invited in. He'd heard similar things his entire life. Apparently, his father was short, as was his mother. Thus it struck many as odd that Jordan turned out to be a six-footer. But his mother often spoke of his father's two taller brothers, and here was the only remaining one, standing even taller than Jordan.

The inside of the house was enough to make Jordan forget he was in Jersey, with knickknacks everywhere and mismatched patterns on the furniture, carpeting, and walls. Vintage coal-region decor.

Nick was happy to show off his pauper's mansion. Gregarious in a nonoffensive way, he seemed nice. Then Jordan met the missus.

Jordan had been warned about Marianne Matino. His mother, who loved everyone, loathed Marianne. She was attractive, if you had a good imagination, but definitely past her best days, with a personality that presented itself in a bad light before she even opened her mouth.

"Marianne, this is Charlie's boy, Jordan."

"Well, thought we'd never see you."

It was said in a less-than-friendly way. She smoked, and the house reeked of cigarettes. That habit was becoming so rare that it really caught Jordan's attention. For some people, smoking is like an additional limb, a method by which to fashion a distinctive personality via the unique way it requires them to move, gesture, and communicate.

Carrying an ashtray in one hand and a cigarette in the other, Marianne was unable to shake Jordan's hand, but motioned with her lit cudgel for him to make himself at home in a nearby easy chair. Almost immediately, Jordan hoped she would not be hanging around.

Neither Nick nor Jordan really knew how to get the conversation rolling, and Marianne acted more like a special guest star than a series regular. The banalities of "How's your mother?," "How often do you get back to Mountain City?," and "So, you're a doctor now," came and went pleasantly enough. Clearly, the gossip about Jordan and Heather being a couple had not reached them yet. The coast was clear. While Jordan had no intention of making this visit about anything but confirming his mother's story, he strayed into issues concerning his father, if for no other reason than he was there and it might be considered odd if he didn't.

The manner in which questions are answered is often more important than the answers themselves. As soon as Jordan brought up his father's name, Nick and Marianne fidgeted. They spoke well of Charlie, but seemingly more out of obligation than passion. Yes, he was okay. He'd had a lot of problems over the years. In the end, he wasn't really cut out for marriage and kids. He wished he'd see Jordan sometime, but was afraid Opal had put terrible thoughts in his head about him and that it would be an ugly scene.

Jordan didn't know if he should feel obliged to ask where his father lived or for his phone number. He chose not to, since his father's whereabouts certainly didn't seem relevant to the problems at hand. Although he did not regard himself as cold, this was the chilliest part of his personality. His father had been lost to him since long before he could remember. To him, the man never really existed.

Nick seemed all right, although he wasn't the handsomest

guy Jordan ever met, even in the old-guy division. Rick George looked like Brad Pitt in comparison. Of course, after thirty-odd years, a lot can change. Nick had a big ol' belly and a dozen chins, but he still had his hair, albeit with a ton of axel grease in it.

Marianne finally got up. She wasn't gracious enough to excuse herself; she just left the room. Jordan leaned toward Nick and whispered, "I don't mean to be rude, but there's a very important reason I came here today and I'd like it if we could speak privately for a bit. Can we take a walk, just you and me? It shouldn't take too long."

Nick tried to look relaxed and cool, but Jordan could tell he was nervous. "Uh, sure. Sure. Lemme get my coat. Marianne! I'm gonna show Jordan around the neighborhood. We'll be right back."

Standing out front, Nick pointed things out to Jordan, the roller coasters off in the distance being an obvious choice.

"Nick, I want to talk to you about the Georges." Nick just looked at him. "Is there a place we can go for a cup of coffee?" Nick had to know where Jordan was going with this topic. Had to.

They got into Jordan's car and went a short way out to the highway and then to a diner less than a mile away. Nick seemed in no hurry for this conversation. "I started dating Heather George a short time ago." With each word, Jordan looked intently at Nick's face, knowing that at any moment the guy could lie when asked to respond. What he saw after only one sentence was stress and anxiety, just as he expected. "That's Rick and Eleanor's girl, you know?" Nick nodded. "We've known each other all our lives, but it never got romantic until recently. On Christmas Eve, I proposed to her." Now Nick looked like he was having a heart attack. His face got flushed and sweaty. He fidgeted and looked out the diner window, unable to face Jordan. Yet he said not a word.

"Do you think at this point you and I have something we need to talk about, or should I keep going?" Jordan was sure that Nick did not, in fact, want him to keep going, but had lost the ability to speak in order to make him stop. This guy could have an actual heart episode, Jordan worried. "Nick, who is Heather George's father?"

Jordan had dropped his bomb and said not another word. His poker face was on, his bet laid on the table. Check or fold, Nick.

Finally he said, "Didn't they tell you?"

"Not really. Not soon enough. I wouldn't be here if it were all laid out nice and neat. Rick and Eleanor have been keeping it a secret and wanted it to stay that way."

"So the girl doesn't know?"

"No. She's completely in the dark."

"Oh my God. Oh dear God in Heaven."

"Let's you and me take this one step at a time. Pretend I'm stupid. Humor me. All I ask of you is honesty. I mean you no harm. I was in diapers at the time and it didn't involve my mother, at least as far as I know. But as you can see, the past is affecting my future and I've got to know. First question: Did you sleep with Eleanor George?"

"Jordan, it was a long time ago and Marianne and I don't want to get involved. She'll kill me."

"I'm not asking you to get involved. I think you can see my dilemma and I just need some straight answers. Did you, way back when, sleep with Eleanor George?"

"Yes."

"Do you believe the baby girl she had is yours?"

"Yes."

"Do you have any reason to believe there was any other guy she was also sleeping with at the time? Anyone else who could have been the father?"

"No. I mean, I couldn't be certain. You're asking about her, not about me. But no, there's never been any real doubt that I'm the father."

"What about Rick George? Why couldn't it have been his kid?" Jordan played dumb.

Nick didn't know whether to smirk or remain contrite. "Rick . . . Rick he . . . you know, guys sometimes they . . . you know . . ." Nick gestured uncomfortably toward his lap.

"Nick, I'm a urologist. I use words like 'penis' everyday, even in mixed company."

"Yeah, that's right; I forgot. Rick George's penis . . ." Nick still whispered the word as if embarrassed, ". . . was all fucked up," "'fucked'" being a word he somehow did *not* have a problem with.

"So this was common knowledge."

"Well, I don't think he went around town bragging about it. And Eleanor, she certainly wasn't happy about it, either. I don't know who knew and who didn't, but *I* didn't know until Eleanor and I got together privately, and we were all, you know, pretty close as neighbors and such.

"It was a mistake. We were all young, way too young. You kids got it right these days, waiting until you're more grown up before you get married. Half the time we were either doing it because we were afraid of getting drafted and killed in some foreign country before we ever got laid, or worried that getting married was the only way we *could* get laid.

"Marianne and me, we didn't really know each other when we got married. Same with your dad and mom. The Georges too. We didn't know each other, we didn't know ourselves. We hadn't lived yet.

"Needless to say, all of us did some things we regretted. We never meant to hurt nobody, but it just happened that way. Eleanor and me, we fooled around and she got pregnant. She swore on the Bible it was mine, not Rick's, and I believed her. Why would she make up such a crazy lie? She wasn't in love with me. She didn't want to break up either of our marriages.

"The most amazing thing is that only your dad and mom got divorced in the end. And that had nothing to do with anyone fooling around . . ." His voice tailed off for a second, as if the last sentence was not quite true. It was more labored than the easy rhythm he had gotten into. But Jordan thought not to pursue it. Other things would just muddy the water.

Jordan had brought a swab for another DNA sample, but it seemed futile now. This was the end of the trail. The shooter was caught and there was no need to go further. Impregnation, unlike murder, rarely has accomplices.

They sipped their coffees in silence. Nick made another request that Jordan not bring up the subject with Marianne, and Jordan agreed. Hell, from what he'd heard about her, why on earth would he want to get on her bad side? What did Nick see in her, anyway? She didn't look too damn bad. But when Nick had the chance to toss in his cards for a new hand, why didn't he do it? Marriage, though, had been that way for a long time in the region. Now the divorce rate was as high as in the rest of the country. Like everything else, it must have been because the region was its typical ten years behind the rest of the planet.

Driving home, any optimism Jordan had felt that morning faded into depression increasing with each mile. Who needed the frig-

gin' DNA at this point? He could hardly wait to tear up the envelope when it arrived. The lab results would only drive the final
nail into the coffin, and that he didn't need. He and Heather were
cousins. They had to be. This many people couldn't be lying. Not
when the lies served to turn their own lives and reputations upside down. Jordan ranked the chances of everyone getting it
wrong as somewhere between slim and none. He had come looking for a confession and he'd gotten one. Dammit . . . dammit to
hell! Now he was numb, scared, and morose. Jordan Matino was
on death row, and he was thinking there might not be a way out.
Now, he had to face Heather.

Bambi walked innocently toward the hunter who had a bazooka
with his name on it. "Honey, I'm home." It was still a reasonable
hour. Jordan had even brought flowers. He had made reservations
at one of the city's finest restaurants, and he checked the movie
schedule for the time and location of a romantic comedy Heather
was sure to enjoy. He was a heck of a guy, he thought.

Heather hated flowers. She had once had a boyfriend who was
a constant screwup. Every time he crashed and burned, which
was frequently, he either showed up at her door with flowers or
had them sent to her at work. To this day, every time a man gave
her flowers she was tempted to say, "What did you do wrong
now?" In this case her intuition would have been appropriate. After giving her the bouquet, Jordan laid out his plans for the
evening. Mustering up as much fake happiness as possible, he
sounded enthusiastic and proud of himself, as well as contrite for
his abandonment and chastity.

"Is that really what you want to do tonight?"

"What do you mean? Yes, I want to show you a good time, a

night on the town. Yes, this is want I want. Why, don't you like it? What do *you* want to do?"

"Jordy, I want to stay here all night long, just the two of us, like we used to. That's what I want."

"But I went to all this trouble. If that's what you wanted, why didn't you leave a message for me at work and tell me so I didn't make reservations and stuff?"

"Why did you assume that's what I wanted to do without asking me first?"

"Heather, you're in this place all day long. I would've thought you'd want to get out."

"I'm in it *alone* all day long. Now you're here. I don't need a big meal and a movie. I want you. That's what's been missing from my day. You."

It was not a vicious argument. Heather had plotted her position. This was a test, and he was failing.

His grade continuing to plummet, Jordan said, "I can appreciate that, but this is a wonderful city and there's so much to do here. I just thought I'd share it with you."

Perhaps because he was older, or perhaps because Heather had for so many years had a crush on him, Jordan may have had the upper hand in their relationship. Now, for Heather, this liaison was reaching an even keel for the first time. She still loved him, loved him more than she could probably love any man. She knew he loved her, too, or at least she hoped he still did. But enough was enough.

"Jordy, I'll give you one last chance. What happened back home? What went on after my father did his thing? Tell me the truth."

And of course he could not. Oh, it crossed his mind to do it then, more than any other time since he had found out—and especially with what he'd found out only that day. But like a card player with only one ace, he knew once it was played he could not take it back. He was still struggling with the onus of being asked to continue to keep the Big Secret from her. Which brought him back to . . . tell her what?

"There's nothing I haven't told you. I've been working . . ." Jordan's head was pounding. They were cousins. He was supposed to break up with her now. But then he'd be the bad guy. He *wasn't* the bad guy. He wasn't *a* bad guy. *Let this cup pass from me.*

"I can't stand to hear about your work or my father one more time. I gave you your chance and you blew it. I'm not calling you a liar. I just feel that if this is how it's going to be, I'm doing you a favor if I give you some space for a while. You obviously have some issues to work out, and you're not going to get there with me hanging around. This week should have been absolutely wonderful, but it's not. I'm going home."

"Heather, don't go. I don't want you to go. I'll make it up to you."

"Jordan, what I want from you I don't want given to me out of obligation. Let me ask you one thing, and please, please don't lie about this: Do you still love me and do you still want to marry me? If you're not sure, I can accept that. Say it, goddammit, but I can't accept a lie of any sort."

"Heather, I swear, I swear on the lives of my unborn children, I love you and I do want to marry you."

"Good. Now don't say anything else or you might start lying again. I'm going out the door and it's a good thing, really. You may not understand it now, but you'll be grateful that I did this. Please don't stop me."

As she moved toward the door with suitcase in hand, Jordan

tried one last plea. "Before you go, you have to answer for me the same question: Do you love me and do you still want to marry *me*?"

"Yes I do, Jordy. But we have to get past this. Don't call me for a few days. I mean that. I don't think we should talk. I want three or four days without you and you without me. We'll see what happens after that."

The cinematic thing would have been to pull her into his arms as she moved past him and kiss her like there was no tomorrow. In life, there are things you envision doing, and then there are things you *feel* like doing. Part of him was relieved that he was getting his home back and the freedom to think without Heather. He grabbed her and kissed her, but it was not a "leave me and I'll die" kiss. It was more in the "Miss you. Don't take any wooden nickles" vernacular.

For the next hour or so, Jordan sat alone in his most comfortable living room chair, unmotivated to eat or to move. It was only then that he realized that Heather's suitcases had already been packed.

Helplessness. Depression. Chuck Edwards, his best pal from Ursinus College, once told him that when he had to put his cat to sleep he returned to his car, sat there for a moment, and then howled. Howled like a wolf in utter primal agony, pain, and heartbreak. So, too, did Jordan right then and there. Like Chuck, he hadn't seen it coming. This was not crying. This was some Klingon death ritual. Only the feeling of a vital organ being ripped from one's body could cause such a sound. Heather's leaving raised the stakes and played brinkmanship with his heart. Clarity began to form. If she were standing before him right now, cousin or no cousin, he would carry her into his bedroom and there they would stay until hell froze over. She had pushed his buttons and now she was gone.

ELEVEN

NUMEROUS OLD FRIENDS were no longer speaking to each other with love and kindness. Rick George knocked and then entered the residence of Opal Matino. Opal strode down her second-floor stairs to an angry face.

"What's going on?" he demanded.

"What's going on with what?" It was a dumb rejoinder, but Opal was stalling for time and mentally arranging her notes.

"Don't play dumb, Opal, you know exactly what. Your son."

"Rick, they've only been gone a couple days. What were you expecting?"

Rick was in a finger-wagging-in-the-face mood. "You should have headed this off right from the start. You know that. You've got the son. It's his fault."

"What do you mean, 'It's his fault'? Fault for doing what? Asking her out? How do you know that wasn't her doing? You think girls are never the forward ones?" This only served to raise Rick's dander to the next level.

"What's that supposed to mean? Is that a dig of some kind? Do you think you're so much better than my wife and my daughter? What are you now, the born-again virgin?"

Rick started to menace Opal physically, like a bear stalking a chipmunk. Turning her back to him, she walked into the kitchen, hoping that her body language was seconding what her mouth now exclaimed. "Go away!"

Rick was enraged. "What, you don't like it when people are talking about you? Well, at least I do it to your face, not behind your back like you do! Don't forget to tell your son about this, too! But make sure you add in all your own transgressions over the years, Miss Perfect!"

Opal was scared of Rick George for the first time in her life. What was he going to do? Hit her? Rape her? "Get out of here! Get out of here now! I'll call the cops, you bastard!" she screamed at the top of her lungs. She was a woman alone. No matter how much her mind reasoned that her friend and neighbor couldn't possibly mean her harm, if something looks like danger, sounds like danger, smells like danger . . .

She put the kitchen table between them. Rick, with almost psychotic zeal, began to circle around her while she fled his advances. "What are you afraid of, Opal? Someone chasing you around a table for the first time in years? Is that why you could never keep a man? Did they all have to run after you like this?"

Their screaming drowned out the sound of Jack Stein bursting through the front door and moving through the living room as quickly as he could, bum leg and all. Rick never saw what hit him. Jack grabbed his shoulder from behind and spun him around just enough to land a blow squarely upon Rick's jaw.

Stein then backed off so he would not get nailed with a retaliatory shot. In his prime and when sober, blue-collar Stein might

have given Rick a helluva match. But Rick was significantly bigger and ten years younger. The age difference meant more today.
Stein had the bad leg, and his knuckles were so gnarled with
arthritis that he held his right hand and winced with pain after
delivering the blow.

"I've been waiting years to do that," Stein grimaced.

Opal stayed in a fight-or-flight mode, ready to save herself in
any way necessary. Rubbing his jaw, Rick came back to earth like
a hysterical person who'd just been slapped across the face, which
was about as damaging as Stein's blow had been. Eleanor and Mildred ran in, too late to catch the big finish.

"What's going on?" yelled Mildred, looking at Stein with the
assumption that if something was wrong, it had to be his fault.

Opal was not covering for anyone today. Staring at Eleanor,
she stated emphatically, "Your husband came in here and tried to
attack me." Saying something out loud has the effect of removing
all chance it was a dream or a mere misunderstanding. Opal began to break down. Mildred pushed past Rick and cradled Opal.

"What?" said Eleanor. It was, indeed, an unexpected accusa-
tion of her husband. Opal was too upset to give details. Rick was
still rubbing his jaw.

"Is this about the kids? Is it, Rick?" shouted Mildred. "You
keep away from her. She's done all she can do. If Heather finds
out, tough. You're nearly sixty. Grow up and deal with it. And
you . . ." Mildred said, turning her glare toward Eleanor, ". . . if
anybody oughta quit hiding in the closet and take responsibility
for their actions, it's you, Eleanor. What happened, happened.
You've more than made up for it. You oughta be the one to tell
Heather the truth."

Eleanor, who had gathered her strength, shot back, "Listen,
Mildred, it's not up to you. Live your own life. If you want to talk

about forgiveness and making up for things, you still haven't forgiven Jack for his old drinking binges and you know you never
will."

There's a point in arguments when the combatants have taken
their best shots and are left to choose among silence, apology, or
ridiculousness. Today, silence won. Rick, who had not said a word
since taking the punch from Jack, was the first to turn and walk
out, followed immediately by his wife. After an awkward bit of silence, Stein mumbled, "I'll be next door," and slowly made his
exit, still massaging his right hand and leaving Opal cradled in
Mildred's embrace. Mildred was big sister, mother, and friend to
Opal, and right now she needed all three. She whimpered and
then sobbed, as if purging all the unhappiness and fear within
her. Mildred patiently waited. Finally she asked, "Did he touch
you? Did he hit you?"

"No, no. I didn't know what he was going to do. He was crazy,
Mil. He was crazy. He said such terrible things. He hates me. I
don't know why. I never did anything bad to him or Eleanor.
Never." And Opal sobbed anew.

"Honey, he hates himself. He hates his wife, too. He says I
never forgave Jack. Bullshit. Maybe in some ways I didn't. But
what Rick did right here, he's showing all of us that he never forgave Eleanor. Every time he gave Jordy a hard time when he was
a kid, he was showing he never forgave Eleanor. And all this
anger about them getting engaged, that's him again showing how
he never forgave Eleanor. He's just taking it out on everyone else."

"Jordy's a good boy. I should have told him years ago. I just
didn't want him to think any less of Eleanor. He always liked
Eleanor much more than Rick. He . . . he shouldn't have to do all
this now. He's never found someone he wanted to marry before,
and now when he does, we drop this on him." The tears poured.

"I know, but he's strong, like you. And he'll always love you; you know that. He'll always be there for you. If Rick ever comes at you again, I'll be here with my wet dishrag. Plus, I always have Jack's hunting rifles."

Opal finally chuckled. Mildred was famous for her Wet Dishrag of Death. When her oldest son, Jerry, was on the front lines in Vietnam, he wrote home, saying, "There's gunfire everywhere, but I still fear Mom and her dishrag more than I do the VC." Back in the days when corporal punishment of children was less frowned upon, Mildred chased those boys of hers throughout her house and neighborhood in order to get them to brush their teeth, make their beds, or whatever, swinging the dishrag over her head like a samurai sword. It was quite unlike Jack getting drunk and slamming his fists on them. This was a feisty mother showing her love in what might now be considered an incorrect way. The Stein boys knew she did it because she cared. Mildred never hurt them. She was just making a point.

The two old friends held each other, neither of them knowing what was to come next, neither of them sure they wanted to be around to find out.

Jordan continued his howling, even if it was now on the inside, where no one else could hear. Taking an over-the-counter sleep aid was of no use. He tossed and turned all night long. The next day at work, he would not have wanted to be one of his patients.

Music in the operating room was pretty commonplace. It served to relax everyone. The surgeon, being highest in the pecking order, got to choose the tunes. Jordan, despite being an avid music lover, tended to go more for ambiance over specific songs or artists. He usually selected classical, new age, or light jazz when he was operating, even though he listened little to them at home or in the car. Today, he told the head O.R. nurse to pick whatever *she* wanted. Excited, she turned on a soft rock/country crossover station. Jordan couldn't have cared less if she'd put on a Megadeath CD.

Banal song after banal song seeped into his consciousness for no good reason until one hit Jordan hard. Maybe it was the lyric; maybe it was the arrangement. It was countryish but piano-driven, without an overabundance of pedal steel guitars.

This country ballad was knocking on Jordan's brain like a Jehovah's Witness with a quota to make. He couldn't quite catch the words, but there was something about this song that made him want to stop, really stop, and put his head right next to the speaker. That certainly would have caused the nurse to call in another urologist to take over. "*. . . Like a song . . .*" the lyrics went—or something like that.

The song ended, and he got back to work. Death metal might have been a better choice this morning. Ballad-heavy radio stations play a heck of a lot of songs with heartbreaking lyrics, songs that could get a desolate surgeon off his game.

After work, Jordan did not want to go straight home to his empty apartment. First stop was an upscale lounge full of other after-work professionals. That scene held his interest for barely two drinks. He then slipped out and tried to find the nearest music store. With his heart in pieces and his mind devoid of any solutions, he had to find that song with the pretty tinkling piano.

It's often difficult to find a music shop staffed by people conversant with more than just music recorded earlier that afternoon. Jordan somehow felt that the song he was searching for had not been recently featured on MTV.

As expected, the first shop's pimply-faced clerk was no help at all. Jordan did not have a complete title or an artist's name. Trying to hum or sing this song he'd heard only once while working on some guy's prostate to a kid with green hair made him feel like an idiot.

On to the next shop and then another. Rejection only made him more determined, a sure sign of mental derangement. The song was not important, not important at all. The song had made him *feel*, and as illogical as that was right now, Jordan needed to feel: to feel bad, to feel sad, to feel enough of a sense of loss to feel completely and totally alive.

The fourth shop employed an older guy. He had a sort of urban cowboy air about him, a trait that Jordan generally loathed. But when searching for bear, bring along a bear hunter, not a stockbroker.

Two hours later, Paul Zeiss entered Jordan's living room to find him sprawled on the floor in front of his stereo, Ronnie Milsap CDs and liner inserts spewed everywhere.

"Whatcha up to?"

"Listen to this." Jordan clicked to the cut he had heard in the O.R. earlier that day. "It's called, 'It Was Almost Like a Song.' It's beautiful." The tune enveloped the room.

After discreetly listening for a while and looking over Jordan's shoulder at the CD covers, Zeiss said, "Ronnie Milsap, huh?"

"Yeah. Heard of him?"

"No. How long have you been into him?"

"This morning."

"I understand." Zeiss sat down on the floor with his best friend and quietly listened to his confession.

"Still not giving me unconditional support?"

"No," said Zeiss, "I'm nothing if not consistent. Preliminary and highly questionable evidence leads you to believe that having babies with your first cousin is not medically irresponsible."

"Paul, the percentage chance of any two people producing a child with birth defects is 3 to 4 percent. With first cousins it only rises to 4 to 7 percent. The difference isn't big enough to merit a prohibition."

"Oh, so an increase of 50 to 100 percent is no big deal?"

"Not when you consider that Jews marrying Jews carries a higher chance of Tay-Sachs. That Africans marrying Africans carries a higher incidence of sickle-cell. People with Huntington's disease have a 50 percent chance of passing it on. Ask Arlo Guthrie whether he'd rather be alive or never born. The whole argument is not based upon good science. Guys like you and I know that someday it may be prudent for *everyone* to receive genetic counseling for one thing or another—cancer, heart disease, mental health disorders, substance abuse. But everyone else is allowed to marry and procreate, everybody but cousins in half the United States. Not even the whole country, just half the states! Do you realize the case someone would have if they got this to a federal court? It's no different than when some states outlawed interracial marriage."

"Jordy, you can run for Congress some other day. You're missing the most important point: The young lady still doesn't know about any of this and is thus not allowed to make an informed decision of her own. How am I supposed to unconditionally support that?"

Zeiss, of course, was right, as he most often was. Jordan had a hard time recalling an instance where Zeiss made an error in judgment. This is quite admirable in a doctor, although expected from medicine's finest minds. In life and love, however, it's a rarity. Paul had flings with girls he should have had only flings with. He avoided situations with women he should have run from. He got involved with great young ladies who were intelligent, attractive, and had the potential to be an asset to his quality of life and his career.

"Paul, how is it that you always manage to have such a tight, responsible rein on your heart?" Jordan and Zeiss had engaged in many heavy conversations over the years, but it's still hard for guys to use words like "heart" and "love" when sober.

"If, unlike my mother, you haven't noticed, I'm terminally single. Does that mean I've got all the answers?"

Jordan's only response was to subject his best friend to "Any Day Now," "He Got You," "Since I Don't Have You," and a number of other country croonings apropos to his dispirited mood. Good friends listen to eccentric music with you and try to hear the feelings within that mean so much when you're in an emotional quandary. Jordan even thought he saw Zeiss's head bobbing to the beat. Wait 'til he pulled out the Patsy Cline.

TWELVE

I F JORDAN HAD gotten into his car the night before to find Heather in Reading, he would have been sitting alone at her place for an awfully long time. Map in hand, she had instead headed north from Philly, much farther north than Reading. Picking up Interstate 81, she blew past the exit for Mountain City, heading ever northward.

Binghamton, New York. She'd never been there, nor did she know a thing about the place. The address was a little outside of town. Following the directions she had pulled up off MapQuest, she knew she was only blocks away from potentially facing down an enigma. Crazy ideas always lead to a point where the protagonist questions why she embarked on the insanity in the first place. Heather was now in godforsaken suburban Binghamton looking for the long-lost father of her fiancé. This had all made perfect sense in Philadelphia. Her goal was to see if Charlie would talk with her, if she could find out his side of the story. Was there something else that happened around the time of his leaving, something that explained Heather's father not wanting her to marry Jordan? This puzzle was missing a piece.

The next turnoff was the entrance to a trailer park. How sweet. Finally, she found the proper address. It was nighttime. She had left Philly around five, and now it was quite late. Civilized people were already asleep. She did not want to go to Charlie's home during the day, though, as he would most likely be out working. That is, unless he had maintained the poor work habits of the tale she'd been told. So, at nearly eleven o'clock at night, Heather approached the door of a strange man's trailer home. She felt like calling somebody to tell them of her whereabouts. She was always so bold and gutsy that it seemed inevitable she'd one day put herself in harm's way.

There were lights on inside. Cautiously, she mounted the wooden steps leading to the door. She decided to knock, then take a step back to make it harder for someone to pull her inside. Was this all a dumb, dumb, dumb mistake?

As a shadowy figure approached the door, Heather thought she might faint from fear and anticipation. The person opening the door looked completely unfamiliar to her. Not that she'd ever seen Charlie Matino, except for age-old photos, but this guy looked nothing like what she'd expected. First off, James Dean he was not. He was tall, lanky, and gaunt, with hollow cheeks, thinning salt-and-pepper hair, and an ugly schnoz. Some things just weren't checking out. Charlie Matino, Jordan's Charlie Matino, was short, very short. This guy was almost as tall as Jordan, who was six foot.

"Yes?"

The man had a gentle enough voice. Charlie was supposed to have been a gentleman. "Um, I was looking for Charles Matino."

"Just a moment, please." He turned away for a second and

then glanced back at her. "Who shall I say is here?" This guy wasn't Charlie, but Charlie was in the house. Charlie Matino was in the house!

"Tell him it's Heather George. From Mountain City."

The tall, lanky man took several steps back. Heather's adrenaline shot up. The real guy could be here; the one no one had seen in decades.

The tall man returned and asked, almost apologetically, "May I ask what this is about?"

It was the real Charlie! It had to be. Anyone else would have said he didn't know anyone named Heather from Mountain City. And it had to be her Charlie because the man inside was scared of what she might want with him. It was only natural, especially after she had come unannounced at eleven o'clock at night.

"Tell him it's okay. I'd love to meet him. I just want to talk a bit. I'm all alone and I don't mean him any harm." She regretted saying that as soon as it left her mouth. Tell two male strangers in a trailer park that the young attractive woman at their door in the middle of the night is alone and doesn't mean *them* any harm. Good one, Heather.

The tall guy walked away again. Heather listened to their mumbling, hoping to decipher it without stepping too close and getting abducted. Finally another man came to the door. This was James Dean. He was short and had that same hair she saw in all the photos. It was grayer now, but the style was the same—a pompadour so out of fashion as to be downright hip and retro by today's standards.

"Can I help you?" He sounded timid. Heather was struck by the genteelness of the two older fellows living in this trailer. Two fellows living in a trailer. What was missing from this picture? Unless they were old Army buddies in separate bedrooms cruis-

ing for chicks at the local Binghamton bowling alley, these guys
were more than just friends.

"Yes, I'm Heather George from Mountain City. Good Street.
My parents are Rick and Eleanor. Is Jordan your son?"

He looked meek and embarrassed, which told her she certainly had the right guy. A denial at this point would have been
absurd. "Do you want to come in out of the cold? It's okay; we
won't hurt you. Come in."

In all her years, she had never been inside a trailer home. The
interior was like a decent-sized boat. Everything was constructed
for maximum use of minimum space. She was led to the front
seating area, which quadrupled as a kitchen, dining room, family
room, and living room. The other fellow got up to leave.

"This is Gil. Gil, this is Heather. The last time I saw her, she
was still inside her mother's tummy."

Finally, any possibility that she might have found the wrong
man disappeared. She began to relax a little.

"Pleased to meet you, Heather. I'll leave you two alone."

"No, that's all right, Gil. You can stay," said Charlie.

Heather figured that was Charlie's way of having a support
system in place. Obviously he was wary of her, having sent this
Gil guy to ask her why she was there. Gil had his back.

"So, what brings you up here to Binghamton?"

"Well, I'm engaged to your son, Jordan."

Boom. His face dropped, the same way her mother's had.
Something here stunk. "What's the matter, Mr. Matino?"

Charlie looked uncomfortable as hell as he scrunched around
in his seat like her students when they didn't know the answers.
"Nothing. I guess I just feel bad when I think about Jordan and
back home. How is he? I hear he's a doctor now."

How the hell does he know about Jordan and his career?

Some coal region underground where messengers deliver information from the front? "He's fine. But I think he wonders about you. If you don't mind me asking, why didn't you keep in touch with him? I can understand divorce; it seems everyone is getting divorced these days. But I know he would have liked to have heard from you."

Again, more squirming. "It was not a pretty divorce. I guess few of them are, but I know Opal wouldn't want me in his life."

As well as she knew Jordan's mother, Heather doubted this. Maybe Opal would not have wanted him there every weekend, but poking his head in once a year or so would have at least made the kid feel more loved.

"Ever since Jordan and I got engaged, everyone has been acting strangely, especially my father. He's stomping around saying he won't even come to the wedding. I can't seem to get anything that resembles a straight answer from anyone. Now even Jordan is acting weird. I know you don't really know your son, but he's wonderful. Fantastic. That's why I love him so much. I was wondering if you might be able to shed any light on it."

Charlie made her wait a long time until he opened his mouth to speak. The man was even more muted than Jack Stein. "I . . . I really can't say for sure. As you said, I really don't know Jordan. I wish I did. As far as your father is concerned . . ." Charlie got this faraway look in his eyes. ". . . Rick and I were best friends way back when. We had some good times together. Fun times. Once, on a New Year's Eve, we all went out to a hotel that had one of those dinner, dancing, and breakfast packages. I guess I had a little too much to drink. So did your father and my brother. He was there with his wife, too. Anyway, I started acting silly, sillier than the rest, and your mother got mad at me. Later, when everyone went up to their rooms, I snuck back down to the ballroom and

stole a bunch of flower centerpieces . . ." His eyes came alive as
he retold his tale. ". . . I brought them back to your parents' room,
knocked on the door, and then ran to my room, leaving them outside their door. The next day, your mother knew it was me who
did it. I guess I was known for stunts like that. Anyway, she wasn't
as mad at me the next morning."

"That's a great story. I never heard that one. Is that why you
never go back?"

"What do you mean?" Charlie's face was tentative and frightened again.

"Are you afraid people are still mad at you there?"

He fidgeted and looked to Gil, who had been silent until this
point, for support. "We have a pretty nice life up here these days,"
Gil interjected. "I guess we've both run away from some old problems." He forced a chuckle, but his face betrayed that he knew
running away from troubles was unseemly.

"This question might seem a little off the wall, but is there
any hereditary disease or something you have that they know
about, which would explain why they don't want us to get married? I'm pulling at straws here. I hope I don't offend you."

"No, I'm not offended. I'm in good health. Gil's in good
health . . ." Why the hell would she care about Gil's health? Was
this guy two sandwiches short of a picnic or what? ". . . As I've
been saying, there're a lot of bad memories back there. I'm sorry.
I never meant any harm to Jordan." The guy almost started whim-
pering. God, he was fragile—like glass or cellophane. She had
made it abundantly clear she was not there to harass him. He literally shook except for the times when he let his mind drift back
to more pleasant days.

"Mr. Matino, I want to marry Jordan. I love him. If there's
anything else you can tell me, any other thing that rings a bell,

that tells you why everyone there wants to stop us from marrying, would you please, please share it with me?" Heather was at the end of her rope. It was late. She was tired. It had been a long drive. Another time, perhaps, she would have wanted to spend more time just chatting and getting inside the guy's head. Within him was, biologically at least, a major part of Jordan. As it was, this trembling fear, this frailty, were traits she had never seen in Jordan.

"No, I can't really say. You seem like a nice girl. Your parents must be proud of you. And you say Jordan turned out fine as well. I'm sure it'll all work out in the end. People get strange sometimes. Pressures, changes."

Charlie wasn't talking about Heather's parents. He was talking about himself. The insight into his psyche was interesting. She had always wondered what this guy looked like. It was also good to know where he lived, that he was indeed alive, and that he was not locked up in some mental institution. He was also most likely gay. Somehow her mother forgot to slip in that one. God, could her parents be so backward as to think that being *gay* was hereditary? Jordan was a lot of things, but gay certainly wasn't one of them—at least not before this past week. Her dad was a bit homophobic, but geez . . . All in all though, this seemed a pretty wasted trip. The real issues remained.

She thanked Charlie and Gil pleasantly for their hospitality, which only made them apologize for not having offered her beverages and food. That was all right. She had no plans to stick around here. Jordan's father was obviously pretty weird, or at least fairly pathetic.

A secret of some sort existed; that she was sure of. Maybe it was as banal as what she'd been told, that her father just had severe issues about Charlie Matino and took it out on Jordan.

Funny how when things really suck and you're not sure why, you think and think and finally come up with a theory that still sucks—but sucks less than anything else you can think of.

Ah, Jordy. Where are you? Why did I only have your heart for such a short, short time?

Gene Pitney. Roy Orbison. The older dude at the record store and Jordan were now goombahs. The only bum steer he sold Jordan was Johnny Ray. The guy simply tried too hard. The liner notes said this Johnny Ray fellow literally cried every time he sang. Jordan listened and, naw, nobody emoted like this. Ray was too contrived, too full of phony bull for his taste. Roy Orbison, there's a truehearted singer. Pitney? An acquired taste, but he dug him.

Why had he developed this sudden penchant for geezer rock? It wasn't as though Jordan felt singers of his generation couldn't write a good heartbreaker. But Top 40 radio played songs to death, thereby causing them to lose their desired effect. Overplay wears out meaning and emotion for the listener. To Jordan, this stuff he was listening to was all new.

It had only been about thirty-six hours since Heather walked out on him, but every second was funereal. These music appreciation lessons augmented his internal howling. Nurses and colleagues occasionally looked at him as though he appeared distracted, devoid of his usual personality and verve.

It was New Year's Eve. Jordan loathed holidays when you were mandated to have fun or do something spectacular. His favorite New Year's Eve was now the one where Heather got drunk and came on to him, even though she was with some other guy.

Jordan and Heather had not formulated New Year's Eve plans. When you're young and not in a long-term relationship, you don't make New Year's Eve plans in September. It was time, though, to give her a call. He'd been a good boy and waited a bit. Okay, so it wasn't the three or four days she requested as she stormed out. Bet she didn't realize that would extend over New Year's Eve when she said it. The time apart had helped him get his head in order, just as she said it would. What was troubling was that it clarified for him that he wanted to marry his cousin.

He frequently went back to cousinsinlove.com. He also tried every other combination of words like "love," "cousins," and "kiss," along with .com and .net. All, with the exception of the one he already found helpful, were porn sites. "Come on in! See private pictures of my cousin and me! There's even some from when she brought along her girlfriend for a threesome!" Yeah, that was now his crowd.

True deviants are often unable to cognizantly acknowledge the right and wrong of their perversion. Pedophiles frequently stump lie detectors when asked if they "abuse" children. Their definition of abuse is to beat or batter. Since they sincerely feel what they're doing is not damaging or done in physically manifested anger, it's technically not abuse to them. Had love so dulled Jordan's sensibilities that he couldn't reason with a society that declared love and sex with one's cousin wrong?

He wondered how Heather felt about it? In the abstract, that is. How do you bring that up in respectable conversation? "Heather, if a person falls in love with their first cousin, do you think it's bad? What if they didn't know they were cousins when they fell in love? Do you think they have to break up when they find out?"

He punched up Heather on speed dial. Telephoning when there's a lot at stake makes the ring sound like Big Ben and the time it takes for the person to pick up to feel like an eternity.

Finally, "Hello."

"I love you. I miss you more than you'll ever know. I was wrong. I screwed up. I allowed things to mess with my head that shouldn't have. I want to make it up to you. I want to spend every minute I can with you."

"Bob?"

The girl was downright hysterical, once you got to know her. "Funny, very funny. I pour out my heart to you, Ernestine, and this is what I get?"

"Are you just calling because you're hard up for a New Year's date?"

"Yeah, the escort services charge double for holidays. Look, I know it's late in the day. Have you made any commitments to this Bob guy yet?"

"Not really. He never wants to make love. He works too much and never has time for me. If you're different from him, I could possibly fit you into my schedule."

"Here's the pitch: no dinner, no dancing, no crowds. Just the two of us at my place, in bed, naked, all night long. There may be champagne and strawberries, perhaps some tunes on my stereo, maybe an old movie or an even older Dick Clark on TV. But really, I don't plan on us having much need for diversions. What do you say?"

"What shouldn't I wear?"

"Everything. You should not wear everything, anything. You in?"

"Only if you are."

Jordan immediately chilled the champagne, washed the strawberries (when he was serious, he was serious), and cleaned the place so that even the most obsessive-compulsive woman would feel comfortable making love on any surface. The CDs got rearranged. Orbison, Pitney, Milsap, Cline, et al. got packed away, replaced with more conventional fare like Ben Folds, Dave Matthews, and Lenny Kravitz. Ray Charles' *Modern Sounds in Country and Western Music*, the only country CD he owned before falling in love with Heather, stayed for sentimental reasons.

When Heather reached the door, he grabbed her, melding with her from head to toe. They stumbled about the apartment as clumsily as two people trying to occupy the space normally taken by one. It appeared this night might supplant Jordan's previously favorite New Year's Eve.

The next morning, Jordan awoke with a start. His body was completely covered in blood. He searched and searched for a wound. Looking around, he noticed that the sheets and Heather were also covered in a red substance. Yet he felt no pain, only a mild hangover. Then he noticed the blood was lumpy and coagulated. Tissue? No, strawberries. Crushed strawberries everywhere the eye could see. Strawberries squashed and rolled upon all night long. He peeled them off his legs, his back, and his arms. The sheets would have to be thrown out.

What a night! The lovemaking was incredible. He kissed her, nurtured her, and gave her his heart as he'd never done so fully before. This was the good news. It was also the bad news. He was a deviant. The best sex of his life had come after he'd accepted that it was with his cousin. True love was supposed to be illogical. This certainly was.

They showered together and made love again. They made the bed up with fresh sheets, on which they kissed and held each other close.

"You seem to have gotten over things."

"Actions speak louder than words."

"When do you wanna get married?" Heather giggled like a child as she said it, like something you do when a phrase is so odd and so new that it tickles your palate.

"I don't know. I never thought about it. When do *you* want to get married?"

"I don't know . . ." If this got any cuter it would break into baby talk, and the Dignity Police would bust in and slap them both silly for being silly.

After indeterminate time spent cooing and ooing, a basic plan was formulated. Heather would move in with him at the end of the school year. They would not make a firm commitment to a wedding date at this time but would continue to discuss it with no feeling of desperation.

The ceremony would be at St. John's. Jordan, while not wanting an ostentatious reception, did not want a typical back-home beer blast either. A coal region wedding reception is typically held in firehouses or cinderblock social halls; the open bar features beer, seven and sevens, and nothing more. No one needs an invitation. You just come. If you have any class at all, you knock back a few drinks but only sit down to eat if you were invited to the ceremony. Food is served family style: kielbasi, meatballs, chicken, city chicken (which is not even chicken), mashed potatoes, canned corn, and overcooked green beans. Music is live, usually a combo where the front man wears an accordion. Although they are primarily a polka band, they occasionally acquiesce and play a piece of real music as well. As with all polka bands, the leader is named Happy Louie, Happy Stefan, or Happy Stosh. Being the leader of a polka band apparently makes one quite happy.

About midway through, a few people get plastered, start fighting, and break up the joint. Chairs fly, dresses rip, glasses smash. Then the men join in and it gets really ugly. It's not a true coal-cracker reception unless the cops and the paramedics burst onto the scene. Then *they* throw a few punches, because most of them are either drunk themselves or have some grudge against one or more of the combatants.

Heather brought up her dad, and Jordan immediately interjected that he would pay for anything Rick would not, up to and including everything. He planned on getting married only once. It was worth it to him.

Throughout this wonderful discussion, Jordan felt only the slightest tinge of guilt and worry. If his brain had been working at all, he never would have participated in this, for he was still stringing along this woman who was his cousin and who had no idea of their blood relationship. He wondered how long he could keep *this* up?

THIRTEEN

⟿

Mᴵᴰ-ᴀꜰᵀᴇʀɴᴏᴼɴ ᴼɴᴇ boring January day, the doorbell rang at 126 Good Street. Mildred Stein, who was alone as usual this time of day, came to answer it. Standing there was a rather unattractive woman who appeared to be in her early twenties. She wore unfashionable eyeglasses, had bad skin, stringy hair, and was a bit overweight, although the heavy coat she wore masked her figure. Mildred had never seen her before and did not know if the stranger was selling something or what, which was why her guard was slightly up.

There are times when someone says something that is so horrible, so unthinkable, that one hears only every fourth or fifth word. Niagara Falls rushes through the ears, but no one hesitates to say "What?" or "Huh?" because they hope it's a hallucination.

The young woman . . . girl . . . Christ, she could have been less than twenty for that matter, took a step backward on the porch, away from Mildred, and told her tale. The words sounded like, "Jack and I . . . working on our house . . . my mom didn't discourage it . . . thought he had money and could take care of us . . . didn't really mean to get pregnant . . . thought he'd help us out . . . doesn't want to leave you . . . I know he's old, but I don't mind . . . I have another child by another guy . . . I told Jack if we couldn't agree on things I'd have to talk to you about it . . . I don't mean to be a home-wrecker, I just want what's best for my kids . . . I don't want an abortion . . ."

Mildred's brain spun. She felt faint. The girl was obviously poor, even by Mountain City standards. Despite missing most of the words—the adjectives and adverbs that give a story color—Mildred heard what she needed to hear. Her seventy-year-old husband, to whom she'd been married through fifty years, three children, and truckloads of disappointments, had caused her the final embarrassment of getting some woman-child pregnant.

Mildred turned to go inside her house as the chubby waif continued to stand on her porch. When the girl said something on the order of ". . . But what . . . ?" Mildred, with a face devoid of any life at all, whispered, "Go away," as she slowly and quietly shut the door behind her.

Back inside and all alone, Mildred could hardly move. Any desire to scream or cry out was impeded by a door slammed over her throat. The same door made her breathing incredibly labored as well. Her limbs would not obey a command to take her next door to Opal's. Instead, she turned and kneeled upon her sofa, pulling herself up to rest her arms and face against the dark imitation-wood-paneled wall behind, and she banged. Over and over she hit her hand against that wall, the wall between their double block, the wall so thin that each family's most embarrassing arguments could be heard as clearly as a radio through it. Opal was at work and not home during the middle of the day.

Mildred had no idea how long she kept smashing her hand against the wall. The pain did not stop her. That she felt only once she stopped and saw the blood and horrible bruising she had caused. Only then did she cry.

No matter the discomfort, Mildred could not motivate herself to move off that sofa. Like a dying person who had fallen and couldn't get up, she sat on that old piece of furniture and simply prayed that Opal or Eleanor would somehow know they were needed and rush to her aid. But it was not to be.

Sunset came and went, and still Mildred did not move. She banged again with her other hand. Opal was still not home from work. Soon, though, someone else would be.

Jack Stein came clomping up the wooden front steps with his inimitable limp. Only then did Mildred rise. She rose, not to greet him at the door, but to go into her kitchen at the rear of the house in order to grab her wet dishrag. She was not going to lose this fight.

Stein never knew what hit him. He never fully entered the house. Mildred came at him like a cyclone, displaying energy she'd been completely devoid of for the past few hours. Just as she had not heard most of the words the girl had said on her porch, she could never correctly recall anything she screeched at Stein as she whipped him mercilessly with the dishrag. Never had she used it so violently on her boys, but she was determined to apply it to Jack as purposefully as one would a lead pipe or billy club. If necessary, she would kill him with it.

She almost did. Between the swinging rag and her forward movement, she pushed Stein away and even down the porch steps. Without hearing anything resembling a complete sentence, Stein did not need to ask or wonder what this was all about.

"Girl . . . fuck . . . young enough to be your granddaughter . . .
Mr. Moneybags . . . old bastard . . . worthless piece of shit . . . I
hate you . . . GET OUT, GET OUT, GET OUT!!!!!!!"

Stein writhed on the decrepit sidewalk where each section
rose from the ground at a different angle thanks to the overgrown
trees lining Good Street. The only words emitted by Stein were on
the order of "I'm sorry . . . I didn't . . . it's not . . . I think I need an
ambulance . . . ," accompanied by sounds of sincere physical
pain.

Mildred began throwing at Stein every item of his that she
could find. The SPCA would be glad to know that his dogs were
too heavy and too self-determined to go flying down the steps after him. Then Mildred turned and closed the door, ending the
longest chapter of her life. She did not know what happened next
to Jack Stein, nor did she care. He could have died on that sidewalk and she would not have grieved a moment. She doubted he
was in any condition to try to come back inside. If he did, she was
sitting on that same sofa, holding one of his hunting rifles, loaded
and ready. Prison did not frighten her at all.

Because of this man, she had lost her children and grandchildren. Whatever little was left of her was now gone as well. Mildred
got the occasional phone call from her three boys, but each had
picked a different corner of the world and called it home. None
was closer than a thousand miles away. She had put herself on a
plane every few years in order to see her grandchildren, dragging
Opal along once or twice. Jack never came, and she knew why. It
was the same reason the kids rarely came back to Mountain City.
Jack felt uncomfortable in their presence, the way a criminal feels
guilty facing a victim. Unlike her, his boys never fully forgave him.
He, in turn, never fully forgave himself. Good Street seemed filled
with people doing penance for the sins of the past.

It was hard to say how much later it was, but Opal eventually knocked on Mildred's door and announced her presence, a fortuitously wise and lucky move of accidental self-defense. She let herself in, as Mildred remained on the sofa clutching the rifle. Seeing a best friend fingering a loaded gun causes one to use smooth, unjarring movements and a soft tone of voice. Mildred, again, would not be able to recall exactly what Opal said, but the essence concerned the stray pieces of Jack's socks and underwear that littered the sidewalk and which made it apparent that something was amiss at the Stein house. The rest, with all the sordid details, eventually came pouring out of Mildred. The rifle was unloaded and placed back where it safely belonged.

On a far happier Saturday morning a few weeks later in Philadelphia, Heather, Jordan, and Zeiss returned from a wonderful brunch. As they entered their co-op, Jordan and Zeiss went to their mailboxes.

Jordan stared at the envelope containing the lab report. He'd made sure to have the information sent to his home instead of his office, lest his secretary open it and inquire as to which patient chart it belonged. He'd given fake names to the lab and had tried to take all precautions to protect his privacy and avoid any gossip or speculation that might jeopardize his reputation, especially his medical license. Now, here it was: The written, scientific proof he had been dreading was now in his hand. And that hand was just inches away from Heather George's.

"Paul, I got another piece of your mail."

"What?"

"Yeah, two doctors in the same building; we get a lot of our mail crossed." That was directed at Heather, who probably couldn't have cared less about the inefficiencies of the U.S. Postal

Service. "Looks like that lab report that you had sent here instead of to your office." That was directed at Dr. Zeiss, whose uptake was quick enough.

"Oh. Oh, thanks." Zeiss shoved it into his pocket.

The three rode the elevator together, with Jordan and Heather getting off first and Paul ascending up to his floor. After a few minutes, Jordan said, "Heather, I have to go upstairs and get something from Paul. I'll be right back."

The elevator couldn't move fast enough.

"When the hell are you going to tell her?"

"I don't know."

"Do it now. This envelope; it's a sign. Do it."

"But . . ."

"What are your alternatives? If you don't tell her, she's going to find out eventually—maybe from her dad, maybe from her mom, or maybe from your mom. And if they all dummy up, she may still find out if you decide to have children.

"You have two choices, Jordan. You tell her the truth or you break up with her. Either way, you may lose her because she has all the rights that you do. And you're denying her those rights. She has a right to decide how she feels about this, too."

Zeiss could have gone on for hours, for Jordan had no arguments or counterpoints. He thought to mention the advice of his turbaned guru from the hospital chapel, but he knew Zeiss would only scoff. Jordan had been given a short respite after he had come to terms with his own feelings. Now it was Heather's turn. The plea from the Good Street crowd to keep it a secret was beyond absurd. The situation had been allowed to become untenable. Before another minute elapsed, he had to do the right thing. No more lies. No more secrets, either his or anyone else's.

"Do you have any of the stuff I printed out for you? I keep

mine at the office." Zeiss scurried around and gave Jordan a few of the printouts from cousinsinlove.com that Jordan had shared with him.

"I'm relieved you're doing this, man. It's the right thing. Whatever happens, happens."

"If you say, 'If you love it, set it free,' I'll kill you."

"Do you want the lab report?"

"I already know what it says. I'm just going to do what I have to do."

Jordan's favorite technique when telling his patients things they did not wish to hear was composing what he called his "caring lack-of personality visage"—a "warm" poker face.

Now back in his apartment, Jordan beckoned Heather to sit down while he placed himself directly across from her. Wiping his expression of any emotion, he asked, "Have you been talking to your parents lately? About us?"

"Kind of. I've been cutting down on my calls because I'm still so pissed at them. When I do call, I try to keep it short and talk about the weather, you know?"

"So you haven't gotten any new information as to why they're against this wedding, right?"

"Right. Why? Did you?"

"Yes." He let that sit a second. It would get her attention and perhaps allow him to continue uninterrupted. In order to do his best, he needed the fewest number of improvisational moments. "I was told something, something incredible, and I wallowed in it a while until finally I checked it out as thoroughly as possible." His pace accelerated. "It seems we're cousins."

She chuckled. "Right. We always called each other 'cousin' when we were kids. Very funny."

"Not really. See, they must have been squirming whenever we

said that because we really *are* cousins. Your father is not your bi-ological father."

With that he paused intentionally. His face showed nothing but premeditated, monotone, vacuous warmth. It worked; she knew he was serious. She would now hit him with a thousand questions, total incredulity, or else shocked silence. He got the silence, jaw agape.

Jordan continued, "Apparently, at around the same time that *my* parents were having troubles, so were yours. Your father is sterile; your parents couldn't conceive. It must have caused a lot of confusion and tension between them. They were both much younger than we are now . . ." Jordan did everything he could to sugarcoat the details, just like he did with patients. ". . . and they didn't have the technology we have today. Situations like that can cause people to react unlike how they would under normal circumstances. I've told people they have terminal cancer and watched them do crazy things like hang gliding and stuff. Anyway, my father's brother, my uncle Nick Matino, lived on the other side of where you live on Good Street. Your mother and my uncle had an affair. It didn't last long. They weren't in love. But your mother got pregnant."

"No. No, you're making this up . . ."

"Heather, my mother and Mildred Stein both told me, then . . ."

"The Steins know? No, they're lying to you."

"Your parents kept you in the dark your entire life. Your father found out about it but forgave your mother. The only caveat he made was that he never wanted you to know he wasn't your biological father."

"Where the hell do the Steins come in?"

"Forget the Steins. That's not important. I think everyone told maybe one other person. I don't know. I didn't believe them at first, either. Even though it explained why everyone, especially your father, freaked out about us, I couldn't buy it. That's why I checked further."

"That was the thing with the Q-tips. That was some sort of DNA test or something, wasn't it? You lied to me."

Jordan knew he'd take direct heat at some point. "I'm sorry. I was in a state of confusion. I also tracked down my Uncle Nick and confronted him. He confirmed it as well."

"Why didn't you tell me the moment they told you? Do you think I'm so delicate? I'm not your little sister, Jordy. I'm a grown woman. I would've gone straight to my parents and confronted them. And if I thought they were making it up, I would have gladly gone with you for testing, right up front. You didn't have to lie about that to me. There was another way."

She was right. And wrong. From the very moment he'd been told this tale, Jordan was doomed. He could do no right. "It's not that cut and dry. I was sworn to secrecy right from the start. My parents and your parents told me it was my duty to break up with you without any sort of explanation. They said if I told you, your father would leave your mother."

Heather wanted to give a quick and cutting comeback, but that last one hit her like a grand piano falling from a tall building. Her faced showed a thousand emotions at once, a horrible image he wouldn't wish upon his worst enemy. Her entire world had been rocked, and she was trying to sort it all out. Jordan wanted so much to soothe her, to comfort her. But he knew there were so many obvious issues to come that she might scratch his eyes out if he did the wrong thing in the wrong way.

She saw the manila folder. "What's that behind you? The test results?"

"No, it's some other stuff."

"Is it for me?"

"Yeah."

"Let me see it."

He offered it up, and she grabbed tersely. "It's research. Stuff about cousins marrying and having children together."

Suddenly Heather cast the folder to the floor like it was a venomous snake. "Marrying? You've been having sex with me and you *knew* we were cousins?" Her look of revulsion was unmistakable. This is what he had feared the most—the lollapalooza.

Jordan took his best shot. "There's this big onus on cousins falling in love, but you know what? It's not about retarded kids and it's not about the Bible, because one's an overblown urban legend and the other actually *supports* it. You know what it's really about? It's about the fact that you can't divorce your cousin. That's it. If you fall in and then out of love with someone who's related to you, what happens to the whole extended family? Who sits next to whom at holiday meals? And you know what? You and I faced that the first time we kissed. Because Heather, you and I are family. We always have been. Blood or no blood. The biggest risk I took—we both took—was that by falling in love we could lose a lifelong friendship. But it was worth the risk. I love you, Heather. I love you."

"You're sick! You're a sick bastard!" She got up to leave. The papers splayed out of the folder and lay on the floor like dead pigeons. She would not pick them up or look at them. He almost went to grab her but thought better of it. This was her opportunity to work it out in *her* head. He couldn't, he shouldn't stop her from doing that.

"I am not sick. You've known me your entire life. You know who I am and you know that I'm telling you the truth."

"The truth? Which truth? What truth? How many times have you lied to me since Christmas? And I've known my parents even longer and look what liars they are!" With that she grabbed her coat and purse and flew out the door.

When he was finally able to move again, Jordan went over to his sound system. Reshuffling his listening library, he moved his musical relics of despair back to the forefront. "Walk Away, Renee," the Rickie Lee Jones version, filled the room. It matched his mood.

As she did once before in anger and confusion, Heather gunned her car northward past Reading. She was 90 percent sure she was heading for Mountain City until she saw the sign for the exit. Then the 10 percent kicked in and she kept going, northward to Binghamton.

At some point she was going to confront her mother and father; that was for certain. Yet she was not ready to do that now. Perhaps she was looking for a practice session, a scrimmage with a weaker adversary.

Skies were darkening when she got off the main road near Charlie Matino's trailer park. On this second trip, she had less anxiety than the first. Now she knew her way around and knew that the two old guys in the trailer were harmless. While pulling up, she remained aware enough to note how hard she had plowed into the gravel-covered parking spot, like a cop on a mission to bust someone. Knocking on the door, she was greeted again by Gil.

"Heather! What can I do for you?"

"Is Mr. Matino home?"

"No, he's not. He should be back in about an hour or so. Would you care to come in and wait for him?"

She thought about it and finally conceded, "Okay," as she climbed up into the trailer.

"Didn't think we'd see you back again so soon unannounced. Is there a problem?"

Heather pondered for a minute before answering. An hour or two suddenly seemed like an eternity stretching before her, and she didn't feel like spending it watching TV or making meaningless small talk with this Gil fellow. "Gil," she said, as she made herself at home, ". . . how long have you and Mr. Matino been together, if you don't mind me asking?"

"Well, I'd say about eleven years or so."

"I don't mean to offend you, but are you two lovers?"

Gil smirked a little before answering. "Yes, we are. Are you surprised?"

"Yes and no. No one ever mentioned it back home, but I got a vibe the last time I was here."

"And you're wondering how Charlie could have a son and an ex-wife, right?"

"No, not really. I don't lead that sheltered a life. I know some people are bisexual and that back in your generation—*sorry*—it was harder to be an openly gay person and many people tried heterosexual relationships in order to fit in with what society expected of them."

"You've been reading, haven't you?" said Gil with that smirk again.

"Reading, living, whatever. Do I sound naïve to you; is that why you're smirking?"

"I'm sorry. You seem like an awfully nice young lady, and I shouldn't make you feel naïve. My apologies. Yes, Charlie and I come from a generation and from places where you didn't march around proclaiming you were gay. And, yes, it is easier today, but not completely. Look at that college kid in Wyoming a short while back."

"Yes, I know. You're right."

"So is that all you wanted to know? Maybe you were lucky you got me and not Charlie, then. Charlie, I love him, I really do, but he's not a strong man. I'm not talking physical strength; I'm talking strength of character. Maybe that's not even right. I'm not a walking dictionary, you know?" He cocked his head self-deprecatingly.

"You know why we live in this trailer? Charlie. He and I both work. Neither of us is rich, but with two incomes we could afford a nice little house somewhere. But Charlie, well, Charlie, he's scared. He's afraid of the neighbors. He's afraid we might change our feelings and all. He's afraid we might lose our jobs someday because someone will rat us out as being lovers. Hell, I keep telling him, everybody already assumes it and doesn't care. Who gives a damn about two old fags living together and not bothering anybody? We keep to ourselves pretty much but not entirely. We even belong to a dart league."

Heather started to relax for the first time since she raced out of Philly, but she still wasn't sure Gil could be of much help to her. She let him ramble.

". . . But Charlie needs his trailer. He needs to know he can make a fast getaway in the middle of the night if he has to, with or without me. Unlike Opal, I guess, I at least understood that about him when we first started up together. A lot of folks think gay people can't be monogamous. But me and Charlie, hell, we never really look around at other people. If Charlie were to leave, it wouldn't be for another man or woman. It would just be old

Charlie running. Running away, trying to find peace. Trying to find a place where nobody would expect too much of him or yell at him over things.

"I accept that about him; I do. He's a good man, a lovely, beautiful man once you get to know him. Oh, even if you never really get to know him, he's fine. He's got no temper. He's no troublemaker. He'd never do anything to intentionally hurt anybody. He's just not mean, you know? The world is full of mean, angry people. Charlie, he's a bit of a depressive, I think, along with his other problems. But that's another thing entirely. He's kind of like a good pet. That's probably not a nice thing to say, but I know what I mean when I say it and I say it with love. Did you ever have a dog or a cat that sits on your lap and lets you pet them all day long? Then a door slams somewhere and they jump up all skittish and stuff. But they'd never bite a stranger and they'd certainly never bite you. No anger, no anger at all. Never. Oh, what do I know? I'm just rambling here, boring you to tears."

"No, you're really not. I'm kind of enjoying it. I don't know a single thing about Jordan's father. Neither does Jordan, I think."

"What, you weren't told about terrible Charlie and all his crimes and transgressions? Yes, when he was younger, he did some stupid things. He knows it. Again, he never meant to hurt anybody. He hated his job, but when Opal had to stop working to have the baby, that's when it all came crashing down on him. That's still Charlie, you know? Pressure, he can't handle pressure. Runs from it any way he can. They say that isn't manly, but I always hated words like that. Manly. What does that mean? That women are allowed to run from pressure, but men have a different set of rules? That's bullshit. Sorry."

"That's okay. I've been known to use some language myself."

"I'm talking way too much. I do that when nobody jumps in

to stop me." There was that self-deprecation again. This Gil guy was all right.

"So, if I can turn the tables in order to get you talking, is Charlie's sexuality the only thing that brings you here tonight?"

"Gil, it sounds like you know an awful lot about Charlie's past. I was asking about it the last time, but now I need to know something else. Something very specific that you might know . . . or you might not."

"Shoot."

"Is Charlie's brother my father?"

Gil made the classic tics of a man trying to avoid answering a direct question; he raked his fingers through his hair, he scratched his nose, he tugged at his ear. Finally, he replied, "Yeah. That's why you were here before. I know. I told Charlie he should have either told you or tried to put you on the right track. He should'a said something to help you out. It was obvious you were in distress, but that's Charlie again. Not a mean bone in his body, but he couldn't, absolutely couldn't tell you that stuff. Here again, I'm lucky it was me seeing you tonight and not him. I'd-a come home and the home would have been gone. Zoom, off on the run again." He laughed at his own joke, but Heather had a hard time joining him in frivolity.

"Honey, I don't know what you know and what you don't, but Charlie speaks very highly of your dad. That's your *real* dad I'm talking about: Rick George. Sometimes I think Charlie misses him more than any other person back in Mountain City. I get jealous." Again that laughter, but Gil was probably only doing it to ease his own tension and maybe hers as well.

"Nick is all right, too. He has some problems with Charlie being gay and all. Can't look me in the eye ever. Like if he did it would be like condoning who we are. But most of that is his wife,

Marianne. Least that's what I think. God, that woman! In a million years, I can't figure out how anyone, *anyone*, could stay married to her. I wish for a day I could get inside Nick's head to figure out what punishment he feels he deserves that he stays with her. I told you he's all right. If he got away from her, I have a feeling he'd be a great guy, a really great guy."

"So everybody knows but me."

"Kid, people did what they felt they had to do to get by. And from what I hear, most of it turned out all right. Look at you and Jordan. Two great kids, all grown up and conquering the world."

"How do you two know anything about me and Jordan and what people back there are like today? Does Charlie sneak back there or what?"

"No, he stays away mostly. But this one talks to that one and so on and pretty soon Charlie's talking to his mother, when she was still alive, or to Nick, or to some old friend who's still talking to him and he gets the latest.

"My sister, she's a divorce lawyer. All day long, people are tellin' her why they want to get divorced. She tries to just keep it professional, but these people, they think she's a shrink, not a lawyer. Yak, yak, yak. She tells me about this one lady the other day. Comes in and says she caught her husband in bed with another woman. Now she wants a divorce. Fine. But she goes on and on. The husband makes a ton of money. He's treated her fine up until this. They live in a big house and have three lovely kids who adore him. He's a great father. They've been together twenty-some years. She had no inkling; they never had any major fights or disagreements. Since she caught him, he's been on his knees, begging for her to forgive her and take him back . . ."

"He just doesn't want to give up half his money."

"No, you're missing the point. When two people are married,

you give up more than half; you give it *all* up. Everything you both have: money, things, your entire being, is shared or completely given to the other person. No, here's the point. Outside of this fling he had, this couple had one of the best marriages anyone could describe. But the wife feels cheated on and lied to and now she wants out. My sister says to her, 'Look, I make a living off of other people's misery. I admit it. But in this case, honey, this man sounds like a gem. You'll spend the rest of your life looking for someone better and all you'll find are guys with a whole other set of problems. Nothing anywhere near as good as your husband. If he's sincerely sorry and promises it won't happen again, take him back. Get out of here and forget divorce.'

"The point I'm making is, a bunch of people made a bunch of mistakes, as I've been told. Some got through it better than others. Your parents—Rick is your father. I don't care what some lab test tells you. They love you and they love each other. That's why they stayed together and got through that whole thing."

"But you weren't there. You didn't know any of this or any of these people. You've never even met them."

"Heather, what do you think Charlie and I do all night long? And get your mind out of the gutter; we're two old men," he chuckled. "We talk. Charlie, if he's not afraid you're going to scream at him about something, he'll talk; talk your ear off. Worse than me. He knows I'm not going to judge him and so he opens up and spins tales of everything he's ever seen or done in his life. I feel I know your father, Rick, like I know anyone I've ever met. Certainly more than I know you, and look what good friends you and I are."

Heather smiled a little for the first time.

"You think that woman in my sister's office shouldn't have taken her husband back? The great father, husband, and provider?

How many men do you know who'd find out their wife was having an affair, got *pregnant* by the guy, and then take her back and raise the child as their own? How many? How many?"

On a dime, her smile turned into tears and they flowed for no reason she could explain, nor would they shut off. Gil reached out and gave her a soft shoulder to soak with her pain. He was gentle and as properly comported as a near stranger should be.

"I don't know what I'm gonna do," she finally said. "I love Jordan so much. Why did this have to happen? If my parents had told me, I would have gotten over it a long, long time ago. And I never would have thought about Jordan that way."

"What is Jordan saying? Did he break up with you?"

"No. Can you believe that? He thinks it's all right. He starts handing me these printouts and journal papers and tries to tell me it's okay for cousins to marry and have kids. He's crazy. Does craziness run in his family?"

"Charlie's not crazy. I don't think Jordan is either. He still says he loves you, then?"

"Yes. He says so. Why?"

"Because some people will tell you that Charlie and I are crazy. Certain people in other places and times would kill us for feeling the way we do about each other. But what harm are we causing? None. Sounds to me like Jordan got something of Charlie's and it isn't insanity. It's being a romantic. Charlie loved Jordan's mom, but she fell out of love with him at some point. As I said, most people might find Charlie hard to stay in love with. He's had his heart broken a number of times. Now Jordan says he's still in love with you and that none of this other stuff matters. That's Charlie for you. I guess it's up to you whether you can get past a few things and love him back like you used to."

"Gil, are you saying it's okay for cousins to marry?"

"Heather, I don't know a lot about things like that. I mean, for one thing, people like me and Charlie don't have to worry about having kids together, you know? But I was thinking about this when Charlie and I were talking after you left here the last time. What if your mother had never said a word to Nick that he got her pregnant? What if she led your father to believe you were his? It's possible; it could have happened that way. People have been known to do that. And then what if years later something tragic happened to your mom, like she got into a car accident and was killed? Her secret would have died with her. You and Jordan would have gotten together just the same as you did. Neither of you knew. Your dad wouldn't have known, neither would Opal, Charlie, Nick, or anybody else. You two would have gotten married, had a big wedding, lots of kids, lived happily ever after, and no one would have been the wiser."

With that, Heather turned on the sprinklers again.

"You see," Gil continued, "if nobody knew, what damage would have been done? Two kids would have been happy and in love."

"But what about when we went for blood tests to get married?"

"Those things just check for venereal disease. You don't have that, do you?"

"No."

"Well, then."

"What about kids? Don't people who marry their cousins have retarded children?"

"Now you're getting into things I don't know about. Maybe you should ask Jordan; he's a doctor. He would know."

"But he wants to marry me. He isn't objective."

"Is he the kind of doctor you'd go to if you got sick?"

"He's a prostate cancer specialist."

"You're splitting hairs on me, lady. Answer the question. What kind of man do you think he is? Is he a good man? Is he mature and responsible? If you knew a man who had the type of problem Jordan treats, would you feel secure sending him to Jordan for treatment?"

"Yes."

"Then why don't you sleep on all this and keep an open mind? From what I've heard, Jordan is the best parts of Charlie *and* Opal. That's a pretty great combination. You're a beautiful girl, but you might have a hard time topping that."

Heather leaned in this time and gave Gil a big, hard hug. "Gil, would you marry me?"

"Sorry, girlie, you're not my type."

"Charlie's lucky he has you."

"I'm lucky, too. Nobody's perfect. You just have to be able to bring out the best that one other person has inside of them. Maybe that explains Nick and Marianne. Something has to."

FOURTEEN

———◆———

TWO PEOPLE LIVED at 122 Good Street in Mountain City, Pennsylvania. Heather George had shared a house with them for more than eighteen years. Now they seemed like strangers to her.

Truth was, a lot of her anger had dissipated after talking to Gil. Unless a big door-slamming drama went down, she would confront Rick and Eleanor, then stay and sleep at her parents' house. Parent. Singular.

Parking her car and walking up the steps, as she had a million times before, she took time to notice as much as the darkness would allow. She gazed at the house next door, not Jordan's, but number 120, the revolving-door house. The fourth house. It seemed that no one lived there more than four or five years before moving again. None of those families ever had kids around her age. Except her, for she was actually the by-product of that house and the one she had forever called home. Never before had she stared so hard at number 120, trying to picture her biological father who had once lived there. Did she have half brothers or half sisters? She had forgotten to ask Gil that one. Siblings, oh, how she had begged her parent(s) for that. Now perhaps she had them. Did they look like her? Think and act like her? Could she ever reach out and meet them? What Gil told her about Marianne Matino scared her, though.

Heather rang the bell, something she never did, and then let herself in with her key. Rick came down the stairs first, flinging a robe around him. Neither of her parent(s) wore anything to bed except a smile. They were always so sexy and frisky together; Heather's ideal of what a marriage should be. Heather had always desired a lover with whom she could be unrestrained, experiencing all the pleasures sex could provide without censure or embarrassment. She had that with Jordy. Now it seemed dirty to her.

"Heather, what are you doing here?"

Rick continued down the stairs; Eleanor followed a moment after. Heather thought she'd wait until they were both lined up before she started the war.

"Honey, why are you here so late at night?"

"I was just wondering when you two were planning on telling me, if ever?"

Bah-dump-bump. High-beam stares assailed Heather, especially from her mother, whose narrow eyes could never hide shock or astonishment.

"What do you mean?" said Rick. It was a stupid, lying, irrelevant question. "Did Jordan tell you something?"

"Sort of. Most of it I learned from his father."

"Charlie Matino? How did *he* find you? What was he doing speaking to you?"

"*I* found *him*. When I couldn't depend on you two to tell me the truth about anything, I had to find someone who would. Even Jordan . . . oh, and by the way, thanks for putting it all on him to have to break up with me. That was really sweet of you, like he ever did anything to deserve that. I found Jordan's father and that's how I finally got the whole story. So, Mom, you ran around on Dad when you were young. That's not how you raised *me*."

Suddenly Rick was angrier than Heather. "That's between the two of us. Don't you *ever* talk to your mother that way! You got more love than any kid I know. You got nothing to complain about."

"How about the truth? How's about saying to me, 'Heather, now that you're not a child anymore, we want to let you know that Dad's not your biological father, but we love you very much and that's why we raised you together?' You couldn't do that when I was fourteen or fifteen? My biological father didn't live around here. It wasn't like I was going to run into him at the supermarket or something. And I *certainly* wouldn't have fallen in love with Jordy. Because of your lies, *I had sex with my first cousin!*"

Rick turned to look Eleanor right in the face. "I told you what I'd do if I ever had to go through this again." He went back upstairs. Eleanor knew it was not because he wanted to go back to sleep.

"Don't you go! Goddamn it, DON'T YOU GO!" Heather shouted up the stairs before chasing after him. When she got to him, he was already changing into street clothes and packing. "Don't you run out and punish Mommy for all this! You stay here and work this out. I'm an adult now. I deserved to know, and now that I do, let's get on with our lives. You made her lie to me. Stay here and be a man."

She had never been struck before. Rick's slap was quick and

left the side of her face red and hot. Shock kept her from feeling any pain. Even her mother had never raised a hand to her, let alone her father . . . or this man, this Rick George guy.

As soon as it was done, Rick regretted it but still kept on with his packing. "I'm sorry. I was made a fool of years ago. I won't put up with it again. She was told. I did nothing wrong. I'm not going to live under the same roof with her after the whole world knows what she did to me and that you're not mine."

Taking deep breaths managed to keep Heather from crying and almost allowed her to forget the shock of just having been slapped in the face for what, she did not fully know. "What whole world? Nobody else knows anything. I'm not telling anyone. Jordy's not telling anyone. Nobody thinks you did anything wrong."

"Then why do you think your mother did this in the first place?"

He was irrational in his anger and couldn't be reasoned with. All Heather could think to do was to try and hug him and let him know, wordlessly, that he was still a father to her and she loved him. She was damn angry too, but she didn't want her family to break up over this.

It wasn't working. He pushed her arms away and continued to pack. It was a mess of a packing job, but he dragged a satchel of things down the stairs. Along the way, he continued grunting under his breath, "I did nothing wrong. I did nothing wrong."

At the sight of him carrying a bag, Eleanor lost all composure. "No, Rick, please don't go. Please! It was a long time ago. We should have known Heather would find out someday. We should have sat down and told her, not like this. This is wrong. You can't leave over this. We've got too much invested in this relationship. We've been together so many years. No, don't leave me!"

She practically threw herself in front of him as he walked

toward the door, half dragging her along. Between that and Heather acting similarly, he couldn't possibly be going through with this utter nonsense. How could his ego be so bruised over something so long ago? He couldn't, he just couldn't leave.

And then he did. "Get off of me unless you want the whole neighborhood to see you like this. Then I'll have to tell them what it's all about; and you don't want that, do you?" With that, he went out the front door and got in his car, as Eleanor and Heather watched from behind the storm-door glass. Heather, fully dressed unlike her mother, felt like making one last dash into the street to stop him. Each moment seemed too surreal, as if at any instant he would turn around and say, "Just kidding," flashing that sly smile of his.

But Rick wasn't kidding tonight, no matter how absurd it was. He packed his car and left. He carried with him hardly enough to function beyond a day or so. Unless he bought a ton of socks, shirts, and underwear, he'd have to come back for more later. Maybe he'd go to some bar for a few hours and then return. It couldn't all end this way.

"I did nothing wrong. I did nothing wrong . . ."

Strangely, Jordan felt less like wailing in agony than he had previously. He felt a slim glimmer of hope. Heather now knew the truth. She knew he had never lost his affection for her, that he had been exposed to the most bizarre of circumstances. He'd gone through a tunnel and made his way out the other side, more or less intact. Now all he had to do was pass a light back and lead her through the same tunnel. Was it possible? Like Linus in the pumpkin patch, he felt his hope rise anew.

In her haste, Heather had left behind all the handouts he'd prepared. Jordan gathered them together and went over his data, seeing if there were any bits or pieces that might lead her back to him. It was methodical, practical work, and love is rarely practical. He had to convince his first cousin to marry him. And he had the pie charts with which to make his case.

It was well past midnight, but he was used to keeping odd hours. Passion for his work kept him from fatigue. Furthermore, his mind was buzzing far too much over the importance of what had gone on today.

Being a doctor, when his phone rang at 2:30 a.m., it startled him less than it might most other people. "You've ruined my life," his mother said through hysterical tears. "You've ruined my life, you've ruined Eleanor and Rick's life, you've ruined everyone's life! You are a selfish, selfish person, and I don't know you anymore. I did not raise a person like you."

There's little immediate response within one's book of conversational phrases that fits well when presented with an onslaught like this. He could hear voices behind her, yelling, talking, and crying as well. Whose they were, he could not be certain, but they all sounded female. One sounded like Heather's.

"Calm down," said Jordan. "What's going on?"

"You know it. You know what I'm talking about. You and Heather. You told her, you told her! I know you told her. Why? Tell me, why did you do it when I told you not to? Why?"

"Look, I'm sorry. You put an awful thing on me, and I did what I felt was right. I never meant to hurt anyone."

He could now hear that it was definitely Heather's voice in the background. The other voice was feminine and crying; that had to be Heather's mother.

"So you *did* tell her, didn't you? It was you, wasn't it?"

"You're all upset. I can hear other people there. Is Heather there?"

"Yes, she's here. Answer the question. Did you or did you not tell her about her father?"

The exchange was so odd Jordan wondered if he was being asked to participate in some scam for the entertainment or confusion of Heather or Eleanor. He lowered his voice. "If everyone's there crying, then obviously you know that Heather found out. If she's standing right there, why are you asking me if I did it or not?"

"She keeps saying it wasn't you, that it was your father. *Your father*."

At this point he could hear Heather getting agitated enough to try to wrestle the phone out of his mother's hands. He tried to hear what Heather was saying. Best as he could make out, she was indeed claiming it was his father who told her.

"Put Heather on." More crying, more unintelligible words. Why was his mother crying? Why was *her* life ruined? "I said, put Heather on now!"

After more mumblings through a hand-covered phone receiver, Jordan finally heard a different voice.

"What?"

"What do you mean, 'what'? What are you doing there? Why are you telling them you've been talking to my father? My father's got nothing to do with this."

"I left your place and went to see your father. I know where he lives. I found him a few weeks ago when you started acting weird. He told me who my biological father is."

Hers was a shaky, jagged monotone, showing anger she wished not to express in front of the others. She was covering for him. Why? He had no idea. Another woman would have hung him out to dry. Unless, of course, she still loved him.

He lowered his voice again. "Look, just give me one-word answers so they won't know what we're talking about. Are you covering for me?"

"Sort of."

"Sort of? You didn't really find my father, did you?"

"Yes."

"Yes, you did find my father?"

"Yes."

"You're kidding me."

"No."

"Why? Where is he? How did you find him? What did you talk about? Did you have a suspicion and ask him weeks ago? What?"

She responded with silence.

"Oh, yeah. One-word answers. Simple questions. Okay, did you see my father *before* I told you and did he tell you about this whole Nick thing before I did?"

"No."

"No, I guess that wouldn't make any sense. So you're telling me you saw him *after* I told you earlier today?"

"Yes."

"So he lives within driving distance?"

"Yes."

"And you confirmed this all with him? Like you weren't sure if I was making it up?"

"Basically."

"And now you're blaming him but they don't believe you? They still think it was me?"

"Yes."

"But it *was* me. Why are you doing this? And why do you think I would *make up* a crazy story like this?"

"I gotta go." The phone clicked into the cradle, ending their conversation.

Whoa. His *father*? Where did that come from? She couldn't have really, really found him, could she? Why would she have thought that was the path to any answers? Uncle Nick would have been the guy to find. But she didn't know there *was* an Uncle Nick weeks ago. And it would have been an incredible feat finding him in the few short hours since she was with Jordan in Philly early that same day. She found his dad *weeks ago*? What was that all about? Who was telling lies and keeping secrets now? It had to be a lie; it didn't make sense. She was covering for him and that meant she still loved him. The slim glimmer of hope was getting full-figured.

Jordan expected someone to call him back the next day, but his personal calls were nil. Perhaps that was for the best. He had heard his mother that upset only a handful of times in his life, and time was usually the best cure for it.

The following day was an early one for Jordan, since he wouldn't be on call that night. The schlepping around was fatiguing and time-consuming, but it might be a good idea to drive up to Mountain City and have an eye-to-eye/heart-to-heart with Mom, he thought. She sounded like she needed it.

He refrained from calling Heather, as he was honoring her space. He had a plan, but it would unfold in due time.

His car knew the way to Mountain City. It was early evening, and by rights his mother should have been home, but she wasn't. Perhaps she was at church. He looked around for Heather's car, but she had obviously gone back to Reading. He was afraid to even look in the direction of the Georges'. Their car was there, and the house lights were on; that he caught from the corner of his eye, as if by looking straight at the place he would be reduced to a pillar of salt.

Jordan's second choice of a place to hang his hat a while was at the Steins'. Mildred greeted him at the door, straight-mouthed. She looked older than she had ever looked to him before. "Come on in."

She led him back to the kitchen, where she was making something to eat. Stein wasn't around, but that didn't spark Jordan's curiosity, as he was often out. Jordan was only intrigued by the absence of questions, including the one he most expected, "What are you doing here?" Instead, he was treated as he'd been his entire childhood: living next door and drifting in from time to time when he was bored, as if he still belonged in Mountain City and on Good Street.

"My lads never come here anymore. Know why?"

"Not really. Why?"

"You really don't know?" she asked, suspiciously.

"No."

Mildred chuckled derisively to herself. "One secret still kept."

Jordan shifted uncomfortably in his seat. "Don't give me any more bad news."

"It's not important. What's important is you're the only one who still comes to see me. No matter what happens, I can't be without that. And if you think I'm bad, you should see your mother."

"Aunt Mil, I've got no reason to ever stop coming by."

"Good, then. All this other nonsense is just that—people and their pride, people and their craziness. You were as wild a kid as most any. But you went to medical school and became a doctor, and none of them other men around this block could ever do that but you. Just don't let it go to your head, and don't let anything that happens around here make you want to stay away. Your mother and I, we need you. She's had to be tough on you because you never had a father. But she's soft on the inside, like most mothers."

"And I had Uncle Jack, too. He's been about as close to a father as I've ever had."

Mildred wilted at the mention of his name, as if someone had pulled out her batteries. Her large wooden spoon hung over what she was lifelessly stirring. "You haven't heard, have you?"

"Heard what?"

"Jack doesn't live here anymore. Rick moved out, too. Just us ladies here now."

"What are you talking about? Over this cousins stuff?"

"That's Rick's excuse. Jack, well, your Uncle Jack is going through his fifth or sixth midlife crisis and I'm no longer putting up with it."

"What do you mean?"

"Your Uncle Jack, who you adore, screwed some ugly twenty-year-old kid and got her pregnant. How's that? Think I'm going to put up with that one?"

"Oh my God. That's unbelievable. This just happened?"

"Yeah, I found out the other day. Threw him down the steps outside. Don't know if he's dead or alive, and I no longer care, either."

"Wow."

"Jordy, you're an adult now. Before, you were a child. Children have a right to some innocence. If something happens right in front of them, you have to deal with it. But if it doesn't, they oughta still get to be children."

"We're changing the subject slightly, aren't we?"

"You know what I mean. Nobody set out to lie to you and Heather. Nobody meant you any harm—quite the opposite. And don't you dare argue with me.

"Some day, God willing, when you have kids of your own, you'll know what I'm talking about."

"But like you just said, we're not children anymore. Certainly once we started dating, someone should have told us."

"Yeah, well, some big-mouthed redhead told everybody nothing would come of it."

Jordan sat back, ironically bemused.

"Don't ever take me to the horse track, that's all I'm telling ya." Mildred came closer to where Jordan was sitting. "Try to make up with your mother. She's upset because she thinks she's the cause of all this. Not the business with your Uncle Jack, but the stuff with your godparents. Let her know you love her, even if she yells at you a bit. You can take it. Can't you?"

"Yeah, I can take it. I'm a good soldier."

"Seems I heard that one before."

"What about the Georges?"

"I don't know. I think Rick's just blowing off steam, but don't go by me. I ain't good for nothin' when it comes to advice and predictions, as you can see. Nobody seems to know where he's staying. Eleanor ran down to the pharmacy to try to talk some sense to him. So did your mother. He's a stubborn bastard. Pride's hurt. Thinks the whole town is going to know everything. Yeah, like you and Heather are gonna go running around bragging about it like you just shot an eighteen-point buck or something."

"Think I should go see him there?"

"Not if you want to give your mom grandchildren someday. He's mad as hell at you. Look, it's not your fault, even if it *was* you who told Heather. Frankly, it would have been almost impossible for you to end an engagement and not tell her the real reason why. Part of it is who you are. You might fib about having a beer when you were underage, but you're not going to do a terrible thing like they was all trying to get you to do to her, me included. I'm sorry about that."

"Did you see Heather when she was here?"

"No, they left me out of that one, thank God. Apparently in the middle of the night she burst in, saying she learned it all from your father. Can you imagine that, saying she found your father and *he* told her all about it? She must really love you."

"Is this a trick to get me to admit I was the one who told her? Because I'm not in the mood to play right now."

"Kiddo, I told you, I don't give a damn who told who what. She knows. She should have been told years ago. Now it's done. Can't take it back."

"Do you think there's any truth to this stuff about her talking to my father?"

"Ask her, not me. She's the one who said it."

"We're temporarily not talking. I'm sure you can imagine why."

"It's tough to take, Jordy. I'll grant you that."

"You and my mom don't know where my father is, do you?"

"No. Really, I know I don't, and I think your mother would have mentioned it to me if she did. There's still a few Guidos in town. They're all related to one another some which way. It probably wouldn't be that hard to find him if one was looking. Why, you thinking of looking for him?"

"Naw, just wondering." Of all the things for her to bring up, that was the last one I'd-a thought of.

"Did you say Uncle Jack got some girl pregnant?"

Opal wasn't too surprised to find Jordan, having seen his car as she drove up. Her entrance was not full of the smiles and joy usually given him by a mother who saw him every three months or so. Neither was it full of the rage and disappointment of the other evening. "Hi. What brings you here?"

"Seeing if there's anything I can do to help straighten out the mess."

"Jordan, what's done is done. I'm sorry I lost my temper the other night. But Eleanor came over here, woke me from a dead sleep, and was hysterical. You should have listened to me."

"I'm sorry. I don't want to sound melodramatic . . ."

"Why not? Everyone else around here does."

". . . But I love Heather. I'm not some teenager with puppy love. I'm a grown man and I want to get married to someone I think is fantastic."

"Jesus Christ Almighty! She's your cousin, for crying out loud. You'll have retarded kids. What's wrong with you?"

"I don't want to bore you with all the details. Not now, anyway. But it's not as bad as you think. Trust me, I'm a doctor." He paused. "That's a little joke we use sometimes. 'Trust me, I'm a doctor.' "

"What's so funny about it?"

"It's kind of like, 'Trust me, I'm a lawyer.' "

"You *should* trust your doctor. I've always trusted my doctors. The few times I ever needed a lawyer, I got all right. I had no reason not to trust him."

"Forget it. I guess people are more cynical in the city. All I'm saying is there's nothing morally or medically wrong with me and Heather marrying or even having children. I'm asking you to trust me when I say that."

"Well, *that* I'm skeptical about. Not that it's coming from you, but that it's true at all. Just doesn't sound right."

"I'll send you some research I've done. It's even in the Bible."

"What do you mean? It's got to be a sin."

"Genesis: Isaac married Rebekkah. First cousins. Jacob married two of his cousins, Rachel and Leah. Same book. Numbers: some guy named Zelophehad had five orphaned daughters. They were all commanded by God to marry cousins. There're a bunch of others. Oh, here's the best one of all: Mary and Joseph. Jesus' parents. First cousins. Hard to argue with that one. If you don't believe me, try to find a passage that damns it. Most people turn to Leviticus. Lots of marriage 'thou shalt nots' there, but none mentions cousins. In the meantime, will you be all right here?"

"Yes, I'll be fine. Don't worry about me."

"I do."

"I'm glad."

FIFTEEN

‧‧‧

Fourth floor: The psycho ward. Never thought I'd be coming to this floor, Rick George thought to himself as he stepped off the elevator. *Once, when he'd had pneumonia, he was on the floor right above this one. Along with the dreams his fever provoked, there was this one crazy woman, screaming and yelling all kinds of nonsense all night long. Haunted mansion stuff. Scared the living crap out of him.*

"Hi, I'm Rick. I'm a friend. You're Charlie. We grew up together." *Rick spoke as if it were to some stray wild animal that he did not wish to frighten.*

"I know who you are. Richard David George. The man with three first names." *Charlie Matino said it without inflection.*

As Rick gazed down at him, Charlie looked so small. The hospital bed seemed to swallow him up. His skin was pale, and the sedatives they'd given him made his voice a slurred, gravely monotone. "They told me you said you had amnesia, that you couldn't remember anything."

Charlie stared straight ahead and heavenward to where the wall met the ceiling. "I remember everything," he said quietly.

Rick pulled up a chair and dragged it toward the bed as close as he could in order to hear his near-whispering friend. "Charlie, why are you doing this? Did you just snap out of it?"

"No."

"Charlie, this isn't cool. You've got a wife and baby now. I've been telling you to straighten up. I'll help if I can, but you have to try, man." But Charlie paid no mind. He continued staring at some imaginary point instead of turning toward Rick, looking as if he would either fall asleep or cry.

The silence wore on Rick George. "Eleanor . . . Eleanor and Nick . . . they . . . they've been fucking around on me."

"I heard."

"Did you know?"

"No. They talked about it in here, but they didn't know I knew what they were talking about."

Rick fidgeted in his chair. "I got problems too, Charlie. Eleanor's pregnant with Nick's kid. My wife's pregnant with your brother's kid. I wanna kill him."

The sedatives continued to make Charlie sanguine. "I wanted to take you with me."

"Charlie, that's not the answer."

"No, Rick, it is. We should run away; get away from this place. Get a new start. Me and you."

"And then what? What then?"

"We'll get jobs. We'll get a place."

"Sounds real romantic, Charlie. 'Cept you can't hold down a job here."

"Eleanor. Eleanor and Opal. They don't love us, man."

Rick remained agitated. "Yeah, but some of it . . . some of it . . .

she's just too young, ya know? She doesn't know what she's doing. Then she gets mad at me and acts like it's my fault. Then she goes and fucks Nick. Like she's trying to prove it's not her fault."

Charlie turned to face his best friend. "She's bad in bed?"

"Yeah, man. She just doesn't know. Then we fight and all."

Charlie took it all in. "Opal, too."

"Yeah?"

"Yeah. We do it, but it's just not as good, ya know?"

Rick looked confused. "Not as good as what?"

"Not as good as us."

"What are you talking about?"

"You and me, Rick. We know what each other likes. We're good together."

Rick began a slow recoil, unhappy with what the sedatives were allowing his best friend to say. "I don't know what you're talking about."

"Yes, you do. The things we used to do together. Sleeping out and stuff. Together. Me and you."

"Charlie, that was about girls. We were talking about girls, that's all."

Charlie never left his soft, slow, monotone state. "No, man. It's us. I figured it out when I was with Opal. I thought about it when you and I were together. Eleanor doesn't make you feel as good as I do, does she?"

Rick began to get out of his chair. "I oughta come back some other time."

"You even had trouble with me, Rick. I know. But now I know it wasn't just me. You need somebody who's patient. That's why it eventually worked out. I can be patient with you, Rick. You and me. Together. No girls messing everything up."

"Shuttup! I don't care how sick you are, just shut up!"

"I love you, Rick. I love you."

"Shut the fuck up, you freak! You fuck! You bastard fuck! You did this to me! You and your fucking brother. Fuck you, Charlie. Fuck you forever!"

Jordan once dated a grant writer. Grant writing is begging for money, albeit in a formal and professional manner. It's much more dignified than it sounds. This woman wrote grants for medical research. Without grant money getting to the right people and places, research doesn't get done, and society's well-being does not increase. As Jordan sat before his computer, he realized that what he was doing was writing a grant proposal for Heather George's affection.

Leonard Cohen, Roy Orbison, Sarah McLachlan, Gene Pitney, Emmylou Harris, Joni Mitchell, and even goddamn Judy Garland played in the background, but he did not cry, nor did he howl at the moon. He simply typed and clicked, neatly compiling statistics, medical data, religious opinions, historical information, you name it. If it had to do with cousins marrying, he analyzed it and decided whether to include it.

Jordan tried to keep an open mind about it all, even if he only wanted to believe the proponents of consanguinity. As a doctor, though, he also wanted to know the truth. Truth—a heck of a word to consider at a time like this. The truth was, he'd grown up in a simple little place where people seemed to go out of their way to appear as normal as possible. Who would have dreamed that boring town was such a Peyton Place? Yet when you went to Mountain City and simply observed, it was like watching paint dry. Everything of interest was just like the coal—buried deep beneath the surface.

Piecing everything together and sending it all at once to

Heather would have been overkill. Jordan began with the simple hope that she would read a single word he wrote. For that reason, his love grant consisted of taking one simple piece of data at a time and mailing it to her:

Albert Einstein married *his* cousin.

Charles Darwin married his. And wouldn't *he* know a bit about genetics and evolution of the species?

No European country prohibits marriage between cousins. Nor does Canada or Mexico.

Twenty percent of all couples worldwide are first cousins.

Cousin couples actually have a lower ratio of miscarriages.

Modern qualms about cousin marriage is misinformed and antiquated, but not so antiquated as to be Victorian because . . . Queen Victoria married *her* first cousin.

To make them ever so slightly less dry and unfeeling, he included in each missive a proclamation of his love and feelings for her. One by one, no less than two days apart, these data went in a stream from Philadelphia to Reading. After about three weeks and eight or nine packets of medical information and odes of love, Jordan finally decided to end his and Heather's break in verbal communication. Dialing her number, Jordan was prepared for anything. He simply had to know if his message was getting through.

"Hello?"

"Hi, it's me. Please don't hang up. I just want to know if you've been reading the stuff I've been sending you, and if it's changing the way you look at things between us."

"Your father is gay and lives in a trailer park!" She slammed down the phone. It was rude, but honest. Honest, like he had failed to be with her.

From Jordan's end, it was better than "I hate you," or "Don't ever call me again; I wish you were dead." That gave him a smidgen of hope. On the other hand, it was the most bizarre piece of raw vitriol he had ever heard.

If a small bit of light was indeed emerging from behind the metaphorical door Heather had just slammed in his face, perhaps he should shift more to the purely emotional in his future missives—how he felt about her, how he couldn't live without her. But hadn't he done that as well? Not enough? What, God, what? Apologies, information, affection. Could she have fallen completely out of love with him? Shouldn't she be listening to the same kinds of music he was? Was her heart breaking like his? Oh, how he wished he could ask her.

He'd sent his mother material similar to what he was sending Heather, *sans* the mushy stuff. He wanted to win her over, too. It was also not unwise to figure that Mom would share this sort of stuff with Mildred and even, perhaps, Eleanor. Information and ideas move around like that. He had launched a propaganda campaign to devilify consanguinity. God, he was losing his mind.

Jordan had nothing left to send. He circled a date, an upcoming day he planned to take off from work. He cleared any chance of a single thing getting in his way. It had to be a weekday, when he knew where Heather would be and that she had no chance of avoiding him. That would be his D-day.

It was a cold winter day in February, but Jordan knew they would still be going outside after lunch for some fresh air at the Atkinson School for the Deaf. Glancing at his watch, he waited, parked in his warm car like some school yard stalker.

Finally, the kids came pouring out the doors and onto the playground. Little bodies bundled up with so many layers of clothing, they looked like bright colored balls bouncing about. Then came the taller ones, the teachers. Heather's blond hair showed from under her knit hat, her eyes squinting from the bright midday sun. Jordan watched as she talked with the teachers and then engaged with the kids. This was the Heather he loved. While other teachers stood together and chatted, Heather got down on the same physical plane as the little ones; signing to them, talking to them, being part of their fun and, through that fun, their learning. What a great mother she would make.

It was that particular thought that almost made him drive away. "Selfish" was the word his mother used the other night. Selfish. Was that what he was being now? Shouldn't he do the noble thing and let it go? Allow her to meet another guy and have strong, healthy children of her own, without the need for genetic counseling? It was all so confusing. Jordan Matino desperately wanted Heather George. Selfish, greedy, sneezy, dopey—it didn't matter. The heart is a hard negotiator.

Like a cat burglar, he crept out of his car. Heather noticed neither his parked car nor him coming toward her. As she played with one child, Jordan wondered when the tot would leave. Otherwise, the kid might witness what could be a very psychologically damaging scene. The little girl stayed and Heather finally noticed Jordan when he was close enough to cast a shadow. She turned without a word and stared at him. Her face, squinting even more now as Jordan stood only partially blocking the sun, was impossible to read.

"I have to talk to this man, Tara. I'll chat with you later," she said and signed. The girl looked at Jordan as he made it a point to smile. He needed all the brownie points he could muster.

A moment passed and Heather said not a word, turning her gaze away from Jordan and instead in the direction of the little girl. He squatted down to be closer to her. "There was this deaf couple and they got married. It was their wedding night and they realized they couldn't communicate when they were in bed to-gether in the dark . . ."

"That's stupid."

"Why?"

"You lip-read with your fingers then. Every hearing-impaired person knows that."

"Oh. But this is a joke."

"It's not funny."

"Well, not when you interrupt like that it isn't."

"It's not funny and it's insensitive."

"I'm sorry." So much for an icebreaker. "I don't care if you're my sister, my mother, my cousin, or my fourth-grade teacher. I'm in love with you and I want to marry you."

No response. He was close enough to feel the warmth of her face even on this frigid day. Words weren't working. He kissed her cheek. At first, she tried to turn away, but his hand guided her face back toward him. His kisses were insistent and passionate, far too passionate for a public place and certainly inappropriate at someone's place of business with children watching. After what seemed a lifetime, gradually the kisses were returned, on lips, cheeks, and all over each other's faces, combined with desperate embraces. It was sloppy, it was uncoordinated, and, finally, it was insulting the laws of gravity. They fell down together, both of them laughing like loons. For a few moments, they rolled on the ground, kissing, hugging, and laughing like the world no longer existed.

Suddenly, a shadow draped over them, and an older adult looked down at this pathetic pair. "Ms. George, are you all right?"

"It's okay . . ." Heather began to laugh so hard she was almost unintelligible, ". . . *it's just my cousin!*" and her laughter contin-ued unabated despite the bizarre looks her coworker gave her, long after the woman had turned and walked away. Finally, as they lay on the ground, Heather rolled toward Jordan and said, "I hate you."

"I love you, too."

"What's the end of the joke?"

"What?"

"The end of your stupid joke. What happens next?"

"I forget."

"You are so stupid. I hate you. I really, really hate you. You think I'm kidding. I really hate you. I am not being funny . . ." But the more she talked, the more she laughed, and the more she laughed, the more they rolled together on the ground and kissed and hugged and acted generally insane. Jordan looked up to see about thirty tykes under the age of eight staring at the two crazy people wrestling on the ground.

"One question. What music have you been listening to?" Jordan asked.

"What?"

"I said, what music have you been listening to lately?"

"Ray Charles."

With that, Jordan dusted himself off, scooped Heather up in his arms, and carried her off the playground and into his car. As they passed by, one of her coworkers said, "Heather, is this your fiancé?" To which Jordan answered, "No, I'm her cousin," and they laughed again like hyenas.

"I want to marry you. Let's start making wedding plans and announcing our engagement."

"You're crazy. We can't."

"Yes, yes we can, and yes we will. All you have to do is say yes. Say yes." Jordan looked down at her hand. The engagement ring was missing. "Where's the ring?"

Heather reached into her purse and pulled it out, hesitating a terrible, terrifying moment before placing it back upon her finger. No more words were needed.

In Philadelphia, Dr. Jordan Matino finally announced his engagement. Paul Zeiss was unforgiven but with good humor when he asked, "To whom?" Otherwise, the mood was celebratory and Jordan allowed himself to partake in it fully.

After spending a very special day and night with Heather, he called his mother. Luckily, his "master's thesis" was melting Opal's resolve incrementally, as it had Heather's. She was, well, not yet happy, but at least no longer beside herself. Not once did she call him selfish. That was a start.

"But what about the law? I thought you couldn't marry your cousin in the United States?"

"That's not quite right, Mom. Don't worry about it. It's under control. You're not planning on telling more people that Heather's my cousin are you?"

"Of course not!"

"Then it'll be fine. I'm sure her parents won't be broadcasting it, either."

"But is it legal or isn't it?"

"Trust me; I'm a doctor."

Heather was also making peace with her mom. Jordan didn't pry, but when Heather wasn't with him and had any spare time at all, she was driving up to Mountain City. Apparently, Heather and Eleanor talked and talked, and generally worked through all the feelings of the situation. All Jordan listened for were sentiments that Eleanor was, in fact, also coming around and warming up to the wedding idea. It seemed to give Eleanor something to hold on to, a reason for getting up in the morning. Yes, at first blush it seemed rather strange. Yet, to people who had been through so much, what was one more scandal?

Eleanor was still talking to Opal. With only Mildred and them living on Good Street now, their bond seemed more fortified than ever. Heather, the only child still coming to visit on a regular basis, became adopted and loved by all three of them, to a higher degree than she'd ever felt before. This wedding, this outlaw wedding, would belong to all of them, these victims of love.

A date was set for late spring—June, to be specific. Cliché, yes, but neither Heather nor Jordan desired a long engagement. Jordan would most likely have to pay for it all, as Rick was still AWOL.

Heather purposefully went to Southern's every time she visited. Her father was always there. Each time, she maturely and unemotionally implored him to return to her mother. Each time, he declined without elaboration. Rick seemed to have chosen to define his life by the imaginary line he'd drawn in the sand, sticking by it no matter what. Heather felt this was nothing more than a waiting game, as Rick couldn't possibly keep up this stupid behavior forever.

Heather made a point of never making too big a scene. She didn't want him to lose his job, for then he would have nothing, not that he had much of anything now, thanks to his own stubbornness. He appeared less angry than simply in need of attention. Regarding the impending wedding, Rick's reaction was wordless. Despite all that had gone on, Heather still harbored the dream of him walking her down the aisle.

Back in Philadelphia, Jordan was finding himself more involved in planning a wedding than he'd ever envisioned. He had become *the wallet*, and thus, his was the final word on far too many things for his own taste. "Spend what you want. We'll live in the infirmary the first couple of years."

A new hotel had just opened in Gibbsville where a department store once stood. Heather went on a reconnaissance mission, and her report to Jordan was positive. It was clean and new, had a decent-sized dance floor, and would serve almost any meal they wanted in any fashion they desired. There would be a real cocktail hour with a full bar serving actual cocktails! The locals would think they were at a Hollywood premiere.

Since there were no non-polka wedding bands in the area, they hired a DJ. This was something Jordan usually abhorred, but he put himself in charge of selecting all the music in advance. Despite complaining every step of the way, he was having the time of his life.

They decided to ask their old pastor, Rev. Lance Paulson, to officiate. St. John's had a new minister, but neither Jordan nor Heather really had a relationship with him. Jordan's mother, who had to interface with the new minister on an almost daily basis, did not have great affection for him either. Rev. Paulson had been pastor during their entire childhoods, and Jordan and Heather both loved him. He'd baptized them, had presided over their first communions, and Jordan knew his mother adored Rev. Paulson. Having him conduct the service would be like completing a circle.

Shortly after they'd both gone off to college, Rev. Paulson, or "Rev" as they both called him even to his face, asked for a transfer to another parish. There were rumors of marital troubles and, indeed, once he left town, he and his wife divorced. Gossip swirled that it was over another woman, but that seemed unlikely; Rev wasn't that kind of man. He possessed a lot of qualities Jordan had always tried to emulate. Their relationship was, as

Jordan's had been with Jack Stein and a handful of other men, more godfatherlike than what he had with his real godfather. Jordan and his mother hated to see Rev go.

Rev. Paulson's ex-wife was okay, but Jordan's mother always thought she was a bit too "out front" for a proper pastor's wife. Opal used to go on about how she herself might have wanted to marry a minister. She had all these theories of how important a minister's wife was and how she should act. To Opal, it was almost like royal protocol or being the first lady.

Why Jordan didn't call his mother first to ask if she knew Rev's whereabouts, he couldn't say. Perhaps he had an inkling that she would try to talk he and Heather out of calling him, due to those damn church protocol issues of hers. She might think it insulting to ask the present minister to step aside for this ceremony. But Jordan, being *the wallet*, did what he thought best. He placed a call to the synod's headquarters and found Rev's present parish. Lo and behold, it was—of all places—in Schwenksville, a little Mennonite village right by Collegeville and Ursinus College.

"Rev. Paulson speaking."

"Rev!"

"Say a little more. I have an idea of who this is, but I still want to guess and guess right."

"When I was thirteen, I told all the girls in our confirmation class I needed to measure their chest for their gowns, and they believed me."

"Jordan! Jordan, how are you? My, I've missed you. How's your mother?"

"She's great. And the best news is she's about to come marching down the wedding aisle."

"You're kidding? After all these years! With whom?"

"With me. Gotcha! I'm getting married."

"Someone should spank you. I'm so happy for you. Do I know the girl?"

"I'll let it be a secret. If I give you too many shocks all at once, an old guy like you could have a stroke."

"Yes, and I certainly don't know any good doctors, do I?"

"Not any neurologists, anyway. Here's the reason for the call. I don't just want your congratulations; I want you to officiate. At St. John's. It's June 22. Would you come back and do it? Please?"

"I'll check my calendar, but if it's a Saturday, I can't recall having any other weddings around then. A funeral perhaps, but they tend to come on shorter notice."

"Can we come by sometime to talk over the service? I've never done this before, but I've heard that's standard procedure."

"Yes, it's my job to discuss the birds and the bees with you."

"You're scaring me."

"No, it's right here in the manual. Sit you both down and ask if you have any questions, concerns, or fears."

"The only fear I have is being excommunicated if you ask too many personal questions on the subject."

"Jordan, this is wonderful news. Your mother must be so happy. Send her my love."

Heather and her mother came to Philadelphia one weekend. Seeing the two of them together was like watching a loving daughter helping her mother over recent widowhood.

Over the years, Jordan had spent little time with his godmother away from her chores and responsibilities to her husband and daughter. Eleanor now seemed happier, if that made any sense at all. As she was still melancholy over her husband living apart from her, something told Jordan that if Rick ever did come to his senses, he'd have a very different dynamic with this wife of his. The idea of her crawling through glass on her hands and knees, begging his eternal forgiveness, seemed less and less likely, as Rick foolishly let time slip by.

Unlike everything else, which was starting to go swimmingly, the whole Rick thing was getting odder by the day. Coal crackers are known for their stubbornness, but this was too much.

Eleanor and Heather spent an entire day hitting every bridal shop in greater Philadelphia, and according to Heather, it was the most giddily fun day they'd ever spent together. Jordan felt like taking out a loan in order to throw even more money at them once he heard them describing the good time they'd had. This was how it was all supposed to be.

"You should start dating."

"What?"

Jordan, Heather, and Eleanor, the person to whom he directed his opinion, were all relaxing together in his Philadelphia apartment. "You're looking great; you're smiling. There's so many doctors your age I know who would die to meet a woman like you."

"My age, huh? What about your age?" And both she and Heather almost convulsed in laughter.

"What?"

"Jordan, darling, I know you've had a crush on me for ages."

"Aww, c'mon."

"Oh, please. You think a woman doesn't know? Every time I went out in the backyard to sun myself, you'd find every excuse in the world to do yard work or stare at me from a window. It's okay. You've certainly got no chance with me now." The two women continued to crack each other up.

"What's up with this? You two planning on giving me some Kate Hudson/Goldie Hawn mother/daughter fantasy here?"

"Not on your life, my intended. You men are just so clueless."

"How do you mean?"

"I mean, we both knew you always liked my mother, you little creep. There you were, walking around thinking we never noticed. And how you never seemed to look at *me*, the hot young daughter . . ." She almost couldn't finish the thought as she was laughing so hard, her head falling in the direction of Eleanor's lap. ". . . Who practically built an altar to you in my bedroom during my childhood?"

"I didn't know you felt that way about me. So shoot me. Maybe I'm just not egotistical."

"Egotistical? Egotistical? Dr. Matino thinks he has no ego?" they said, almost in unison.

"Aunt Eleanor, really, I know this one surgeon. He's about your age. He doesn't even have a comb-over. He just shaved it all off. He's got that Kojak/Michael Jordan thing happening that all the young chicks dig. And he's loaded, lives in a mansion on the Main Line, has a vacation house in St. Lucia . . ."

"I don't need a man with money. My daughter's marrying a doctor. He'll keep me in furs and diamonds, just like he will for her."

"Uh, in that case, I *really* think you should meet this guy. I can't keep two of you in the lap of luxury."

It was laughter, it was fun, and the three of them had never quite been that way with one another before. It was very, very good.

The day came when Jordan and Heather had a date with the Rev in Schwenksville. They knocked on his office door at the rear of his new church. When he opened it, there was general jubilation and much pandemonium. These were two of his flock, the true flock only a pastor who really knows how to reach people has. It was only once they were seated before him that Rev gathered himself and actually noticed who was occupying the chairs across from his desk.

"Heather, what brings you here with Jordan?" He delivered this so straight, without a hint of humor, that it was almost disconcerting.

"We're getting married. Jordan and I, we're getting married. Didn't Jordan tell you?"

The look on Rev's face told everything. It was heartburn and indigestion from an undercooked piece of something almost toxic. Finally, Jordan piped up. "You know?"

Silence.

"You *know*? Even *you* know?" He gaped at Rev, hearing nothing as the man fished for words. "You know that Heather is . . . not exactly who people think she is?"

Finally, he replied, "Yes," and nothing more.

Heather's face turned crimson. "I told you that you should have told him you were marrying me. Do you know how this feels? Every time I turn around, I find everyone knew this deep, dark secret about me but me."

"Rev, I was led to believe we could account for everyone who knew about this: Heather's family, mine, the Steins. Where do you come in?"

"Jordan, your families are very dear to me. I've counseled them both over the years. A minister is called during spiritual and human crises as a moral and ethical sounding board. Just like priests, we hold many secrets, which is one of the reasons we're sought out in those times."

"So you know we're related," said Jordan.

"As do you both, I see."

"I think we should leave." Heather, visibly upset, began to push away her chair and rise.

"You know, years ago I used to do a little moonlighting."

Heather stopped to see where Rev was going with this. "You did what?"

"I had a kind of side job. Your parents knew about it. Your dad was the only one who seemed to have trouble with it, but we respected our differences of opinion. I used to perform gay and lesbian weddings. I didn't do them in St. John's; that would have caused a scandal. But I did them when no one else would. Our denomination has always been very liberal in the areas of love and commitment."

"Where, then?"

"Wherever. People's homes, college chapels, the occasional pub. Heather, I'm sorry if I embarrassed you, but what I'm saying is, I'm open to discussion of the issue. What do your parents think?"

Jordan took this one. "Well, as you can imagine, it's been rough going. Heather's dad bounced off the wall. I won't get into the whole gory mess, but suffice it to say . . ."

"I figured. Remember, I know the entire history. How in the world did you two manage to get together and become engaged in the first place?"

"We didn't know and they didn't tell us until it was too late."

"Makes sense. God . . ."

"You're blaspheming."

"No, I'm grabbing His attention. He should hear this one. So Mr. George is peeved. What about everyone else?"

"Believe it or not," said Jordan, "they're starting to come around."

The Rev rubbed his chin, engrossed in his own thoughts. "Do they know I'm being asked to officiate?"

"No, no one knows, since you haven't agreed to do it yet," answered Jordan.

"Kids, I really want to help you out. But you're going to have to give me some time on this one."

"Is it just about the cousins thing or what?" asked Jordan.

"Actually, that's not at the top of the list. Although, have you looked into the legality of it yet?"

"Yes. It's okay." Heather wondered why Jordan seemed to hedge so much whenever he was asked that question. He answered it, but there was always a hesitation in his voice, the way a person talks when they're lying and they know it. Rev. Paulson's eyes bored a hole through Jordan's, bugging her out even more.

"You're sure?"

"I've researched it. I'm confident. We'll show up that day and place a marriage license in your lap."

The showdown stare morphed into a knowing grin. "You will, will you?"

"Yes, I will. Can we count on you?"

"Are you two really in love, or is this just deferred teenage rebellion?"

"Rev. Paulson, this is no game." Heather looked on the verge of anger again, ready to bolt out the door.

"Heather, if I were to say 'no' and if you were to walk out that door right now, upset with me, what would you do next?"

"What do you mean?"

"I mean would you call it off? If I sat here and gave you a hundred reasons why you two shouldn't do this—and I could—what would you do?"

"We'd . . ."

"Quiet, Jordan. I'm asking Heather a question."

Heather looked not at Rev, but at Jordan. "I love you, Jordy. I can't live without you. If you want to marry me, I want to marry you."

"I do."

"You did that well," said Rev. "Sounds like we've had our first rehearsal. Let's get together a little closer to the date so we can go over the rest of the vows. In the meantime, I'll figure out how to further destroy what had once been a very promising career in the ministry."

That was more than an off-the-cuff remark. Heather and Jordan came out of their own worlds for a moment to focus upon someone else's troubles. "How is Junie?" Junie was the Paulsons' only child. Almost ten years younger than them both, Jordan and Heather had each baby-sat her when she was a little toddler and they were in their teens.

"She's okay, Heather. She's completing college in upstate New York right now. We're very proud of her." He paused and then continued for the benefit of those from whom he did not have to hide his own vulnerability. "It's been difficult. Ministers rarely divorce and when they do, it's usually pretty dignified. But that's not been the entire case with BJ and me."

Jordan's mother always rolled her eyes heavenward at the mention of Barbara Jane Paulson's choice of moniker. "BJ! BJ! A minister's wife tells people to call her 'BJ!' I shall not. I don't care if she corrects me every time I say it; I will either call her Mrs. Paulson or Barbara Jane, but I will not call this woman BJ."

"I'm sorry, Rev. I hope you and Junie still get along, though. She's great."

"I'll tell her you were asking about her, Heather. I wish I spoke to her more than I do, but that's part of what I'm talking about."

"Rev, if I could be so bold, maybe this is hitting close enough to home for all of us to understand one another. Without being clichéd or funny, I feel your pain. Heather and I love each other, and we love our parents. There're some rough patches we've gone through and there are others we're still going through. But we'll all get through it. That's why we want you there."

"Jordan?"

"Yes, Rev?"

"Please don't ever, *ever* feel my pain. Promise?"

"Rev . . ."

"Heather, if you're thinking of writing your own vows, will *you* please do the honors? Have Dr. Matino stick to medicine," Rev said as he playfully pushed them toward the door.

"But Rev . . ."

"Goodbye, Dr. Matino, Ms. George. I'm going to stay here and feel some more of my pain. I'm sure you can find your way back to the turnpike."

SIXTEEN

———◆———

As WINTER TURNED to spring, plans for the Matino-George (Matino) wedding moved steadily forward. Rick was still not back with Eleanor. Heather continued to stop at Southern's Pharmacy to implore him to return, yet Rick would not budge. He acted civil, treating the situation like that of a man who had just completed a very amicable divorce. No hard feelings, just don't want to be married to her anymore, okay?

Strangely enough, Opal seemed less enthusiastic about the wedding than did Eleanor. For Eleanor, it was the only thing getting her through her days. For Opal, there was a continuing feeling of cynical dread.

"I support you, Jordan. But I keep thinking that your heads are in the clouds and something awful is bound to happen. I don't know why; I just do."

"Well, that'll be your job. You worry. I know it doesn't pay well, but people should do what they excel at. Me, I gotta look for some banks to rob."

Stein was rumored to be living with the twenty-something who was having his baby. Those said to have seen him claimed he looked a mess, certainly not like a man trumpeting his virility and good fortune. Even in actually doing something swingin', the likes of which Rick George probably fantasized about, Stein would still not discuss his sex life with anyone.

Mildred remained on Good Street. Her mood improved incrementally each day. Unlike Eleanor, she did not wish to repair her marriage. Furthermore, this ridiculousness of Jack Stein's made her feel neither ashamed nor inadequate. She was seventy years old. This affair of her husband's was not competition, it was abomination. All those who knew them both seemed to side with Mildred, even Stein's hunting and fishing buddies. Some appeared to be spending an awful lot of time "consoling" poor Mil. This gave Jordan a bit of a tickle. Was this how people in their seventies got jiggy? Making condolence calls on lonely older women?

"Dr. Zeiss?"

"Yes, Dr. Matino?"

"My best instincts tell me not to do this, but would you be my best man?"

"Of course."

"Does that mean you're finally giving me your unconditional support?"

"Absolutely not. You're breaking laws of nature, if not those of our American legal system. You're risking getting someone pregnant, whether intentionally or accidentally, and having a higher than normal chance of creating a child who may need intensive medical care or have a shortened life span."

"So why are you agreeing to be my best man?"

"You don't understand me yet, do you, Matino?"

"You Jews be fuckin' crazy."

"My people thank you, coal mine canary. What shall I be wearing to this shindig? Bib overalls?"

"No, that's only for the groom. You'll be in hip waders and a Richard Petty cap. And make sure you arrive drunk."

With Zeiss as best man, Heather and Jordan decided to have three pairs of attendants. Jordan made his high school best friend Danny "Puddin' " Poleschalk and college roomie Chuck Edwards his other two choices. That done, Jordan felt it quite appropriate to make his first additional invitations to . . . The Boys.

The Boys were, individually, Ed "Ed Z" Ziegler, Carl "The Bear" Stoltzfus, and Kevin Covalesky, although it was difficult for anyone who knew them to think of them separately.

As each was a highly motivated achiever in his own way, each did not simply enlist in the Marines, but also went to either a full-fledged service academy or ROTC. The Bear went VMI, brainy Ed Z went Notre Dame ROTC, and Kev, the most hard-core one, went Citadel. Each graduated with military, if not always academic, honors. Although they weren't able to arrange to attend the same service academy, they managed to attend jump school and survival school together, scoring the highest in their class. It must have been magnificent to see.

Being that each of The Boys could potentially be found on any of the four corners of the world at any one time, contacting them as far in advance as possible was imperative if you really wanted them to be somewhere. This was Jordan's next big project. One by one, he caught up with them. Each felt honored, and that is the word he used, being as how honor meant so much to him. Jordan wanted The Boys, in their full Marine Corps dress uniforms, to be ushers. Each gave a hearty "Hoo-rah!" when Jordan gave him the go-ahead to wear his dress blues instead of a tux. This was going to look fantastic.

How a Philadelphia doctor had three gung-ho Marines as some of his very best friends deserves a little explanation. The truth is that Marines, unlike what a common assumption holds, are not born. They start out like every other child in the world, only to come under the sway of devout service to their country in the most dedicated fashion at some point in their lives. In most ways, they are more analogous to a place like Mountain City than was a big-city doctor like Jordan Matino. But that was Jordan's conundrum. They remained friends with Jordan because Jordan remained friends with Mountain City.

It came as quite a surprise to Jordan when Kev, in high school, became the first to announce his military career intentions. Bear and Ed Z were drifting until then but now had a cause that tickled their fancy as well, and The Boys was born. Jordan and Puddin' never felt left out of all this military stuff, then or now. Neither gave a second of thought to joining up, but The Boys never made them feel excluded. Indeed, whenever they were all in one place at the same time, they went out en masse—all five of them.

When out together at Lantenengo County guy bars to get some cheap liquor before hitting the singles clubs, The Boys were greeted like visiting royalty. There was no mistaking they were Marine officers, even out of uniform. In singles bars, however, it was a bit different. Crowds did part when they entered, but there was always some badass or badass wannabe who thought he could make his stripes by beating up some Marines. Dumb, very dumb. Almost every foray into the clubs ended in a brawl worthy of some Hollywood western, complete with broken chairs and bottles. The badass wannabes rarely found anyone covering their backs. The other locals, even if they did not personally know The Boys, were incredibly patriotic and felt it un-American to help some toothless jerk beat one up.

When Zeiss heard of these adventures, he always said, "Please, whatever you do, don't invite me out with those guys. I bleed too easily." Now, thinking about his role as best man, Zeiss said, "I don't have to take you out for a bachelor party with those Green Berets do I?"

"Green Berets are Army, so please don't say that around them if you value your life. Believe me, if you ever party with them, you'll never feel safer."

"I feel safe now. I go to my father's country club and no one ever throws a chair in my direction, even if they just shot a 120."

Jordan may have had no interest in visiting *his* father, but he dreaded Heather's asking for the same opportunity.

"What is your Uncle Nick like?"

"He's okay. He's much larger than I've been told my father is. Got a pretty big belly on him now, too. But he's kind of handsome. Not too bad a guy. I have to admit, I kind of put him in a spot the way I cross-examined him. Probably didn't see him at his best."

"I want to meet him."

"Don't. I think it's a bad idea. I get the impression his wife's a bitch, and you don't need that."

"But I want to see what my real father looks like. I need closure." Closure: a word no man has ever uttered.

"I understand, but I don't advise it. Things have been really good lately. Why mess it up?"

"Jordy, why do you feel the only way to be happy is to put your head in the sand?"

"Fine, do what you want. I'll come with you."

"No, I want to go by myself."

"Why?"

"I don't need a guardian. No one's going to hurt me. I just want to see him and say hi. I'm not mad at him if I'm not mad at my own mother. I just want to see him and let him know I turned out okay."

"He already knows that."

"I'm doing it anyway. Please give me his address."

Reluctantly, Jordan did. He knew if he did not she would eventually get hold of it anyway, so it made no sense to keep it from her. He continued to insist on accompanying her, but she had an idea in her head and would not be dissuaded.

As continued to be her modus operandi, she did not call ahead. The element of surprise appeared to be working fairly well for her, and so she stuck with it. Pulling up to the suburban New Jersey tract home, she thought it seemed like a nice enough neighborhood, newer than Good Street, that was for sure. Clean, safe, it might have been a decent place to grow up.

What if Daddy had not taken her mother back? Would this Nick guy have left his wife for Eleanor? Would that have been her mom's second choice? Did she even *have* choices? Mom told her she never really loved the man, that it was just foolish, young sex. But who knows? Heather could have grown up on this street instead of next door to Jordan. They might have never known each other. They may have never fallen in love.

Approaching the door, Heather felt more frightened than when she was in Binghamton late that first night. Here, she knew she had the right address. Here, it was daylight and a typical suburban neighborhood. But she also knew that there was at least one person living here who must despise her.

And then that person answered the door. Heather had no opportunity to say as much as a word. She thought to lie and say she was selling Avon or something, but Marianne Matino looked at her as if she were Satan herself. One look, one long-lasting look of hatred, and the door was slammed in her face. Door-to-door salesmen joke about this, but few people ever have it happen to them, particularly in a completely wordless fashion. This woman, this Marianne she'd been warned about, had fire in her eyes.

The door was slammed so hard it did not shut properly. Heather stood in front of it, entranced for a moment as it hung slightly ajar. She took a deep, full breath and boldly entered, prepared for anything short of gunfire.

"Mrs. Matino?"

"Go away!" Marianne had retreated from her, and the voice came from a room unseen. Heather continued walking inside, going against her better judgment.

"Mrs. Matino, do you know who I am? Is that why you slammed the door?"

"I said, get out of my house. You're trespassing. I'll call the cops!"

The house reeked of cigarette smoke to an almost nauseating degree. Did her husband smoke, too? If so, more bad news: a biological link to substance addiction. Wonderful.

"Mrs. Matino, did someone tell you I was coming? I don't want to start anything. I just want to see your husband and then I'll go. You'll never have to see me again." Heather tracked the bellowing voice to the dining room. There sat Marianne Matino with her back turned away, quite purposefully, it appeared. The woman responded no further. She had teased, dyed black hair and wore a formless housedress. Indeed, her left hand held a lit cigarette.

Slowly, Heather continued her approach. "Mrs. Matino?"

"I told you to go away. I know who you are. I knew what you would look like if I ever saw you. A bleached blonde with little eyes, pale skin, and a jut butt like your mother," she harrumphed in disgust.

"Is your husband here? I only want to see him for just a moment. I promise. Then I'll leave you alone forever."

"Then for the first time, a George girl won't be getting her way. Nick isn't here. You shoulda called," she cackled like a witch. Heather had not a word to say in response when Marianne finally turned to face her again. "Gonna marry your cousin, are ya? We'll see about that; I plan on making a few calls. Put an end to that right quick."

"No. No, stay away from us."

"Me? Me stay away from you? Who's in whose house? Listen little lady, you forget where you were today and maybe I'll forget I ever saw your face. Leave my Nick alone. He wants no part of you. Just get out of here. Now!"

The only military strategies of George Washington still taught today in war colleges are his retreats. The man knew more about strategic retreat than almost any other military commander who ever lived. Heather George had no frontal assault or ambassadorial reasoning left to draw upon. Retreat was her only option, and so retreat she did. It was a clean, wordless exit, with no dramatic pauses or final flourishes of "I shall return." She did not stop or even turn to look back until she was safely within her car and halfway down the street. Bleached blonde! She did *not* bleach. She *highlighted*. At the bottom of the road, she pulled over and had herself a good cry. She only wondered how many more good cries were in store for her.

Jordan attempted to get his own mother more involved in the wedding festivities, but everything he tried tended to backfire.

"Why did you talk to Rev. Paulson without asking me first?"

"Because it's *my* wedding and it's Heather's and my choice. I thought you'd be pleased. He sends his best."

"You should have discussed it with me first. You always do things like that. Running around behind my back, acting like I'm some idiot who has to have things hidden from her."

"Do you *not* want him to marry us?"

"No, I want you to tell me these things ahead of time. Those sorts of things affect me. I'm the church music director. I have to know all this. Who do you think is going to have to tell the new minister that he's not presiding over your wedding?"

"I was hoping you were."

"Exactly. Make me do the dirty work after you've run off half-cocked. Do you know how uncomfortable that's going to make things for me, having to work with this man day in and day out?"

"So I'll do it. I'll just tell him we have a special relationship with Rev and that it was my choice. Nothing personal. Let me be the bad guy. I don't care; I don't even know this new guy."

"What do you mean, 'special relationship'? With who?"

"Me and Heather and the Rev. Who else would I mean?"

"Nothing. Then I have to get someone to play for me. Or do you want me playing for the service, too?"

"Will you please stop being so cranky? This is so not like you."

"Jordan, I just feel dread. I can't tell you why; I just do. I know you love Heather, but if you had just gotten off it when I told you to, it would be so much easier around here. Now Eleanor has no one, Mildred has no one . . ."

"Don't lay that one on me. I had nothing to do with Uncle Jack bedding twenty-year-olds. *I* don't even do that any more."

"I just think we're all cursed or jinxed or something. I'm having an awfully hard time being happy for you."

"Great. Makes for a wonderful wedding."

"Honey, did I ever tell you why I didn't go to college?"

"Yeah, 'cause Nan and Pap couldn't afford to send you."

"Right, but there's more. I actually got a partial scholarship to Boston Conservatory of Music. Didn't I ever tell you this?"

"I hate it when you say that. It makes me think you're going to say, 'Oops, well, you're really the bastard child of Bobby Kennedy and Ann-Margret. Didn't I ever tell you that?' "

"No, it's nothing like that this time. Anyway, I always felt in my heart that if they really wanted to, they could've afforded to add to it. Maybe borrow some money to send me there. But this was when girls around here didn't go to college. And if they did, it wasn't for something as flighty as music. The worst of it was that all they harped on was going so far away. 'You'll never get to know your family. You'll be just like your Uncle Louis.' "

"Uncle Louis moved to South Carolina and had a fine life. Big family, good job, traveled all the time . . ."

"Right. But all your grandparents ever said was, 'He never knew his family; he never knew his family.' He knew his family. There were a handful of us here, and we never did anything and we never went anywhere. What was there to know? Your grandparents thought if you went outside of Lantenengo County, you'd fall off the edge of the earth."

Jordan settled in and gave his mother room to explain. He couldn't get too comfortable, though, the way shoes kept dropping, one after another.

"I always thought that along with the ignorance, there was

some selfishness thrown in as well," Opal continued. "I was an only child and I was a daughter. I was supposed to take care of them once they couldn't take care of themselves, which is what I did. I loved them and I didn't spend my entire existence resenting it, but it always plagued me: A life not lived to its fullest."

"Sorry. I know. You're bright. You could have done anything," said Jordan empathetically. He was always quite proud of her.

"Then there was you. Ever wonder why I kept telling you not to come home every weekend from college? That's what most of your pals around here were doing. Home every weekend, as if they weren't really away from home at all. I figured if I could have sent you even further away, I would have done it. I wanted you to get out of here and see the world, and you pretty much did. You went to New York; you went to Boston for a while. I loved hearing about it all from you.

"I always thought you'd meet some girl there and settle down someplace nice and exciting with lots of things to do and see. A good place to raise your children, where they'd have all the advantages you and I never had around here in the coal pits.

"When your Nan and Pap died it was very upsetting, but it was a blessing of sorts. Not that I ever wished them ill. But I always said, especially as long as I was still single, that when they passed and if I were able, I'd move out of Good Street. Maybe I'd end up somewhere around where you were, if you didn't mind. I don't want to move in with you or anything like that, heaven forbid. I just figured you'd be getting ready to settle down around now or sometime soon. Then I could be a help if I lived closeby. Baby-sit when you needed it or something like that. But I'd have this new life of my own too. You could be like my friend, not just my son. I wouldn't want to be a burden on you . . ."

"Like you thought they were on you."

"I hate to put it that way, but yes, that was a lot of how it was. God knows, I don't know if I could have raised you without their help. But what happens is that just as soon as you finish raising a child, you're suddenly raising your parents. You're never really free to do what makes *you* happy.

"Then all this happens. Mildred throws Jack out. That's not your fault, but now I feel I have to be there for her. She's seventy; she's older than me. Then there's Eleanor. That, well, maybe that you had a bit more to do with. I'm not saying that to make you feel bad. It's just what it is. Now she's all alone, too. Then you decide to marry the girl next door. How's she going to feel about her mother being up here by herself? She'll be bugging you in no time to pick up and move back. We'll all be stuck here on Good Street."

"The last time Aunt Eleanor came to Philly, I suggested she move down there."

"No, you tried to fix her up with a doctor. That's not right."

"I'm sorry."

"You better be. What the hell are you doing fixing her up and not me?"

The Boys were all going to be able to attend, an incredible coup, as occasionally they missed even major holidays because of duty. Zeiss, Chuck, and Puddin' were lined up, as were Heather's attendants. Opal found another organist to fill in, her first choice even. Rev. Paulson was a lock, and the reception at the new Gibbsville hotel was shaping up.

Heather continued to implore her dad to walk her down the aisle. Each time, he begged off, saying he could not put on a hypocritical show. Instead of becoming depressed over this it became Heather's challenge. No one knew where Rick was sleeping. He was pleasant yet firm with Eleanor and Heather. That was one of the more confusing aspects of it all. It allowed them both to believe his resolve might be melting. Yet he gave them nothing, not a thing to cling to. All they knew was that he could be found, five days and forty hours a week, at Southern's Pharmacy.

One week before the wedding, Jordan and Heather drove up to Mountain City to get their marriage license and finalize wedding details. Heather again ventured in to Southern's, this time to demand, not ask.

"The wedding is next Saturday at noon. You will be there. You will wear a tux. You will march me down the aisle. You will give me away. You are my father. It is your duty."

"I think you should get someone else."

"No, I will not get someone else. It will be you, period. You *will* be there. I don't care anymore what you do afterward. You don't have to stay. You don't have to go to the reception. You don't have to move back in with Mommy. That's between you two. But you will march me down the aisle and that's that. If you're not there, I will stand there and wait until you do. And if I have to wait forever, I will."

The trip to get the marriage license in Gibbsville was what gave Jordan the greatest trepidation. The courthouse was ancient; it was like going into a building in Colonial Williamsburg, only this place was not for tourists. It functioned actively five days a week, like any other courthouse in the world.

Jordan had previously downloaded the standard Pennsylvania marriage application. Upon arrival at the courthouse, he handed Heather the blank form.

"You fill out one side; I fill out the other. Your side says 'bride.' "

"Gosh, Mister, thanks! They never taught me how to read when I was getting my masters in education."

There were two things Jordan was anxious about. Two lines on the application. At a quick glance, the form appeared stereoscopically identical on both sides, but in fact, it was not. Like a child who hadn't studied for a test and was trying to crib off the kid next to him, Jordan kept looking over at Heather as she filled out her part. Down the form she went. As Heather answered the one particular question, Jordan thought he would leap out of his skin.

"What?" asked Heather.

"Nothing."

The moment she dropped her pen, Jordan quickly snatched it up and began filling out his side. Meanwhile, Heather busied herself by pulling out her birth certificate and driver's license. Good.

Jordan was nervous as a jewel thief with treasure in his pocket awaiting the getaway car. It was almost over, almost a done deal. Finally, he came upon the other line he worried about, the only question that, inexplicably, was on the groom's side of the form and not the bride's: "What is the relationship of the two parties?" That's where they try to catch the cousin marriages. That's the only way the government knows if two people are related to each other. They ask for a confession.

Heather wasn't looking. Jordan left it blank.

The registrar looked the forms over and asked for supporting identification documents. Minutes slowly ticked by as the paperwork was checked and their documents photocopied and returned. Husbands-to-be are supposed to be happy leaving a courthouse at a moment such as this. Jordan was ecstatic.

Heather vacillated from euphoric to blue during this, her wedding season. At times, she was the giddy bride about to don her whites; at other times, she was the realist who knew she was about to make a lifelong commitment to a man she had just found out was her first cousin. Jordan was not oblivious of the mood swings and made a point of being as reassuring as possible. There was no more he could do to solve the problem. He simply gave her his love. His throwing in supplementary tidbits such as, "You know, in most Asian nations, marriage between cousins is quite common, even in modern-day Japan," added little. In the end, she was doing what she wanted; marrying the man she loved. It was similar to most everything we dream and occasionally have the good fortune in life to get: It rarely lives up to its hype and is never without its flaws.

"I have a gift for you." Jordan handed Heather a long jeweler's box, the kind commonly used for a necklace. Heather's eyes widened. With what Jordan had spent on her ring and was now spending on the wedding, another big gift would require him to pick up three shifts a day in order to get out of hock.

Inside the box was not a necklace but a very official-looking piece of paper. "Open it."

It was his medical license. "Why are you giving me this?"

"Because I want you to understand something. I've spent my entire life working for this piece of paper. I left home, went wherever I had to go in order to get it, and then I finally achieved it. I love what it allows me to do. Up until now, it's been the most important thing in my life. But it's just a piece of paper."

Jordan reached out and put his hands on her forearms while staring intently into her eyes.

"I understand there's still some trepidation about this whole marriage thing. I'd love to wish away that you're related to me. But I want you to understand that no matter what the circumstance, you mean more to me than anything else in the world. That marriage license we just got is far more important to me than the license in the box. My future is you."

Heather looked into his very soul, calm now; no longer afraid some new dilemma would rear its ugly head. The boy from next door would do anything for her. Anything.

SEVENTEEN

—◦—

WITH ALL THE planning and such, Jordan had arranged to take off the entire week before the wedding, as well as two weeks after for the honeymoon. His medical practice was in order and he was back in Mountain City, sleeping in his childhood bed under his mother's roof. It felt odd; it felt good. He knew he would never feel this way again.

One of the last details of the wedding remained. For the first time in years, he walked the route that Rick George had walked every day of his adult life, from Good Street to Southern's Pharmacy on Nahas Avenue, the main street in town. What Jordan passed along the way shocked him. What once had been a homey little main street was now Hiroshima after the bomb. A building that had obviously been vacant for years stood next to two that were burned down and left in cinders. Next to those was what might be one sad and lonely little family business, looking barely alive and hardly viable.

The remaining stores were, in their own ways, even more

pathetic than the abandoned and incinerated ones. Their window displays seemed unchanged since Jordan's teenage years. The crepe paper was faded, the display bases covered with dust, and their merchandise now more valuable to collectors on eBay than as current retail items. It was a town where time stood still. Yet there had been no singular incident, no great fire or explosion that residents could look to or talk about. There was, instead, this incredible, creeping malaise that had overtaken Mountain City. Encourage the best and brightest to escape, and escape they would, leaving behind . . . nothing.

Towns have Golden Ages, too. Jordan could not say he had seen or caught so much as the tail end of the coal region's. Author John O'Hara used to write of Gibbsville and Lantenengo County of the 1920s, but Jordan could not relate much to that. O'Hara had made mention of the immigrant coal miners, but the bulk of his tales seemed more concerned with the lives of the coal barons and wealthy industrialists of the region. Jordan had searched for that of which O'Hara spoke, but for Jordan it was never to be found. The Gibbsville Club was now in a failed ski lodge, its original location having been gutted by fire years ago. Lantenengo Street in Gibbsville, where "mansions" had once stood, was now merely livable. Tract homes in suburban New Jersey stood finer. Social class was hardly an issue today: most were poor. If any sons or daughters were shipped off to the Lawrencevilles, Mercersburgs, or other tony out-of-region prep schools, they were no longer *of* the region and were made invisible by their absence.

Southern's Pharmacy now stood alone between a bulldozed lot and an abandoned store. The lot had once contained a supermarket until it became obvious that supermarkets needed a stand-alone location with lots of pull-up parking. The store was once a jeweler's where Jordan had bought his mother costume jewelry for five dollars or less on her birthday or Mother's Day. A few doors up from Southern's was a residential double block, odd in its location right on the main drag. On one side had lived a little Chihuahua who performed in the picture window, pirouetting after its own tail over and over again if a kid came by and simply stamped his foot upon the pavement in front of the house. The double block had also burned down. Jordan hoped that the trick Chihuahua made it out alive.

Rick George's eyes rolled with disgust and impatience as Jordan entered his domain. Since Heather had continued to be a weekly visitor with her plea, Rick knew that nothing new was to be expected from his future son-in-law. "This is a place of business. I don't want a scene here. I've spoken to Heather, so just peddle your papers elsewhere. I have nothing to say to you. You disrespected my wishes."

The place was empty, just like the entire downtown area. Unless Cal Southern was in the back eavesdropping, no one could hear their conversation. "Listen, I'm going to say my piece. I'll keep my voice down. Heather insists you walk her down the aisle on Saturday. You'll cause more of a scene if you don't show up than if you simply go there, do your thing, put on a happy face, and then go about whatever it is you want to do with the rest of your life. Don't bite my head off for saying you owe her something, but this is the last thing she'll ever ask of you. All things considered, I don't think it's asking too much."

"I can't believe you're going through with this. This is wrong. It's not only wrong, it's illegal." Jordan simply looked at him and said nothing. "It's illegal," Rick repeated again.

"What makes you think that?"

"Go through with it and I'll report you. You could lose your medical license."

Jordan stared his godfather down, not with hate but almost sympathetically and with a total feeling of masculine self-confidence. "What did you do, look it up?"

"Yes, I did. I'll be doing Heather a bigger favor if I put a stop to this than if I participate in having her make the biggest mistake of her life."

"Breaking her heart, that's a better gift to her? Is that right?"

"I'll do what I have to do."

"I figured if anyone would do it, it'd be you. Recognize this?" Jordan pulled a photocopied piece of paper out of his pocket. "Heather's birth certificate. Know what's on it? Father: Richard D. George. Signed: Richard D. George. This is a legal document, signed by you. You, a pharmacist, licensed in the Commonwealth of Pennsylvania. Now as far as laws go, a licensed pharmacist knowingly falsifying a legal document is far worse than marrying one's cousin. I mean, if the pharmacist forged one document, one only wonders how many other documents he's forged over the years. I'd say that would certainly be a call for revocation of one's license. And if you have no license, Uncle Rick, you have absolutely nothing. You've given up your wife; you've given up your daughter. What do you have left but your ability to earn a living?"

"And *you* signed an application for a marriage license."

"That I did. Every question I answered, I answered accurately and truthfully. For example, I put down the names of both my parents. So did Heather. She wrote down your name and Aunt Eleanor's. No coaching from me. Did it all by herself. Honest mistake, I'd say. But now it's part of the legal record. Guess you'd have to accuse her of falsification of records, too. Could cost her her teacher's certification. That would be a horrible thing to do."

"Heather said you two took a DNA test."

"I John Doe'd the names. The only paper trail of who Heather

really is is this birth certificate and her statements on her marriage license." Now it was Rick's turn to stare and say nothing.
"Seems in order to cause me a little bit of trouble, you'd have to
first implicate yourself and Heather in something the eyes of the
law see as far worse. If that's what you're prepared to do, go for it.
But something tells me you're smarter than that."

It was not checkmate, but it was check, and that would appear to be enough. Jordan had bent the truth with conviction,
putting Rick in a box from which he might not dare to escape in
order to bring down Jordan's life. Young man and old man each
waited for the other to blink. Finally, Jordan turned to walk away,
satisfied that he had made his last request of Rick George. Satisfied, too, that he had vanquished his last impediment to marriage.

"Why did you do it?" Rick's tearless cry was just that, a last
whimper from a defeated foe.

Jordan turned around to face his godfather, man-to-man, no
longer boy to man-bully. "You ask that like you think this is all
about you. Well, it's not. It never was and it never will be. You
ceased to exist for me years ago. You and my father both made a
choice of being out of my life. Or in your case, by just being an
asshole to me. Fine, then. I learned to be a man by looking
around and seeing what *not* to do. I got together with Heather
without a thought about you. What happened, happened. We fell
in love. I couldn't care less if she was the daughter of Hitler, let
alone you. Everybody on Good Street screwing one another years
ago means nothing to me, except that it made both our lives in-
convenient."

"I never screwed anybody."

"I'll let that one go; it's way too easy. I love Heather. She loves
me. We're getting married. Be there; not for me, for her."

Jordan had one more important errand to run, and again he ran it on foot. He had no idea what this twenty-year-old's name was, so he couldn't look for Stein at her place. All he had was Stein's shop a few blocks from Good Street, up toward the Little League baseball field.

The walk to the shop was as depressing as the walk to Southern's. Front yards and porches looked like garbage dumps. Inveterate do-it-wrong-yourselfers made garish and sloppy attempts at home improvement. Plastic pink flamingos would have been a step up.

Finally, Jordan reached the cinderblock building from which hung the sign STEIN ROOFING AND SIDING . . . CUSTOM GUTTERS MADE. Indeed, Jack Stein had put his life in just such a customized gutter of his own making.

The building did not bustle, nor did it appear to have any life at all. The place was locked up tight, with only a few small lights left on inside. It appeared recently inhabited, thus Stein had not ruined his life to the extent that he was no longer in business. But there was no Stein around for Jordan to see. This actually came as a bit of relief to Jordan, as he had no idea what he would say to the old man. He slipped the wedding invitation under the front door and walked away.

He felt quite nonjudgmental about the whole Stein situation. Sure, it was wrong, what he did. Adultery, one of the ten biggies from Moses' tablet. But Jordan looked at Stein the same way he looked at the region. Hell, Stein *was* the region. Jordan had nothing in common with it anymore, as if he ever really did, and yet he accepted it and it accepted him. The region never meant Jordan any harm and vice versa. He asked nothing of the place except that it allow him to gratefully accept whatever it had to offer. He also knew that he forgave Stein, as Stein would most certainly forgive him for what he was about to do, or anything, for that matter, that he might ever do.

And if Stein was the region, then Rick George was the city. Educated, professional, cultured; a ladies' man, Rick was everything Jordan had aspired to be and everything that the region was not. Because Rick had treated him shabbily and Jordan now knew his most embarrassing secrets, today Jordan Matino, M.D., was the victor. He had body-slammed Rick George and raised the championship belt above his head in victory. For Jordan the Prick, it was an awful feeling.

Friday, the day before the wedding, pandemonium ruled the land. But it was good, for this was exactly as weddings should be. Bride and bridesmaids were getting final fittings. Mothers of the to-be-weds rushed around, expending energies on the damnedest of things that were suddenly of life or death importance. Jordan browbeat banquet coordinators to see whether the vegetables were going to be canned commercial slop or fresh, tasty, and attractively presented.

People streamed in from all parts of the world. The Boys were getting in, one by one, and Jordan was helping coordinate airport pick ups and rides to Mountain City. Some of the guests from Philadelphia had decided to come in the night before to avoid getting lost, which only meant that they would get lost one day earlier. Most who needed hotel rooms had been long ago accommodated, but there were always those free spirits who landed on the bride or groom's doorstep saying, "Hi, can you find us a place to stay?"

In the midst of his errands, Jordan swooped into his mother's house on Good Street without knocking or ringing, just as he'd always done. Swoop was an accurate description, as he took two leaping bounds across the small living room and was at the base of the stairs to the upper floor in one second flat.

"Mom!"

The response was frantic, muffled, and included much physical activity. "Don't come up!"

Strange, it was the middle of the day, and even if Opal was trying on clothes, all she had to do was close her bedroom door. No big deal. But there was more than one voice. Both Eleanor and Mildred had rather low speaking voices for women, but it was neither of them. Curiosity forced him to ignore instructions. Jordan inched slowly yet discreetly up the stairs.

There he saw them. They were almost decent by the time he reached the second floor. Jordan could not say a word. Nothing of high moral outrage or even pithy humor found its way from his brain to his mouth.

"Jordan, I'm sorry," said Rev. Paulson as he walked past him, exceedingly careful to not so much as brush against him.

I stand so close to him as we talk. I lean back into him as I point something out. That's the flashpoint. That's the moment when I feel what it would be like to be his lover. I'm that close. My breath is trembling. I'm trembling. He's trembling. I'm not a tease. He doesn't think I'm a fool. Something terrible or wonderful is going to happen right now.

Jordan's jaw remained agape as his mother came to her bedroom door to reiterate, "I told you not to come up!"

Time stood still until Jordan raced down the stairs and out the front door, following the path just taken by the Rev. A car began to pull away, foiled in its quick escape by the larger than usual number of cars on the street at this time of day. Jordan hit his palm against the driver's side window and then came around to the passenger side.

"Lemme in," he said, and the door's lock released. Inside, Jordan looked at the Rev and simply said, "Drive. Up a few blocks."

The two rode in silence, as the Rev looked completely uncomfortable, searching for words that would not come. Finally Jordan pointed, "Here. Pull over here," and the Rev did. They were a few blocks away and in full view of passersby. Rev. Paulson could thus be fairly well assured that this young man whom he had known since he baptized him would not start beating the crap out of him in broad daylight.

"I'm sorry, Jordan. I don't know what else to say."

Jordan was strangely placid, almost dreamlike, in his response to this shock. Maybe it was getting so that nothing sexual could faze him any more. "I've never believed in spontaneous combustion. This wasn't the first time, was it?"

"I'd really feel it more proper if you were to discuss matters of your mother's social life with her and not me. It's not my place."

"Oh, please. We're not in church. We're in a car now. And it's both your social lives, not just hers. This wasn't the first time; I gather that from your answer."

Sheepishly he replied, "No, it wasn't."

Jordan spoke slowly, digesting every moment as if he planned on remembering it forever. "And that was one of the reasons you left St. John's?"

"Yes."

"You moved away and thought maybe you could patch up your marriage, but it wasn't successful."

"Right."

Jordan stared ahead and tried to make some sense of his life. "You remember back when I was in my teens? I was going through my rebellious period and my mom sent me to talk to you. Were you two involved back then?"

"Jordan, your mother is a wonderful woman. I cared for her very deeply for a long time. It began as a working relationship, but then it grew to much more. Neither of us wanted it to happen. It just did. There was an attraction on many levels . . ."

"I . . . really don't need to hear intimate details, thank you. So the answer is yes, it was going on back then. Am I right?"

"There were lots of stops and starts. There were years when we tried to keep apart and just be friends. I don't remember the exact chronology. Why?"

"I thought it was stupid, so insulting that she sent me to see you. I never thought of myself as a problem child . . ."

"You never were; that was what made it ironic. Your mother went through a lot raising you on her own. If you had been a girl, maybe she could have related to you more. As it was, she didn't even have any brothers as a reference to draw upon. No husband. A father who worked all night and slept all day. You were this strange new thing in her life. Once you started to have a mind of your own, she had trouble dealing with it. She told me I was the only man she could talk to about you. She was hoping I could be a sort of father figure."

"I know. What's funny was that I really enjoyed those talks. Yeah, I knew I wasn't going to end up in reform school just because I didn't feel like doing my chores the second she said 'jump.' But it was the closest I ever came to having a father-son talk with somebody, anybody."

"Thanks."

"Not to say you weren't corny as hell. I remember when she thought I was having sex and I hadn't even gotten to second base yet. You sat across from me at your desk with this serious look on your face and said, 'Jordan, is there something you need to discuss with me? Something you'd like to confess?' "

"Yes, I vaguely remember."

Jordan chuckled, "I only *dreamed* I had something worth confessing." The Rev finally understood that he was not going to get a beating from an overprotective son. "Tables turned now."

"I'm sorry. It's hard to see people you look up to being just as human as everyone else."

"Why don't you take her out on a date?"

"What?"

"I said, why don't you ask her out on a date? Take her out to dinner some time."

"Jordan, it's a little complicated. People at St. John's were starting to talk around the time I took my leave. If they were to see me out with your mother it would only confirm their suspicions. I couldn't do that to her reputation."

"Well, I can't speak for her. She might feel the same way. But if it's something more than just sexual . . . I'm making you uncomfortable, aren't I?"

"Yes."

"Good. Now you know how *I* felt when I was fourteen. Anyway, I'd like to suggest, if I could be so bold, that maybe you consider it. Let her be the one to say no. You like my mother, don't you?"

"Yes, very much."

"Fine. Are you involved with anyone else right now?"

"No, not really."

"Good. Then think about it. She loves to dance. Do you dance?"

"Not very well. Ministers don't dance very often."

"You could start a trend. She's very good, excellent in fact.

Even if you're not, I'm sure she could teach you. She tried to teach me years ago, but there's this whole stigma to dancing with your mother."

"Yes, it's more socially acceptable to see a break-dancing minister."

"Good one." Jordan chuckled at the mental image.

"Jordan, this is very embarrassing. I'm glad you're making it as painless as possible. We never should have done what we were doing on the day before your wedding. I feel completely mortified."

"Secrets and lies, Rev. Secrets and lies. This strange little burg is full of them." Both men paused for a moment of quiet contemplation. Finally, Jordan summed up his feelings in a question. "Rev, when a person chooses to lead a double life, how does one tell which is the double and which is the life?"

Rev stared into the steering wheel. "I'm supposed to know the answers to those kinds of questions, aren't I?"

"It's okay. It's probably like a philosophy exam. There really is no right answer. Just answers. All of them right; all of them wrong. Tomorrow I marry my cousin and have to keep it a secret from the world."

"How'd you get the license?"

Jordan turned and stared a hole through Rev's right eardrum. "Why do you ask?"

"Jordan, I know it's illegal. So do you. I could tell it in your voice when you visited me. Was it difficult?"

"Not really."

"Why did you do it? You could have crossed the state line and not have had to resort to deception."

"I know. That was Plan B. But try to understand what I was trying to give her. Heather deserves the fantasy—the big wedding in the hometown church. I wanted to give her that. Any other guy could have. I know, we could have gone to Jersey, gotten a license, had a civil ceremony there, then come back here and had a church wedding just for show."

"I would have gone along with that."

"Yeah, and I'm sure Heather would have, too. But it's not fair. Not fair to her. She'd always know, always know the big one was unofficial. If we had no other choice, fine. But the laws are wrong."

" 'Submit yourselves to every ordinance of man for the Lord's sake: whether it be to the king, as supreme; or unto governors, as unto them that are sent by him for the punishment of evildoers, and for the praise of them that do well. For so is the will of God, that with well doing ye may put to silence the ignorance of foolish men.' 1 Peter 2:13–15."

"So I did wrong."

"Yep. But with a good heart, which is how most of us do wrong, most good people, anyway."

"If you knew it was illegal, why didn't you rat me out?"

Rev smiled a little. "That's not how we work, Jordy. We of the cloth only *prevent* sins in extraordinary circumstances. Otherwise, our job is to listen and counsel so that our flock will learn from their mistakes. So I take it that Heather doesn't know exactly what's going on, either."

"No. I promised her a marriage license and I delivered."

"Try not to keep too many secrets from Heather, Jordy. I know sometimes it's hard. I'm trying not to be a hypocrite here. Maybe I should just stop before I make a fool of myself."

"It's okay, Rev. Everybody around here seems to think I'm judging them all the time. Truth is, all I've ever wanted was for them to judge *me* kindly."

"You're a good boy, Jordy. Any man would be proud to call you his son."

Every time his mother saw him, she tried to explain herself. Jordan was quick to cut her off and say, "Relax, I'm getting married. Everything's cool. I love you; you love me; we're a happy family . . ."

"Is that a song?"

"Recent pop-cultural reference. Don't worry about it. I don't want to talk about your torrid sex life right now. Got a wedding to mess up."

"My sex life is not torrid . . ."

The rehearsal went well except for the father of the bride being AWOL. Everyone not already in the know was given a sanitized version of the events. Rick and Eleanor were having marital problems and had temporarily separated. In answer to the question of who would walk Heather down the aisle, Heather herself was quick to respond, "My dad will. Don't worry. I'll walk down alone for the rehearsal, but I'm sure he'll be here tomorrow. He probably doesn't want to socialize a lot this weekend and that's why he's not here tonight. It's uncomfortable, the timing and all, but there's nothing we can do. Let's just get on with it."

Most everyone took the bride at her word since it's bad form to upset the woman in white on the eve of her wedding. Still, the whispers were everywhere in the tiny chapel as all speculated as to whether Rick would, in fact, show up tomorrow, or what to do if he did not. It cast a pall upon the proceedings. That upset more than a few people, Jordan and Heather primarily.

"A minute, please?" Jordan could see from Heather's face that she was not having the time of her life. After begging everyone's indulgence, he gently took her by the elbow and asked her to join him in the minister's office off the main sanctuary. "Tell me everything you feel."

"I'm being a big baby and I don't care. I want my daddy here. I want my storybook wedding."

"Good. So do I."

"Then why did you have to be my cousin?"

"Wasn't my choice. All I know is tomorrow I'm marrying the greatest girl who ever lived. I'm not settling; I'm getting the best. All the other stuff is minutiae." As Jordan spoke, he gradually moved closer to her.

"It's wrong."

"If you believe that, I'll tell everyone to go home and I'll promise never to see you again."

"Can't you just send them all home and still be my buddy?"

"Is that what you want?"

"No, I want you to not be my cousin and to marry me tomorrow."

"I can only do one out of two. What's your pleasure?"

Heather started to pound emphatically, yet gently on his forearms, "How can you love me when we used to fight all the time when we were kids and I used to kick you in the shins?"

"My mother told me those were love taps. Its a girl's way of showing she likes a boy."

"She's right. No matter how much I hated you sometimes, I still wanted to marry you. When I played Barbies, you were always Ken."

"I never played Barbies with you."

"Of course not, Jerk-off. You would have pulled Ken's head off and used it as a baseball. I played Barbies with my girlfriends. We all picked our favorite boy to be Ken. You were always my Ken."

Jordan wrapped his arms around her. "Wanna marry Ken?"

"Okay. Just stop being my cousin. And bring my father back."

"I'll try. I officially divorce you as my cousin."

"You can't do that."

"I just did. Now come on, let's get out there or people will think we're not getting married."

"What about my father?"

"I'm working on it."

Indeed, as the rehearsal ended, Jordan swung into his next plan for Rick George. He asked everyone's indulgence once more as he grabbed The Boys and herded them into one of the Sunday school classrooms at the rear of the church.

"Guys, listen up. As you heard in there, Heather's mom and dad are having problems. And it's a lot uglier than we've been letting on. Her dad was a no-show tonight and Heather's really worried he won't be here tomorrow. That really sucks."

"Damn. What can we do?"

"Glad you asked . . ." Suddenly Jordan was no longer a urologist with no military training. He was Jimmy Doolittle planning the bombing of Tokyo. "First, we don't seem to know where he's living right now. We could fan out now, but I don't think that's fair of me to ask you the night before the wedding."

"We'll do whatever you want. We're brothers; that's why we're here."

"I know that and I thank you. Anyway, let's just try to have a good time tonight, but I have a mission for you tomorrow. Here's how I see it: You guys remember what Heather's dad looks like?"

"Yeah. Tall guy, mustache, dark hair, late fifties, medium frame."

"Good. We do know he's still working at Southern's Pharmacy. If he's there tomorrow before the ceremony, it's a no-brainer. We send someone in to get him and drag his ass here, clean and simple."

"Done."

"If he's not there, what I suggest is some recon and intel. Ask old man Southern, maybe some other staff or customers. If that doesn't work, maybe work a short perimeter, see if anybody on Nahas has heard anything. Someone else could work the phones, call people who might have a clue, 'cause we sure as hell don't. If he's blown town completely, we're screwed and that's that. It's a small town, though. If you can ID the target, get him in here. I don't care how he's dressed; just escort him in as professionally and nonconfrontationally as possible. The next part may be a little trickier. I can't tell you much more. Details are on a need-to-know basis."

"Understood."

"He might try to cause a disruption during the service. I don't have to tell you how much that would hurt Heather, and I won't stand for it. I'll need someone posted by him once he gets into the sanctuary. You can't be too overt or show hostile intention. It's got to be more like an embassy guard detail."

"Dude, I just finished one of those in Moscow."

"I knew I drafted the best. Anyway, we want him walking Heather down the aisle. You heard that tonight. If he does that, great; it's most likely he'll behave. Even if he does, though, I think we should have a man posted right behind him once he's seated to assure order. If he decides to cause a disturbance, I'm thinking it would be at the traditional place where the minister says, 'If anyone here objects to these two being joined in holy matrimony, speak now or forever hold it.' "

"That part is optional." It was Rev. Paulson, who had snuck

in, Marines or no Marines. "It's more of a tradition, really. I use it very rarely these days. If you want, I'll leave it out. If Rick is waiting for that, he'll be thrown, and you'll have the element of surprise on your side. He'll be waiting for a portion of the service that'll never happen."

"Outstanding."

Jordan looked at his fallen father figure, standing as tall as ever in Jordan's eyes. Hey, maybe it wasn't too late for his mother to get together with a guy who could be a dad to him.

" 'Tino . . . bachelor party?"

"Hey, I know I mentioned things being on a need-to-know basis, but if you knew what's been going on in my life over the past few months you'd be giving me soda, ice cream, and Disney movies tonight instead of booze and strippers."

"I don't know about Disney movies, but I could go for *The Magnificent Seven*."

"*Butch Cassidy*!"

"There we go," said Jordan. "Porn isn't the only type of guy flick in the world. There's stuff with guns and tanks and revenge killings. Stuff most girls *never* want to watch with us."

"Food. My mom's church just had a pierogi sale. We've got leftover halupkis, too."

"I'll get the ice cream," said Bear. "Teaberry and White House, the kind I can never get when I'm away from home."

"Hey, this almost sounds like the sort of party a minister could attend and not be excommunicated for."

"Rev," said Jordan, "the honor would be all ours."

EIGHTEEN

———◦———

D-DAY. WITH NO hangover to nurse, getting up and ready was a breeze for Jordan, despite only an hour or two of sleep. The night had run long, as Kev had insisted on going to his parents' house at 3:00 a.m. for his personal copy of *American Graffiti*. They debated whether it deserved a place in the Guy Flick Hall of Fame, but there was camaraderie to it, a return to feelings of innocence and departure that struck a chord in all of them on a night like this. *Diner* would have been even better, if someone had it. Unfortunately, Blockbuster closed at midnight.

After shooing the guests out, Jordan breakfasted with his mother, who had spent the night at Mildred's. She had on this beautiful little Virgin Mary smile that almost combined with a blush.

"You look happier," he said.

"It's growing on me. It takes a while."

"I know. It took a while for me, too. A lot of that had to do with feeling I was going to lose something very special."

"Some things *were* lost. Rick still isn't around."

"I know. I'm sorry; I really am. I'm trying to do what I can about it."

"I don't know, Jordy. Maybe it's a good thing in the strangest way. I love Eleanor and Rick, but he was a tyrant with her and he wasn't much of a godfather to you. I think that blaming you for Nick was taking things farther than was necessary. Nick was just your uncle. If it was your father, I could understand. But Rick and your father were best friends. They never had any conflicts."

"Maybe I should have been more of a good soldier about it."

"Jordy, it was never my job to make the world easy for you. It was my job to make you strong enough for the world."

"I don't have a rejoinder for that. Thanks, I guess."

"Beneath it all, I think Rick's a very complicated man."

There were 160 RSVPs to the wedding. Not too big, not too small.

In the coal region, besides the wedding invitees there are always some people who come to the church service anyway. Usually it's parishioners who come whenever there's a wedding involving another parishioner's family. Seeing the additional influx of people made Jordan feel warm and loved.

He popped in and out of the minister's office, full of nervous energy. The Rev, Zeiss, Puddin', and Chuck Edwards bided their time there, going over their cues. During a lull, Zeiss joined Jordan outside for a chat.

"I have a wedding present for you."

"You could have waited until the reception. It's okay."

"Not this one. I found it a few days ago when I was cleaning out one of my filing cabinets. I apologize for opening it."

Zeiss handed his best friend a white business envelope. It all came rushing back to Jordan. "You call this a wedding present? No way!"

"Way."

"No! Why didn't you give it to me immediately?"

"Like I said, I only found it a few days ago. I had forgotten about it, too. I had to open it. Once I saw what it said and that you had already gotten your marriage license, well, in the eyes of the law, you're already married. The ceremony is just a formality."

"Are you sure about that?"

Zeiss paused in deadpan thought. "I've never been married and I specialize in treating yellow fever, typhoid, river blindness, malaria, sleeping sickness and cholera. Maybe I'm wrong, but right now I'm the best that you've got."

"I don't know whether to kiss you or kill you. Let me see it." And so he did. "We're not cousins. We're not fucking cousins!"

The Wisnewskis, passing by at that very moment, would recall this quite vividly as their most memorable moment at the Matino-George nuptials.

"I can't believe it! Oh my God, I have to tell everybody."

"Jordy, do you think that's the best play? Everything worked out anyway. Everyone's accepted it. Besides, everyone thinks you already read the genetics report. Now you have to tell them you forgot. On your wedding day. Not cool."

Jordan was confused and frantic. "Paul, go inside and get the minister."

Zeiss obediently obeyed. A few seconds later, out came Rev. Paulson. "Getting the jitters?"

Jordan's face betrayed that something was far more serious.

"C'mere." He signaled Rev even farther off the beaten path, where they could not be easily seen or heard. He whispered, "I just got this," and held up the lab report. "Heather and I aren't cousins."

"I thought you already confirmed that you *were*."

"Anecdotally. Look, it's a long story, but here's the bottom line: I just found out, scientifically, that we're not cousins. What should I do?"

Rev went into a pondering mode that lasted what seemed like eternity. Finally and sullenly, he replied. "Nick is Heather's father."

"No. I have the proof right here."

"That says you two are not related."

"Right."

"It doesn't say who your parents are, does it?"

"No, of course not."

"Then it's wrong. Or should I say, it's not telling the whole truth." He paused. "How is it done—blood, urine, or saliva?"

"Saliva."

"Need a kit or something?"

"A regular Q-tip and a plastic bag would do in a pinch, why?"

Just then, Ed Z came by from perimeter duty. "Eddy, do me a favor."

"Anything, Rev."

"Go to one of the neighbors' homes and ask someone for a few Q-tips and Baggies."

"Yes, sir."

Jordan turned back to Rev, "You want me to run the test again? It's pretty damn conclusive."

"Jordan, Rick George is sterile. I know this. They came to me many times for counseling; I told you that. And before you get into any medical debates, remember what we're talking about here. We're talking thirty-odd years ago in the coal region and people who are by no means wealthy."

"Do you remember what exactly the problem was?"

"Circulation things. Something about varicose veins and his sperm not being mobile."

"Varicoceles. And that's 'motile,' not 'mobile.' That would explain how he could be impotent as well as sterile without having any feminizing traits. When I first heard, I started to wonder whether his mustache was fake and he was strapping down his breasts."

"It was easier and less expensive to work on the impotency problems first. Rick also felt it was the most important thing because he thought that was the reason Eleanor strayed in the first place, not that she wanted to have a baby."

"It would also explain a lot of his social overcompensation."

"That's a tactful way of describing Mr. George's manner. But they did have sex, apparently, and they did try to have another child, but it never took. Never. Then, as technology progressed and became more effective and affordable, Eleanor felt she was getting too old, so they just let the baby thing drop. But I'm telling you, Jordy, Heather is not Rick's child. I'd bet my life on it.

Just then, Ed Z came back with Baggies and Q-tips. Rev must have known that no Mountain City person would say no to any request, no matter how odd, from a Marine officer in full dress uniform.

"So, how is this done?"

Jordan grabbed one Q-tip and bag from Rev. "You just swish it around your mouth like so"—demonstrating as he narrated—"then place it into the sterile vessel—the Baggie—and seal."

"Like this?" Rev mimicked Jordan's exact actions. As he

dropped his Q-tip into another bag, Jordan stared at him with a quizzical, furrowed brow.

"What did you do that for?" The Rev's eyes dropped ever so slightly without response. "You and my mom? Way back then?"

"That was the beginning. I'm sorry. I told you I'm sorry."

Jordan's head turned from side to side, looking for heroes or gods to intercede. "Were you the reason my parents' marriage broke up?"

"Hardly. Things were going badly for them before that. Then your father ran off after you were born. I know you've heard that part; it's true. And it wasn't because of me, or him thinking that I was your father. I know that. He never knew. No one ever knew. No one."

"The Georges? The Steins? My mother told no one?"

"It's the one secret she kept from everyone. She did it for me. Jordy, if she were having an affair with the milkman, it would have been one thing. But things like this can ruin a minister's career. That's her talking, not me. She made a conscious decision to protect me. This must have been part of it, too."

"What do you mean?"

"When it happened, when she got pregnant, I asked her if it was mine—if you were my son. She said no and I believed her. But all these years, I wondered."

Jordan was doing a downward spiral into oblivion. "Then *she* caused all this! All she had to do was tell the Georges and they'd still be together, and Heather and I could have gone through all this without the tumult. We almost didn't get married."

"Jordy, I don't think you're getting it. You've got to remember who your mother is. She would never cause other people pain like that. She'd always take the fall herself. No, I think she really wasn't sure. I guess she should have checked, but again, this was a long time ago. If they did blood tests and stuff, she wouldn't have been able to protect me as she did. I think she just took a guess, a leap of faith that it was your father's and, as time went by, ceased to question it. You even look more like him than me."

"I'm taller."

"But handsome like him. Better-looking than me."

"Smart like you. Harder-working and more responsible than him."

"You're more your mother's son than anything else. To me, she's the greatest woman in the world. That's why I've always loved her . . . and I've always loved you." They looked at each other strangely yet serenely. Rev finally broke the silence. "Let's keep a lid on this until you get the results back. I think that would be most prudent."

"You know, I'd like to start a new precedent with this marriage: truth and clean living."

"I'd be very proud if you did that. As far as Heather goes, though, I'd still wait until you get the new results before you say anything. And *read* them this time.

"Here's a parable: A beautiful princess falls in love with a frog. Frog says to princess, 'Look, just so we're clear on this: I am *not* a handsome prince. You can kiss me from dusk 'til dawn and I shall not, I shall *never*, turn into a handsome prince. Got it?' Princess marries him anyway, accepting him as he is: green and slimy. One day, the beautiful princess wakes up and finds that the frog really did turn into a handsome prince. And hey, it couldn't have happened to a nicer girl. Am I right?"

"Is that from the Book of Paulson?"

"You get the point, I hope."

"Thanks, Dad."

Ten minutes until the first wave of the invasion and still no Rick George. Jordan wondered if the proceedings should be postponed until he was found and could be informed that Heather and he were not cousins. But consanguinity was never Rick's primary issue. It was Heather and Jordan finding out his secrets.

Bear ran in. He'd been to Southern's, and Rick wasn't there, having taken the day off. Ed Z kept bugging that they should have gone for a road trip in the middle of the night to Langley, Virginia, so he could pick up some wireless transmitters like the Secret Service wears. There's nothing like having friends with security clearance high enough to go on shopping sprees at Langley.

As Jordan and his groomsmen sneaked looks from outside the minister's study, as well as inside the church, a tall, hefty man was spotted. It was Nick Matino.

"Son of a bitch!" Jordan popped his own hand over his mouth. "Paul. Outside again. Now."

"Hey, you two having a party we're not invited to?"

"Trust me, guys; you don't wanna know." Once outside, he said, "Paul, my uncle is here."

"Which one? You call everyone here 'Uncle.' "

"The one who might be Heather's dad."

"But he's *not* Heather's dad."

"Don't be so sure."

"What?"

"Later. But most importantly, *he* thinks he's Heather's dad!"

"What do you want me to do?" For a moment, Zeiss wasn't kidding. He understood the gravity of the situation.

"Why didn't we get those cordless mikes last night? The Boys could've had him bound and gagged by now."

"Do you think he'll do anything?"

"Go inside and make sure it's him. Tall Italian dude with dark hair. A big, heavy guy with Brylcreem all over his 'do. See if there's a woman with him. Dark hair, too. Wicked bad dye job. Teased up to the sky."

"Why would I expect to see such an attractive couple in a nice place like this?"

"Do it!"

Zeiss retreated back into the minister's office to peer through the door into the sanctuary. In a few seconds, he returned.

"I think I saw him. He appears to be alone. There's a guy who matches the description wandering around in the back, looking like he doesn't know anybody."

"Does he look angry?"

"Jordy, why would *this* guy, of all people, want to show up and ruin your wedding?"

"I don't know. But his wife threatened Heather."

"The wife, I might understand. But like I said, he looks like he's alone."

"What the hell is he thinking?"

In the back of Jordan's mind was a cornucopia of concerns. Jordan worried all night long about Rick pulling a *Graduate* scene at the wedding. Now it might be Nick Matino instead. Nick was here and Rick was not. How ironic was that?

Next to come was Jack Stein. It seemed that being thrown down his front steps had done its due, as he was walking with a cane and his limp was much worse. It was not just that, though. Stein looked absolutely ancient. He wandered in and stood in the back. The guy meant a lot to Jordan, warts and all. Jordan wanted him here.

Stein had to have been shocked when he saw Nick Matino

prowling the same rear vestibule. What Jordan would have given to hear that greeting. Stein had never mentioned Nick, but obviously everyone knew everyone else in the four houses.

Without use of wireless transmitters, The Boys simply knocked on the office door from time to time in order to give updates regarding the search for Rick George. It was high noon, and the man was nowhere to be found.

"I think for the benefit of everyone here, we have to begin. I'll stall a few minutes, but tell the bride to start making her way toward the rear of the church," said Rev. Paulson.

Bear was called in last from perimeter duty, while Kev and Ed Z had pulled in earlier so they could begin seating guests.

Mildred Stein had a most unpleasant morning, as the first thing she saw inside the church was her estranged husband. She refused to meet his glance. He stayed his distance, careful not to cause a ruckus out of respect for Heather and Jordan. Then Mildred nearly fainted at the sight of Nick Matino, who also saw her and discreetly kept away. Mildred's next adventure was more mundane yet caused her significant grief.

"Guest of the bride or guest of the groom?"

"What?"

"Guest of the bride or guest of the groom?"

"I heard you the first time. How the hell am I supposed to choose?"

"Groom is to the right; bride is to the left."

Mildred stood frozen in the middle of the center aisle. "Jesus Christ," she blasphemed under her breath as she slowly wandered down the aisle, shrugging off the offer of a formal Marine escort. Friendly as she was with the mothers of the soon-to-be betrothed, she knew she was expected to sit close to the front of the sanctuary. Her old seat in the rear would not do. Slowly, tentatively, she made her way up the aisle until she was nearing the altar. Finally, she took the first seat in the second row, groom's side. She felt horrible, having to choose between her two best friends.

Two other late stragglers came in and did the wandering-in-the-rear-vestibule bit, also politely refusing to be seated by the Marines. Jordan would not have been able to recognize either of them, although one may have resembled an old family photograph or two. It was Charlie and Gil. Gil looked understated, which helped him blend in well with the large local contingent. Charlie, on the other hand, was having some sort of nervous breakdown and had to literally be held upright by Gil. Gil was stoic about the whole thing, trying his best not to attract attention.

Heather had some secrets of her own. Unbeknownst to Jordan, she had sent them an invitation and enclosed a very personal handwritten note:

Dear Charlie and Gil,

Yes, it seems Jordan and I are going through with it after all. I love him and love is crazy. It causes us to do the sorts of things others might think are horrible mistakes. Somehow, though, I could never picture being with Jordan as a mistake of any sort. We're at our happiest when we're together.

I know Jordan has never really seen or met either of you. Mr. Matino, I know this is hard for you and I'll understand if you can't see yourself going through with it. It can be any way you want it to be. Even if you just want to stand in the back watching, somehow I think it would be a very special thing. For you, whether you realize it or not, as well as for Jordan and me, whether Jordan knows it or not. You're his father. Nothing can change that. On his wedding day, I don't expect him to have any hate in his heart. Frankly, having known him all my life, I don't think he's ever had hate in his heart for anyone. That's one of the many reasons I love him so.

Gil, you're the best, and whether you know it or not, you're one of the reasons I'm getting married to Jordan. I loved the talk we had that night I found out who my real father is. I'll never forget you for that.

Please consider coming and joining us on this very special day. Even if I can only catch a glimpse of you, it will make me so very happy. And you know, you're not supposed to disappoint a bride on her wedding day. So please take this as my very personal invitation to you. If you want to stay and make a day of it, which I hope you do, it would be my greatest pleasure to dance with you at my wedding reception.

Listen to me; I'M GETTING MARRIED!!!

Love,
Heather

In the rear vestibule of St. John's, the reclusive, assumed father of the groom walked around with his gay lover, chatting for a time with the secret biological father of the bride, watched over by the seventy-year-old cradle-robber who used to live next door. A notorious crew, to say the least.

The mothers of the to-be-weds began their walk to the sanctuary from the rear dressing rooms. If Mildred was aghast, it was nothing compared to how Opal and Eleanor felt. Entering in their lovely dresses, they greeted well-wishers. Both then caught a glimpse of the back vestibule crowd and almost went into shock. Out of the corner of Opal's mouth to Eleanor came, "Did you see . . . ?"

"Yes."

"How did they . . . ?"

"I have no idea."

"I'm going to kill my son."

"How do you know it was Jordan? Did he say he found his father?"

"No. But didn't Heather say that *she* did? I thought she was making that all up. And Nick's here. That's got to be Jordan."

"Who's the guy holding up Charlie?"

"I have no idea."

"Do you think they're here to make a scene?"

"I hope not. I mean, I'd have no idea why. Jack Stein's here, too."

"Should we go down the aisle or should we go over and say something to them?"

"If we go up and start talking, people will hear. I don't want that. Let's just smile at them and start down the aisle. If they give us dirty looks, we'll know this could be a debacle."

Opal and Eleanor painted on smiles, glancing for only a second or two at Charlie, Nick, and Stein, and then queued up to be escorted to their seats by The Boys. Their entrances indicated that the wedding was about to begin. Once seated, they realized they were unable to whisper to each other with an aisle separating them. As Opal sat, Mildred immediately tapped her on the shoulder and said far too loudly, "Did you see who's here?!"

"Shhhh!"

Finally, as they'd not yet heard Pachelbel's *Canon*, Mildred grabbed Opal by the shoulder, stepped out into the aisle, and pulled Opal with her, pushing Eleanor in and seating the three of them together on the bride's side. "Move it, Eleanor. We're comin' over."

"We shouldn't be sitting together. The mother of the groom is always in the front row on the right; the mother of the bride is always . . ."

"Opal, who gives a damn about seating arrangements? Nick is here and so is Charlie."

"We know. We saw them. What about Rick?"

"Mildred, turn around. The mothers of the bride and groom shouldn't be turning around."

"Jesus Christ, Opal. Who do you think you are today, royalty?"

"For a day."

"I don't see him."

"If he doesn't come, I don't know what we're going to do. Heather was adamant. She said she wouldn't walk down the aisle without him."

"Well, did you do anything about it?"

"For the sake of Heather, I went into Southern's and did everything but get down on my hands and knees and beg."

"What did he say?"

"He said no."

"Did you offer him sex?"

"Mildred! If that's what he wanted, all he had to do was ask."

"We know."

"Shuttup, Opal."

Finally, the bride made her entrance. Heather looked luminescent. Her gown fit her like a glove, and her hair and makeup were exquisite. Those still milling about oohed and aahed as she floated past them. Her smile was demure, more a demonstration of how tense she was than anything else. When she saw Charlie and Gil, she almost ran up to them.

"I'd give you both great big kisses, but I don't want my lipstick to smear until after the ceremony. I'm so glad you're here. You made my day."

Gil was sincerely flattered. But Charlie only seemed to wilt more, barely able to keep his feet under him.

"Mr. Matino, you made me very, very happy today. Please be happy. You're being a good father." Charlie tried as best he could to collect himself. It was a losing battle. So great was his emotional trauma, he appeared as if he was suffering from some physical incapacity. It was a sad sight.

Heather now set her focus upon looking for her father. She didn't seem to notice the large man standing near Charlie and Gil. Nor had she seen Stein, who stood further off to the other side. Spying the bride, latecomers quickly seated themselves. All who remained in the rear were Heather, Gil and Charlie, Nick, Stein, and The Boys. Heather frantically looked from side to side, and her anxiety showed. "Did anyone see my father?" she asked to the air, as she faced no one, nor was anyone close enough to hear what she said in such a plaintive, muted tone.

She moved to the center of the aisle, her only other motion being a quick shake of the head "no" to the organist, who was waiting for Heather to signal the start of the wedding march. The others were now discreetly behind her and off to the sides, so she stood alone. Her head no longer turned to search for her father, the one who had raised her. He must now come to where she was standing. Only a fool would not know where he was supposed to be right now.

The bride waited. What must have been only a minute or two seemed interminable. Rev, Jordan, Zeiss, Puddin', and Chuck made their entrance from the minister's office to their places in front of the altar. So, too, did Heather's attendants from the other side. They all looked down the aisle at Heather and immediately guessed what was happening. Rick wasn't there. The son of a bitch didn't show. The selfish, prideful, stubborn son of a bitch.

Suddenly, Nick Matino stepped forward. No, not that. *Anything* but that, thought Jordan. But Nick only seemed to sense Heather's feeling of panic and for God-knows-what reason picked that moment to whisper to her, "You look lovely today." Nothing more.

She turned to see who was speaking and saw an unfamiliar yet pleasant face. Nick smiled a warm, friendly smile that had the odd effect of relaxing her ever so slightly. Maybe it was just the need for some sort of distraction. Then he discreetly stepped back. The color returned to Jordan's face.

Heather cast her eyes up toward Jordan. He could see the disappointment in her face. She had refused a backup plan, a fallback position in case Rick pulled this stunt. Now she must have wished she had one.

She did.

Jordan looked right at her, nodded, gave her a calming, confident smile, and continued to stare lovingly into her eyes. What happened next caught everyone completely off guard. Kev Covalesky, the former captain of the Citadel Sword Team, stepped in front of the bride and withdrew his blade. His move from aside her to in front of her was precise as a Swiss clock. The creases on his dress uniform could cut skin; the shine of his shoes was blinding. His sword looked like a light saber from *Star Wars*, so immaculate and free of smudges or fingerprints.

With Kev in front of Heather now, Jordan nodded his head to signal the organist to begin, as the entire congregation turned to face the bride. Kev, perfectly in time with the music, drew his sword up to his cap brim. With exacting definition of movement, he turned his wrist as if he were a mechanical being instead of a mere mortal and deliberately took his first step forward. His stride was too magnificent for words. Each rise of the foot was the same height off the floor as the following one. On descent, the foot landed flawlessly within centimeters of, but without scuffing, the other.

Bear lined himself up behind the bride, perhaps a wedding faux pas, but this demonstration was so impressive in its choreography that no one was about to start consulting *Modern Bride*. Bear unsheathed his sword and mimicked Kev's movements as if they were one person. Ed Z, with equal aplomb, stepped to Heather's side and took her arm. Each of The Boys was totally expressionless, consummate Marines in formation.

Heather looked as surprised as the entire congregation. Tentatively, she allowed Ed Z to take her arm as he assumed the position normally reserved for the father of the bride. She was in awe as she looked at Ed Z and Kev, and she even turned to look at Bear behind her. But her gaze never strayed far from Jordan's, as he silently urged her up the aisle with his caring eyes. This was the back up plan, developed sometime between *The Dirty Dozen* and *The Magnificent Seven* the night before. Kev casually mentioned the sword team, and the plan just took off from there. The Boys spent an impressively short time choreographing their moves, and now they executed them outstandingly.

So grand was this wedding march that in the two minutes or so it took to travel down the aisle, flashes went off, video cameras whirred, "ohhhhh"s arose to a much more audible level, and some even applauded. The brilliance of it all was that it was possibly the only Plan B that could make every person there forget to ask, "Where's the father of the bride?" No way could this have been an accident. It had to have been by wonderful, original planning and design, this military escort. That neither the bride nor groom was or had ever been *in* the military was a detail no one bothered to consider as they watched the beauty of it all.

Jordan was most impressed by Heather, who was the completely unrehearsed Ginger Rogers of this production number, faking it with her three Fred Astaires. Even the organist seemed to play off The Boys and drove his beat to metronomic exactitude. It almost seemed as if there was an invisible drummer drumming in cadence as all four made their way down the center aisle.

Even Rick George saw it. During this stunning parade, he had managed to slip in through one of the side doors of the church. His demeanor was stoic, irritable, bitter, and resolute. He did not crane his neck to see the full length of the bride's march nor did he rush in order to be part of it. He slowly made his way to the rear of the center aisle in order to get an unobstructed view, leaning against the back wall of the sanctuary next to Stein, who acknowledged his presence with silent surprise.

It was then Rick who was surprised when he glanced to the other side of Stein and saw first a stranger, then, of all the damn people, Charlie Matino. And then, of all the *completely* damnable people, Nick Matino. The sight of Charlie caused him almost to turn and exit whence he came. The sight of Nick made him want to begin brawling. But Stein, despite his fragility and need to be supported by a cane, must have anticipated this, for he suddenly latched onto Rick's right underarm and held tightly. With a quick, strong pull of his arm, Rick could have sent Stein sprawling, but such physical effort was not within him at this moment. Reluctantly, he stayed, leaning with even more reticence against the wall, arms crossed in a stance of indignant posturing.

During the actual ceremony, no heads turned to the back of the church. But those at the altar could glance and see the standing-room-only tableau in that rear vestibule. Jordan knew

Nick and Stein were there, but he became surprised and nervous once he saw Rick. He also noticed two other men in the back: typical-looking local fellows whom he did not recognize as St. John's regulars. They were properly dressed, at least. The tall, thin one looked pretty nondescript. The other guy, hoo-boy, that pathetic soul was already drunk to the gills, it appeared. That guy could hardly stand up but for the help of his skinny drinking buddy.

Anyone who knew the faces and stories of these five men would have been treated to a Mount Rushmore of male frailty and fallibility. Rick George still leaned against the wall, depressed, angry, wistful, and defeated. Jack Stein's face was a blank slate onto which one could write so many different stories. His red eyes, with no tears in sight, were looking at the end of his first seventy years, looking for the last time at a world from which he'd been expelled for his own human weaknesses. Gil, Gil from Binghamton, was unknown to most all. A secret angel who prodded, begged, and finally dragged a man to see someone he thought was his son getting married. Charlie Matino was not, as macho poets might say, "a fine wreck of a man," but rather, simply a wreck of a man. Charlie wept silently. Barely able to stand, he was held in a semi-crouch by his lover. Why the tears? There were numerous reasons likely: shame, regret, embarrassment, discomfort, self-loathing, and deep, deep pain in his heart for himself as well as for what he had missed and what he had abandoned. A baby whom he once denied now stood as a fine, tall, handsome man. Self-sufficient, strong of character, and secure in who he was, Jordan had become the kind of man Charlie would never be. Charlie's brother Nick was perhaps the oddest sight. With one hand helping support his weak younger brother, he paid rapt attention to the same things his brother saw but reacted to them in an opposite fashion. He too, watched the child he had abandoned from birth. But Nick witnessed this ceremony as a man proud that he had somehow helped place upon this earth a wonderful young beauty who was now marrying a doctor. Nick Matino had on his face the happiest Santa Claus smile; it lit up the room.

Heather never shot a glance to the back of the church, but she saw Rick as she finally turned to go back down the aisle as Mrs. Jordan Matino. By the time they reached the rear vestibule, married, relieved, and happy, all had dispersed but Rick. As the new-lyweds greeted the throng, Rick George did his best Rick George imitation possible under the circumstances. "Awfully sick. Almost thought I'd have to ask them to postpone the wedding. But that would've been too selfish of me," he said to all who asked. His was a lie disguising a secret, and a lousy one at that.

Heather made one quick dash to the door, followed immediately by Jordan, before starting the reception line. "Charlie! Gil!"

"Charlie?" asked Jordan, looking in the direction of the two fellows from the rear vestibule heading down the sidewalk away from the church.

"It's your father," Heather said as she pleaded with her eyes. "Catch him."

Jordan was dumbfounded once more, moving promptly, though, to catch up with the two men making their getaway.

"Hey!" The two finally stopped and faced him. Gil was pensive and ready for anything. Charlie was still shivering and scared. Jordan studied Charlie's face, wordlessly letting it all wash over him for a moment. A million times in his mind this scene had played out. He dreamed of screaming, punching, insulting, and abusing him. Yet even if he had not seen the genetics report, even if he had not had doubts cast upon whether this man had helped bring him into the world, he felt differently now, although he did not know why.

Finally, he stuck out his hand: neither a fist nor an embrace, but a simple hand to shake. "It's okay."

Charlie Matino took Jordan Matino's hand and gently shook it. He said nothing. Jordan added no more. Aware that Gil and Charlie's body language still indicated they wanted to leave, he allowed them to.

"It's okay" were the first and last words Jordan would ever say to Charlie Matino. Heather occasionally kept in touch with Gil, but Charlie was loath to get more involved. Two years later, Charlie died when the trailer caught fire while he napped alone. Gil was inconsolable.

Rick kept up appearances by coming to the reception and continuing to "Hi-hello" guests as if he had a damn thing to do with the success of the entire operation. Later, when he was finally forced to look Heather in the eye as they participated in the ritual father-daughter dance, all he could say to her, sober-faced and with little emotion was, "You look lovely today." Rick uttered verbatim the only words said to Heather by Nick Matino, a stranger to her. Ironically, she took those words from the man who raised her in a more superficial fashion than she had from the stranger. Heather compartmentalized Rick for the rest of the day. The moment he failed to walk her down the aisle, he crossed a line he might never be able to uncross during his lifetime. Rick had drawn his line in the sand. Heather had since drawn hers.

Rick later beat Eleanor to the punch by moving out of Mountain City first. They divorced amicably, and he managed to get a job with a pharmacy chain somewhere. He was rumored to have taken up with a younger woman who knew nothing of Mountain City, nothing of Nick and Eleanor, and nothing of his youthful nights with Charlie Matino. Although melancholy at losing touch with Heather, the young girl he raised so well, he seemed, for the first time in decades, comfortable within his own skin, courtesy of his belated fresh start and clean slate.

With Nick Matino nowhere in sight and relieved his wedding had not been turned into a brawl or an inquisition or broken up by the Pennsylvania State Police, Jordan was as totally spent as his bank account. He would have welcomed Jack Stein had he come to the reception. But Jordan understood that one.

The hors d'oeuvres included fresh and smoked kielbasi, skewered, appropriately enough, by sword-shaped plastic toothpicks.

Days later, while on their Bermuda honeymoon, Jordan was thinking out loud while sunning himself next to his new bride. "Do you think everyone thinks where they come from is boring?"

"I never thought about it. I haven't traveled as much as you, but probably. A lot of people I met in college and at work and stuff talk pretty much the way we do about where they come from, although we have some stories that are funnier. No one believes that our dentist never used novocaine."

"Yeah, but what I wonder about is, is it the *place* that's boring? I even went to school with some guys who thought growing up in Manhattan was boring."

"Wow. I guess they were just in a hurry to get away from their parents."

"Exactly! When you're a kid, what is it that makes the place you live, the place you live? It's the adults, starting with your parents. Then there are the neighbors, your parents' friends, your teachers. And they're *all boring.*"

"They're *all* boring?"

"Yes, because being a parent means keeping secrets."

Heather didn't like the sound of this. "Jordy, I'd like us to have kids someday, and *I* don't plan to keep secrets."

She played right into his trap. "Oh really?" Jordan grinned with bemusement. "So you're going to take the last six months of our lives and lay it all out for our kids in gory detail? You're going to tell them everything?"

Heather pouted. "That's not fair. What happened to us this past year is beyond the beyond."

"Ah, but it wasn't all about us. Most of the secrets weren't even ours. They belonged to those boring people back in boring Mountain City. The place where crickets chirp and the front page of the local newspaper is about how some guy caught a big trout. My theory . . . are you ready for my big theory?"

"Go ahead, big genius doctor."

"My theory is that when people are young, they have adventures and misadventures. And some of that stuff is pretty damn exciting, in its own way. Then they get a little older and decide to settle down and have kids. Emphasis on the 'settle down' part. And they start off saying, 'We're going to tell our kids everything.' Then they remember what 'everything' is and realize there's no way they can tell their kids that. So all they tell their kids is, 'Drink milk, stay in school, don't do drugs.' And their kids grow up saying, 'This place is boring. I can't wait to get out of here.' And the cycle begins again."

"In other words, Jordy, you think that getting married and having kids eventually turns everyone into a hypocrite?"

" 'Born To Run' . . . 'We Gotta Get Out of This Place'—there are a million songs about it. But the real culprit is not the place. It's the people *in* the place and what we don't know about them and the circumstances of their lives. The behind-closed-doors stuff."

Heather let out a depressed huff. "Maybe we should move to an amusement park. Then we can be as boring as we have to be, but our kids will be entertained by the surroundings."

Jordan chuckled. "Maybe that's why Nick and Marianne Matino moved out of the fourth house and decided to overlook a roller coaster."

The Rev's parable would stick in Jordan's mind more than he suspected. A nice, relaxing honeymoon seemed a great opportunity to come clean about his not having initially read the DNA results. Then, on their third day on the island, Heather had a small, unfortunate accident while out mopeding. Attempting to avoid a tiny animal, she suffered a minor crash, scraping up her knees in the process. Coming to her aid, Jordan noticed she'd not only bruised herself, she'd hit the poor thing anyway. A few feet from his beautiful princess lay a frog, squashed and dead in the middle of the hot-tarred road. Now, there's symbolism and then there's SYMBOLISM. At the very least, he would wait for the new test results before discussing whether he was Heather's prince or not.

Throughout the years, both of them would remember the feeling as they swayed to their very first dance as husband and wife. Striding out onto the floor completely alone, they were just as they were the very first time they danced together. Most couples have to invent a song, "our song," for their wedding reception. But Jordan and Heather Matino needed no contrivance.

You give your hand to me,
And then you say, "Hello,"
And I can hardly speak,
My heart is beating so.
And anyone can tell,
You think you know me well,
But You Don't Know Me.

ACKNOWLEDGMENTS

———⚬⚬———

A FEW THOUSAND years ago, a teacher by the name of Ron Grutza handed a junior high schooler an extensive reading list, a magical treasure trove that opened up new worlds and daydreams. It was my first introduction to serious literature, and for that, I shall always be grateful. That list was added to by wonderful teachers such as Pat Thompson, Bob Judd, Joe Yarworth, Margaret Mary Brown, and last but not least, the late Steve Stedman. Great teachers don't get paid a lot, but they are remembered forever.

To my family—Amy, Ryan, and Jason—this is what I was doing staying up past your bedtimes. I love you all.

A big shout out to Mary Hall Mayer, my agent, my friend, and the first person to believe in me—outside of friends and family who, of course, are obligated to do so. Also, the second person to join up—my wonderful editor, the legendary Carole Baron. A page to carol my writer friends, starting with Donna McCrohan, as well as the inimitable Gerard Jones, whose name I shall probably be blacklisted for mentioning.

To my friend V, owner of the world's biggest heart (metaphorical, not anatomical), whose mid-life revelations about his true lineage so inspired me to write this book.

Speaking of friends and family, to those back in the coal region, this one's for you. The list is long, you know who you are, and your last names are hard as hell to spell. Let's meet up at a block party and have a pierogi sometime. And to those who've passed on by, I lift a boilo in your memory.

Finally, I would be remiss without thanking author John O'Hara. This Mountain City boy enjoyed sharing Lantanengo County with you, in life and in letters. We both ended up in New Jersey. What's that all about?